VIGILANT

VIGILANT

WILL BOWRON

For Mom & Dad

*Thank you for dealing
with my chaos*

PROLOGUE

HAMINGTON—A woman was fatally shot in the head outside her East Hamington home Thursday night. The victim, twenty-eight-year-old Alice Walters, was caught in the crossfire between a vigilante and a man previously sought for questioning in connection with a string of armed robberies in the area. Two female bystanders with Walters also sustained gunshot wounds and were in stable condition at a hospital early Friday morning. According to a police spokesperson, the vigilante suffered minor injuries and the robbery suspect was transported, under arrest, to the intensive care unit.

The shootout marks the fourth violent confrontation in East Hamington between vigilantes and suspected criminals in ten weeks. "I just don't understand what's happening to our town," a witness said. "You expect this kind of thing to happen in West Ham, but not over here."

East Hamington Chief of Police Daniel Forrester made similar comments at a press conference, stating, "The past few months have seen an unacceptable increase of violence for our city and township. West Hamington's citizens may embrace these vigilantes as their means of safety, however, the people of East H do not. Our police force will redouble its efforts to make our streets safe for East Hamington families and ensure that the law is upheld by those legitimately employed by the city."

Forrester's comments highlight current tensions between the Hamington township governments West and East of the Baldwin River. Despite a growing number of accusations, District Attorney Logan Parker has repeatedly denied rumors of collusion between vigilantes and police in West Hamington, citing lower crime statistics and police complaints than comparably sized cities throughout the country. "I honestly have a hard time trying to—look, why would the police force associate itself with—there's rarely even enough crime in Hamington to warrant the size of our current police force. Look at New York City, look at Chicago. Not even in their most peaceful years have their numbers come this low."

In his press conference, Forrester did not disclose if he believes the West Ham government funds vigilantes. "At the end of the day, what does it matter? A woman in our city, on our side of the river, is dead. Two others are gravely injured. Whether these vigilantes get a pass from cops in West Hamington doesn't concern me. The safety of our neighbors on this side of Greater Hamington does."

The fiancé of the deceased woman refused to comment.

PART ONE

OF CATALYSTS

CHAPTER ONE

TAYLOR

Beneath the conference room table, Taylor Gardner's foot drummed a violent rhythm. He flipped through copies of the email, still warm from the printer, waiting for everyone to arrive. It had finally happened. After all this time.

The station's producers and writers trickled in, brows furrowed in confusion or annoyance at his request for an immediate meeting. Anchors were only the pretty faces and baritone voices hired to read the teleprompter. He didn't have the authority to tell anyone to do anything or go anywhere. A few glanced at him between questions to their coworkers about how long they thought this would take. They never asked Taylor directly, probably expecting to receive the same silence he'd given everyone over the past few months.

When someone knocked on his office door to notify him of a story change, his only response was a polite smile or distracted nod. If asked about weekend plans or the hottest sports highlights, the reaction was the same. These were unimportant questions. Intrusions to the task at hand. His body might stand before them, but his mind was at his desk, tucked between pages of law books and connected to his phone and filtered into various email folders and sorted through stacks and stacks and stacks of research. All in pursuit of this moment.

Jake shuffled in last, asking everyone to sit down while peering over his glasses at the phone clutched in his swollen fingers. "Taylor's asked us to meet today for what I assume is a very good reason." He placed his glasses on the table and leaned into his well-worn chair, interlocking his hands across his gut. A soft smile crossed his face.

Jake still handled Taylor with kid gloves, long after everyone else at the station moved on and stopped trying to connect. But whenever Taylor brought it up, the man just shrugged and acted like he didn't know what he was talking about. "What's on your mind, Mr. Gardner?"

Taylor licked his lips. His fingers quaked as the pieces of paper refused to separate from each other. He cleared his throat.

"I got him. I got Hudson."

A producer stopped typing copy into his phone. Another slowed the rocking in his chair, and turned to his neighbor, whispering. Jake narrowed his eyes. His chair creaked as he leaned forward. He pressed his hands to the table, spreading his fingers.

"You *got* him?"

"Yeah. Well, I mean I got him to email me back. Or his assistant at least. A woman named Linda Howard." Taylor sent the stack of emails around the table. Paper rustled as producers snatched copies off the pile. Jake kept his eyes on Taylor until the stack came all the way around the table. He placed his glasses back on his nose and read the page aloud, despite everyone already dissecting it. Taylor's foot continued to shake underneath the table.

"'Mr. Gardner. Please find Mr. Hudson's response to your emails below. Please excuse the...' yada yada yada... Okay, here we go: 'It has been my pleasure to watch you present nightly news in Hamington over the past few years and get to know you through your interactions with local citizens. Your dedication to the city and its commitment to you through difficult times is encouraging, and, in a way, a confirmation of my lifelong goals. I'm writing now to acknowledge your plentiful emails and…'" Jake paused and looked up at Taylor.

"Are you sure this is real?"

"Positive," Taylor said. "I checked everything this morning. Verified the email address with his old advertising agency and the station's security software detected nothing suspicious. It's real."

Jake adjusted his shoulders and continued reading. "I'm writing now to acknowledge your plentiful emails and to accept your request for an interview. I have reached the age when I would like my story to be told, and I believe you are the person who would do that story the most justice." He stopped short of reciting the rest but continued in silence. Taylor watched his gaze travel down the page, his brow furrowing the closer he got to the end.

Jake folded the paper in half, covering the words no one in the conference room could look away from. Taylor did not move. Did not participate. He simply stared at the top of his boss's head while the man deliberately folded the paper's corners like origami, back hunched and stomach rolling over the end of the table.

The producers' discussions started as whispers. What questions should be asked in the interview? What kind of equipment would be necessary? What would be a good release date for the special? Is there any way this could finally be actually happening?

"Excuse me, everyone," Jake said. "You can all go back to your offices now. Mr. Gardner, will you sit here with me for a moment?"

The producers evacuated the room, finally able to speak outside the parameters of hushed voices and jotted notes. Jake closed the door behind them and returned to his seat. He lifted the paper between two fingers like a soiled diaper.

"I cannot have you do this."

Taylor's foot ceased its vibrations. "You're not serious."

"I've allowed you to pursue this on company time because I thought it would be good for you to have some closure. It was a managerial decision for the development of an employee. I never thought… Hudson hasn't made public contact with anyone in almost twenty years. He's only granted two interviews his entire life."

"Three."

Jake rolled his eyes and tossed the paper onto the table. "Okay, sure. If you count a two-minute radio call when he told the press not to bother him anymore."

"I don't understand. Doesn't that make that make this more important?"

"Of course it's important." Jake pointed at the folded square, keeping his distance. "This story is a whale for viewership and ad revenue. I don't even care that he's demanding to set the when and where, and how all the logistics are handled. This has potential to be an historical moment in broadcast history. But I'm talking about you, Taylor. This... this is not healthy for you."

"You read the email. He said it has to be me. No cameramen. No sound guys. That's it. There shouldn't even be consideration about this. If it were anyone else, you'd be right in the conversation planning out how to best—"

Jake stood and ran his hands through his thinning hair.

"Stop. You're not listening to me. You shouldn't be alone with this guy. I hoped the process of researching and keeping your mind on something would be helpful, but I honestly never expected anything to come out of it. And now? You... you get an email that says you have to be at his house in less than twenty-four hours? That's no time to prepare for a standard assignment, nonetheless something much bigger than that.

"I wholeheartedly understand what you're trying to pursue. We both know that you aren't the same person you were before... Alice. But I have to say, for the last time, this is not healthy for you."

Hearing her name didn't sting as much as it had immediately after she'd died, but it still took him by surprise, even with Jake saying it as softly as he could. The kid gloves needed to be removed, even if Taylor had to rip them off himself. The sensitivity was a kind gesture, but it was only needed or tolerated for so long. An interview with Hudson could help Taylor put his career back on track and put an end to the puppy-dog looks of pity from passersby that followed him wherever he went. And it could help him understand why it had happened. Where it all started

Taylor rose from his seat to match Jake's height. His voice was steady. "You don't understand. You can't. I appreciate your concern, but I didn't set this meeting so you could have an opportunity to talk me out of something. You read the email—he wants to do this tomorrow morning, and I need producers to help me develop the right questions. I need tech to talk me through how to work sound and camera equipment. This needs to be done now. And if it doesn't happen after everyone in this meeting read that email, they'll know it was because you killed the biggest lead on a story this station has ever had."

Unfamiliar sensations flooded through Taylor's body. His heart beat heavily. He tasted copper. Adrenaline prickled in his veins.

"I don't..." Jake said. His shoulders dropped and he shook his head. "Talk to your producers, make your meetings. Do whatever you need to do. Please just remember that I tried." He closed the door quietly as he left.

Taylor breathed heavily. Maybe he'd gone too far by threatening him, especially after Jake had been so patient. But no number of good intentions could separate Taylor from the answers to his questions. They kept him awake at night, flitting above his head like moths. Sleep would not come easily until they'd been exterminated.

He sank his face into his palms, rubbing his eyes. Shook his head. There was no time for exhaustion. No time to be distracted by guilt. He had to be ready. Tomorrow he would meet the man whose existence had haunted him for months. Timothy Hudson. Tomorrow.

Sleep almost came for Taylor around two in the morning, but a man and woman started screaming at each other outside his townhouse and all hopes were lost. Sweat accumulated in his sheets. He kept feeling for a puddle to roll out of, but even the other side of the bed was hot and sticky. He stared at the ceiling, watching car lights pass between the curtains every few seconds.

Famous images of Timothy Hudson refused to leave his brain. Front pages, cereal boxes, magazine ads. A man with a hero's clean, white smile on top of a tall frame with broad shoulders that seemed capable of holding up the city itself. An invincible human being. This was the man he was supposed to confront.

He rolled over, grabbing at the pillow on the other side of the bed, unwrinkled from a night's tossing and turning. Wrapped his arms around it and breathed in deep, hoping he would smell something different than clean cotton.

He told himself he wasn't nervous when the clock alarm went off, but his chin refused to stop bleeding after he cut it shaving and it took several attempts to knot his tie. He missed the keyhole more than once when locking the door as he left.

The sun had barely peeked between the buildings on his block. It was a quiet morning but wouldn't be for long. West Ham rose early. Runners, cyclists, and newspaper deliverers controlled the streets for now, the steam from their lungs casting a mist over the city. Plumes of exhaust grew long from the tailpipes of taxis, and the few people walking to work had grabbed an extra layer before leaving the house. Taylor took the steps from his front door and joined the working world on the sidewalk. Street vendors were beginning to cook for the inevitable passersby who had woken too late to toast their own bagels.

He bumped his briefcase against his thigh while waiting for the signal to cross. No one carried briefcases anymore, but this one was lucky. A little bent and torn on the corners with the leather worn out on the bottom, it helped him look older and more mature when he brought it to his first interview for Action News 3 in college. Even now that it was falling apart, he knew he'd never get rid of it. If a day finally came when it was only held together by string, unable to carry anything more than the memories of the college graduation day when it was given to him, it would still have a special place in his home, in the side closet full of clothes and pictures and stationery he couldn't bear to throw away.

Pedestrians started crossing the intersection and Taylor retreated from his thoughts. It was too early to get lost in them today. And he was too early for the interview. Five minutes early was good, half an hour was desperate. As he rubbed his eye with the heel of his hand, he decided to stop for coffee to waste time on the way to catch a cab. He took his normal turn though the alley that was the fastest way to his Starbucks.

The homeless man who had been there for the past week stretched beside a garbage can as he rose from the ground. Taylor accidentally made eye contact with him and looked away, walking faster as he passed. When would this guy leave? Some hobos would pass out from a night of cheap boozing in the alleys and beg for change as people walked by, but most stayed in the underpass, confined to their own area. This one had made the alley his home and tried to talk to Taylor every morning, almost yelling at him when he passed.

There were mornings when Taylor considered changing his route, but with everything he'd gone through, a harmless wino wasn't going to be the thing that pushed him to change.

"Hey man, you got the time?" The hobo tapped his naked wrist. Taylor shifted his shoulder, hoping the sleeve of his blazer covered his watch. He continued to look straight at the exit of the alley.

"Did you hear me? You know the time?"

"Nope. Sorry."

The hobo pointed at Taylor's wrist as he walked by and said, "I can see your watch right there!" He followed him. "Come on, man. Just help me out. What time is it?" He kept following. Kept asking. Close enough for Taylor to feel his breath. "What time is it? What time is it? What time is it?"

Taylor's heartbeat pounded. He picked up his pace, turning

the corner onto the sidewalk as the hobo called him a fucking asshole before stopping at the mouth of the alley.

Taylor released a deep breath. The homeless from the underpass never followed him or deviated from the usual beggar's script. Change or food or smokes. This guy was like the rest. There was always something he wanted. Today he said it was the time, but Taylor knew he was asking just to get his watch out in the open so he could easily steal it.

He readjusted his jacket over his neck to combat the cold. By the time he stepped into the coffee shop, his only thoughts were if he should be polite and get Hudson a cup, or if the man could rot in hell with or without it.

CHAPTER TWO

SAM

As the suited man left the alley, Sam kicked a garbage can over, spilling its guts onto the concrete. There wasn't anything to eat in there. He'd already checked last night. But if he had to eat another fucking can of cold, thick tomato soup, he'd puke it right back up. Other cans of food—vegetables and baked beans and cinnamon apples—all added weight to his bag, but it was mostly full of soup from a church food drive. Some old bitch probably died with a storm shelter full of Campbell's and her kids didn't know what to do other than drop it at the feet of their Lord and Savior Jesus Christ, more excited to get it off their hands than to help the hungry. It was better than half-eaten trash, but not by much.

He untied the garbage bags and looked for anything useful he may have missed in the darkness last night. A jacket, pants, anything. If he didn't get some warmer clothes he'd freeze to death in a few weeks. He rubbed his arms, wondering again what time it was.

This time last year, he could have just used his phone or checked his own watch. Wouldn't have had to beg some guy committed to ignoring him day after day.

But then he had to run from the cops after they'd found him and he had to abandon the apartment and couldn't charge his phone and finally sold it for food money that turned into quarters and dimes and evaporated without ever really ending the hunger, making him beg strangers for the time, unable to thank them with anything but a treasure trove of tomato fucking soup in an alleyway. It was all bullshit.

The Salvation Army didn't open until nine. The pennies in his backpack wouldn't be able to get him anything even from there, but hopefully they would let him trade work hours for extra clothes. Or at least a shower. He knew he smelled like shit, and if he could smell himself, he didn't want to know what other people thought.

Violet always said that. When Sam met her in his first few days in the underpass, she asked, "Can you smell me? I can't smell me yet, but you've gotta smell you."

A couple turned to jog down Sam's alley. He looked up from sifting through the garbage. "Hey! You two!" he yelled. The man stopped short, grabbing his girl's arm and shook his head. "You got the time?" Sam asked. They turned out of the alley.

He didn't understand why no one would speak to him. He just needed to know what time it was. He ran his hands through his hair and rubbed hard at an itch on his forehead.

When he and the neighborhood kids were young, they would hang around and talk about what superpower they wanted. Everyone picked super-strength or flight or some other stupid shit, but Sam loved the idea of being invisible. No one would watch and laugh when he was chased out of an electronics store for standing in front of the TVs for too long. Cops wouldn't slow their cars down and stare at him over their sunglasses when he and the boys sat on the steps of the project block. And being able to do whatever he wanted and never get in trouble? Nothing better.

His friends didn't understand him, no matter how many times he walked them through it. "Man, you could be rich. Walk into a bank, grab shit, and leave. You never have to pay for anything, just take it."

Life has a weird way of giving you exactly what you ask for. Super-duper invisibility powers. That guy in the suit with the briefcase and the thick, shiny hair. Those runners. Violet, when Sam was right in front of her screaming for help, knuckles raw and bloody. Invisible to everyone. Everyone except the cops. The only people he actually wanted to disappear from.

No clothes or food had magically appeared in the garbage can overnight. He kicked it again and slid down the wall, his thin Hawaiian shirt catching on the bricks and tearing new holes. He had to get a jacket.

He dug through his backpack and found a can of SpaghettiOs somewhere in the sea of tomato soup. A rat scurried against the wall opposite the alley from Sam, around puddles of dirty water and broken slabs of concrete, poking its nose into trash piles. "Squeak at me if you find anything," Sam said.

After he poured the last of the pasta in his mouth and licked sauce off his fingers, the empty can went back in the bag. Never knew what could end up being helpful, and there wasn't enough in his bag for him to worry about it getting too heavy. A half-empty water bottle, a few pairs of stolen socks, some food. Too empty. He had to get a jacket.

He wasn't as thin and starved out as the hobos living in the underpass, but without anywhere to get food or money, he would be soon. The desperate ones shook change cups on the steps leading to the subways. Some lay like corpses, faces shoved to the ground with their skeletal hands held out until someone dropped a quarter and the hand slid the coin into a hidden pocket.

Sam wasn't good at the begging thing.

He'd be nice to people who walked by, ask them how their day was and if they had any spare change, holding tight to the politeness Davey preached when Sam was still in the underpass, before quickly falling back to accusing—yes you do, you lying piece of shit, give me your fucking money before I beat it out of you. And no one gave him what he needed. He wanted to yell that he liked begging to survive as much as they liked him in their personal space. But it was just what he had to do. Manners wouldn't get him anywhere.

Violet said it was his face. That he looked scary. That he looked like the kind of guy who would convince a person to give him a dollar, then steal the wallet it came from. Fuck her, though. Violet had gone through college and everything, but still ended up right with Sam in the underpass after losing her money putting bad bets on shitty poker hands. She didn't know what Sam had gone through.

But with all that education, maybe Violet had been right. Maybe Sam scared people. He practiced smiling as he thought about the Salvation Army shield flashing in neon outside the store window. He had to look nice if anyone would help him find a jacket. Had to look like a nice person. Not scary. He scratched some grime off his front teeth. A shining white smile. Davey always said that was the key to getting back in the real world.

Sam zipped his bag up and left the alley. Even if The Salvation Army was still closed when he got there, he'd be warmer in the sun. But he'd be back here later. It was a good, safe spot: far enough away from the underpass that he didn't have to worry about running into someone who would rat his location to Davey. Two exits onto busy streets made it easy to see if someone was coming, and there were plenty of trash cans and dumpsters to find things in. He'd give it a few more days then see if a better place came along. There was no reason to run yet.

The entrance to the Salvation Army was on a street that acted like a damn wind tunnel, air whipping around the corner of the building, cold as a motherfucker. Sam's eyes felt like they would dry and shrivel up before he even got a chance to wear the jacket he'd been so worried about. He rubbed his arms, trying to warm himself until he got inside.

Nothing blocked the wind. The buildings were all smooth glass and concrete in this area. No alcoves or recesses to step into and hide from the weather. So he stood, waiting outside the front window of The Salvation Army. Finally, he saw the lights inside flicker on and workers walking around, laughing and peeling off layers of thick woolen clothes. Laughing because they were comfortable. Because their fingertips weren't freezing off. Sam rubbed his ears with his palms to try and defrost them.

When he knocked on the glass door, a man inside tapped the unlit "Open" sign and mouthed, "Just a few minutes," before sinking away, farther into the store where Sam couldn't see him. They didn't care how cold he was, or that he would be a fucking popsicle in just a few minutes. He wouldn't need a jacket then, N-O, no he would not.

More movement inside. They had to be opening soon. He needed a jacket.

His teeth felt like they were going to chatter right out of his head.

He wiped condensation off the window with his fist and cupped the glass to see through it. Workers were strolling around, half asleep, drinking steaming cups of coffee. They could at least open the fucking door and let him in since they weren't doing anything. He wouldn't bother them. Just stay on the welcome mat by the entrance, happily melting in the warmth, staring at all the crap people had given away.

Clothing racks lined the length of the building, filled with all the random things left behind when people moved because they couldn't be bothered to take five seconds to throw them in a box. Why'd they even buy all this shit in the first place if they were going to throw it away? These things cost money. And money takes time and you pay for your things with the hours of your life. They made no sense to him, these people. Throwing away days and weeks of their lives. Made him sick. If he had a few more hours every day, he'd probably have a home. A family.

The bell above the door politely rang as an employee let him in. Sam pushed past her and inhaled the warm inside air, ignoring whoever greeted him from behind the counter. He wasn't there to chat about the weather and tell people good morning. He had to get a jacket.

Sam ran his hands through the racks of winter clothes, only seeing things that wouldn't fit him. He was smaller—all sinewy muscle and bone. These clothes would swallow him and make it difficult to move. Attract attention from the wrong people. Cops couldn't care less if he wore clothes that didn't look like his. But the vigilantes looking for someone to attack in their free time would.

"Sir." A short old woman wearing a red Salvation Army apron stood in front of him with clenched fists on her hips. "I said you have to leave your bag at the front counter." The employees were all looking at him. Probably had seen people do crazy shit before.

Sam shrugged. "Yeah, that's no problem. Just don't go through my things."

Her scowl melted into a sugar sweet smile as she reached for the bag. "Of course not, sir. Let us know if you need any help!" Sam grunted and returned to the clothing racks. Could she smell him?

He tried a jacket on. It was dark with a high collar and thick enough to bundle up in. It would work.

"I'll take this one," Sam said. Inside, the jacket made him almost uncomfortably warm. The man behind the cash register looked up and asked Sam to take the jacket off so he could check the price tag. Seventeen dollars. Sam's stomach clenched. "I don't have that much money. But I can help you guys here. Or spend time volunteering to pay for it. Or something? I need this jacket." He stared at the man behind the counter, daring him to look him in the eyes. Ignoring his clean Salvation Army polo shirt. This bastard didn't know what it was like to not be able to buy things. Especially not at a fucking Salvation Army.

"Unfortunately, sir, we can't sell it to you if you don't have the money," he said while folding the jacket. "How much do you have? Maybe we can find something that'll work for you." He sounded bored. Looked bored. His unsympathetic eyes searched for more coffee to heat his bones, even though he'd been in the warmth while Sam was stuck outside waiting in the biting wind.

The man didn't understand. Nothing else would work. This was the jacket. Seventeen dollars stood between Sam living and dying. "No," Sam said. He tapped the counter with his finger. "I want that one." The worker looked over Sam's shoulder. Still no eye contact. Still didn't see invisible Sam in front of him, bargaining for his life. The man nodded and Sam turned to see what he was looking at.

"Is there a problem here?" The manager looked like the stupidest one in the store, his eyes droopy and half-lidded, his body made of waves. A bulging gut curving out the front, then into a slouch bending forward at a harsh curve. Sam recognized the bloodshot look in his eyes. Knew about getting high in order to start the day. This guy didn't give a shit about Sam. He wouldn't help him. Nobody here understood what he needed.

The cashier repeated that Sam didn't have the money for the jacket. "Sir," the manager said, "if you didn't have the money, how'd you expect to buy the jacket?" His slow speech pissed Sam off. He wanted to grab the man's large, shiny, spit-covered bottom lip and rip it off.

"I have to get a jacket."

The manager's head rolled from one side to the other. In the same bored, stoned voice, he said, "Sir, that doesn't answer my question. How did you expect to buy this piece?" Sam clenched his fists. He'd answered the question, just not how the fat bastard wanted. He had to get a jacket and he would be leaving with a jacket. There were ways he could have paid, but these weren't the type of people that would work with him. Just like Davey and Violet. If no one would help him, he'd just have to help himself.

He angled his head down, keeping his eyes on the manager. In the side of his vision, Sam saw the jacket folded next to the cash register. He adjusted his weight onto his left foot. The manager tilted his head and pursed his lips. "Sir, we would be more than happy to help you find a less expensive item."

Sam slammed his fist into the manager's temple. It popped to the side and his body followed, tumbling over. A woman screamed. Sam swung his elbow into the other side of the man's head as he fell. There was a solid connection, and he crashed to the floor, groaning. Sam grabbed the jacket off the counter and ran, colliding with the glass door, swinging it open in the wind. Someone yelled. He sprinted down the street. Faster. Faster. Smiling.

He had a jacket.

He ran blocks down the road, down an avenue, turned here, two streets more around a corner and then hid by a dumpster. Listening. Calming his breaths and heartbeat so he could hear any following footsteps or dumbasses who wanted to play superhero. He waited.

Waited.

There were none.

It felt good. He couldn't remember the last time something worked out for him that easily. And it had been so damn easy. He reached for his bag to drink a sip of water while he caught his breath.

The backpack wasn't there. Of course it wasn't.

The short woman at the store. She told him to take it off and now she had it. The Salvation Army had it.

He'd been so stuck on the jacket that he'd forgotten everything else he owned. Water. Tools. Even the tomato soup was gone. He crouched and leaned against the dumpster, lightly banging his head on it. "Fucking. Bitch. Fucking B-I-C-H, bitch."

He couldn't go back. No way. He'd hurt that man. The elbow landed hard on his head. A loud crack had rung out from his face when he collapsed. There might even be police there. Or worse, the people who pretended they were the police.

His hair felt slick as he ran his hands through it. Had to figure out his next move. This area wouldn't be safe for long. It was too close to the store. Davey and the others would look for him harder now. He had to get going if he was going to survive. He had to get food.

CHAPTER THREE

TAYLOR

IT WAS DIFFICULT for Taylor to flag down a taxi. He waved his briefcase above his head to signal for a ride as cabs sped by, trying not to let the coffee in his other hand spill as yellow car after yellow car passed him without slowing. Before, black SUVs with heated leather seats and the morning's paper would pull up outside of his townhouse to take him wherever work needed him. He didn't want those kinds of luxuries anymore. Too many people stared and noticed who he was, rushing over before he could get in the car to tell him they were so sorry for his loss and that their thoughts and prayers were with him.

The less attention, the better, and as long as he could look Timothy Hudson in the face and ask the questions he'd been waiting for, Taylor didn't care if he took a limousine or a cab or had to walk the entire way. He would get to that man's house, one way or another.

A cab finally careened to a stop in front of him, its driver jabbering into his Bluetooth, barely acknowledging his passenger as he started the meter.

Taylor's phone buzzed in his jacket. "Hudson House, please," he told the cabbie before answering the call. Jake's voice came out rushed and choppy.

"How are you feeling? You have everything you need? All set all across the board?"

"I'm fine. All fine. Bill's meeting me at the house with the cameras and helping me set up. Everything's on schedule."

"Okay, good. And how are you doing? Still alright about this?"

"I'm fine, Jake."

"Alright. Just... just call me if you have any issues."

Jake was known around the station for his micromanaging. He stepped in to fix problems before they even existed, then continued probing until he found more issues to massage into solutions. Taylor used to complain with the other anchors that he made them feel like kids going out for a solo drive after barely passing the driver's exam. Today was the first time he'd felt Jake's prodding in months. Maybe their conversation yesterday had done the job and he'd realized he couldn't afford to mishandle a story this big.

It was all lining up. Taylor would meet Hudson. Interview him. Tell him that Alice's death was his fault. Prod and accuse until he finally had his answers. And if everything went perfectly, Taylor might even be known as more than just the guy on the news with the sad story.

It was still possible to get through this without moving out of Hamington and starting from scratch somewhere else. He watched as the city passed by his backseat window.

The cabbie drove them through Taylor's favorite part of Hamington, where the skyscrapers and office buildings of West Ham made way for the suspension bridge crossing the river to more suburban East H. It was more than the quiet strength of the river or the aesthetics of the mountains in the distance, but something in the way that both sides of the city had their own personalities that met along the natural division in the middle. Towering skyscrapers and city streets on the west, residential houses and private schools tucked among rolling hills on the east.

Taylor stared out over the water. He hadn't crossed the river in months, content for it to be a shield that kept the eastern half of the city and all its memories away from him. But now he was ignoring the divide and going right in.

"You know it's not a museum or nothing right?" The driver's voice brought him back from the distant mountains.

"I'm sorry?"

"Hudson House. The guy lives there. It's not like a tourist spot."

"I'm interviewing him for Action News 3." He met the cabbie's eyes in the rearview mirror. No glimmer of recognition. Taylor released a breath he didn't realize he'd been holding.

"No shit. That'll be a hell of a story, huh? Most people I drive there are tourists that just want to take pictures in front of the house, or pay their respects, like it's a royal palace or something. This one time, I took a family and I heard this guy tell his kid it was where the most powerful man in the city lived. When I told him it wasn't the mayor's mansion anymore, he just shook his head. It's like people worship the guy."

Taylor tapped the story into his phone as the driver continued. It wouldn't get into the video interview, but might work as a good opening for the piece. Timothy Hudson. The most powerful recluse in the world.

The driver rambled on, talking over a radio spot for the newest superhero movie, first on his Bluetooth and now to Taylor. He was one of those people who couldn't stop words from pouring out of his mouth, like a constant stream of over-familiar word vomit, rather than a little spurt here and there. It didn't take long until he started complaining about the crooked cops that pull him over for this and that and the jerk who didn't tip after a long drive out of town. But the abrasiveness of it comforted Taylor. It was the only piece of West Ham that travelled with him across the bridge.

Nothing on this side of the river ever seemed to change. People watered their lawns behind white picket fences, small yellow flags marking invisible dog barriers, a mid-life crisis sports car on every other block. The only differences were the colors of the car and the breeds of the dog.

Things moved slower here than in in West Ham. He'd loved it before, in a nostalgic sort of way. There was no rushing to get around. Everyone looked relaxed and well-rested and safe as they walked down the driveway for their newspaper. They embraced the slower ticks of the clock, as if it actually gave them a little longer to live. It made him sick.

Taylor noticed a wrinkle in his suit as they got closer. He stretched the fabric, tried to press it smooth, and rubbed it before giving up. His foot tapped a rhythm on the floorboard of the taxi. The nerves were setting in.

The cab turned left off the main road and began driving up a long, crawling hill. Sharp turns and dense trees kept them moving slowly. As they passed by a Hamington Historic Landmark sign, Taylor wrenched his neck to try to read it, but it disappeared in trees as they rounded a final turn.

And there it stood.

The Hudson House. Alone on a plot of healthy grass behind a black iron fence with spikes at the tip of every rod.

The house towered before old pine trees swaying with the breeze, four stories tall. Columns framed the face of the red brick building. Twin staircases wrapped down from the middle of three balconies, around groupings of trees on the front lawn. The stone driveway wound its way from the front steps past a fountain down to where the cameraman, Bill, stood in front of the gate, adding another cigarette to the pile already at his feet, his van parked in the middle of the drive.

"Why isn't everything ready to go in the house?" Taylor asked as the cab drove away.

Bill flicked his cigarette to the ground. "I got here an hour ago to unload and set everything up, but they said I couldn't come in. I couldn't call you because cell phones don't work with all these trees and mountains around here, so I've just been sitting on my ass, wasting my damn time." He snatched a coffee from the carrying tray in Taylor's hand.

"I talked to his assistant this morning and she said we were all good. Let me call up and see what's going on. Don't worry, we'll get it figured out." Taylor gritted his teeth as he walked to the intercom system by the gate. What the hell did Bill do to get locked out?

He pressed the solitary button on the console. The fish-eyed camera lens above the system hummed as it adjusted to focus first on Bill's face over Taylor's shoulder, then on his. "Hello? This is Taylor Gardner with Action News 3, here to interview Mr. Hudson?"

He recognized Linda's voice, sharp and clear through the speaker. "Good morning, Mr. Gardner. Please dismiss your film crew. Mr. Hudson has decided he does not wish to be on film for the interview." Bill threw his hands up in the air and returned to the van before tearing a half-empty pack of cigarettes out of his jacket pocket.

"I think there's been some... confusion," Taylor said. "This was supposed to be a filmed interview special."

"Yes, that was the original plan, but that is no longer the case."

Taylor's stomach dropped. "This was not what we discussed. You can't just change the agreement at the last minute. And my cameraman has the audio equipment too. I don't have any way of recording the interview in full quality without him."

"Mr. Gardner, we have not signed any contracts or memorialized any agreements. You can either dismiss your colleague and come in by yourself, or both of you may leave. We have a sufficient recording system for you. Please let us know your answer promptly. Mr. Hudson is not interested in prolonging this discussion and will not stand for insubordination."

He wanted to break the camera. *Insubordination.* Like some military nutjob, cooped up in his mansion. This man didn't understand anything. Unless it was a slow news week, audio-only interviews didn't have any place or popularity on TV, no matter who they were with.

Maybe he could convince him once he got inside. Change Hudson's mind and let in cameras another day, for nothing else other than stock footage panning over the house or of Hudson contemplating life while looking off in the distance, starkly lit for the most dramatic effect. If the man wanted his story told, audio-only was no way to do it.

He shook his head and pushed the professional instincts out of the way. Taylor would get in that house, no matter if he wasn't allowed to bring cameras or audio or pen and paper. Maybe it wouldn't be the career reviver he'd hoped for, but this was more important than the story. If he could convince the recluse to change his mind and understand the importance of visuals to the story, that'd be helpful. And if he didn't, at least Taylor would be able to look him in the face and ask him what he needed to know. He told Linda to hold on while he spoke to Bill.

"There's nothing we can do," he said. "We either have no camera or no story."

"What? I have to pack it in and don't even get past the front gate? This story won't be shit without video." He sucked in a deep breath on his cigarette and blew it in Taylor's face. "That took two seconds for you to give up. You didn't even try to fight them on it."

He felt his heartrate quickening. His fists clenching. Bill didn't understand.

Taylor concentrated on breathing calmly and slowly said, "I don't know what to tell you. I thought we were good to go, just like you. But I have to get in there and talk to him. I'll try to convince him to let you set up the cameras next time, but for right now, this is the way it is. There's nothing I can do about it."

Bill rubbed his forehead with the back of his hand. "Look, I..." He held a finger up and returned to the van, coming back around from the driver's seat with a manila folder. "Would you mind asking him to sign these for me? I know it's... you know... it's unprofessional. But my kid loves him. He's got the comics and the movies and everything. You know how much this would mean to him." Taylor had met Bill's son before but couldn't remember his name. He was about five.

His chest shuddered as he imagined the boy's room. Decorated with cartoon posters over twin beds. Toys scattered across a carpeted floor. A LEGO table in the corner. Things Taylor would never see in his own house.

"I'll try," he said, "but only if it's going well."

Bill said he understood as Taylor grabbed the folder. As he put it in his briefcase, his chest finally began to loosen. What was the kid's damn name?

The van coughed a cloud of exhaust fumes onto the stone driveway as Bill peeled out. Taylor waited until he could no longer see it on the drive before returning to the intercom. "My man is gone. Can I come in now?"

There was a moment of silence, then the black, iron gate shuddered and began to rattle open.

The driveway beyond the gate wasn't as long as the side open to the public, but it was steeper and soon turned Taylor's steady breathing into shallow pants for air. He pushed off his knees as he took big strides up the hill. Sweat accumulated on the back of his neck and ran down his suit, despite the cool wind making the trees sway. His briefcase gained weight with each step. He tried to distract himself by checking his email, but Bill was right. No signal. He put his phone back in his pocket, his hands feeling empty without it.

He focused on his breathing and the questions he'd been waiting to ask. There was no film to study. No audio to prepare with. He had no idea if the man would answer in short, clipped responses, or if Taylor would have to shepherd him back to the question as he drifted away from the answer he was looking for. Not like a normal interview that he had time and content to prepare with. But nothing about this was normal.

Taylor took the stone staircase to the front door slowly as he smoothed his suit and readjusted his tie. He wiped sweat off his forehead. His palms were sticky.

"Just breathe."

The brass knocker felt full and heavy in Taylor's hand. He knocked twice, much harder than intended. Silence followed. Somewhere, a bird chirped. Still no answer.

He smoothed his hair, inhaled, and reached for the knocker again.

Multiple deadbolts moved inside the door. As it opened, a voice on the other side said, "You know it's not the eighteenth century. We do have a doorbell." Taylor saw the owner of the voice. His muscles clenched. Dread filled his bones.

Taylor recognized elements of him from old pictures—the shape of his face, the solid angles of his jaw—but everything else was different from the last time he appeared in public. What used to be a man with an athletic body and a grin made for the movies was now a ghost. The waif in front of Taylor was swallowed by a wheelchair, his legs covered with a plaid blanket that didn't conceal the fact there was nothing from his right knee down. His right hand, mangled and twisted, laid in his lap, not gripping anything; his left arm ended below the elbow. His hunched back moved his face farther toward Taylor, making it impossible to avoid a closer look at the hole where his right eye should have been, probably caused by whatever left the long scar slashing across his face. This was Timothy Hudson. This was the man he was supposed to confront.

The longer the silence, the deeper Hudson's scowl grew. He stammered, "M-my name is Taylor Gardner, it's ver—"

Hudson's phlegmy laugh interrupted him. He knocked his left elbow against the wheelchair's arm rest, like slapping his knee. "Ah, I was just fucking with you. We don't have a doorbell." The nurse behind Hudson gave Taylor a thin smile and looked back at her feet. Hudson waved him into the house with his nub and said, "Come on in. You're letting all the bought air out. Timothy Hudson. Damn glad to meet you." He extended his right hand, the one still attached to his body. Taylor delicately grabbed the arthritically curled hand and shook. The formality must have hurt him, but he made no sign of it. He just said, "Ah, you'll have to excuse the hand. Doesn't work quite as well as it used to," and coughed out another laugh.

The house opened up into a foyer with ceilings at least thirty feet high, illuminated by a crystal chandelier hanging in the middle. Formal and uncomfortable-looking chairs and seats were scattered around the room, covered in fine fabrics of deep reds and blues. A marble staircase at the side of the room went up to the second floor, the railing for a stairlift chair running up the wall the only indication that a cripple lived here.

"It's not a problem at all," Taylor said.

Hudson waved his nurse to start wheeling him down the hallway. "I probably should have told Linda to warn you about all this," he said, motioning to himself. "Truthfully, it's been a long time since I've met anyone, and I wanted to see if you think I look as bad as I think I do." The nurse gave him a light slap on the shoulder and began pushing his wheelchair over the ornate rug leading down the hallway.

Taylor's stomach turned in knots. The man had no problem calling him out on his unprofessional first impression. But even worse, Taylor felt guilty about it. How was he supposed to do anything here if he felt guilty for nothing more than looking at him too long? "I'm sorry if I offended you," he said. "I just... honestly had no idea that this had happened. No one's seen you in twenty-something years." Taylor glued his eyes to the pictures and memorabilia on the walls as they continued down the hallway, at first only feigning interest to avoid Hudson's gaze and refortify his gut, then quickly becoming captivated by everything he saw.

Oaken wainscot panels lined the hallway beneath dark crimson walls. Tables featuring framed pictures and newspaper articles were punctuated by closed doors for rooms that Taylor assumed looked similar. He saw Hudson shaking the hands of people he didn't recognize and read headlines both famous and unfamiliar to him. The cab driver had been wrong earlier. Hudson might have lived here, but this building was most definitely a museum.

"It's really not a problem. You can't be sensitive with me. No offense taken," Hudson said. Out of the corner of his eye, Taylor could see him watching his face as he looked around the house.

"Now, before we go any further, I want to clear the air. I'm sure you're angry, or annoyed, or frustrated with me about changing the details of our discussions. And I'm fine with all those things," Hudson said. He held his nub against a wheel to slow the nurse's push and readjusted in his seat to stare at Taylor with his one eye. He shrank under his gaze, glancing at the nurse, but found no solace there. Her eyes were locked to the chair in front of her. "But you have to know that I will do things like that from time to time. It's a necessity for me. Not just because I'm some ornery old man, but you don't stay alive as long as I have, doing the things I've done, without being careful. Please don't ask me at any point about cameras being allowed into my home. On this, I will not budge. Are we clear?"

The discomfort Taylor felt made way for the anger from outside to bubble up again. But he had to remind himself that the cameras were not the priority. His career and the final news story would always fall behind what he was really here for. As long as he had opportunity to find out what was needed, nothing else mattered.

"Not a word about it."

Hudson threw his hands in the air in celebration, the military firmness gone again, and said, "Terrific! Now, tell me a bit about yourself. I know you as well as just about anyone else who watches the nightly news." Taylor forced a smile.

As Hudson was rolled down the wooden-slatted hallway, Taylor described his path to his job at Action News 3. Born and raised in Hamington, attended Hamington University, majored in journalism, then worked his way up to where he was now at the station. He didn't mention his fiancée, even though Hudson probably knew her fate just like the rest of the city. Didn't mention his inability to focus on work. Didn't mention the fact that he hated everything Hudson represented. Not yet.

The nurse led them into a sunroom soaked in natural light. It was mismatched from the rest of the house. The one wall connecting it to the mansion was made of exposed brick, and the rest were only glass, like stepping into a giant, transparent cube. No curtains or paintings lined the walls. No ornate rugs on the floor. Just glass and furniture.

The purpose of the room became clearer as Taylor followed behind the wheelchair. Trees lined the property on all sides, as if they were in the middle of a forest, except for an opening at the west side of the property that looked over a view of West Ham. He could see the Baldwin River, the skyscrapers, and in the distance, could even make out remnants of the abandoned factory. Taylor couldn't imagine there being a better view of the city.

He breathed it in. This city. *His* city. It had everything. The nature, the industry, the character, the people. It supported him after all that happened. He meant to repay that debt by holding a magnifying glass to it. Examining it. Finding out why things were the way they were here. And the only person who could answer those questions was in a wheelchair, barely able to function.

He pulled his eyes away from the skyline and back to Hudson, for the first time noticing a hospital bed with an IV and blinking, beeping machines attached to it. The nurse had rolled Hudson to a table in the corner of the room next to a station of audio recording equipment. Taylor had worked a similar setup in college. It wouldn't be a problem.

He joined Hudson at the table and the man clapped his stump into his remaining hand. "Now. This was supposed to be a series of how many interviews, Linda?" The nurse held up three fingers. "Right. Three. Now, I'm willing to extend that number by as many as you like since we won't be having the cameras. I know that takes away a pretty important aspect of TV news," he said.

"That would be helpful," Taylor said. The more time he was able to spend with him, the more information he'd be able to wring out. He turned to the nurse. "And I'm sorry, I didn't realize you were the person I'd been speaking to. It's nice to meet you." He stuck out his hand for her to shake. She didn't move.

"There are some guidelines, though," Hudson continued, ignoring Taylor's introduction. "If we come to a topic I don't want to discuss, we will not discuss it. This is just like your cameraman. If you push me on any of these topics, we are done. You will no longer be welcome in my home.

"You are not to interact with any of the people here besides myself. They do not exist to you. Take Linda here, for example." Hudson motioned to his nurse as she filled his glass with water. "My staff has already been notified of this, and will not acknowledge you unless I directly ask them, like, 'Linda, would you mind pouring Mr. Gardner a glass of water as well?'"

A polite, practiced smile crossed her face as she poured, her eyes never meeting Taylor's. He had always suspected there were legitimate reasons Hudson was never seen. Maybe security or travel or financial reasons. But it went well beyond any of that, or the injuries and publicity concerns. This man was psychotic. Controlling and delusional, just as Taylor should have predicted. But his rules were the rules, and if he was going to get anything done here, he'd have to follow them.

"Are we clear so far?"

"We're clear, Hudson." Taylor waited to see if he had any further requirements or comments. The man only looked at the ground, the room finally silent.

"I think that should cover it then," he said.

Taylor opened his briefcase in his lap, waiting for some sort of objection or addendum to the statutes Hudson had recited. But he didn't move. Didn't speak. Taylor prepared his materials.

Notepad on the table, pen in hand, he sat poised. "Are you ready?"

Hudson breathed deeply and nodded. His eyebrows furrowed. He looked up from the floor.

Taylor turned on the recording equipment. "Mr. Hudson. Tell me: how did you become Hamington's first vigilante?"

CHAPTER FOUR

SAM

Sam's stomach continued to make noises as he pulled all the same trash out of the can that he'd dug through earlier in the morning. Nothing new. Just more reminders of how stupid he was.

A warm jacket wouldn't be any good if he starved to death. The soup in his backpack, the tools and loose change he'd been able to gather, all of it sitting at the Salvation Army, probably taped off and surrounded by cops and boy scout vigilantes playing dress up, pretending they could help the city. He couldn't go back there. He didn't remember seeing a security camera, but there had to be one, either hidden in a back corner or underneath a dark lensed bulb in the middle of the store. Well-off people don't help others unless they could make sure their own asses were covered.

Déjà vu rolled over him as he kicked the garbage can. No one had thrown away any more trash, and the bags were full of the same hamburger wrappers and torn up utility bills he'd seen this morning. At the center of everything, homelessness was just more of the same, day after day. The stench of uncleanliness, the hunger cramps, the aches and bruises from sleeping on a layer of thin cardboard. Every day. More of the same. More of the same.

He couldn't afford to be patient and wait for someone to

throw out a stale slice of pizza or mold-covered vegetables. Running from the store tired him out more than it should, even with the can of SpaghettiOs filling his stomach. If he didn't find something soon, he wouldn't stand a chance if one of those masked and costumed fuckers attacked him in the name of keeping the neighborhood safe.

He couldn't stay out in the open either and beg passersby for change. Too many vigilantes were hunting for him. And he was too weak to take anything from people by force. He was out of options.

This was all Davey's fault. Davey's and Violet's. When he was kicked out of the underpass, Sam asked for her help, but she just stared at him with those big empty eyes and shook her head. She could have done the right thing. Stuck her neck out for him. Hid him in her tent until the anger died down. Instead she froze solid and pussied out. Wasted precious seconds while Davey and the rest were tearing through the underpass looking for him. All because Sam was trying to help.

Maybe he could use that.

Yeah.

Violet's guilt always ran deep into her core, coiling around her guts like vines. As a self-proclaimed good person, she should have helped Sam. But she didn't. She was too afraid or worried about Davey then. She panicked. And now Violet owed him. It was risky, but it was all he had.

Violet had to help him, or he was going to die.

Sam left the alley and started crossing the street before cars finished passing. A woman leaned out her window and yelled as she swerved around him. He laughed. Getting hit by a car would have meant charity. A hospital room and food for the night while nurses came to him whenever he asked? Heaven. His jacket was warm, but nothing would be better than staying somewhere with four walls and clean sheets. And food. He needed food.

Sam dropped to the ground across the street from the underpass and cupped his hands out. He wouldn't get any money here.

People here lived too close to the underpass to feel bad for every hobo they saw. But he could watch everyone entering and leaving the tent city as he sat, the collar of his jacket pulled high to cover his face.

Nothing had changed since the night he ran out of there, swinging the nearly empty bag of food over his shoulder as he tried to wipe blood off his shirt. The tents sat in the shade of the highway overhead, undisturbed and unoccupied as they usually were during the day. These were the hours most of the hobos left to look for jobs, or a bottle of hooch, or dropped change. All the same as it had been months ago.

Back when he still had an apartment and a job and a life, he'd started moving up the heroin business chain. It paid well and he was good at it, but he'd reached a boulder in the road. His main connect standing between him and next level money was a fool. He wasted product, always using his own supply, not returning calls when people were desperate for their smack and offering to pay triple the street price. It hurt Sam's business.

And Sam had worked for that position. He deserved it. Earned it. It was his right.

So he broke the man's neck with his own baseball bat. Stole his stash, cut it two and three times, and sold it at a high rate. It was just one score, but the dough flowed his way, living in tall stacks in the corner of his bedroom. Enough to start up his own connections.

But the cops found him somehow. He apparently left fingerprints or hair or sweat or some other CSI tracker bullshit at the murder, and they tracked him down. It was blind luck he wasn't there when the cops busted into his complex.

He'd come around the corner from the grocery store, paper bags full of foods he'd never been able to afford before, and there they were. Cars outside the building, splashing red and blue light into the neighborhood as men stood around in black uniforms. There were no thoughts. Only actions. He was running in the other direction before the bags hit the ground.

He'd tried to get too hot too fast. Couldn't afford to be stupid anymore. So he adjusted.

Instead of calling his friends or family, the first people the police would expect him to contact, he went off the grid. Didn't reach out to anyone he knew, didn't leave any tracks to be followed. Stopped trying to pull money out of his frozen bank accounts and became a ghost. He slept in doorways, empty trucks, and churches before he came to the underpass looking for a place to permanently stay.

After existing for years, the underpass tent city had figured out a sort of government. And Davey was king. It was the unbreakable rule that before anyone moved in, they had to meet with him to gain his approval. Approval, like Davey thought the underpass of a bridge was the kind of place that required thorough vetting to weed out the undesirables.

"The first thing I always ask people that want to live here is how they came to be on the streets," Davey had said. He smiled a lot and his milk-white teeth made Sam want to scrub his own with sandpaper. People with teeth like Davey's couldn't be trusted. They focused too much on themselves. King Davey wouldn't let him stay in the underpass if he knew the truth about the things Sam had done.

"Well, I got laid off from work, couldn't find another job. That, combined with alimony payments to my ex-wife and everything involved with that pretty much crushed me. Couldn't afford the house, had to sell it, couldn't rent an apartment without a job, and now I'm here. I'm sure that's the story for a lot of these people."

Davey chuckled. "Yeah, that sounds pretty familiar. You ever spend any time in jail, or are you currently wanted for anything?"

"Nope. Downloaded a lot of illegal music a few years ago, but not sure if they're still trying to snag people for that."

"Drugs?"

"I used in the past, but I'm clean now."

Davey made a face. It would have been better to tell him

he'd never touched a thing, but the track mark scars on his arms wouldn't lie.

"Any sexual stuff I need to know about? We take very good care of our women here."

"I'm more focused on getting back on my feet than anything else. You don't need to worry about anything on that front."

"Diseases or medical issues? Our city has some pull with the police department. If we keep quiet, keep to ourselves, they get us basic medical assistance when they aren't overly busy." Sam's thoughts immediately turned to smack, but he shook them off. If he wasn't going to have anywhere to live, he didn't need the drugs to become a problem for him again. No, Davey. No conditions that needed help. He'd be a model tenant, tent city member, or whatever made up name he wanted to call them.

They toured the underpass. There were more people living there than Sam expected. It looked smaller from the outside. "We have a nice set up," Davey said, "but it took a lot of time and work to get that way. Police used to clear everyone out and we'd return within days. Climbed fences, knocked down barbwire, whatever it took. We even started organizing protests and sit-ins to use free speech and the Occupy movements to deny eviction. Occupy the Underpasses, we called it. After a while the government stopped trying and just embraced it all."

Crime spiked in the areas surrounding the underpass and the neighborhoods fell apart, but it made things easier for cops to monitor. The rest of the city felt safe with most of the homeless population enclosed in a square block, all confined to their shanties and tents.

The tent city had started when Davey built a hut in the middle of the underpass where the mud was thicker. It spread outward as more people joined, setting up tents on pallets and wooden platforms to keep them from sinking into the mix of water and dirt underneath. Even with the wet mess underfoot, the center was the best place to live. Sleeping in the middle meant you could leave in any direction necessary. It was quieter. Cleaner. A lot of the garbage that people threw into the underpass didn't reach them. The shelters on the outside were made of ponchos and trash bags and sticks and shopping carts. The closer to the middle, the nicer things got, until reaching real tents with zippers and insulation and privacy.

It was a seniority system into the middle. When someone moved out or died, their spot was taken in a few hours by someone living closer to the edges. A meeting area was cleared out in one corner of the underpass with a wooden fence separating the homeless from the real world of West Ham. Police could come there to talk to Davey if they needed to. It served as a good middle ground and a reminder from the cops: they would only come into the designated area of the underpass unless the homeless started problems for the rest of the city. Then they would tear through them like a storm.

Sam's tent was on the outer rim, vacated by a guy in his fifties who had died earlier that day. Well, Davey called it a tent. Sam called it a miserable shithole of garbage stacked on garbage to make something even more uncomfortable than sleeping out in the city. A rusted piece of fence, covered by a moldy shower curtain, reeking of mud, piss, and mildew. But it was shelter, and he had to put the time in if he ever wanted to live closer to the center. He just had to wait for people to die. The farther in he lived, the less likely the cops would ever find him. He thanked Davey and unpacked his bag.

Months passed and seasons changed. The summer was horrible down there. The mud stank as it dried and cracked, the evaporating water bringing the rancid smell into everyone's nostrils. Overhead, the bridge that usually protected them from nasty weather kept everything humid and made it difficult to breathe. Desperation flooded the camp, and during the day more of the residents stayed outside the underpass than in it. In the heat of day, people gave less to beggars, always quickly walking past them and averting their eyes until they could get somewhere with air conditioning. The tent citizens had to stay out hours longer to get the same amount of money as before.

Crimes happened more frequently as the temperature rose. Nothing serious, but enough to notice. Sam came back to the underpass after an unsuccessful day of panhandling and saw Davey getting yelled at by a lady cop. She had bars on her uniform and looked important. She kept poking Davey in the chest, prodding his sweat-soaked shirt. As he sank back toward his hovel, she wiped her finger off with a handkerchief. A meeting with the community was held that night and Davey passed the buck to the tent citizens, screaming that they had to stop fucking with the cops and the law, or it would fuck them right back.

It was hard to stay angry at Davey. He was good for the underpass, taking the role of a hobo and turning it into a strange version of leadership. His underpass, his community, his rules, his responsibility. It never went to his head, but he enjoyed the position like a politician, shaking hands and waving hello. People listened to him. When someone passed along a request for a favor that had come from Davey, it was priority. When he announced a rule, it was gospel.

But that night, the summer heat and humidity turned his cry for order into a slap in the face. Back in their tents, residents complained and argued. Fuck with us? *We* will be the ones to fuck you back.

The next day, Sam's neighbors were more aggressive on the street. One pushed a man that didn't give him money. A group of three stole cases of beer from a convenience store. The cop was back that night, but this time she was the one preaching from the meeting area. The police hadn't talked to them since Sam had started living there.

As they gathered around the platform where she asked for their attention, Violet whispered to Sam that living in the tent city was technically squatting and the government couldn't officially condone or even acknowledge their living in the underpass.

She was breaking the law herself by speaking to them. Sam kept his head low to avoid meeting her eyes.

She asked for quiet, waving her hands with expensive nail polish. Yelling through bright red lips, her face layered and caked with makeup, slightly plump from too much food. This rich, beautiful woman who had decided to be a cop, asked for their attention. "We understand that you are all in difficult situations. However, that does not mean you do not have to abide by the law. I have no interest in getting my officers to search through your property, or to force you out of here. But if your behavior continues to disrupt the rest of West Hamington, we will have no other choice."

Sam ground his teeth. He'd only been in the underpass a few months, but this was his home. He didn't want to leave it. He didn't have any responsibilities, any pressures, and he had shelter. This bitch was not going to steal it away from him.

He ambled out of the crowd, disgusted as the cop continued her lecture. This pretty bitch wearing pearls and a diamond ring had no place to tell the homeless people living in the community what to do. He walked outside of the underpass, looking at the buildings around it.

The lights in the city were all out. People were probably sleeping comfortably, knowing they would get up tomorrow, work for a few hours, and bring home some money. Their office buildings would have air conditioning and they would complain about the sun beating on their necks during the walk to the subway. The cop probably lived in one of these apartments with air conditioning. Or a nice house in East H, her husband asleep under a thick blanket. The distribution of things was not even. The distribution of things was not fair.

He turned the corner of the underpass. The wooden fence stood between the meeting area and him. He could hear the cop droning on about their responsibility to the city. He leaned against the fence and listened. "We are all the same. All residents of Hamington. If you're unhappy, we're unhappy, and vice versa. We have to work together to improve the city."

Improvement. Like her version of the world was the same as theirs. Like she cared about their lives being improved. He wouldn't have it anymore. She would not take away their home. The wooden fence was at least twenty feet high. He began to climb, using broken boards as footholds.

Her back was to him as he gripped the top of the fence. She would have turned around if she had actually been paying attention to the people she was lecturing. As soon as Sam swung his second leg over, they all looked above her and stared. She didn't care. She didn't see where they were looking. Didn't see a group of people trying to survive in a muddy hell. This woman saw a distraction and a pit stop on the way home from the office.

Davey stood next to her, looking at his people. When their gazes rose to Sam, he turned. Davey saw him. Their eyes met.

A pleading look crossed Davey's face as Sam turned his eyes to the cop's pretty ponytailed hair. He launched himself off the fence and his knees landed between her shoulder blades. Her head snapped backward as she fell, and then forward when her chest hit the ground. Her chin split open as it crashed against the wood beneath them. Sam rolled over, his knees screaming from the impact, but he wasn't finished. She would not take this place from him.

He grabbed that pretty ponytail and slammed her face into the broken wood with it. Stood and kicked her in the ribs. Brought his foot back for another. She grabbed her stomach and cried out.

Davey tackled him before he could kick her again. He straddled Sam, pinning his arms down with his legs. The underpass residents scattered back into the tent city like roaches.

"This is our place, Davey. Fuck that bitch," Sam spat. He tried to get out from under Davey's knees.

Davey shook his head. "No, this is *our* place. Not yours. You have to leave. We can't have you here. It's bad for all of us."

His home was gone. Taken from him by that bitch and Davey. How did he not understand? Sam was the one trying to help them. Sam was the one doing what was necessary for all of them to survive.

He yanked his arm away and shoved Davey off. He sprinted through the city to his tent. Davey was yelling for people to find him, hold him and don't let him leave.

He collided with someone and they both fell. Sam got to his feet and his eyes met Violet's. His friend didn't move, just held her hands up in surrender. "Help me, Vi. I was just trying to make sure we didn't lose this place. Let me hide in your tent." She didn't move. Just stared and shook her head with those hands raised in fear. Long seconds passed. Sam spat on the ground and kept running to his tent. His backpack was still half-empty when he fled the underpass.

All that blood and violence had passed, and now he was right back. Sam readjusted from his prone panhandling, the concrete under his feet making his legs go numb. There was no reason to wait any longer. The underpass looked empty enough. It'd have to do.

He breathed deeply as he walked across the street toward the embankment into the tent city. His ankles screamed as he eased his way down the slope into the underpass and took the last steps quickly, using his momentum to slide in behind one of the tents. No one saw him. He risked a glance out of his hiding spot. As long as he stayed out of sight from the middle where Davey lived, he'd be alright.

He crouched low as he ran through the thick mud, hiding behind one tent, sliding around another. The main path through the underpass was a branching network of pallets and cardboard. He wanted to steer clear of it, but each step was announced by a loud wet sound as his shoes sank deeper. Even if the city looked empty, he needed to hurry.

He waded through the underpass looking for Violet's tent. When everything happened, she'd nearly graduated out of the garbage teepees in the outer rings. She'd be closer to the middle now, in the tents held together with duct tape and makeshift sewing. Closer to the middle, and closer to Davey.

Sam looked for a tent with a voodoo doll hanging over the front flap. Even when she was living on the outside in a refrigerator box, Violet hung it up and told Sam it represented temptation or something. Hopefully she still had it. There was no other way to find her.

Minutes went by. It was taking too long. She had probably died or gotten too close to Davey or moved out into an actual shelter. Sam was fucked. No options for food. No options for safety.

And then he saw it. The temptation doll. He breathed deeply, his stomach's cramping briefly forgotten. Sam had never felt so happy to see something so stupid. There were no witnesses as he ducked through the front flap.

The lazy woman was still asleep, wrapped up in a garbage bag to keep the moist air of the underpass away. Sam nudged her with his foot and said, "This is probably why you don't have a job."

The body under the plastic groaned, rolled over, and saw who was in her home. Violet jolted and pulled the garbage bag tight against her dirty clothes like a shield. "Wh-what the hell are you doing? You can't be here."

Sam crouched and yanked the garbage bag off. She started saying something and Sam talked over her. "Shut up. Shut up. I won't be here long. I just need some food. I'll get out of your hair after that."

Violet motioned around to her tent. "Are you serious? I don't have anything. I'm sleeping because I have to go raid the dumpsters tonight before the trucks pick them up." Her tent was filled with trinkets and other trash. The kind of things a lot of hobos thought would be useful and then just ended up taking space. Empty cans, small baskets, baggies of twist ties. Sam noticed a stack of fabric in the corner, waiting to be sewn together. "Hey. Look at me." Violet grabbed Sam's face, her fingers reeking of something rotted and horrible. "You need to go. Now. Davey will kill both of us if he knows you're here."

Sam waved the threat away. "Davey won't do shit. He's afraid of me. And he should be. I cracked the skull open of some manager at Salvation Army this morning to steal this jacket. Imagine what I would do to Davey after everything he's done."

Violet shook her head. "The people that actually care about us and try to help us, you steal from? How are you going to get off the street if you keep dealing yourself bad cards?"

Sam gritted his teeth. Violet's path to homelessness was covered in shitty poker hands and smoky casinos. She used card and gambling metaphors when talking about finding a place to live, like all she needed was just one good hand, then she'd win the pot and bet her way out of the underpass. It was disgusting. She'd had everything, then threw it away.

"I was never dealt anything. I had to take it all myself," Sam said. He gripped his hands tight, wanting to throttle something. Violet leaned backward, tighter against the corner of her tent. She looked terrified. Reminded of what Sam could do when pushed. "Just help me get some food and I'll be gone. I've already found a good place to stay, I just need you to help me out. I lost my bag and all of my stuff. All I have is what I'm wearing. And you owe me." His new jacket had already gotten muddy from crawling through the tent city. Just entering the underpass made him smell like mildew.

"I owe you? Are you serious? I... Look, I don't care. I just want you out of here. What do you need?"

Five minutes was all it took. Making Violet change her mind was the easiest thing Sam had done since running from the tent city. It was the fear that did it. The face people used to say was so scary. Violet was afraid of him, and there were only inches between the two of them. Not enough space to protect herself from an attack. Sam should just take her for everything she had.

But then his emergency line would be finished. He needed to keep that last-minute option open. Someone that would help him if things ever went really bad. Even more than that, he needed to learn how to catch fish on his own, not just steal someone else's. And to catch fish, he needed…

"A rod."

"What?"

"I need a rod. A way to get money."

"Sam, I can't help you get a job."

"I'm not talking about a job. Help me get a weapon."

Violet's eyes skittered around the tent like balls on a pool table, refusing to look at Sam until she finished thinking. Same as always. Shitty, shitty poker face.

"How am I supposed to help you find a weapon? That's not exactly my skillset."

"I said it before. You owe me. Help me with this, and I'm gone. Cashing out, as you would say."

She didn't laugh at the joke. Sam knew she was weighing the options out in her head. She could either give Sam money for food and guarantee he'd be right back for more, or help him get protection and never be bothered by him again. Violet's eyes flicked back and forth, like she had narrowed down to two possibilities in front of her. Her eyes finally met Sam's. They were tired. Droopy. Pathetic. Sam owned her now.

Violet groaned. "Fine. What kind of weapon are you talking about?"

CHAPTER FIVE

VIOLET

INSTANT REGRET. IT wasn't an unknown feeling. When the cards were flipped or she snapped at her husband or pressed the green button on the ATM. Violet regretted asking the question as soon as the words tumbled out of her mouth.

She had been on the verge of just giving Sam some money out of the Chef Boyardee can behind the books in the corner, but she knew what would happen. Sam would return tonight when she was out searching for clean food in the backs of restaurants, and by the time she got home, the rest of the money would be long gone. No cash for food. No cash for booze to help her blur the edges and feel like a normal human being. So she'd given in. Said she'd help. Words Sam would never let her forget.

She cringed as Sam ground his teeth, the sound like two bricks scraping together. He probably didn't even notice he was doing it. Most smackheads didn't.

Other than the grinding, Sam looked clean. Before, he always had the jitters and eyes that darted around, looking for the next score. He must have handled the withdrawals by himself. It was impressive. Violet had seen some guys almost die from the sickness, even when they did have help.

But this was Sam. He was probably only off the stuff because he didn't have enough cash to buy it or was too busy running from people he imagined were chasing him. It had been months since he was kicked out of the community and nobody had orders to search for him anymore, but whenever a tent citizen saw him, he started running. Always running.

Constantly avoiding everyone you used to know would make anyone paranoid, lead you to make stupid decisions. People who were thrown out of the tent city usually ended up in jail or died on their own, but weaselly Sam had managed to keep on moving. Right back to Violet's doorstep.

"Do you have any connections to get a gun? I mean without leaving a trail. I can always find a pipe or a two by four or something, but that doesn't have that intimidation factor for cashiers that a good pistol has, you know? I need something small that I can hide. Pull out quickly and wave around to scare people."

"A gun? Sam, look around. The most valuable thing I have is a fresh roll of duct tape. Do I really seem like the kind of person who would know how to get a piece? I thought you meant something easy like a knife or a blackjack."

That teeth grinding sound again. "What about that pawn shop? The place you used to sell all your shit."

"Jakob's?"

"Sure, I don't know."

"I mean, yeah, I know where a pawn shop is, but you still have to pay for the thing. I don't get a frequent seller discount or anything." Jakob had always been excited when she came to visit, desperate for card money and willing to part with her belongings for cheap. It started with personal mementos and prizes she'd won in casinos, then slowly escalated to jewelry and family heirlooms. She came into the store once and recognized almost an entire shelf of her earrings and necklaces. She swore to herself she'd never go back there again. That she would turn it around and buy it all back.

It took a month for her to return to Jakob's, pawning her wedding ring.

She tried to get help, but the addiction never really left. She'd pass a casino and find her hand rustling through her bag for the soft feeling of loose cash. She canceled her debit cards to avoid ATMs and then lied to her husband about things she needed money for. It was worse now, even without the money to play, because now, after all the long days of politeness and panhandling to save enough and get out of the underpass, now she really knew the only way to get her life back was to win a few games. It could take the money away fast, but it worked the other way around too.

Sam fingered open the front flap of the tent and peered out. "How well do you know him? This Jakob guy."

"Met him a few times in my card days."

Sam scoffed and let the flap fall closed. "Your 'card days?' Shit, Vi, you'd still be gambling if you could cut your own hand off and trade it for chips. Is he a good guy? Hard worker? Anybody that really depends on him?"

"Not that I know of. Why?"

Sam smiled that nasty smile again, grinding his teeth from side to side. "So no one that would immediately call the cops if something happened?"

She had to draw a line. No one was going to get hurt because she mentioned the name of their store. Especially not after seeing what Sam had done to that poor policewoman.

They were all terrified they would get kicked out of the underpass after the attack. There were rumors that the city would fence it up again and station police nearby to teach them a lesson. Some of them even packed up their things and left. But the cops did nothing. Tracking down one person in a city the size of Hamington would have been too much work for too little pay. It was the vigilantes the underpass had to be afraid of.

They harassed the tent citizens, beating them up sometimes, convinced they knew Sam's location. Within a few days, there was another violent crime outside the underpass. Then another, and another, and the vigilantes soon stopped paying attention to them. All back to the way it was before.

Sam thrived in violence. That lifestyle worked for him. He found people that had something he needed and used them until they were dried up. He was trying to do the same thing now, but Violet would get in front of it. That was the damn truth.

"Nothing's going to happen to Jakob. There's no reason for it."

The smile left Sam's face. "Violet, stop. Don't be a coward. You need the money, and I need you in order to get this done," he said. "You've been there God knows how many times, you should know the place well. You help me, I'll get you a gun, you'll get some nice cash, and you can go back to throwing it away in some dirty casino."

Violet's gut pulled at her. He was right. All she needed was a little buying money to get on the table, and in a few hands she'd be able to consistently pay for a shelter. Maybe even one of those apartments they set people up with. Three meals a day.

The violence, though. She'd done so well to avoid trouble, rarely even getting in arguments with people who did her wrong. Now Sam was trying to take her past arguments. Past fistfights. Something she'd never even considered. A peaceful life served her well. Kept her from worrying about cops or vigilantes coming after her in his sleep. But she still lived in this damn swamp, under tons of concrete and metal overhead. Maybe something needed to change.

"You're a bastard for trying to pull me into this. You know that," Violet said.

Sam shrugged. Silence sat heavy in the tent.

"I need your word on something," she continued. "You have to promise me that if I help you, you won't talk about it. Like I was never there. And I don't owe you anything after this. If you come to me with anything else, I'll let Davey know, and you'll be cooked."

Sam moved in closer to her. An electricity in his eyes that

hadn't been there before. "If this thing goes well, I won't ever have a reason to bother you again."

It felt too clean. Too easy for Sam to come in to her home and drop a few questions, a few "pleases," some desperate stories and guilt, and change everything that she'd worked so hard to avoid. He kept calling it this "pawn shop thing," but this was robbery. Assault.

If she could keep Sam under control, keep things straight-forward and easy, her life could be back to its straight-edge lines—with a little extra cash in the process. You need to take a few risks to come out big on the other side of the table.

"Violet. *Vi*. Are you going to help me." It wasn't a question. It was forceful drag out of her thoughts.

She shook her head and looked around her tent at the pile of tattered books. The thin, stained mattress tucked beneath a full garbage bag. Layers of soiled clothes sitting in random balls all around her. She suddenly felt tired. Exhausted from constantly trying to swim out of the mud of the underpass. The idea of money and central heating and thick, clean blankets had snuck back into her head. She couldn't live like this anymore, under a bridge, worrying about freezing or starving to death every night. No human should.

"Yes. If it means you leave me alone, you leave my home alone, and you stop coming around here... then yes."

Sam clapped and rubbed his hands together. "Thank you. I really do mean that. I would die out there on the street without you."

"Sure. But... but you promise you won't come back after this?"

"Of course. I'm sorry to have to force you into it, but I needed help. And you're the closest thing to a friend I have."

"You're just all heart, aren't you Sam?"

He extended his arms out wide and said, "Nothing but love." The smile on his face faded and he leaned in closer. Violet was already tucked into a corner of the tent and couldn't move further away. She forced herself to stay still. Sam's eyes were a pale blue framed in his head.

"Tonight. It has to be tonight. I'll be here."

Sam took one more peek out the front flap and was gone, footsteps in the mud squishing away from the tent. Violet waited for the steps to fade into silence, then grabbed the soup can in the corner and poured out its money. A few quarters, a couple of bills, some pennies. Couldn't have been more than four or five dollars. All of her savings. The cost of one fast food meal. And then what? She tried to steady her gut and fight the nausea of her decision.

"I don't have another choice," she said aloud. "I don't."

She turned the can over and put the money back in, letting each coin drop one at a time.

CHAPTER SIX

TAYLOR

"No. That's not how we're going to do it."

Taylor turned off the recording equipment and rubbed the bridge of his nose. His heart pounded with anger and adrenaline. He tried to control his breathing and forced a patient smile onto his face.

"Just to clarify," Taylor said, "you contacted us and said you wanted to do a biographical report on the nightly news. Specifically a video feature. Then you ask me to send my camera guy away. And now you don't even want to talk about what we agreed to discuss." Taylor had to get Hudson on track early. If not, the old man would try to run the show and none of this would be any help. It was falling through his fingers.

"That's not it. If this is going to happen, we're going to do it my way. I don't want to forget anything, and to ensure that, I'm going to take the wheel. So," Hudson said, leaning forward and turning the recording equipment back on, "why do you, Taylor Gardner, want to interview me?"

"I'm sorry?"

"Why. Do you. Want to interview me? Think of this as my portion of the conversation." He leaned forward in his wheelchair, smiling politely and crossing his arms behind his back like a one-eyed Larry King.

Taylor fought a scowl from crawling across his face. This man didn't deserve to know his thoughts. To know what he'd been through. "Every journalist in the world wants this job."

"You're telling me you're only here because I personally requested you?"

"No."

"So, why do you want to be here?"

For almost anyone else, it would have been a simple question with a straightforward answer. Timothy Hudson was the first openly operating vigilante in a city that ended up embracing and putting its trust in unofficial law enforcement over the real thing.

Hamington's justice system had a reputation of pervasive laziness and corruption, from top to bottom. One rigged judge was voted out and replaced by another. Local police acted like they weren't worried about figuring out what was happening in the city and keeping people safe. All of it, top to bottom, round and round it goes.

Hudson went outside of all that. There was no money to make from throwing himself into dangerous situations to try to help people. No health care or life insurance benefits from trying to break up crime organizations and drug rings. People believed the vigilantes who actually help the city all started with a single person's selflessness. That person was who defined the entire city. Everything the vigilantes did was because of him. The good and the terrible.

"I just wanted to learn more about Hamington's local royalty."

Hudson shook his head. "Honesty, especially as we begin this process, is vitally important. I'll be as honest with you as you are with me. I know there's more than that. If you can't tell me why you're here, I'm afraid I won't be able to tell you anything at all."

Taylor stared at him in silence, ignoring the empty eye socket looking right back.

"Mr. Gardner. I cannot help you if you are not truthful with me. If you have no interest in sharing your reasons for being here, please feel free to leave."

His mouth opened and closed. Throat felt dry. Honesty? This man didn't deserve honesty or respect or any other conversational niceties.

But Taylor knew that if he wanted answers, if he wanted to finally be at peace, he would have to meet this man halfway.

Her face forced itself to the front of his mind. Alice.

Memories he'd tried to forget bubbled back to the surface. Meeting in college. Travelling the world. Trying new foods, new adventures. Their house. His proposal.

Taylor looked down at his hands. Picked at a dry scale of skin on his knuckle.

"When... when my fiancée died, everyone knew about it."

He heard the words come from somewhere far away. Nausea rolled in his stomach. He felt himself sinking deeper into his chair. "If they weren't watching when I found out, they saw it later. YouTube and video clips, things like that. 'News anchor learns about family death mid-broadcast.' It went viral, as they say. The worst people, the really insensitive ones, they'd tell me they were sorry and asked how I was doing. Asked me how I felt. What it was like to have a loved one die because she got caught in a gunfight between two people who believed they were doing good for the world by taking the law into their own hands. What it was like for no one to even pretend to try to find and arrest them." His vision blurred. He blinked quickly. Cleared his throat.

"And I had no answer. I understood why they asked. I even used to think like that. To everyone else, Alice... she was a statistic. One number in a sea of other numbers that clearly said—screamed even—that the vigilante presence in Hamington is a good thing.

"But there were other people too. People who cared for me after everything happened. My parents were long gone, I was an only child. Alice was my only family. And people who watched me on the news started sending me cards. They brought food, flowers, hell, some even started a scholarship in Alice's name at the university. They felt bad for me but followed up by reminding me that this was just the way the city worked and I was just unlucky to catch the bad end of the stick. Like they had to justify to themselves why they were still happy with masked, armed men patrolling their streets.

"I tried not to get angry, because I understood. I used to be right there with them. Got wrapped up in their same feelings of awe and that warm safety when someone who looked like he belonged in a comic book helped the world by stopping a mugging or walking little old ladies across the street. I never expected anything bad to come from it. Because I didn't understand it. Didn't look at it straight on.

"There was a point when it all changed for the worst. Long after you started. Long after others joined in. When the police began embracing the vigilantes and allowed them to take on the more dangerous jobs. When people believed they were safer because the vigilantes were doing the protecting and serving the city paid the cops for. When the rumors began that police were using vigilantes to get around the laws they were supposed to enforce.

"But it started with you. You, your name, your image. They were all symbols of safety. Of the uniqueness of our city. And they made us proud—me, proud."

Taylor's hands were shaking. He mindlessly grabbed the pen and paper off the table in front of him, trying to find some kind of stability. This was all too much. Finally being here. Confronting this man and telling him everything. It was too much but he couldn't stop it. Words kept pouring out like blood from a fresh wound.

"You know... we had talked about getting pregnant. Wanted to try from day one on the honeymoon. It made sense for us, our career paths, our age. The wedding was only a few weeks away when it happened. Those... lawless animals stole that from me. Stole my future family."

Taylor wiped his mouth with the back of his hand. He was sitting forward in his chair, clenching the pen in one hand, the other pushed flat and tight against the notepad in his lap.

"You want to know why I'm here? I wanted to talk to you. Because you're the one who made an entire city believe that the defined rules of right and wrong weren't really rules at all. That common, decent laws don't matter if no one will judge you guilty or innocent. It all started with you. I see this as your fault. Your doing.

"People romanticize it. In movies and comic books and everything else. You've been on a Wheaties box, for God's sake. But beyond the costumes and stoicism and speeches, there's a dirty violence. Tracking down and assaulting gangsters. Crippling, paralyzing people that are still yet to be proven guilty by the justice system, because a man in a cape or a mask believes that someone is abusing his wife, or laundering money from his company, or stealing possessions from unoccupied homes.

"I want people to understand what that really means. I want to understand. What was it that started all this? Caused it. If it was all worth it. I just... I just want to know why."

He fell back into his chair. He felt spent.

The equipment on the table blinked, still recording through the silence.

Hudson showed no emotion. He thumbed an edge of the scar that slashed across his face, gazing through the glass wall into the woods. "I appreciate your candor," he said. He pulled a handkerchief from his pocket and dabbed at the corners of his mouth. The old man blinked, his left eyelid closing over his eye as a normal one would, his right hanging loose like a curtain being pulled up and down. "And I would be happy to answer your questions. I feel like it's the least I could do. Not sure if there's much else to say."

Cooperation. Finally. Taylor released his grip on the pad of paper and tried to sit up a little straighter in his chair.

"But I'll be honest and tell you right now. It might not make a lot of sense. It barely does to me. But it started because of my family. They were strict Christians, with a moral compass stuck in one direction. Whatever they decided was wrong, was wrong. Nothing changed their minds. I'm getting ahead of myself though. I guess the best place to start would be when I was in college. My school had an honor code. If you were caught lying, cheating, or stealing, you were immediately..."

CHAPTER SEVEN

HUDSON

"...In a fuck ton of trouble," Brian said. He dropped his head into his hands, wiping tears from his eyes while Timothy sipped a beer and watched football on the muted television set. "It was one fucking question. And everyone knows Professor Andrews asks those obscure, ridiculous questions on purpose. Even if I had read the chapters, how the fuck are we supposed to remember every sentence?"

Some of the other brothers crowded onto the fraternity house couches mumbled their agreement. Timothy remained silent. It was difficult for him to feel sorry for someone who knew the rules of the school, knew the consequences, and still refused to follow them.

"Is there going to be a jury or something?" someone asked.

Brian sniffed snot back into his head. "I go before the honor council next week to plead my case. And then, you know... if I'm found guilty, I'm gone."

"All over one question on a test? Seriously? That's such bull-shit. Who hasn't cheated before?"

"One. Fucking. Question." Brian took a long swig of beer. "Any idea who ratted?"

Brian rested his drink against his knee and leaned back into his seat. Even with the threat of expulsion hanging over his head, he looked like he was enjoying having an audience. "Oh yeah," Brian said. "I know exactly who it was. There's only one person it could have been. We were all spread out in the classroom. I was on the edge, Rick was in front of me and never saw me look at his test, and the only other person anywhere close was that piece of shit, Dennis."

"Wait, Dennis like our pledge? Dennis Rhodes?"

"Dennis fucking Rhodes."

The mumbling began again.

"We shun him," someone said. "Force him to quit or blackball his ass and make sure everyone on campus stays away from him like he's got the fucking plague. Make his life miserable." More mumbling. Louder this time.

Timothy shook his head, staying intently focused on whatever commercial was playing on the TV between quarters to keep his mouth closed. These guys always escalated things so quickly.

"We could do it tonight. Punish him," Jonah said. There was no mumbling now. The brothers spoke and nodded and smiled.

Jonah was hard to say no to. He had a way of speaking that invited only agreement. "We could tell him that we appreciate him coming this far, especially for making it halfway through Hell Week, but we don't think he's the kind of brother our house needs."

Whether it was Jonah speaking or Brian or anyone else, it felt wrong. Dennis had done everything asked of him and never complained. To put him through an entire semester of cleaning the house after parties, sending him on cigarette runs, random menial tasks, and the constant, unencumbered harassment of pledgeship, only to be denied brotherhood days before the end because he'd done what was demanded of him by the school. It was wrong.

"You... you can't do that." The words escaped Timothy's lips before he could stop them. He kept his eyes on the television, hoping no one heard.

Brian leaned forward in his seat and pointed this bottle at

Timothy. "What do you mean 'we can't do that'? This kid's a snake, and I'm probably not going to graduate from this school because of him. Is that the kind of person you can trust as a brother?" The house was quiet. No one on the couches moved. Too many pairs of eyes, heavy on him, waiting for him to respond. His heartbeat quickened.

He finally turned and acknowledged the question. "What do you want me to say? You cheated on a test. We all knew the rules coming here. You cheat, you're gone. You see someone cheating and you tell the administration, or you're gone. That was Day One, man. How are you going to punish him for doing exactly what he's supposed to do?"

"Because no one needed to know!" Brian said. "He could have looked the other way. He could have kept his eyes on his own test. He could have stuck his fucking thumb up his ass and diddled himself all the way down the road! This is his fault and he betrayed the people that he was supposed to be closest to. How do you not see that? Everyone else here does."

Brian stood up and shouted. "If you think this douchebag Dennis no longer deserves to be a brother, stand with me." Brian's roommates Arnold and Paul leapt to their feet. Jonah got up after them, eyebrows raised as he looked at the rest of the brothers seated on the couches. Despite all of their mumbling and agreements, no one joined the four dramatically standing in the center of the room.

"Well... fuck all of you too. You pussies," Brian said. "We're going to take care of this shit after tonight's event. Force him out." He stomped out of the room, slamming his beer bottle into the bonfire logs in the backyard. The other three followed. Hesitant laughter simmered around the room.

None of the four who stood had positions of power within the fraternity. They had no say over whether Dennis would or wouldn't become an active brother and no ability to punish him as a pledge. "That's kind of embarrassing," someone said.

"I'd be surprised if they even show up tonight," another laughed.

Unease sat high in Timothy's chest. He didn't like arguing in public and having everyone in the house pay attention to him. But his discomfort ran deeper than that. Brian's anger was contagious. And irrational. That kind of anger spread like a fire. Timothy need to make himself scarce during tonight's Hell Week event. No good would come from running into that, accentuated by alcohol and fear of expulsion.

It was a good excuse to get some homework done and go to bed early. Every night for the past week, he'd been alongside his brothers at the fraternity house, drinking cheap beer into the early morning and laughing at the pledges' mild discomforts. It was exhausting.

The lights in his apartment were off by eleven, but sleep wouldn't come. When he began to drift off, he heard Brain's words, each syllable exploding in his ears.

Dennis fucking Rhodes, followed by a swig of beer.

We're going to take care of this shit.

Swig of beer.

After tonight's event.

Swig of beer.

That was hours ago. How much did Brian have to drink since then? And Jonah and Paul and Arnold?

Timothy grabbed the clock beside his bed and squinted at the numbers in the dark. It was that blurry time of day, either late at night or early in the morning. The pledgeship events would be over by now. There was no harm in checking to make sure Dennis was alright. If not, Timothy's mind would keep diving deeper into a rabbithole, imagining atrocities worse than could ever come to pass. There would be no sleep until he confirmed Dennis was fine. Timothy grabbed his sweatshirt and left quickly, wanting to clear the uneasiness from his chest and get some sleep.

As a freshman, Dennis had to live on campus. The brothers knew the locations of all their pledges' dorms in case they needed to find someone who could buy beer or cigs at a moment's notice, but when Timothy entered Dennis's dorm he was worried he wouldn't be able to tell which room was his. The lights were all dark at this hour.

He stepped down the hall, running his fingers against the cinderblocks on either side. Stairwell exit signs tinted the hallway a low red. He turned a corner and saw light flooding from underneath a door. His stomach dropped.

This was Dennis's room. He should have been asleep by now. All the other pledgees on this hall were. Why wasn't he?

Timothy placed his ear against the door and heard groans from inside. He tapped a knuckle against the door.

"Ah, uh sorry, who is it?"

"Timothy Hudson. Can you let me in?"

"Door's, ah, door's open."

He turned the knob and saw Dennis, stripped down to his underwear, lying facedown in bed. His body screamed a bright, violent red, from his calves all the way to his neck. Blisters bubbled on the back of his arms and knees. Bile rose in Timothy's throat.

"Jesus Christ. What happened?"

Dennis turned his head to look at Timothy, a visible line separating the red from the back of his body from the front. "They stripped me down and made me stand close to the bonfire. Asked me a bunch of questions. It's not awful, it just stings when I move. Like a bad sunburn."

"No, this... this is an actual burn, Dennis." Timothy could feel the heat off his skin by just holding a hand over him. It looked stretched and crisp, like dry leather. "We need to get you to a hospital."

"A hospital?" Dennis laughed, then winced. "It's really not a huge deal. I burn easily, then I tan. It'll be fine."

Timothy eyed a trio of blisters on the kid's triceps, filled with something viscous and yellow. They'd grown that large in only a few hours. What would he look like by morning?

"No. We need to leave now."

Dennis grasped the sides of his bed like a child. "I'm not going anywhere. Please. I already messed up by turning in Brian. Anything else will be worse. It's all just part of the game."

"Look at me. Dennis? Look at me. This is not normal, okay?"

"I don't care," he said. Tears welled in his eyes. "I messed up, it's my fault. I'll get through it, but I'm not going anywhere."

Timothy tried to grab his arm to pull him off the bed, but Dennis let out a sharp cry as Timothy's hand wrapped around one of the burns. "Please leave," Dennis whimpered.

The sides of Timothy's mouth curled downward. They'd done a number on him. Tortured him, then made him think it was his fault for doing what he was supposed to. Timothy clenched his fists. Nothing would change Dennis's mind right now. Not when the pain and guilt so tightly enveloped his thoughts. He backed out of the room, looking at the blisters and redness that covered Dennis's body.

The lights were still on in the fraternity house as Timothy drove past. Smoke rose from the bonfire pit at the back of the property. He smashed his foot on the brake pedal and pulled off to the side of the road.

What if they were still there? All four of them, laughing because they thought they'd won and taught the kid a lesson. Something had to be done. If Dennis wouldn't take care of himself, Timothy would do it for him. If his brothers didn't understand what they'd done was wrong, Timothy would make them. He slammed the door of his car and strode into the house.

They were still there. Silent with wide eyes. Timothy's chest rose and fell heavily. His heart pounded.

Brian was the first to speak. "We went too far, man. Did... did you see him? How is he?"

"He has burns and blisters all over his body. It sounds like you made him stand right next to a bonfire. What did you expect? And for what—payback? I told you not to do anything."

Jonah winced. "We didn't know he was that close to the flames until after we pulled him away. His skin… it was hot to the touch. We wouldn't have done it if…"

They kept talking. Jonah explaining, apologizing, Brian chiming in to contribute, Paul taking over the reins, all around in a circle. Timothy couldn't look any of them in the face. They were disgusting. There had been no foresight in their actions. No consideration of the consequences.

It was more than violence. More than burns and blisters. They made Dennis feel like the one who needed to apologize. Made Dennis feel like the guilty party.

The four of them would say their condolences, take him out to dinner and say how sorry they were. How it all got out of hand and the fire was hotter than they thought and they never could have imagined that it would have done that kind of damage. But apologies from them weren't enough.

As they kept trying to explain and justify themselves, Timothy focused on the Christian calmness that his father taught him and tried to channel it. He searched for that peacefulness as they continued apologizing to Timothy for something that didn't happen to him. He thought about the lessons his father had tried to teach him.

Kindness to strangers. Do the right thing. Protect your friends and family. And most importantly, if someone did a person ill, it was Timothy's job to make things right, any way he could.

He searched for the kindness and reconciliation the situation required, but a tension built inside him, coiling like a snake. And then released.

The first strike knocked Brian backward. Timothy grabbed Jonah by the back of the neck and slammed his fist into his stomach. He threw another punch at Arnold and kicked Paul in the kidney.

The four of them tried to fight back, throwing wild, slow strikes, but Timothy had only started. This was their punishment. This was what they deserved. Fists strengthened by anger and disgust.

When he left the fraternity house, his shirt was torn and covered in blood, knuckles raw, hands shaking from the adrenaline. Brian was unconscious. The others were battered and bloody with no will to chase after him as he walked out the door.

It didn't take long for word to get around. About Brian and Dennis. About Timothy. The dean of students left a message on this answering machine only days later, setting a meeting in his office.

His father was there when Timothy walked in. Apparently Brian and the others had gone to the dean, turning themselves in for what they'd done, explaining how Timothy had punished them in the process. The dean had already filled in his father while they waited for him to arrive.

"While we do not condone or allow any type of hazing to happen on this campus," the dean said, "that does not give you the right to physically assault your classmates. They will receive punishments from the school, along with your more... unique message. But you were in no place to determine how they were to be reprimanded."

Timothy tried to argue and make him understand, but nothing worked. His father sat silently the entire time and only listened. At the end of it all, the dean shook his head and said, "Due to the severity of this incident and the condition of your classmates, I have no option but to suspend you for the rest of the semester." And it was over.

When they got home, his father sat him down at the kitchen table, the same seats as an uncountable number of lectures before. He poured Timothy and himself a glass of water, waiting for his son to speak first. Maybe to offer an explanation. Timothy didn't have anything to say. His father had just sat there while the Dean had accused him of all these things. Didn't come to his defense. Didn't try to protect him.

"Timothy. What were you thinking?"

"You were the one that told me if a person hurts someone, it was my job to do something about it, right?" Timothy asked.

The one lesson he'd succeeded in banging into his head was that if a friend was hurt, you did whatever you could to fix it. All he had done was correct the problem when no one else would. Even the dean was reasonably sympathetic. But his own father wasn't? How did he not see that he was wrong?

"Your heart was in the right place. But you have to be careful."

"Careful of what? I was the one who walked out of there with my head held high. They barely even tried to fight back. They knew what they had done was wrong."

"And tell me. What was it they did?"

It felt like this had been going on for hours. Days even. Arguing with Brian. The dean. And now finally at home, with his father. Timothy threw his arms in the air, leapt from his seat. "Are you serious? They burnt the shit out of a kid for doing what he was supposed to do. He was smaller than they were and he was terrified to fight back. That's no good reason to hurt someone."

"Exactly. Now tell me how that's different from what you did."

"But that's not the same thing. They hurt him, and I hurt them so they wouldn't do it again. That's it."

"No," his father said. "Those boys, friends of yours, Timothy, were not going to do anything to that boy again. They cooperated with the school. Turned themselves in and pled guilty. I don't—"

"After it was over. They weren't going to report themselves for anything. They only did that to get me in trouble and wrap me up in it."

"You don't know that. They were punishing themselves, and you had no right to step in and impose your authority over what you thought needed to be done. It was none of your business."

"I saw a situation and was fixing it. Doing something like you told me to."

"No," his father said again. "You weren't pursuing justice, you were pursuing retribution. You couldn't have tended to Dennis's burns? Taken him to the hospital? Sat with him and made him comfortable? Getting payback is not the same thing as fixing a problem. That is a slippery slope that many men have descended and been unable to climb back up again." He crossed the room for the Bible that lay on a nearby table and flipped through it. Every room had one, to ensure that the Hudsons were able to call upon scripture at a moment's notice. Timothy couldn't believe it. Not only was his father lecturing him, but now he was getting Jesus to.

"'Hear, my son, and accept my words that the years of your life may be many. I have taught you the way of wisdom and I have led you in the paths of uprightness. When you walk, your step will not be hampered, and if you run you will not stumble. Keep hold of instruction. Do not let go. Guard her, for she is your life. Do not enter the path of the wicked, and do not walk in the way of the evil. Avoid it. Do not go on it. Turn away—'"

"What, so you think I'm evil now?"

His father looked over his reading glasses at him. He spoke softly. "Of course not, son. I want to protect you from the evil that is out there. The things that are present and in front of you, as well as what is not so easy to see. The sinful misinterpretation of words to fit one's own goals is one of those straight paths of the wicked, for it involves not only yourself, but those who originally spoke them. 'My son, be attentive to my words. Incline your ear to my sayings, and let them not escape from your sight. Keep them within your heart.'"

He crossed the room and put his hand on Timothy's chest. His eyes tore across the page.

"'Keep your heart with all vigilance, for from it flow the springs of life. Ponder the path of your feet and your ways will be sure. Do not swerve to the right or to the left. Turn your foot from evil.'"

He took off his glasses and put them down with the Bible. He knelt in front of Timothy and held his hands. Timothy had a hard time meeting his father's eyes. He was not comfortable with him kneeling before him. "Be vigilant, son. Evil is around every corner. It is up to good, Christian men like us to slay it, even when it touches us. *Especially* when it touches us. It is not always an easy thing to discern good and evil actions from one other. Constant vigilance is necessary." He used Timothy's arms as a support and rose from his knee. Without another word he left the room.

The silence pressed on Timothy's ears.

That was it? That was the big justification for his father believing he was wrong to protect his friend? Suggest that he was on a pathway to evil and leave him in silence with nothing but an old Bible to keep him company? Christianity didn't understand how friendship worked. Jesus never had to fistfight anyone. He just sat there and prayed and apparently made miracles happen on a daily basis. Timothy wasn't a miracle worker. He was just a person. And a person had to do things that might make others squeamish.

The Bible on the table mocked him, its thin pages still parted open, a silk bookmark in the crease. He grabbed it and scanned through the words until he found what he was looking for. Keep your heart with all vigilance. Turn your foot from evil. His father's heart was in the right place. He was wrong, but his intentions were good. All vigilance. Be a good person.

Timothy's actions fell in line with those words. Be vigilant of evil. Be a good person. Run, don't stumble. Act with surefootedness.

His father had tried to guilt him with a Bible verse, but all he'd achieved was confirming that Timothy's actions were the right ones. He checked for the verse number. It was...

CHAPTER EIGHT

TAYLOR

"...Proverbs, chapter four, verses 10-27," Hudson said. "He jumped around a bit, but the meaning was still there. I've read that passage every day since, despite the fact that I've never called myself a 'good, Christian man' like my father. It became a beacon for me.

"I don't know what it was about that moment. Maybe the words rang true within me or it was one of those times signaling newfound maturity and a transition from childhood to adult. I honestly don't know. But from then—"

"Excuse me."

Linda had returned to the sunroom and apparently felt it necessary to interrupt Hudson's story. "I believe that's enough time for Mr. Gardner's visit today." Taylor checked his watch. It had been an hour since Hudson started telling the story and the only information he'd obtained was that Hudson had gotten in a fight in college, followed by a guilt trip from his father. That was nothing. Taylor had been in his share of fights in college. Gotten lectured by his own father. There were plenty of people just like that. That didn't turn them into revolutionaries or cultural phenomena. It couldn't have all just started because of some frat house brawl.

He couldn't be forced to stop so early in the first meeting. There had to be more. A better explanation of why.

He opened his mouth to ask Linda for fifteen more minutes before reminding himself of Hudson's first rule. Do not speak to the help.

"Linda will show you the way out," Hudson said. He looked away from Taylor, through the glass walls of the sunroom, over the crest of the hill to the city and beyond. He seemed deflated after telling the story.

Taylor turned off the recording equipment. "Is it alright if I take the audio of today's interview?" Hudson waved his hand and told him to do whatever he needed to, keeping his eyes on the skyline of West Ham.

The change in behavior was concerning. Just seconds ago, he wouldn't stop talking, digging into the past, gesturing with his hands to accentuate certain details. He was deep in the story. Then Linda entered the room and he became withdrawn and quiet. "Will the same time tomorrow be alright?" Taylor asked. He needed to keep Hudson's mind here. In this room. Couldn't afford to lose him now.

"Linda?"

She pulled a notebook from her scrubs and said that would be fine. Hudson grunted and readjusted farther away from Taylor. Didn't see if he needed anything else or ask if he'd felt like it was a productive session. Hudson was done with him.

Taylor stood and deposited the tape in his briefcase. He turned to leave, then glanced back at Hudson. He was still turned away, gently rubbing the bottom of his scar with his thumb. Taylor swallowed his disgust and placed his hand on Hudson's shoulder. Pushed away the anger at the man for forcing him to talk about Alice. The only thing that mattered right now was making a connection with him. If he didn't, he wouldn't learn anything and all of the time pursuing him would be for nothing.

"Thank you. For sharing with me. I'll see you tomorrow."

The man curtly nodded. And nothing else.

Linda escorted Taylor out of the room. Farther down the hallway, out of earshot from the sunroom she said, "I've called a cab for you."

Her voice surprised Taylor. "I thought we weren't supposed to acknowledge each other."

She shrugged. "My father never followed the rules. Why should I?"

"Wait... I'm sorry, did you say your father?" he asked. Taylor didn't see the resemblance, but it was hard to see Hudson's similarity to anything other than a cutting board. Linda had prominent cheekbones and Hudson's were sunken and dented with damage from years of combat. His jaw jutted forward at an angle, probably due to being broken and set incorrectly, while hers was pointed and polite. Taylor couldn't imagine how difficult it would be to helplessly watch a parent get whittled down over years. He wouldn't wish Hudson's condition on anyone.

She smiled politely. "Yes. The one and only Timothy Hudson has a daughter."

"And... you're his nurse?"

Linda glanced at her feet instead of straight forward. A small break in composure most wouldn't notice, but it was a tic Taylor recognized from interviews. "Sure," she said.

They continued down the hall in silence, Taylor replaying the morning in his head, looking for any clue about the relationship's existence. There was nothing but Hudson's strange silence when Linda abruptly announced it was time for him to leave.

As she guided him to the front door, he slowed. "What happened back there? Did I do something wrong? He just shut down. You said it was time for me to leave, and then... nothing."

She turned back to face him and narrowed her eyes. "I'll be completely honest. I didn't want this interview to happen. And it's not a personal thing, I didn't want anyone here. He'd been getting by fine, finally starting to embrace his schedule, not depressed about his health. And then suddenly he told me to get in touch with you. Called you 'that reporter that won't take a hint,' because of all those emails and letters you sent. He and I are in a bit of a fight over it. Nothing to do with you."

Linda continued to the door and opened it for him. His taxi was idling at the bottom of the hill, past the black iron gate. "I know he said he'd be open to as many interviews as necessary, but I would ask you to hurry up, get your sound bites, and be done with this. I'm sorry about what happened to you and your fiancée, but he needs as much rest as possible."

Nothing was given other than that. And none was really needed. A daughter didn't have to defend her attempts to protect her unwell father from a vulturous reporter. But something felt off. Her jumpiness when he asked about her being his nurse. The way she dismissed the rules Hudson had defined so clearly.

Something had happened there. She'd lost her composure and felt the need to shuffle him out as quickly as possible. A sharp change, in the middle of Hudson's story.

How long had she been in the room? Taylor had been so focused on the man himself, he wasn't quite sure. Was she listening the entire time, or had she just looked at her watch and decided he had been there long enough?

The door closed solidly behind Taylor as he left the house. The driver of the cab peered past him to the mansion at the top of the hill as he got in. "Damn, how'd you get in there? I've never picked anyone up from Hudson House before."

"42ND and 4TH, please. And it's... just a job I'm doing." Taylor didn't pay attention to the beauty of the city on the way home, or the driver telling him that he'd seen the YouTube videos of Taylor finding out about Alice on air and he was so sorry about what happened. He didn't even linger on Linda's immediate shutdown.

His mind was stuck on Hudson. On his story. He just couldn't figure out the man's catalyst.

In all of his experiences interviews for the station, his subjects had identifiable catalysts. Events that caused them to be unique and deserving of sharing their stories. People could look back on their lives and point out a specific instance when their paths

changed. The crazy guy with the show dog obsession. The philan-
thropic humanitarian. The award-winning second grade teacher.
Maybe it wasn't always a direct influence from A to B, but
through a certain chain of unique events, something happened,
or a decision was made, and their lives were put on different tra-
jectories.

Hudson's story, at least the way he'd told it so far, didn't have
a catalyst. There had been no change in his character or decision-
making when he decided to fight his fraternity brothers. That was
a direct reaction from the rules given to him by his religious family with a strict moral code. That was it. He continuously moved
in the same direction over the course of his life. No scarringly
early death of parents by criminals in the night, no catastrophic
event, just an idea that was constantly in place within him, until
he found an opportunity to act upon it.

Not good enough. That was not a good enough explanation
for everything that followed. A direct line, a direct path was no
journey at all. He made the decisions he felt were necessary to live
with the morality and responsibility imprinted upon him by his
family and knew that if something was wrong, it was his job to fix
it as well as he could. It was clear and foreseeable. And if everyone in this city had a similar experience, then by that reasoning,
no one would worry about laws, and would only do what they felt
was right.

And according to Hudson, it all started because four guys had
been on the wrong side of that. Hell, four guys he'd called his
friends. Dennis was almost a stranger compared to them. But
he chose to fight his friends because of something he personally
believed was wrong.

Chose his beliefs over his people.

He had to have known the fraternity brothers were going to
be punished. Things like that always made their way back to the
administration. Instead, Hudson went to them first and tried to
do to them what they'd done to Dennis.

Even knowing all of this, there was still so much missing. Why had he not wanted to be filmed? What were the topics he didn't want brought up? The man was an enigma and Taylor was no closer to finding out why Hudson started the vigilante movement. No closer to answering Taylor's questions.

At home, he listened to the interview again, writing down his thoughts and emotions while they were still fresh. His phone occasionally buzzed as Jake called to check in and Taylor silenced it each time. Couldn't be bothered. He'd rather drown in a pile of notes and a detailed account of the experience than be distracted by Jake and only be able to work off dull memories.

The phone rang again. Missed call number thirteen. Taylor realized it was dark outside and tried to rub the shadows of his computer screen from his eyes. He picked up the phone, and the first words he heard through it were, "This is a clusterfuck, Gardner. I've got Bill whining in my ear about how he was kicked off location and isn't allowed back for the rest of the interview, and now you're ignoring my damn calls. Please tell me you have some news that'll make me a happy man."

It felt like Jake's kid gloves were finally off. At least Taylor had made some progress there.

"I'm not sure if I do. We'll have as many sessions as we want, but the drawback is no cameras and I'm the only one allowed in the house and can't speak with anyone there besides Hudson."

"Seriously? Not even the woman who helped set up the interview?"

"Yeah. He was pretty adamant about that."

Linda's casual dismissal of the rules entered his mind again. Their conversation on the walk to the door. Taylor wasn't sure why he didn't want to tell Jake about her.

The other end of the line was silent. Taylor peered at the clock in the corner of his computer screen. Eleven at night and Jake sounded like he was still at the news station despite arriving at six in the morning, just like every other day.

He spoke slowly. "Taylor. Please. Tell me something good. You know I don't do well without having some control. Tell me anything good about today."

He scanned his notes and recounted the interview. Hudson's health, the mementos lining the walls, the fight with the fraternity brothers, the conversation with his father. No mention of Hudson forcing out his memories of Alice. No mention of Linda.

At the end, Jake said, "You better get that camera inside. This broken hero you're talking about? No one's going to give a shit about that guy until he's right in front of their faces. That audio by itself isn't going to have an effect on anyone. One old man sounds like every other old man in the world. We need the damage, the sacrifice, in front of the viewers."

"Jake, I don't think you understand. He's not messing around. If I push him on the cameras he'll pull the whole thing. He's threatened to do it already. There's not a lot of flexibility here."

After the call, Taylor shut down his computer and began packing to do it all over again the next day. As he opened his briefcase, a manila folder fell out. He opened it and remembered that Bill had given it to him before gunning the news van off the property. Taylor still couldn't remember the name of his son who wanted the items signed. He crouched to pick up the folder and its contents.

Three comics had fallen out, all wrapped in plastic and supported by cardboard, like museum pieces. They were the first three issues of *Hudson*, the series originally based on the vigilante's adventures. The writers used to scan the papers for any reports of Hudson's involvement in stopping criminals, then used the articles to create storylines.

The comic was one of the things that spurred Hudson's popularity so early, even though parents were angry about it. Real life crime was too dark for children to read about. Rape and murder and powerful people using their resources to slowly make other people weaker. Kids needed stories to have superpowers and romantic dialogue to distract them from all of that. Not a man dressed in all black, attacking people in the night.

Taylor loved that costume when he was a kid. It wasn't like Superman or Spider-Man in their bright, cartoony spandex. This was a real person using regular clothes as his uniform to fight crime. Things anyone could buy. Kids made their own Hudson costumes for Halloween and had Hudson-themed birthday parties and pretended to beat each other up.

It was a simple outfit of all-black boots, jeans, jacket, gloves, and baseball hat. Not much of a disguise, but the contrived silhouette with the hat pulled low became iconic. Back when camera phones and the internet were still things of science fiction novels, it was difficult for anyone to discover the true identity of Hudson. Even before he retired and announced who he was, he simply told people to call him Hudson and they had no idea it was his actual name. What kind of psychopath would assault violent criminals and then tell them his name?

Taylor tossed the comics on his desk and ran his hands through his hair. Add it to the pile with all the other unanswered questions.

It had only been one session, but something about today made him worried. The way Hudson controlled the conversation. What if at the end of it all, Taylor had hours of recordings and conversations and still knew nothing about the man? Nothing that he needed to know to let him sleep at night. To justify all that Hudson had done to the city. To the people that lived here. Taylor had sworn to himself that he would understand it one day. And if now wasn't the time, speaking directly to the core of the vigilantes, it never would be.

Taylor refused to believe that.

He would find his answers. He would drag them out of the man. No matter how hard he fought to avoid giving him the knowledge.

And what if there were no answers? What if there was nothing to be learned from him? If he had no more knowledge of why he'd acted than anyone else did? Taylor's stomach rolled. The idea of it made his vision blur. He closed his eyes and took a deep breath in. Held it. Released.

He opened his eyes and saw the comic. This idea of a super-hero. Taylor would defeat him.

CHAPTER NINE

VIOLET

THE BELL ABOVE the door jingled as they walked into the pawn shop. The bars on the window were more rusted than Violet remembered and there was an arcade game in the corner of the store, but nothing else had changed since she last owned property she could sell off.

The shop looked like someone's garage sale had thrown up into categories. Generators were lined up next to lawn mowers, which were across the aisle from the wall of hanging guitars. The iron gate over the jewelry display separated the rest of the shop from the back office and cash register. Shotguns, pistols, and hunting rifles were propped on display behind the counter, a metal lock running through their trigger guards. Sam started walking toward the counter, staring at the guns like he was caught in a trance, then swerved away to look at bobblehead trinkets on a shelf.

Jakob came out from the back office and peered through the bars separating him from the rest of the store. He called out, "Oh shit! Hey hey! Miss Violet! How's my favorite customer? It's been a long time! You're looking good! Thinner!" Sam glanced at her and scoffed. Violet walked toward the iron divider and tapped on the jewelry display separating them.

"How's it going, Jakob?" she asked absently. She scanned through the display, an old habit from when she used to visit. She saw a number of wedding bands, but none were hers.

The day she pawned off her ring was only a few weeks before her husband kicked her out. She held on to her ring longer than a lot of the bad card players she knew, but she eventually had to have some extra scratch. It was in the display for the next five or six visits. Every time she came in and saw it there, a sense of relief washed over her body. If she was able to win a few games she could still buy her old life back. Her ring, car, marriage. They'd all fall back into place. The day she came in and couldn't find her wedding band was an ugly one. Jakob asked her to leave and not come back until she'd gotten her shit together. She moved into the underpass three weeks after that.

"Ah, SSDD, Violet. Same shit, different day. What can I do for you? Need a little walking money? Or are you looking to take something home?"

Violet's cash pocket itched. "No, I'm just visiting the old stomping grounds. Heading out of town soon. Gotta get a new start somewhere else. How's business been?"

"Oh, I'm sorry to hear that. I'll miss you here. And business is just fine. Little bit of this, little bit of that. I did just get that big arcade machine over there." It was straight out of the nineties, the Teenage Mutant Ninja Turtles painted down the sides in action poses. Sam glanced at it and turned his head back to the Stratocasters hanging on the wall.

"They used to have one of these over at the Pizza Palace," Violet remembered. "I had more than a few late nights of beer and pizza with my college friends there. I actually wasn't terrible at that game. That's a nice find."

"You want to play? For old times' sake before you get out of town. I can pay for a couple of sessions." The register rang as he grabbed a fistful of quarters. Sam twitched when he heard the drawer open and close. Jakob came out from behind the counter and relocked the door behind him with a key attached to a ring on his hip. Sam passed them and Jakob nodded, telling him to let him know if he needed anything. Sam smiled.

Jakob's eyes lingered as Sam crouched and looked at a rack of baseball bats. He placed his hand on one and pulled back almost like it burned him.

He was being stupid. Acting like someone who had never been in a pawn shop before. No one ever shopped around, looking for something to spend money on. They came on a mission, either to recover what they'd pawned or find something specific they'd been searching for.

Violet got Jakob's attention again and reminded him about the game. They booted it up, and the theme song crooning about turtle power played through the store. Waves of nostalgia, thin and wispy, washed over her. Everything on the screen was déjà vu. She remembered seeing things in the game when she was younger, but only after they happened, and she could never remember what was supposed to come next.

She was rusty. Her turtle kept kicking and punching by itself in the corner, while Jakob's took out hordes of attacking ninjas. Jakob laughed at her and told her to get back in the fight. Get in the game, Violet! He'd obviously had more than a few quiet hours in the store to play. Violet was able to bring her character back into the mix as the battle was ending. The main villain of the level came on screen and started monologuing about how the turtles would never stop him. She was so sucked into the game that she forgot why they were there until Sam grabbed Jakob's hair and slammed him onto the floor.

They collapsed together, Jakob gasping as the wind was knocked out of him, a thud reverberating through the linoleum as his head cracked against the ground. Sam pinned him down with his knee on the man's chest, one hand around his throat, the other pulling the keys from his hip. He tossed them to Violet and wrapped both hands around Jakob's windpipe. "Remember. The door, the guns, the money, the tape."

Violet made the mistake of looking at Jakob. His stare burned her gut. Jakob had given her a pretty good deal on the things she'd brought in. Always tried to pay her enough so she could play a hand or two more, and now she was doing this to the man. Jakob's face was turning red, eyes big in their sockets. Violet ran to the front door and locked it.

"Let go of his throat," she told Sam. "Just hold him down." His teeth were gritted, lips pulled back in a violent grin as he barely loosened his grip. Violet wanted to push him off, but she had to flip through the key ring and find the one that unlocked the back office. There must have been dozens of keys. Her fingers fumbled, trying them as fast as possible.

A few were too big for the keyhole. Others she had to punch into the lock to see if they fit. It took longer than she liked. Jakob gagged. The keys clanged and danced in her shaky fingers. One finally clicked home and released the door.

The lock for the guns was easier: a big key that didn't need a lot of searching. The trigger guards clicked loudly as she pulled away the chain holding the guns in place. She grabbed pistols, two at a time, and slid them through the opening in the bars. Sam was still on top of Jakob. Violet called out, "Don't do anything stupid, man!"

"Then hurry the fuck up!" Sam yelled. He slammed his foot onto Jakob's free arm that was trying to push him off. His face was inches from Jakob's, hand still on his neck, sneering and whispering.

This was a mistake. Not like Sam said it would be. Jakob's legs swung around, trying to catch leverage or hit his attacker, while his breaths came harsh and quick. Violet's pulse pumped faster as she punched keys to the register. Someone was going to try to come in and find the door locked and look through the glass and see her behind the counter and Sam strangling Jakob and call the police and they'd all go to prison. The Ninja Turtles grunted and cried out in pain as they were attacked with no one at the controls to defend them.

Jakob wheezed. Violet had to move faster. She stripped the

register of all the cash and put the money with the pistols. She grabbed boxes of ammo and slid them through too. Jakob ran a cheap security system with a VHS tape and video camera in the corner. Violet ejected the tape and put it with everything else. She called to Sam for a bag. There was no response.

Both of Sam's hands were still around Jakob's neck. His face was a strange purple color. Violet yelled at him and ran through the door. Shoved Sam off. Sam pushed back. Fists clenched, tangled in each other's limbs. Violet looked down at Jakob as she shoved Sam away.

She'd never seen someone strangled to death before.

Death by starvation, overdose, drowning, those things happened all the time to people without homes. Murder was rarer, but stabbings and shootings weren't uncommon during the hot months of the year. This was something different.

Jakob's throat was already bruised from Sam's grip, his eyes pointed in different directions and bulging out of his head, all red from busted blood vessels, his face swollen. There was no movement. No breath. Just twitches in his limbs as the final nerves fought for oxygen. Violet didn't need to look for a pulse to know he was dead. She felt sick.

"His shit's all fucked up," Sam said. "We gotta get out of here." Violet turned to see him standing by the door, looking at the body. His face and neck were scratched and bleeding. There was no remorse on his face, no fear.

Tears welled up in Violet's eyes, and the burning in her chest made her want to scream. "You put me in this. You involved me. This was a decent human being," she said quietly. Sam walked past her without acknowledging her voice and swept everything off the counter into a bag. "What the hell is wrong with you?" Violet yelled.

"I did this for us. This is the way it had to be done. We have weapons, we have money, and we don't have some asshole to call the cops on us. He knew who you were. How long do you think it would take for him to find you? It's not like you kept any part of your life a secret from him, always coming in and whining your ass off. I made a decision to keep you safe. You would have been a robber, I would have been an accomplice, and this guy would have had the cops looking for you in no time."

"I was the robber? This was your idea!"

Sam shook his head and raised the bag. "Videotape in here says otherwise. You're a thief, I'm a murderer. That's just the way it goes. But we leave here, there's no evidence, and nothing will ever put us at the scene of the crime. You and I are finished. Debt repaid. You don't have to worry about me anymore. Hell, with this cash, you might even be able to work your way into a few more card games. This is a turning point for us, Vi. This is where we make our moves."

Sam dragged the body behind the counter where it couldn't be seen from outside. They turned off the lights and the neon "Open" sign. Check through the window for anyone walking by and locked the door with the ring of keys, leaving calmly. Quietly. And slowly. It would be days before anyone wondered where Jakob was.

Sam kept trying to talk to her as they walked. At first reminding her to keep calm, not to run, not to look too hard at any police officers or vigilantes patrolling the streets. But it felt like everyone they passed was staring at her. Knew what had happened. Thought that it had been her hands around Jakob's neck. Groans and cries started forcing their way out of her throat. Sam hissed at her to get her shit together.

Sam pushed her into a through-pass alleyway with a dumpster and some trash cans. Maybe they should have hidden the body better. In a dumpster or something. The body of the man they had killed.

The image forced his way into Violet's thoughts. Jakob's body. Rotting in the dumpster. Its popped eyeballs being chewed on by rats. Asking Violet to play a game. For old time's sake. To celebrate her getting out of town.

She ran to the exit of the alley and vomited. People on the

street didn't ask if she was okay or if he needed help. Just walked around her, ignoring the poor crying mess of a woman on the ground. She wiped flecks of vomit off her chin.

Sam grabbed her shirt collar and dragged her back into the alley like a dog. He pushed her against a wall and began pulling everything out of the pawn shop bag, evenly dividing and stacking up the pistols and ammo and cash between the two of them. Violet stopped him. She spat leftover acidic saliva onto the ground. The idea of bringing a killing machine into her tent made her skin crawl. "I don't want any of the guns. It feels wrong. Just... just give me my half of the money."

Sam cocked his head at her. "Half? And none of the guns? I'm not trying to give you a shit deal here. I wouldn't have any of this if it wasn't for you."

If it wasn't for her. She felt like vomiting again. "No. it doesn't feel right. It feels dirty. I don't want the guns. I really don't want any of it after what you did, but going through all of this... a man dying, robbing a place, I should... oh God, I should at least have something to show for it."

Sam ground his teeth as he looked at her. Just kept grinding and grinding and grinding them until he said, "You'll get two-thirds of the cash. No guns."

"Half," Violet said. She wiped away snot running from her nose. "Don't try to get generous on me now." She needed to get away quickly. This change terrified her. Sam suddenly trying to be charitable and give away money after strangling a man to death. There was no stability in his line of decision-making. She needed to get away from Sam and away from this dumpster she kept imagining Jakob's body in.

Sam put his hand out to shake as Violet left. Her skin tightened at the sight of it, imagining it around Jakob's throat. Violet took her money from the bag and exited the alley without a word.

There was a calming comfort in the cash. The heavy, soft weight of it. There hadn't been that much money in her pocket since before she lived in the tent city. It wasn't until she was back in her tent, the bills stored and hidden in the usual place, that she allowed herself to pull a ring from the pawn shop out of her pocket. It was too small for her finger.

People cried in the tent city all the time. Wept, moaned, and sobbed like animals. Violet didn't have to worry about someone being suspicious of her behavior. She fit right in.

CHAPTER TEN

SAM

TWO HOURS AFTER the robbery and halfway through counting the ammo, Sam knew Violet had screwed up. Big time. When she was behind the counter, she must have just grabbed whatever boxes of bullets she saw and piled them up with the guns and the money. Two Glocks, a Desert Eagle, a snub-nosed revolver, and boxes and boxes of ammunition. But with the same shit luck Violet had her entire life, not a single bullet fit.

They were either too fat for the magazines or rattled around like candies in a Pez dispenser. Sam hadn't bought a lot of bullets before, but he at least took the time to see if they fit in the damn gun when he did. Violet had somehow even grabbed a box of shotgun shells in all of her random grabbing and throwing and packing. Completely useless. He ought to go back to the city and tell her they had more work to do. To forget what he said. Violet still owed him since she'd messed up so badly this time.

But the look on her face when they were splitting the money didn't make Sam feel safe. She had that same guilty, worried grimace from the night of the underpass.

Violet was going to tell Davey, if she hadn't already. Life was going to get tougher very quickly and Sam needed to roll out of the neighborhood before it squeezed too tight. No one would look for him until Jakob's body was found, but he needed to move. Get ahead of all the hobos and vigilantes and cops that would be searching for him. It was a mistake bringing Violet to the alley he'd been staying in, but it was the only place Sam could think to hide her while she was crying and blubbering, attracting attention with every step they took.

It was the bullshit way of things. Find a place that works, live there for a while, something happens, then grab your shit and find somewhere new. It happened with the underpass when he'd tried to protect it and got thrown out, and now it was happening to his alleyway.

And the alley had been a good spot. The shade kept him cool during the hotter days and he'd found some decent meals in the dumpster. Not many hiding places would be as good as this one. There was a reason most of the homeless flocked to the underpass rather than fend for themselves. It would be difficult to find a replacement, but after one last night's sleep, he had to leave.

He opened the dumpster's lid and began climbing in to hide from anyone who would start looking for him. A wave of stench knocked him backward. He coughed the smell out of his mouth. Someone had dropped more trash in after he'd gone to find Violet. Loaded it with something smelling between used diapers and rotten milk. Still nothing edible. Back to the bullshit way of things again.

He sat on the broken concrete of the alley and leaned against the dumpster. Rested his head on the pawn shop money as a pillow, holding one of the pistols by his side.

They were worth killing Jakob for. It was just a matter of protection. No one was going to make sure Sam was safe but Sam. And if one of the vigilantes managed to find him, even an unloaded gun to the face would make him pause. Pistols all looked the same whether they were empty or not. And they all made that same beautiful sound.

He pulled the slide back on the Desert Eagle until it locked, then pressed the release. It snapped into place. The smooth click and pull of the hammer. A cocking pistol had to be the most recognizable sound in the world. That sound on its own would scare the shit out of anyone he ran into. He rubbed the edge of the trigger as he lay in the darkness and fell asleep, tucked between the shadows of the alley.

Sunlight had just started coming between the buildings when a stiffness in Sam's legs forced him awake. He stood to stretch, wondering what time it was.

Time.

When that suited asshole came through yesterday, all Sam wanted was the time. It wouldn't have been that difficult to look at his wrist and tell him three numbers. But every day since Sam had landed in this alley, that asshole kept walking through, acting like he didn't exist. Treating him like he was invisible until Sam got right up on his ass yesterday. The few others that walked through at least acknowledged him with a nod or some change thrown at his feet. Those people would have told him what their watches said.

He would scare the guy. Just a little payback for all the times he'd ignored him, then head out of the alley. Let himself have a little enjoyment before focusing on surviving again. It'd be a nice end to his time here. Shit, it would be hilarious. Sam had to stop himself from laughing. He tucked himself tighter beside the dumpster, hiding in the shadows.

When he heard footsteps coming down his alley on the pavement, his body tensed, then released when he saw it was only a delivery guy starting his day early. Not a businessman in his suit. Not the asshole. Sam laughed every time he imagined the man passing through. Shook with laughter. Kept checking that the gun was tucked in his waistband, under the jacket.

And then there he was. Mister high and mighty. Mister blind and deaf and dumb to anyone who wasn't as rich as he was. He turned down the alley like always, staring at his phone, stepping over puddles and broken concrete, not aware of anything. Sam stood out of his hiding place. The movement made the man look up, stumble a little, and then keep walking. Eyes back on his phone. Ignoring the human being right in front of him.

"Hey. Hey, man," Sam called out. "You got the time today? You're looking at a phone, I know you gotta have it. You're dressed pretty nice, you gotta have a watch too. Gimme the time, man."

Sam could see him pursing his lips. Trying not to admit that Sam was there. Just this nice, homeless guy asking for the time. Polite as could be.

Sam smelled himself as the asshole passed him in the alley. A stench wafted over him. He yelled in the man's ear, "I'm talking to you, man. Do you hear me? See me?"

Sam started following him. Closely. Two strides behind.

"Hear me. See me."

The man coughed and started walking faster toward the exit of the alley. Clicking his clean shoes on the concrete. Keeping his briefcase close to him. In his tightly buttoned suit.

This wasn't enough. This man wasn't afraid of him. Sam was just an inconvenience for him. A minor annoyance on his way to wherever he was going. He thought he was better than Sam because he had money and a phone and a house.

Sam shoved his hand into the back of his pants and wrapped his fingers around the pistol grip.

He screamed. "I am right here! Behind you!" The words screeched from his throat, something strange and inhuman. "Look at me! Hear me! See me!"

The man turned. Their eyes met. Heat grew in Sam's bones.

CHAPTER ELEVEN

HE ONLY TURNED around out of instinct. He knew he shouldn't have. There was no reason to give attention to the screaming man.

It was the same one that always asked him for money in this alley. The only one he ever saw this far from the underpass. The twisted face with pale blue eyes. Grinning wildly, his hand hidden behind his back. Taylor's muscles tightened. The screaming was what made him finally turn. That terrible sound.

The man's hand jetted out and grabbed Taylor's tie, shoving him against the wall of the alley. His right hand emerged with a gun, thrusting it under his chin. The force of it pushed Taylor's head against the brick behind him. He gagged against the pistol. Smelled its metal. The hobo smiled and breathed on him, rotten and acidic. "Got the time now, motherfucker?

Taylor dropped his briefcase and put his hands in the air. His bladder felt full. "Please. P-please don't shoot me." His vision blurred as tears pushed their way out. He would do anything. Anything to not have it all end in a dirty alleyway. The hobo's shaky hand pressed the gun harder, making it difficult to breathe.

"I-I have ca-, I have some cash in my wallet." Taylor slowly reached for his back pocket. The pistol moved from his throat to his forehead, squeezing his skull against the wall. The rough bricks ground at the back of his head. He pushed harder. Pressure built. Taylor's head screamed and threatened to crack open.

The hobo kept smiling, shook his head, and slowly said, "I don't want your money." The man cocked the gun, his eyes flicking back and forth. Taylor's knees started to give. The ground slipping away. All he saw was the smile. The crooked teeth. The dripping saliva.

"Nononono, please don't shoot. What do you need? What do you want?" The pressure lightened, but his head kept pounding. The man's grin faltered slightly. A chance there. Opportunity.

"Nothing. I'm just some crazy hobo, right? Just a beggar for change, nothing else." He started breathing heavier. "Right?" he yelled in Taylor's ear. Made it ring. The attacker glanced at the alley openings. No one noticed anything happening. There was no reason to look down this alleyway. No reason to get involved. No cops. No vigilantes.

If Taylor cried for help, he'd be dead. If he tried to push the man off, he'd be dead. The only thing he could do was beg. There was no shame in that. The pistol moved to his temple. He squeezed his eyes shut. In his mind, he saw his brains parting for a bullet like the Red Sea. "Look. At. Me."

Taylor opened his eyes. All he saw were the man's, so close nothing else mattered. Their noses touched. He kept himself from gagging at the smell. If he moved, he was dead. The man's bloodshot eyes were peeled wide open, taking it all in. Homeless, desperate. Angry. Nothing to stop him from killing Taylor. No one was going to save him.

He was alone.

"Good. Now, you see me. You see me." Taylor felt spittle hit his lips. The man stepped back, releasing the gun from Taylor's skull. He felt a wave of relief before the gun crashed into the side of his head and the world turned to static.

When everything came back into focus, he was on the ground, watching the hobo pick up his briefcase and put it under his jacket as he walked away, the gun still pointed at Taylor. He kept still, lying in a puddle. The hobo still smiling. Taylor waited until he was around the corner before starting to move.

He tried to push himself up the wall. Lights danced in front of his eyes. He sank back down to the ground. Felt the side of his head where he'd been struck. It seared with pain and his fingers came back bloody. He saw the man's eyes again. Smelled him. Felt the spit on his lips. Taylor threw up into his lap, unable to move his head without falling over. *You see me.*

He could have pulled the trigger. Just shot him, walked out of the alley, and disappeared into the city. Relief. That he hadn't killed him.

His eyes. His eyes told Taylor he wouldn't have been the first.

Some time passed. Still, no one came through. No one noticed him struggling to keep his head from pumping out blood. He was the only person who would be able to get himself help.

Taylor pushed up the wall again, steadier this time, keeping himself from falling back down. Slow steps brought him to the entrance of the alley, where it only took moments for a woman to notice the stumbling man in a suit with vomit dribbling down his chin and blood dripping off his face. She helped wave down a cab to the nearest hospital. Let him lean on her.

They were wheeling him into the operating room when he remembered the comics in his briefcase. Trevor. That was Bill's kid's name. Trevor. He wondered how much they'd cost to replace before passing out.

CHAPTER TWELVE

VIOLET

Jealousy washed over Violet whenever she went to Davey's place in the middle of the city. He didn't live in a trash pile, or even one of the tents. When Davey first moved into the underpass, he built a shack out of wood he'd scavenged and stocked the surrounding area with abandoned furniture like some kind of hobo patio. The hut was small—smaller than even Violet's tent—leaky, dark, and lacked any kind of insulation for the winter. But there was something about having solid walls instead of fabric ones that made it seem better. Four solid walls and a roof made an actual building. It was barely passable, but Davey had a building to live in. He had a home.

The entire thing shuddered when Violet knocked. Davey pushed the door open with his toe, a foamy toothbrush in one hand and a water bottle in the other, his hair sharply combed. Not wild or matted like the other tent citizens'. He almost looked like he belonged out there in the real city. "What's up, Violet? Happy Friday."

She immediately regretted her decision to come here. Things would be so much easier if she just let them progress by themselves. But she had to get rid of this guilt somehow. She couldn't deal with it for another night. Her insides rotted with the knowledge of what happened and her throat was hoarse from the night's sobbing.

She looked down at her hands, trying to find a way to start her confession. "Davey, I... please don't get mad." Davey stepped out of the shack and spat into a puddle. A thin bubbly layer of foam spread over the surface. He sat on one of the stained and cushionless couches outside of the shack and waited for her to continue.

She exhaled, still looking at the ground, then began speaking in a quick monotone, knowing if she stopped she wouldn't be able to start again. "Sam came back and forced me to rob a pawn shop with him. Things got crazy and he killed the owner and stole the guns. He-he threatened to kill me and find my family if I told you or anyone else. I just can't deal with it any longer."

She looked up at Davey. The man's lips were pressed together into a thin white line. The threat was a lie, but she had to sell something to get Davey's pity.

"You talked to Sam?" Davey's voice shook. Violet nodded. "You helped him steal? And he killed someone?" She nodded again. Davey's face quivered. "*Shit*!" He threw his toothbrush into the dirt and rubbed his knuckles against the side of his head. "We had been doing so well, Violet. This is bad. This is very, very bad."

He leapt from his seat and started pacing in front of his shack. A couple of residents leaving to look for jobs stared at them as they walked past. Davey was known for being collected and measured. It was one of the reasons he was in charge of the city. He could talk to police easily, deal with problems, calm down tensions, all with a smile on his face. He never lost his temper like this. Not even when Sam attacked the cop.

"Do you know where he is now? Did you leave anything behind? Did anyone see you?" She answered no to all of the questions. Davey took a large breath, held it, then exhaled, pacing faster. "The problem we have here, Violet, is that now I have to take a gamble. Which, huh, as you should know, can go really badly for us. We let things roll, forget about it, and hope the police think it was just a random robbery, completely unrelated to us, or we go to the cops. Talk to Jessica about it head on. Which could go really badly, since, again, as you know, Jessica doesn't have a whole lot of love for Sam. She still has that terrible scar on her face from when he jumped her."

Violet remembered it clearly. She'd been right there with everyone, cheering for Sam as he soared through the air, crashing on top of her and beating her senseless. And then refused to help him as he tried to hide in the underpass.

Davey continued rambling to himself. "But, that could go either way. She could hurt us for even interacting with Sam. Or she could throw us a lifeline for giving her the killer and thief in a crime she wouldn't be able to solve by herself." He rubbed his knuckles against the side of his head again.

"Davey, I told you. I stole the stuff. He forced me to, but—"

"No you didn't. What are you talking about? You just bumped into him and he was bragging about it. You had nothing to do with it. You didn't take any of the guns, right?"

"Right."

"And you didn't take any of the money, right?"

Violet hesitated. "I took half."

Davey rubbed his face with his hand. "Let me ask you again," he said, emphasizing each word. "You didn't take any of the money, right?"

Violet winced and said, "Right." She'd come to Davey with the truth, trying to alleviate her guilt. Now it was getting smeared out of existence.

"Right. Okay," Davey said. If he kept rubbing his knuckles against his head like that he'd go bald soon. "We'll go see Jessica and tell her what Sam's done. Maybe she'll throw us a bone."

Violet stiffened. She'd never voluntarily walked into a police station before. She'd been taken there, arrested for gambling in illegal casinos and thrown in the drunk tank, but never of her own free will.

"Do we have to? It's not like they'll do anything to help us. You might as well tell the vigilantes so they can go look for him."

"There's really no difference between the two," Davey said. He grabbed some things from inside his shack and locked the door before they left. Locked, with an actual key. If someone really wanted to steal something, they could kick the door in and it would fly off its makeshift hinges, but the lock was like the solid walls. It made the place a home.

Violet remembered her routine to secure her house, back when she still had one. Making sure the kitchen lights were off, checking the hallway mirror to see if anything was stuck in her teeth, then sorting through her purse to make sure she hadn't forgotten anything. Davey still had his routine. The man wasn't a tent citizen, finding temporary refuge under a dirty bridge. He was a mortgage-free homeowner.

Of course he would want to go to the cops. People with more than others always trusted the police.

The station usually seemed empty when Violet walked by. A solid monument made of marble, pretending to stand for law and order, even though she struggled to remember ever seeing someone without a uniform climbing the big concrete stairs to the front door.

A police department was supposed to be a place of resolution. A place where people entered with a frown, exited with a smile, all their problems fixed somewhere in between. There were plenty of problems in Hamington, but the answers wouldn't be found here. She could count more positive interactions with the vigilantes than times the police had even acknowledged her. If something needed to be done, the vigilantes were a better option.

She'd seen them helping the tent city homeless before. Anything from giving them food or money, to physically defending them against people interested in taking advantage of the weak. Some of the vigilantes she'd met were good people. They wanted to actually make a difference.

Davey strode into the police station like a man attending a

business meeting. He stopped at the front desk and before he said a word, the man pointed down the hall and said, "Go on back." Violet turned as they walked away and saw the cop holding his nose with one hand and waving in front of his face with the other. She sniffed her clothes. She should have bathed in the river this morning. It would have washed the stink off her.

Farther down the hallway, Davey quickly rapped his knuckles on a door with a brass nameplate reading "Jessica Sanders—Community Relations Officer," and opened it without waiting for a response. The woman inside stood from behind her desk.

"Dammit, Davey. I can't have you disrupting my day like this. You were just here last week. I'm not even supposed to be talking to you, much less dealing with your squatter complaints. And who the hell is this?" She looked Violet up and down.

The officer's eyes felt hot on her as she followed Davey to the chairs in front of her desk. She adjusted her weight to try to get comfortable in the seat. Tried to avoid looking at the puckered scars crossing the lower half of the cop's face, still angry and red from when Sam ripped her chin in half at the underpass.

"This isn't a 'squatters' problem,'" Davey said. "This is a real, serious situation."

Jessica peeled her eyes from Violet and focused on Davey. Violet could almost feel the pressure release. Her gaze had a weight to it, heavy and full of judgement.

"What is it? Please tell me you have your crew under control."

Davey's eyebrows furrowed with concentration. "Trust me, this guy is not a member of our city." He motioned to Violet. "Would you mind filling in Officer Sanders?"

She froze. Her throat felt coated with cotton. Jessica's mouth turned into a sneer, pulling the scar tissue into inhuman lines.

This woman hated tent citizens. Her face showed the same disgust as the people who laughed when she asked for change or something to eat. She needed to stay as far away from her as possible. Nothing good would come from being here.

Davey leaned over and pleaded in her ear. "Come on, just tell her what you told me."

Violet glanced at Jessica, met her eyes, then tore them away before she could see the truth. She bit her thumbnail.

"God dammit, Davey," she yelled. "You bring some crackhead into my office who's about to go through the shakes and shits? I can't deal with this right now. Get the fuck out of my office."

She thought they were all the same. Looped them all together, because they didn't have homes. And in her eyes, Violet was the same as Davey and Sam and everyone else in the underpass. She either didn't understand that they were different, or worse, knew and just didn't give a shit.

"I'm not a drug addict," Violet said. "I had a gambling problem and now I'm homeless. But I don't do drugs. I don't destroy my own body."

Jessica forced her hands through her hair. "Then what do you want? Please! Tell me, so I can have some peace. Jesus."

"Sam," Violet said, pointing at Jessica's chin, "the same Sam that gave you those nasty lines, has killed someone. And robbed their store."

The anger vanished. Paleness pooled in Jessica's cheeks. She sat heavily in her chair. The police uniform that had been taut and cared-for when she stood suddenly looked worn and baggy "Where?"

"A pawn shop," Violet said. Seeing the fear in Jessica made her stronger. Jessica was just a human being, like her. Violet's words made her afraid. She rested her chin in her hand, covering the scars.

"The strangling," Jessica said. She leaned back into her chair and crossed her arms, staring at the wall across the room. "Are you kidding me, Davey? I told you this guy would be a problem! You said you'd get rid of him. What happened?" She pointed at Violet and her voice cracked through the air. "Were you there?"

She jolted and words tumbled out of her mouth, keeping her eyes focused on the outstretched finger. "He was going through a trashcan nearby and I saw he had a gun. I asked him where he got it and he started bragging about how he'd killed a pawn shop owner and stole a bunch of pistols."

Jessica closed her eyes. "A *bunch* of pistols?"

"Glad I came to you now?" Davey leaned farther back in his chair with a smirk. She opened her eyes and scowled at him.

"Get out," she said. "You, fidgety. You stay." Davey's jaw went lax and his eyes darted to Violet.

"No, I need to be here," Davey said. "You and I are supposed to work together to make the underpass better."

"I'm going to have her help me, since she was the last one to see Sam," she said, pointing at Violet again. "If we need you for anything else, I'll make sure she lets you know."

Davey winced like he'd been physically wounded by her words. The politician in him must not have liked how easily she'd brushed him aside. He leaned over Violet as he stood and whispered, "It was only Sam." She nodded. Her heartbeat picked up speed. How was she going to do this without Davey here?

Jessica called someone when Davey left, asking him to come to her office, then turned to her computer. She didn't acknowledge Violet again until her office door opened.

"Oh Jesus," the new officer said. "Did something die?" The thin man wore his uniform crisply, like he took pride in it. Shoes shined, armpits stainless.

"Yes, asshole. Johanson, this is…" Jessica trailed off. She hadn't bothered asking for her name.

"Violet."

She thought she saw Jessica roll her eyes. "Right. Violet here knows who killed our pawn shop owner last night. It was a hobo, used to live in the underpass on 5TH."

"Anyone we know?" Johanson asked.

Jessica glanced at Violet and said, "No. It's a new guy. Most of the bad ones have already been locked up."

Violet's brow furrowed. Why was she lying?

"Well that sucks. Ready to spend the rest of the year writing paperwork? Hobo crime equals your paper time."

"I was hoping you'd share it with me. Who's your vigilante who works that area?"

"Which area?"

"By the underpass."

Your vigilante? What was happening here?

Johanson looked up and bounced his head from side to side, like the ceiling would have the answer written on it if he just looked from the right angle. "I'll have to check. I think it's Silky O'Sullivan, but that doesn't give me a lot of confidence."

Jessica shook her head. "We need someone more subtle. What happened to that Victor guy?"

"The Hudson copycat? Shit, Jess, he got capped six months ago."

"Shame."

Violet's eyes flicked between them. It was like they'd forgotten she was even in the room. And why were they talking about vigilantes? She just wanted to tell her story and get out of there.

"I don't know what to tell you. No one is going to be as quiet as you want, and as efficient as you need, when dealing with a murder. Layer the underpass situation on it too, and that brings another level of difficulty to the table. You should send it up to the chief."

"No, Jesus. Come on, Johanson. Fuck. That. I'm not going to tell him I have an armed, murdering hobo running around West Hamington with multiple sidearms. We'll get one of the crazies to figure it out for us."

Johanson shook his head. "The underpass is your deal. I'm not touching it. But if you won't tell the chief, you can figure out terms with one of them yourself." He left the office and Jessica rested her chin in her hand again, staring at the computer screen.

"Excuse me," Violet said. It was the first time she'd spoken since Johanson walked in. Jessica didn't acknowledge her. She stood from his chair. "Can... can I leave?"

She looked up from her computer. "No, you can't fucking leave, because otherwise, who else am I going to blame for this?"

Her nerves started firing hard and fast. She knew. Her eyes widened, looking for the door in his peripheral vision.

"I'm kidding, idiot. I need your help. You know him well?"

"Sam?"

She seemed to twitch at the name. Her lips curled downward. "Yes."

Poker face. Poker face.

Violet shrugged. "Yeah. Well, no, not well. But I knew him." She scratched her head, dandruff snowing onto her shoulders and chair. She looked around her office, trying to appear casual.

Davey should have never brought her here. Without him, Violet's only hope was that Jessica didn't see through her lies and realize she'd been there when Sam had murdered Jakob. If she figured it out... if she figured out that she was lying and that she'd been there and was tied in with the man that attacked her, Jessica would make sure she never saw the light of day again.

And this woman, with her disgust at the people living in the underpass and her history with Sam. She'd smile as she threw her in the cell.

CHAPTER THIRTEEN

JESSICA

JESSICA OPENED A window, stuck her head out of it, and took deep breaths. This new one, Violet, reeked even worse than Davey. It reminded her why she only worked with one of these underpass people. Throwing another into the mix would take up all of her time. She might as well change her title to Hobo Management Officer. Davey had gotten too comfortable with the relationship, and this was the result.

She went back to her desk, keeping the window open to help filter out some of the underpass stench Violet brought into her office, and flipped to a new page of notes before asking her questions, trying to keep her voice steadier than before.

She fired them quickly, one after another. The faster she could move past this, the better. Did she have any idea where Sam could be? What he could be doing?

She didn't expect to get any of the answers she was looking for. The homeless were all fucking idiots and this woman Violet was no exception.

Violet. Not even a name, just a color.

"Like I said, I know him—knew him—but we weren't close. Before the underpass he sold dope. When he killed his dealer, he killed any of those connections he had. I don't think he has any-one to get in touch with."

"Does Sam strike you as the kind of person who would use the stolen weapons himself? Or would he sell them off?" She felt her chin throb every time she said his name. Her ribs and belly burned. She'd just started getting back to normal and here the bastard was again.

"Either. I can't see him getting rid of all of them. He'd keep at least one of..." Violet paused and fidgeted in the chair. "...them. Yeah. He'd probably hold on to one of them."

Jessica squeezed tighter on her pen. Every time Violet fidgeted in her chair, she rubbed the smell in even further. It'd taken days for that rotted smell to go away last time Davey stopped by to complain about some hobo problem. Now with Violet squirming around every time she answered a question, Jessica would have to throw the chair in a damn furnace when she left. But she dealt with it anyway, because it was her job to listen to every whimper and complaint from the people of her fair, shining city. At least for now.

"He'd probably go north," Violet continued. "He's not stupid. Probably putting as much distance between himself and the rob-bery as possible."

North. If he went too far it'd be outside of her jurisdiction and she'd have no other option than to use vigilantes anyway. She could get ahead of it and offer terms in the area. Put a price on his head too good to ignore. Not only to make sure she could sleep at night, but for everyone else in the city too.

As soon as Davey had started talking, she had a feeling this was going to be bad. He usually tried to act like they were friends. Overly chatty, asking how things were going and if she could so kindly help him with this small little issue, please, thank you, could I have s'more please? The last time he spoke in focused short clips like today, some dipshit from the underpass was leav-ing dirty used needles in a church playground.

These people were awful. The hobos ruined the city and made

her life miserable. Causing dozens and dozens of times more trouble than they were worth.

This could have been a simple armed robbery and murder case. Some gangbanger needing cash and knocking over the closest, cheapest spot available. Instead it was a homeless problem in her district. Involving Sam. And she was the one who was supposed to make sure the homeless stayed to themselves, under control under their bridge. She couldn't handle this fucking asshole going on a rampage and selling people tools to kill each other on top of everything else. People could get hurt. Children could die.

The cold ball in her stomach settled deeper and Violet scraped at her teeth with a dirty fingernail. Disgusting.

But she knew Sam, which at least made him better than Davey. That one was worthless. How hard was it to control people who didn't have anything to live for? He couldn't do it when she was attacked, and he still wasn't able to now. She needed help finding Sam, but Davey would clog up the whole situation with his sanctimonious horseshit once he realized she was asking the vigilantes for help. This Violet woman was her best option.

She'd make her describe Sam to the vigilantes—what he was wearing, where he was going, how he was acting—and then send her on her way, back to live in the mud. That was all she needed. But if she kept wasting time, acting fidgety and distracted, Sam would be halfway across East Hamington before she found a vigilante to accept terms. This was her only option. It disgusted her, but without Violet, she was walking blind.

She crossed the room to the door and yelled at Violet as she put her jacket on. "Let's go!" The hobo jolted in her seat and rose like a scorned puppy. The officers at the front of the station gave them looks as they left. Jessica wanted to hang a sign around her neck that read, "THIS IS NOT MY CHOICE."

They walked past the pool of cop cars to the parking lot of personal vehicles. She tried to push away the thought of how much worse Violet would make her car smell by the end of the day. Just another reward for being stuck on hobo duty. She swept trash from the passenger seat onto the floorboard and rolled down the windows as soon as the engine turned over. She could deal with the cold. Maybe the smell could air out.

Violet stood outside the door of the SUV, looking unsure of what she was supposed to do. Probably mentally incapable of figuring out how to open a car door.

"We can't drive around talking to vigilantes in a police cruiser," Jessica said. "Get in."

She looked ready to piss her pants. Maybe it was just the way hobos had a hard time trusting the cops, but the closer Violet got to her, the more her eyes darted around, like she was looking for an escape route.

They pulled out of the parking lot and Jessica dialed the cell numbers she had written down back at the office. She mostly left quick messages telling the vigilantes to call her back. It was early, and these people preferred to roam the streets into the darkest hours of the night rather than rise with the sun.

When one finally answered, she pulled a U-turn and started heading toward his territory in midtown. She noticed Violet swallow deeply as she weaved between cars and sped up through a yellow light.

"Best perk of being a cop," Jessica said. "Even if you get pulled over, you never get a ticket." Jessica grinned and looked over at Violet, but her eyes were glued to the road. Jessica wiped the smile off her face. No sense in trying to make her feel comfortable with small talk. "We're meeting with some of Johanson's vigilantes to talk. Don't ask any questions, don't say anything without being prompted. These guys are cagey enough as it is when dealing with the police. We don't need them to be paranoid about you being with me."

Violet scratched at the back of her head and a flurry of dandruff floated onto the fabric of her seat. "If I'm not supposed to talk, why do you need me at all? I don't want to be involved with this if I don't have to. Davey just made me come to tell you what happened."

They stopped at a red light. Jessica stared at it, waiting for it to change, rubbing her stomach under the seatbelt.

"You're the best way to find him. If any of the vigilantes ask something I don't know, you'll be able to fill in the gaps better than I will. Trust me. If I didn't need you here, you wouldn't be."

They turned a corner and she muttered curses under her breath. A small crowd surrounded a man in an army helmet, football pads, and large flannel shirt. A reflective visor attached to the helmet left only his mouth exposed. He smiled and gave thumbs up to cameras while people posed with him. Some seemed excited, others mocked him with their friends after taking the picture. Jessica felt the skin on her chin tighten. She knew that kind of laughter well.

"I swear to God, half these guys are fucking braindead," she said. They parked and walked past the crowd, Violet trailing behind her like an obedient pet.

Jessica didn't acknowledge the vigilante or break her pace even when he started calling her name. She and Violet waited for him around the corner of a building, near the back door of a restaurant. Violet waved to a woman rifling through the dumpster, dressed in dirty and torn clothing. Jessica fought the taste of acid climbing her throat.

The vigilante caught up with them and said, "Good day, officer. I apologize for my tardiness, a number of civilians were informing me of problems in their communities."

"They weren't telling you their problems, they were taking selfies with you. Either way, I don't give a shit." She looked him up and down. The costume looked even stupider up close than it had when they drove by. "Do you always crave this much attention?"

His response was automatic. "We in the vigilante community must make our presence known to both the law-abiding and lawbreaking citizens. We do so by employing costumes and outfits that do, at times, attract gratuitous attention." She rolled her eyes and introduced Violet. When they shook hands, the man announced his name as Colonel Hamington.

"You don't have to call him that," she told Violet. "His name is Harold Rosensweig." The vigilante opened his mouth as if to argue, then locked it closed again.

Jessica explained the situation and Violet filled in everything about Sam beyond her knowledge. Jittery and shaky, but not as bad as before. Maybe freaks felt comfortable around other freaks.

Finally, the man who called himself Colonel Hamington stroked his chin with a gloved hand, dramatically rolling his fingers across his cheek, and said, "I see. Pursue murder suspect. Apprehend. Deal justice?" He asked the last question to Jessica.

"You can do whatever you want."

"I see. Officer Johanson does not usually employ such open language in our dialogues. What are the terms on this case?"

"Seven and a half and two months."

His chin stroking stopped. He tilted his head. "I appreciate your seven point five, but two is not enough if I am to deal justice at your discretion. I need at least six."

"That's too bad. I can give you two."

Colonel Hamington puffed out his chest, the football pads sliding halfway off his shoulder, and said, "Unfortunately that will not be enough. I shall continue to protect our citizens as currently operating. Please do not hesitate to contact me if you are able to adjust said terms."

"Oh, fuck off," she groaned. She turned to leave for the car and Violet followed behind her again before she had to remind her. Good dog.

They walked a block before she said, to no one in particular, "These fucking assholes think they can wrangle stronger terms than we can possibly pass off. What a crock of shit."

"What are terms?" Violet asked. Her voice roused Jessica from her thoughts. "That guy asked you about them earlier too."

At first she didn't answer. She didn't need to know. She could follow her around all day and be clueless about the numbers she was giving vigilantes. But she needed Violet to trust her. She knew more than Jessica did about Sam and without that information and that trust, she was screwed.

She sighed and answered slowly, measuring out each word before they left her lips. "Terms... are deals. Or, offers we make vigilantes for their... services. These people technically work outside the law and in order to have them do what we specifically want them to, we give them terms.

"It's one thing if someone's in a fight or getting mugged, and the vigilantes step in. There are witnesses, they can say it was for self-protection or something. There are a lot of ways to weasel out of getting in trouble, especially the way our justice system works. But when a crime is already committed, and we know who did it but don't have the evidence or witnesses yet, we can't touch them due to the rules that come with legally carrying a badge and a gun. So Johanson persuades the vigilantes to do it. Off the books. It's not communicated with the rest of the police force, which can cause some... issues. With communication, I mean."

Violet shook his head. "I don't understand. Why would you sneak around your own police department if what you're doing is helping?"

"It's not sneaking," Jessica said quickly. How could she explain this to someone as simple-minded as a hobo? They walked another block before she started again. "Look... if a vigilante gets caught assaulting someone who isn't actively involved in a crime, or gets seen kidnapping a person to uh... drop off at the police station, according to the rule book, what they're doing is illegal. And getting caught happens way more often when you're dressed in tights and a mask like you're going to a comic book convention. Most of these guys come into run-ins with the police force while doing their job. If they don't say anything about the arrangement, the police in the know can talk to prosecutors or judges and convince them to be lenient. If the terms are mentioned, or rumored, or even whispered about, their deals are cut and not only are they forced to deal with the bullshit of the justice system, but they lose their main source of income—us."

"So you're just paying them to do what they'd already be doing."

"I wouldn't say paying. Maybe... incentivizing. To continue being good members of the Hamington community. We make sure they get time off a prison sentence if they get caught illegally doing vigilante things, like assaulting a citizen who is technically innocent despite their cut-and-dry status as a murder suspect—an evil fuck like Sam for example—or some money will disappear into the black hole of government accounting and re-appear in their pockets. Usually, it's a mixture of both. Colonel Dipshit from earlier refused seventy-five hundred dollars and two months guaranteed out of prison."

Violet stumbled at the numbers. "Seven... seven thousand five hundred dollars?"

Jessica had slipped up. Started talking faster than she should have. She could practically see the dollar signs spinning on Violet's eyeballs. "It's not about the money," she tried to explain. "Don't focus on that. When terms are on the table, there are fewer crimes. Vigilantes are a pain to deal with, but they're a necessary evil. Without them, crimes spike. They're able to get places and do things outside of what the police are permitted do. No need to wait on warrants or the lengthy trial process to deal out punishments. People are safer. They're going to do what they're doing anyway, so we try to at least point out the bad guys and lead them in the right direction."

She looked at Violet in her peripheral vision. She was staring at something in the distance, her gaze foggy, probably thinking about all the shit a hobo could buy with that kind of money. Jessica needed to downplay it. Stop her from thinking about it. The more people who knew about the terms, the more complicated her job was. But she still needed Violet to tell the vigilantes what she knew about Sam.

The next vigilante they talked to, Killa Fist, passed on the job too. Another one, Catman, who had long blades attached to the fingers of his gloves said he'd consider it. Their last guy never showed.

Jessica slammed the door as she got back in the car after the final meeting of the day. "I will never understand these people. They claim they want to help keep the city safe, but don't have the balls to follow through with what they promised."

Violet nodded silently, still miles away from the conversation.

"I'll drop you off at the underpass. If I need you, I'll get in touch with Davey," she said. Violet nodded again.

She turned down 5TH and could see the bridge all the hobos lived under, only blocks away. Cheap paint flaked off its sides as cars passed overhead. These people woke up in a shitpile, begged for the coins that people would rather toss in a jar when they got home, then went back to sleep in a shitpile at the end of the day. What a pointless fucking existence.

"Could I get terms?"

The sudden break of her silence surprised Jessica. "What?"

"Could I get terms? To find Sam. Money, get out of jail free, the whole thing."

Jessica didn't immediately respond. They drove in silence until she parked in a spot across the street from the underpass. "Why should I offer that to you? I didn't tell you all of this to turn you into a pain in the ass."

"None of your people have taken the offer. I know more about him than anyone else. I don't have anything to lose. You don't have anything to lose. We could either walk around for the next week and beg people to do the job based on information I'm giving them, or I can just do it for you."

She narrowed her eyes. "That doesn't exactly convince me."

Violet got out of the car and held the door open. Her smell lifted off Jessica like a weight. "You're looking for a vigilante. I can be that. Or you can keep trying to find someone else and by that time, Sam'll be almost impossible to find." She rocked her weight onto either foot waiting for her response. Jessica chewed her nails.

Narrowed her eyes at Violet. Was she playing her somehow? No... That big stupid face would show a lie clear as day.

"I'm not saying the answer is yes, but if it is, you'll get much less than we give our standard vigilantes. They've proven themselves useful. They have our trust. You have nothing."

"That's fine. Anything is something."

She chewed her nail again. This was too much, moving too fast. A nice morning had quickly turned into an almost-forgotten nightmare coming back to life, with the cherry on top a hobo from the underpass trying to weasel her way into their vigilante system.

"I have to talk to Johanson. Come by the station tomorrow morning. I'll let you know what we decide." A large smile crossed Violet's face. She emphatically nodded and closed the door, waving before turning to go back to the underpass. Happier than a pig in slop at the mere suggestion she could be helpful.

Jessica hated even considering it. Hobos looking for hobos was worse than the blind leading the blind. But she couldn't disregard it as a viable option. Violet had the most knowledge of the perp. And she was right—if no one else took the offer, what other choice did Jessica have? Detectives didn't like getting their hands dirty with low-end murders, the chief would have her head if he knew someone connected to the underpass had committed a capital offense, and this woman was willing to take shit pay. No opportunity cost, no better option.

The light was still on under Johanson's office door when she got back to the station. He hadn't left for his early Friday afternoon drinks yet. She was never asked to join him and the other officers when they got drunk a few hours before the weekend really started, but it was a blue blood boys' club ritual she let them get away with. There were more important things for her to worry about on a Friday night than gender equality.

She let herself into his office and collapsed into a chair, waiting for him to get off the phone. Something about developing a vigilante network in East Hamington. That would be more trouble than it was worth.

He finally hung up and said, "That was the fumigators. They'll get to your office next week, but until then you should leave a bunch of open cans of tuna in there. It'll probably smell better."

She groaned. "Very funny. I was with that woman all day, and I swear she kept walking in the direction of the wind so that I would get a big mouthful every time I breathed. She acted like she didn't know, but she knew. Oh, that little bitch knew."

"Were you able to hook up with any of the guys from our list?" It was usually Johanson's job to find vigilantes that would take on terms, but the involvement of the underpass put it square on her desk.

She gave him the rundown of her day with Violet. "No one, huh?" he asked, scribbling on a notepad. "That's disappointing. And I'll have to check on TerraLink. He's usually pretty good about showing up."

Jessica nodded, her teeth tearing at a corner of her thumb. She'd gnawed the ends off all of her nails today, but needed to keep chewing. It was either that or smoke again, and she'd rather chew her fingers to nubs than have the coughing return. Smoking was a dirty habit she'd picked up after Sam happened. Talking about him again brought all the old cravings back.

"The hobo though. Violet," she said, "She was there the entire time telling people about Sam. Listening to the conversations all day. When no one accepted the terms, she asked if she could have them. We could low-ball the shit out of her, Johanson. Keep it at a hundred bucks or a couple of nights out of jail. But she knows Sam well. Might have better luck than any of these other guys."

Johanson leaned back in his chair and laced his fingers behind his head. He breathed deeply. "You didn't really tell her what terms are, did you?"

"No. Of course not. She figured it out herself. She may be a hobo, but she's not the stupidest person I've ever met," she said. Johanson nodded. The lie came smoothly, like the others she was used to telling her coworkers every day. He didn't need to know that she'd explained to Violet the entire process from top to bottom, and he didn't need to know that the murder Davey had brought to the station was because of the same fucker that attacked her only a few months ago. He'd worry. Think she was too close to make rational decisions. "So what do you think?"

"My first thought is that I don't like picking up new crazies as the weather gets colder. Crime goes down on its own and having too many of these guys on the street at once sometimes leads to them fighting each other to turn in perps for terms. It could be more harm than good, and would probably result in more bull-shit paperwork to deal with.

"On the other hand, it doesn't sound like this girl would have that media-greedy attitude. She won't be going for publicity. She knows our perp. All she wants is her money and time off." He rubbed his forehead. "Do you think we can trust her? She's not going to screw us, is she?"

Jessica thought back through the day. Violet was quiet, like she'd asked her to be, but always listened. Pretending to be uninterested and focus on something down the street when she wasn't talking to her. But she was a shit actor. Beneath her dirty clothes and matted hair was someone who cared about her own well-being and nothing else.

"Honestly, I don't know any way she could. She doesn't have any reason to go to the media. They wouldn't believe a homeless woman's story about police passing up a murder investigation to pay vigilantes, especially if she claims to be the one they hired. If she finds this suspect and gives him a heads up that we're looking for him, we're back in the same position we're in right now. And she didn't even ask what standard terms were. I told her they'd be lower than normal, and she didn't seem to care. Nowhere to go from the bottom but up, right?"

Damn right it was right. Jessica and Johanson discussed terms and whittled them down from small to laughable. Two hundred fifty dollars, two nights out of jail, and a weight off Jessica's shoulders. No more Sam to worry about. No dealing with Davey on this topic. Just a vigilante doing what they always did—throwing herself into violence for little personal reward. "You know you owe me, right?" Johanson said. "Using my vigilante network to solve your underpass problem. You owe me." He rubbed at a spot beside his nose. She rolled her eyes and told him to hold on.

When she returned to her office, she punched the door lock and collapsed into her desk chair, her feet throbbing. It had been a long day of walking and talking and dealing with the insanity of people who actively searched for violence. She unlocked one of her desk drawers with its custom key, pulled it fully out, and reached behind and above the drawer. Same old Johanson. Once a problem was solved, or even seemed like it would be at some point, he wanted to celebrate.

She returned to his office and locked the door behind her. A small bag of pale powder appeared from her pocket. Jessica leaned over his desk and wiggled it in front of his face. "My little homeless problem still isn't fixed. But I guess you have to get yours before it is."

CHAPTER FOURTEEN

TAYLOR

An alarm screamed and Taylor jerked awake, throwing off damp bedsheets and sitting up quickly to escape images in his head of gnashing teeth and cold pressure. His skull throbbed a quick rhythm and forced him to lay back down with a groan. He slapped at the screen of his new replacement phone to silence the sound.

The doctor had warned him of possible "strong headaches" over the next few days, but Taylor hadn't expected anything like this. Three days after the attack, and he still felt like his brain was trying to break free from his head. He squeezed his eyes shut, feeling the pain pulsing along the path of his veins.

Years ago, during an undergrad Christmas break, he and Alice went on a skiing trip with another couple and he'd broken his leg on the first day. Hours later, he was able to limp his way around the hospital, and when they flew home, he maneuvered through the airport without so much as a wince. He'd always had a high pain tolerance that helped him get over injuries quickly, but this felt like it wasn't going anywhere soon.

His fingers searched across the bedside table, grabbing for pain pills and a cup of water. He sat up again, slower this time, and took his medicine, willing to stay in bed as long as necessary for the throbbing to subside.

The pain was peaceful compared to what he'd woken from. In his dreams, a man with jagged yellow teeth was slowly pulling the trigger of a gun pressed against Taylor's head. He was doing everything he could to make it stop, pushing and punching and screaming, but the man kept tightening his grip on the trigger. The alarm was the only thing that stopped it from firing.

He laid there as long as he could to let the pain pills kick into action. When he finally had to use the bathroom, every step sent waves of pain down from the crown of his skull. His reflection looked little better than it did after he'd left the hospital yesterday. He narrowed his eyes against the lights, noticing bags and dark circles that had moved in as he slept. A section of his hair had been shaved above his temple to put in the stitches. He leaned closer to the mirror, trying to see as much of the cut as possible. It was a nasty one, like jagged lightning branching off in different directions. But he couldn't complain. It was all he'd received after being threatened and mugged by a psychopath. Stitches and headaches were better than his brains being splashed all over a dirty alleyway.

His phone dinged its text message tone from the bedside table as he took soft steps out of the bathroom. It was Jake, suggesting questions and stories to ask Hudson about during the day's interview. Taylor tossed the phone back on the bed without reading through them.

His boss had called him at the hospital when he heard what happened, briefly voicing his condolences before switching to business mode. Only a split second lived between his question of, "Are you alright?" and, "Is this going to delay your Hudson interview schedule? Are you going to be able to anchor on Monday?"

"I'm ready to work whenever you want me. You should know though—I have stitches in the side of my head. They had to shave off a square patch of my hair to put them in. It looks a little rough."

"I'm sure we can figure out a replacement anchor so you can rest and recover," Jake said. "Your health is the most important thing. No need to push it too hard." Taylor forced back a scoff. This wasn't Jake putting his kid gloves back on to treat him with respect or caution. He just didn't want his anchor's appearance to scare the viewers while he talked about missing person cases nearby or car bombs in a foreign country. It would make everything too real for them as they drank their morning coffee. They were comforted that the scenes of desert firefights and mourning parents were happening to someone else, only intruding on their days between commercial breaks. Never thinking the violence could happen to them around the corner of their homes. Or on their way to work.

Jake made sure to clarify that taking some time off didn't equate to taking a break from the Hudson interviews. Anchor positions could be moved around. Nothing, not life, death, or anything in between would become a priority over Taylor's work with Hudson. Jake ended the conversation with a request for an update as soon as the day's interview session was over.

The whole thing was so abrupt that even Linda had been more conversational when Taylor called to let her know he wouldn't be able to make it for Friday's interview.

Taylor finished getting dressed, knotting and readjusting the length of his tie while imagining the scenes Jake would make if he showed up to anchor his time slot and forewent the interviews. He pulled the tie tight around his neck. He felt the mugger grabbing it and forcing his chin into the barrel of the gun. Grinning at him. Squeezing the trigger.

He couldn't breathe. Couldn't think. His fingers fumbled for the knot. Too tight against his throat. He ripped the tie off. Unbuttoned his shirt. Chest heaving. Claustrophobia. He leaned over the bathroom sink. Ran water. Drank some. Splashed it on his face. Dug the heels of his hands into his eyes.

He breathed.

He was alone in his home.

Breathed deeper.

No one was there.

One more large breath. He looked at himself in the mirror, face pale and dripping with water. There was work to be done now. He had to get over it. Just no tie today.

His heartbeat didn't return to its normal tempo until he left the townhouse. The morning air felt crisp. The small walls of his home, narrow and made of exposed brick the alleyway, didn't lean in around him. He welcomed the openness of the outdoors. But after locking the front door, he couldn't force himself to walk down the steps to the sidewalk.

The street wasn't aggressively busy. The normal early risers were walking their dogs or speed-talking on their phones as they passed by his front steps. Traffic was light. No one took any special interest in Taylor or his blocked-out haircut, lined with stitches. But he felt something.

Where was the man that mugged him? Did he leave the neighborhood or was he still in that alleyway, only minutes from where Taylor was supposed to sleep at night?

This place wasn't safe anymore. And if that man was still there, if he wouldn't leave, Taylor's home wouldn't be safe. He would find out where Taylor lived, break in, steal all of his worldly possessions, murder him, and no one would know until the stench of his bloated corpse was so potent that people walking on the street could smell it through the windows.

He tried to steady his breathing. Think rationally. There was no other way to stop the downward spiral of paranoid thoughts than to find out. He'd walk past the alleyway—very quickly—and make sure the man wasn't there. Of course he wouldn't be. He'd committed a crime, he couldn't stay there anymore. Could he?

Taylor's legs shook as he descended the stairs, fighting against the logic of his brain. Panic. Adrenaline. They had a way of setting the body into autopilot that he had to force off. He ignored the need to run back to his home and triple lock the doors. Tried to think about something other than getting back into bed and sleeping for years. His hands quaked as the dark, gaping mouth of the alleyway came into view. The throbbing pain in his head quickened.

This was a bad idea. Why did he have to live in this neighborhood? Obviously it was a dangerous place, full of criminals and worse. He should put his house up for sale, and he would never have to see this damn street again. There was no shame in keeping himself safe. He stopped at the intersection one block down from the alley, the traffic light counting down until he could cross.

Fifteen seconds to make a decision. He could turn around now. Go the long way to a street with taxis, avoid the alley, and contact a realtor after deadbolting his doors for the night. But what kind of person would that make him?

Nine seconds.

The kind of person that would go out of their way to avoid fears and problems? Or someone who cautiously approached situations, aware that every decision had a ramification?

Four seconds.

Why couldn't he be both?

The orange palmlight faded to black and the signal to walk appeared. Taylor had to force his leg to take the first step forward. The next was easier and less shaky.

His breathing stopped as he walked past the alleyway, peering into it. He saw the place where his life had almost ended. Where he'd been attacked. Not a soul looked back at him.

Empty alley after empty alley, he walked. And when Taylor finally reached the end of the street, unoccupied taxis painted a happy yellow passed him in both directions. His heartbeat was even. His hands steady. All was safe.

The cabbie was quieter than the one he rode with last week. He kept looking at Taylor in the rearview mirror, opening his mouth like he had something to say, before glancing at the stitches and closing his mouth. Taylor downed another painkiller and ignored his journalistic instinct to encourage the driver to speak.

As he climbed the steep private drive to the house, the wound felt tight on his scalp and his head pounded. He had to take breaks and wait for the throbbing to subside. It would be good to get back into the rhythm of work and distract himself from the pain.

"You bump your head and all of a sudden you have to wait an entire weekend before you come to work?" Hudson asked as Linda opened the door. He motioned to the eyepatch he was wearing to cover the empty eye socket. "Sorry I forgot to put this on last time. It's been a while since I've had guests and needed to wear it. Nurses around here are used to things like that."

Taylor told Hudson not to worry about it and tipped his head toward the man to point out the ugly gash. "They had to stitch me up."

Hudson leaned forward in his wheelchair. "Oh, that's just a scratch. If it was a real cut, they'd use a mattress stitch, not that continuous stitch crap." He waved Taylor's injury away with a laugh. "No big deal there, but I'm glad you're alright."

"I guess. I was in the hospital for two days." Linda wheeled Hudson back and they began walking toward the sunroom.

"What'd he use? Gun or a knife?"

"Gun. He... he put it to my head and then pistol-whipped me."

"I take it that's the first time someone's stuck a gun in your face?"

"Well... yeah."

Hudson shook his head. "Gun's nothing to be worried about in a mugging. If someone has a heater pressed to your noodle, one little pull of that trigger and it's lights out, no question. There's no pain, no life or death struggle, just the end of your story. A knife though. There's no fast death with a knife. You feel like you got punched, then the warm blood starts pouring down your body, and only then does the pain start. You'd do well to remember that."

This legend in his wheelchair and all of the pictures of him hanging in the hallway seemed to stare and judge Taylor for his fear of physical assault. He looked to Linda for some support, but she kept her eyes locked straight ahead. As long as Hudson was nearby, she would continue following his no-interaction rule. Taylor felt his teeth clenching. "Nothing to be worried about? I had a nutjob put a gun to my head. He told me he didn't want my money and then bam. Lights out."

"It's wrong to automatically dismiss evil for insanity. They are each dangerous and unpredictable in their own unique ways. This man was either, or both. But his mental state shouldn't matter to you anymore. He's miles away from here by now. You'll never interact with him again. What matters is how you'll go forward from this event. What matters are his actions and the justice he deserves. What do you think he deserves?"

"I don't know. It was assault, so jail time?"

Linda parked Hudson beside the table at the side of the sunroom like before. It felt so much less oppressive in here than in the rest of the house. The open glass walls let in sunshine that the dark wooden entranceway seemed to stifle with Hudson memorabilia.

Linda went to the hospital bed in the corner of the room and started working on machines she'd probably plug Hudson into once Taylor left. The man was a puppet, kept alive by strings of monitors and IV fluid.

"Not the charges, pressed against him. What does he deserve?"

"Jail... jailtime. I'm not understanding your question."

"I don't mean what he would receive if he were caught by the police," Hudson said. "The justice system here is broken. Even if you don't have enough money to hire a lawyer and convince people you're not a criminal, they still don't do enough to punish the guilty. I mean what do *you* think he deserves? What would you do if he was here right now?"

Taylor saw the gun in his face again. Felt the man's presence in front of him, the encompassing stench. The pressure of the gun against his temple. Sweat covered his brow. His heart beat faster. Flexed and unflexed his hands.

"I'd break his fucking neck."

He released his clenched fists. Felt himself inhale sharply.

Where had that come from? Did he really believe he would kill a man, even after what happened to Alice, after people acting outside the law were directly responsible for her death? He stammered an apology for his language and Hudson ignored it. "There's nothing wrong with speaking strong opinions, as long as they're what you truly believe."

Taylor nodded. It was what he believed. The man deserved it. He had a gun to Taylor's head and could have killed him. And now Taylor had to concentrate on controlling an all-consuming fear. A paranoia that made the skin on the back of his neck prickle. There was no pain medicine he could take for fear, no stitches that could seal together his contentment with walking on the street. Violence seemed to follow him wherever he was in this city. Whether it was a few blocks away from his home days earlier, across the river years in the past with his fiancée, or at this very moment, speaking to the man that solidified the public opinion that a badge wasn't necessary to determine the legality of a person's actions, it was everywhere. Right now, he had no other option than to live with the fear. And the criminal deserved to pay for it. But Hudson was wrong. No matter what happened in the past, it wasn't Taylor's right to take the law into his own hands.

Hudson's eyes narrowed. "You know, before I really started fighting crime and doing the vigilante thing, I had an experience not totally unlike yours. I was trying my best to get back into shape before my suspension from school finished. I wanted to earn back my starting spot on the wrestling team, and..."

CHAPTER FIFTEEN

...Needed to go for a run. On top of the usual bloat that went with Thanksgiving overeating, the lack of daily practices with the team meant he had to work even harder on his own to get back to his weight class before the start of the spring semester. Coach had written multiple letters to make it clear he was pissed that Tim had gotten suspended and wouldn't hesitate to toss him from the team completely if he couldn't get back to where he was before.

Tim looked through his dirty clothes for workout gear that didn't reek of sweat. The laundry duty standoff between him and his mother was reaching a tipping point. She refused to put his clothes into the wash for him, and he was equally stubborn about doing it himself. If she was already running the machine, why couldn't she just add a few things in? It had been like that all semester, one small thing after another. If she was able to make life harder for him during his suspension, she would, just to prove a point. "Cleanliness is close to godliness," his mother said the last time she picked his dirty clothes out of the hamper, leaving them in a pile next to the laundry machine. "It's one of the few things that divides us from the rest of the animal kingdom. And that's something you have to take care of by yourself."

The only clean clothes he could find was a set of all-black

sweats. He looked out the window at the setting sun. The last time he'd worn dark clothes on a night run, he'd almost been hit by a car. The jackass rounded a corner too fast and Tim had to leap into someone's front yard to avoid becoming a hood ornament. When he complained about it to his parents, his mother only shrugged and said, "You can't be mad at them. It's common sense, Timothy. No one can see you if you're out at night in dark clothes. Please use your head."

He pulled the black sweatshirt over his head as he thought about the argument that had followed. Nothing bad was going to happen just because he was wearing dark clothes. And he'd rather get in the same argument again than endure his own mildewed stench.

He checked the mirror while stretching. She had a point. It was hard to see even a sliver of color. His black running pants covered the tops of his dark running shoes, and his black hoodie covered the rest of him. He'd just have to run through the park tonight instead of on the road. Everyone avoided Overton Park after dark, but potentially running past drug dealers and thugs would be better than getting hit by a pickup truck and left on the side of the road. He'd go for a run, roll his eyes when his mother complained that he wasn't listening to her advice, and show her that she was wrong, yet again, when he came home safely. Nothing was going to happen to him.

The air felt warmer than it had the past few nights. Dry wind had been making his ears ring and left him with a hacking cough for hours after he finished his workouts. It still wasn't optimal running weather, but tonight the sharp, cold air didn't stab his lungs every time he took a breath. Moonlight and occasional streetlamps illuminated the walking path in strips that managed to break through the trees. Birds slowed their chattering as he approached, then picked back up again as he passed. The trail was lined by the expansive park on one side and woods on the other. The world was quiet and still. Everything flowed easily.

It allowed his mind to wander, rather than fixate on how heavy his legs felt after a few miles. His breathing and footsteps beat a rhythm on the sidewalk as he thought about Dennis, wondering if the kid ever considered the sacrifice Tim had made to get justice for him. He thought about the guys he'd hurt. Friends. Wondered if his parents understood the reasons for what he did, or if they felt comfortable with not caring and just being angry. And then he heard a noise.

Tim slowed his steps and stopped, taking the hood off his head to listen better. Had that been a person screaming? He heard only the wind rushing by his ears. Dead empty branches clicked together in the quiet. It was nothing. People playing a game, or a sharp laugh from someone taking a late walk. He felt the muscles in his legs start to tighten. He pulled the black hood back over his head and tried to find the rhythm on the concrete path again.

He played the sound back in his head. He'd probably imagined it. Mistook a dog's sharp howl for something sinister. His thoughts had already ventured on again when a scream of "Rape!" swept through the park. Closer than before.

He continued running in the direction he thought it came from, the trail winding into a more heavily wooded area lit only by the moon. His legs pumping faster. Stayed light on his toes. The crack of a slap carried through the wind. "Shut up, bitch," a voice growled. He slowed his run and tried to calm his breath. Where were they? He hadn't seen a soul the entire time he was in the park.

Tim crouched by the side of the trail and listened. A woman's yelling was muffled to the right of the path, within the trees, no more than twenty or thirty feet away. Tim froze.

His mind went to a case they'd studied in psychology—Kitty Genovese. She'd been raped and killed in the courtyard of an apartment block, perfectly visible to everyone who lived in the building. No one called the police. No one tried to help her. They all thought someone else would step in. All of those people, and it would have only taken one to help. Overtaken the criminal. Done something. There was no one here who could help this woman, besides Tim.

But if he stepped off the path and into the trees, branches and leaves would crackle and scream underfoot, and the man in the woods would find him and beat him into oblivion. Someone needed to do something, but Tim couldn't insert himself into a situation if he was going to get killed because of it.

He started walking down the path to continue his run. Tried to ignore the images in his head of what was happening, and what was about to happen because he wanted to continue on his way without any inconvenience. His gut constricted.

What did she look like? What would she look like after the night was over? Scarred? Dead? And if he stepped in, he might end up the same way. He didn't know her, it wasn't any of his business. He should ignore it. Put it out of his mind. Keep walking.

Keep trying to push away images of a dead woman in the woods.

The trail branched apart, one side continuing his direction toward the open park in the distance, the other veering deeper into the trees, curving back the way he'd come. Back toward the screaming. He stepped onto it.

Tim heard the words in his head, like they'd been searching for an opportunity to present themselves: "Keep your heart with all vigilance, for from it flow the springs of life. Ponder the path of your feet and your ways will be sure." His heartbeat pounded in his ears. He made sure his hood covered as much of his head as possible and forced his feet to move down the trail.

Ahead, he saw an ember glow from the end of a joint. Another burned beside it. Tim's eyes adjusted to the lack of light deep in the trees. Someone struggled on the ground, her arms held down by a third man while another was pulling at her clothes. Jesus. Four men. It still wasn't too late to leave. They hadn't seen him.

The woman wrenched her arms and kicked her legs, trying to find any leverage to escape. Her chest heaved as she screamed into a rag they'd tied around her mouth. They would take their turns with her. Take their turns and then get rid of her like a piece of garbage. They joked to each other that she would wear herself out and then it wouldn't take long. Like it was a casual evening. Like it had happened before. Bile rose in Tim's throat as he grabbed a heavy tree limb off the ground. He crouched, waiting. He had to move quickly. The first joint burned bright. Then the second one. They wouldn't see him behind the glow. He sprinted.

The first strike glanced off the man's shoulder and solidly struck his head. Tim swung the stick again, taking out the other's knees. He raised the limb over his head and smashed it against both of their faces. A gunshot roared. Something punched him in the arm. Caught him off balance. He fell. Scampered to his feet as another shot rang out. He tackled the man trying to pull his pants up. Two more gunshots. He rolled onto his back, holding onto the man from behind. Keeping him between himself and the shooter. He stood him up, holding his throat in a tight grip. Tim's left arm was weak. Couldn't see the shooter in the dark. Another shot was fired. The man Tim held screamed. Warmth ran down his legs. Tim dropped him. Sprinted toward the muzzle flash.

He ran into the shooter and slammed him into a tree. Something knocked Tim's head back. He smelled metal. Blood ran into one of his eyes. He couldn't see. He grabbed for the gun blindly and crushed the hand holding it against the tree, bending the elbow the wrong way until the man dropped it. He landed punches to Tim's ribs. Tim twisted the gun arm once, twice, and then a third time, hard, further than it should have gone. Something snapped and it went limp. The shooter used his other hand to try to push Tim off. He knocked it away, then slammed the man's head into the tree twice. He let himself fall, dragging the face against the bark. He landed with a raised knee, shattering the man's nose against it. The rib punches came harder, more desperate. Tim held the man's head against the tree and swung his leg around, his knee connecting with the man's temple, crushing it into the tree. He collapsed.

Tim fell to the ground. Listening. His breath came in heavy cloudy bursts. Pain in his shoulder that he hadn't felt before flowered down his arm. The woman cried. The gunshot victim moaned. He went to the woman and let the man bleed. "Are you alright?" Her silhouette nodded in the dark. He helped her stand and stood back as she brushed herself off. She took a step toward the path and cried out in pain. He tried to give her support for walking, but she refused. He silently walked beside her to the path and then to brightly lit street, where she thanked him...

CHAPTER SIXTEEN

TAYLOR

"...And then she just... walked away." Hudson sighed heavily and leaned back in his wheelchair. Silence settled into the room as he drank from the glass Linda brought over almost an hour ago when he began talking. His voice had started going hoarse as he neared the end of his story. The physical exertion of its telling draining him of energy. The red light on the recording equipment blinked silently.

When it was clear the man had no more to add, Taylor spoke for the first time since Hudson started. "I have to be honest, I wouldn't say that you getting shot in the process of saving a woman's life was a 'similar experience' to me getting beaten up by a hobo. What'd you do about the gunshot?"

"Are you kidding?" Hudson took another sip from his water and used his nub to help readjust the glass in his arthritic hand. "I was a child back then. What do you think I did? I went straight to a hospital and told them what happened. Told them I'd been taking a run at night and gotten jumped. Doctors are legally and morally obligated to help anyone who walks through their doors. You'd do well to remember that." He took one more sip and placed his glass back on the table.

"I was lucky. The bullet only grazed my shoulder and didn't

do serious damage. Even so, my parents barely let me out of their sight for the next month. My mother stopped being so harsh toward me. My father quoted bible verses to me whenever he could. Proverbs in particular, over and over again. Even Coach Snyder made a trip to the house to ream me out for being stupid, running through the park at night. He wanted me off the team, not dead."

"And after that?"

"Well, you know... around the time everything healed and my parents weren't so overbearing, my suspension finished up, and I was back at the university. So I kept at it. The area around the school was the worst place to be after dark. A lot of young and stupid college kids for bad people to take advantage of. It was a while before I returned to the park by my parents' house. When four men are found barely hanging on to life somewhere, police tend to monitor it a little more and crime seems to magically dissipate." Hudson chuckled and released a small phlegm-laden cough.

He shook his glass to clink the ice and Linda was there seconds later refilling it. She kept her eyes down, locked onto the glass, and returned to a chair in the corner of the room that Taylor hadn't noticed her sitting in before. Hidden just out of sight, like the first day he visited Hudson.

She scribbled something on a notepad. Probably the amount of water he'd had to drink or notes on how bad his cough sounded. She'd been silent while Hudson was telling his story, but close enough to hear if he needed something.

Had she heard these stories before? Taylor tried to imagine listening to his father describe getting assaulted and shot or attacking other people like an animal. His stomach turned. It couldn't be an easy thing to sit through.

"Once the crime scene in the park was cleared out," Hudson continued, "and the police eventually stopped monitoring it, I filled in where I could. It didn't always get as violent as that first night. Mostly just people here and there dealing drugs or mugging and attacking people stupid enough to be in the park at night. It took weeks of work, almost months, but rumors started getting around of a person who dressed in all black and came to the park ready to fight. If I saw people, either on the trails or the park's open spaces, I would head their way. When I was close enough for them to see me, the ones getting into bad shit knew they had to split. Slowly, they learned their lessons and it got cleaned up. Last I heard it's a popular place to spend time during the evenings for cookouts and parties."

"Why?"

"Well it's a park, Taylor. That's sort of the point of those places."

Even between stories of attempted murder and assault, the old man refused to drop the smartass routine. Taylor forced a laugh that came out sounding like an exasperated breath.

Something pulled at him. He didn't come here for jokes or trivial conversations. He had to know the answer. This man had to justify how it all started. Taylor leaned forward in his chair. "No, I mean why did you do it? Why did you continue on after what happened to you the first time? You were a college-aged kid and you got *shot* for trying to do the right thing."

"People always used to ask me that question," Hudson said. "At least, back when I still talked to people. That was always the first thing they said that had a clear question mark at the end of it. You can hear it, you know? 'Mr. Hudson, it's great to meet you,' *period.* 'Oh my goodness, can I get your autograph,' question mark, *exclamation point.*

"But when the shock of meeting a celebrity—and like it or not, that's eventually what I became more than anything, a celebrity—when that finally wore off, and people had time to think about what they actually wanted to say to me, what they actually wanted to ask, it was almost always, 'Why did you do it?'"

"And what was your answer?" Taylor heard Linda shuffle in her seat outside of his line of vision.

"Oh you know, 'the city deserves better than the cops' or 'I'm just trying to make my city a safer place.' Something nice and canned like that. Good for the audio clips. You know how it is.

"But in reality... I think it was because I was greedy. It made me feel good, saving that woman. And that's a terrible thing to say. It took me a long time to embrace it. To understand that I wasn't doing it solely out of the kindness of my heart or for the betterment of the human race or any of that. The safety of the city was the goal, but it was also the byproduct. I did it because I was able to. I did it because no one else was doing it and I was making a difference and because it made me feel good."

Hudson brushed his hand across his forehead, gliding a finger across the edge of his eyepatch. The scar across his face flushed white under the pressure. He leaned forward in his wheelchair. "Let me make something clear," he said. Every syllable was choppy. He said them forcefully, baring his teeth. "There is no such thing as charity. People who go to sub-Saharan Africa on their own dime to give check-ups to starving children, people that donate hundreds and thousands of dollars to non-profits, down to even the people who drop a few coins into a beggar's cup—none of that is charity. That's someone who's making themselves feel better by alleviating another person's shitty situation a small amount. Patting themselves on the back for a job well done so they can sleep well at night with a warm fuzzy feeling of accomplishment in their belly. There is nothing special about that. Nothing charitable about reaffirming your place in the world by looking down at someone else and saying, 'I am helping you because you are worse off than I am.'"

Taylor could feel an anger, a bitterness, oozing out of the man. It curled Hudson's mouth down at the corners into what criminals must have seen when they encountered him in the dark—the face of a man disgusted at what they were doing, how they were behaving. Disgusted he hadn't moved fast enough to stop what had already happened. It was the strongest reaction Taylor had seen from Hudson since walking through the front door.

"I'm not afraid to admit that," Hudson said. "There's a pleasure to it. It's self-serving. That's the only reason anyone does the things they do. I just acted on that need differently. If I always paid attention, I could notice things that were going on. People acting like they were about to commit a crime or like they had done so recently. And if I felt like something wasn't right, I'd do everything I possibly could to stop it and the people doing it. Because it made me feel good."

Taylor nodded. He'd found it. The catalyst.

Hudson's father telling him to become more focused on doing good for others. His realizing he could do it in the most direct sense possible, ignoring the danger that came with it, because his father's words bounced around his head a few too many times and he knew it would make him feel better after being stuck in a miserable environment with his family. Being a captive audience to messaging that he was responsible for creating a better world however he could.

It wasn't dramatic. It wasn't a superhero origin story. It was a search for relief from a situation. Maybe it started with trying to improve the lives of others, but in the end, all of the vigilante, superhero life-saving came down to simple, self-centered greed.

Greed and desire to make himself feel better by helping others at the expense of people he decided were not deserving of his help. Repeating the process for years, on an escalating scale, resulting in a man whose body was slowly shutting down after decades of abuse and damage in the name of the greater good of a city. The man who first stopped a rape in the woods and over time turned into the person famous for tearing down an organized crime syndicate.

This was not a hero sitting before him. Justice or crime fighting or whatever he called it was just a byproduct. Greed was what started it all. What kept everything going. Not just with Hudson, but everything surrounding him. The rapists in the park. A city full of thieves and crooks and drug dealers. Years of it. Onward and outward over time, all the way to the man who'd shot Alice when chasing after an armed robber because he was greedy to get on the nightly news as a hero following in Hudson's footsteps. All of it was greed.

The whole thing made Taylor sick.

It was the first of the answers he was searching for. Not a clear one, but the question of why someone might ignore his comfortable life to become a person who threw himself into overwhelming, dangerous situations was answered. And for Hudson, all of that had been diluted down into one phrase that made him want to try to fulfill that need by making a difference.

"Constant vigilance," Taylor said. Proverbs. The bible verses from the first day he'd interviewed the man. The words Hudson's father had repeated and focused on when lecturing him.

Hudson nodded and readjusted in his wheelchair. His mouth opened into a smile, interrupted only by the scar crossing his face. "That's right. Constant. Vigilance. The determination to always be aware and watchful of your surroundings in order to identify a problem and fix it before something truly goes wrong. It's something that must be trained.

"Take right now, as an example. Your brain is processing and ignoring all of the information that isn't necessary to your survival. The temperature of the room is not a threat, so you aren't thinking about it. The seat underneath you doesn't pose a source of danger, so you've forgotten about that. The leaves outside, drifting gently with the breeze aren't even a tick on your registry. It's a matter of evolution. Adaptation. To allow you to focus on what's important.

"Right now, your survival depends upon getting good information from me, and reporting it to your producers. The better job you do, the better your career will be, the better your salary, and the better your odds of not facing the same fates as your ancient ancestors: dying out in the wild, weak, hungry, without shelter, after being hunted down by a wild animal. You're concentrating on what's important to you. And back then, I made the decision to consider everything important to my safety and the safety of people around me. I tried to be aware of everything. It's overwhelming at first, but you get used to it."

Linda cleared her throat as she made no effort to quiet her steps to the table and announced it was time for Hudson to take his pills. The old man's brow furrowed and he glanced at the sun shining through the trees. "Now? It's too early."

"Or maybe you're just not as good at tracking the time as you used to be," she said.

He took them down without another complaint. One pill, one matching sip of water. One pill, one sip, in a slow rhythm. Taylor's eyes moved from the pill tray Linda held, up to her face. She glanced at him only once and returned her gaze to her father's movements. One pill, one sip.

When he was finished, the angry Hudson had been replaced by the passive one from the end of their first session. His eyes returned to the limbs of the oak tree outside, swaying in a heavy gust of wind. Taylor followed his gaze. Watched the individual leaves move, reacting to every shift of the limbs and the wind. He had to stop himself from shaking his head in frustration. There was no way anyone could focus on every aspect of the world around them all the time. It had to be a lie. All of it, just greed and lies.

Long minutes passed. Taylor forced himself not to push Hudson into speaking. He looked out the other side of the sunroom at Hamington in the distance. Past the rose bush, past the river. A world away.

When the wind stopped and the tree settled, Hudson broke his silence. "As I kept finding criminals to fight, throughout the rest of my college years and afterward, other vigilantes showed up."

"How did that make you feel?" Taylor asked. He had to build the momentum back again. Easy questions. Open ended. An old man's silence wouldn't get him anywhere.

Hudson chuckled and used his stump of an arm to rearrange the legs underneath his blanket. "'How did that make you feel?'

It's bad enough that I'm talking to a reporter. If I find out you're a shrink too, I'm kicking your ass out the door."

"No, no," Taylor said, "just a guy trying to keep his job."

Hudson waved away the lazy rebuttal. "We both know that as long as you come to this house on a regular basis your boss will treat you as a sacred cow. Or at least like the guy interviewing the sacred cow. There's nothing wrong with acknowledging the situation at hand.

"But dealing with the other vigilantes later in my career was… a bit of an adjustment for me. My ego had to deal with the fact that I was no longer the only one in the game, but at the same time, as they became more prevalent, the justice system became less clogged. Fewer violent criminals lined the hallways of the courthouse waiting to be processed and released after judges were paid off or juries intimidated.

"There's a reason Hamington is the only place in the country with a vigilante community. And it's not just because I happened to live here and be stupid enough to start this whole thing. Judges in this city have always been shady. Everyone knows it, but there's never enough evidence to bring a case against them. You know this right? As part of the news you have to."

Taylor rubbed his cheek with his palm, the wedding ring on his hand prodding against his jawline. The tips of his fingers brushed the sewed-up gash above his temple. "I haven't reported many courtroom cases, but I know it seems like every time a wealthy criminal is on trial, a judge conveniently reverses the jury's decision or throws the case out due to tampered evidence or some other… well I guess the technical term is bullshit."

"That's right. But vigilantes don't take criminals to court. Not now, and not then. Some drop them off, bound and gagged on the front steps of the police department like some sort of Robin Hood, stealing the criminals and dropping them off to the authorities, but most settle things on their own."

The face of the man who had accidentally shot Alice flashed in front of Taylor's eyes. He'd tried to settle things on his own. And

Taylor's life was ruined as a result. He cleared his throat and tried to refocus on Hudson.

"You mean like what you did in the park."

"Yes. I was never one to help put criminals through a justice system hoping they wouldn't come out unbothered on the other side. I would—"

A quiet alarm sounded from behind Taylor and he heard Linda rise from her seat. "I think that's enough for today," she said. "Would you like me to walk Mr. Gardner out?"

"Oh, I'm fine, you don't have to do that."

"Yes, please," Hudson said to Linda. He turned back to Taylor and said, "It's a complicated house. Wouldn't want you to get lost in it."

Taylor thanked him for the day's interview and stood. Hudson responded with the same affirmative grunt he had when the previous interview session had ended. His gaze was directed out past the wall of windows to the city in the distance as Taylor and Linda left the room. She closed the doors quietly.

When he thought they were out of earshot, he asked Linda, "Does he always do that?"

She glanced back at the closed sunroom doors behind them. "Do what?" she asked. It was almost a whisper. Her paranoia of being caught breaking her father's rules remained no matter where they were in the house.

"Just shut down like that. He was talking and talking for what felt like hours, and then nothing."

"I don't know." She kept her eyes to her feet. Their footsteps were quiet on the carpet that ran down the long hallway. Hundreds of Hudsons stared down at them from photographs and news articles. "Did he seem strange to you today?" Linda asked.

"Strange?"

"Yeah. I mean, I know you've only met him twice, but did you notice anything different about today?"

"I... he's an ex-superhero celebrity. I don't know how you define 'strange.' This whole thing is strange."

She shook her head. "No, I mean his speech. The way he said things or talked. I'm asking you as a reporter that's used to interviewing people."

"Nothing really stands out. Why?"

She chewed her bottom lip, eyebrows furrowed. She slowed her steps and stopped in the entrance hall, the tall ceilings and chandelier towering overhead. "The things he told you today... they were different than when I've heard them in the past."

"Different how?"

"The details. The way he told the story. He's told me about that night in the park more times than I can remember. It's just one of those stories people ask your parents a lot, so as you grow up, you hear it over and over again. They say things the same way, down to the word, like it's a rehearsed and memorized script. But today seemed like he messed up some of those details. When he told it before, he'd been more injured. The rape had gone further, to the point where he had to physically carry the girl out of the woods. And I definitely don't remember him telling me he'd been pistol whipped. It was all just... different."

Taylor clenched his teeth. Today felt like it was going so much better than the first visit. For most of the day, the anger and disgust he felt toward the man only simmered in the background rather than at the forefront of his thoughts. He'd gotten caught up in the man's charisma. And now Hudson was just like every other interview subject Taylor had ever spoken to. Embellishing to make himself look better. Tweaking things to make them more dramatic. First it was the insane concept of being aware of all things at all times. Now it was the story itself. *Greed.* "So you think he's lying."

"No. I'm worried it's worse than that. His body has always been the thing that held him back. He has to get his lungs drained every six months, he can barely move because of his arthritis, all of his organs show signs of internal damage. Everything gives him trouble. He didn't even make it to sixty before he had to get a pacemaker. But what if it's his mind now?" Linda glanced back down the hallway toward the sunroom and started walking Taylor to the front door. She closed it behind them. A cab idled down the driveway beyond the gate. She must have stepped away at some point and called for one before ending the interview session.

"I'll be perfectly honest, I didn't want you to come here. He's in bad enough shape, he doesn't need any extra stressors to exacerbate things," Linda said. Her voice was louder outside. Stronger, like stepping out of the house had lifted a weight off of her.

"He's never cared about the publicity," she said. "Never wanted attention after he knew it wouldn't get him anything else. It's always been very straightforward. And then, all of a sudden, he tells me he wants an interview. That he wants you to interview him, that it can only be you. I don't know why, I don't know where it came from, and he always ignores me when I ask. All these things happening at once... I'm worried he's had dementia or Alzheimer's and it just wasn't bad enough to notice until now."

Her eyes wandered from Taylor's to the trees to the front door and back to him. He couldn't tell if she was worried because of what she was telling him or because he was breaking Hudson's rules.

"You seem like a good doctor, so I doubt—"

"Not a doctor."

Taylor waved the correction away. "Doctor, nurse, whatever. Medical professional. I doubt that you would miss something like that only to realize it after I arrive. Stories change sometimes when people get in front of a camera or a reporter. Usually it's because they want to be seen as the best version of themselves, not the most realistic. It's not something you've missed. It's probably just how he wants to make sure I tell his story."

She kept her eyes to the ground and nodded. "Maybe. Anyway, you need to go. Can't be out here too long and have Dad thinking I'm breaking his rules by talking to you." Linda offered a weak smile and went back inside.

Taylor ignored the flow of questions about the Hudson House

and eventually the cab driver settled into silence as he crossed the bridge over the Baldwin River. Maybe there could be a way to separate out the lies. There had to be. Take the information he'd been given and boil it all down to the truth at the core of everything. For his sake and for Alice's. He would find it. He had to.

148

CHAPTER SEVENTEEN

SAM

Sam crouched in the dark between two cars parked outside an electronics store, waiting for someone to come his way. It was almost closing time and he could see a line of people at the checkout counter through the windows, all wanting to hurry up and buy their hundreds of dollars of shit they didn't need so they could go back to their heated houses, throw it all in a corner, and forget about it until months later when cleaning up their stockpile of things they'd never used. He'd never been in one of those houses, but he knew that's what it would look like. People with money were all the same. They didn't need all that cash. But he did.

Sam still had almost all the money from the pawn shop. He'd bought a Coke and a sandwich at a gas station after attacking the suited man in the alley, but kept to looking through dumpsters and trash cans for leftovers to eat. It was solid money—almost five hundred bucks even without Violet's half—but Sam wasn't like those people in the electronics store. He couldn't afford to waste a dime.

Whenever the thought of Violet wandered into his head, Sam felt the urge to spit. All that pathetic whining after the pawn shop. The crying in the alley. It attracted too much attention.

Made people's eyes hang around too long. She'd almost ruined everything, even though she knew from the beginning what was going to happen in the store. She was a gambler, not an idiot.

She probably didn't even have her money anymore. Probably went straight to a casino and gone all in on the first hand. Either that, or she'd just gone back to the tent city and cried into it like tissues. Looked at it, making herself feel guilty about what she and Sam had done. How they'd hurt somebody. Not understanding it was what had to be done. And with all that moaning and crying, she'd probably run and told Davey, forcing Sam to move.

Violet's emotions made it risky to stay in the alley long enough for the suited man to come back. But it was worth it. For every time the man in the suit had walked past Sam and ignored him, refusing to answer simple questions or drop change into his cup, it was worth the risk. Sam had a hard time not laughing at him when he'd put the gun in the asshole's face.

He smelled like fear. Pissed his pants and the gun wasn't even loaded. And when Sam hit him with it, he cried like a bitch. It was probably the first time anyone had stood up to him. He was used to telling people beneath him what to do, as he wore his expensive clothes, rubbing it in their faces that they'd never be as good as him. Never expecting anything would happen to him on his way to his cushy job.

His briefcase didn't have anything Sam could use. A notepad with a bunch of scribbles on it, some old newspaper articles about vigilantes in Hamington, kids' comic books, and a phone. He thought about keeping the smartphone but remembered hearing somewhere that the police could track them. He smashed the screen with his heel and slammed it against the concrete, its mechanical little guts flying everywhere, then tossed the rest of it in the garbage. No, he didn't get anything useful from the suited man, but Sam felt better now with that image of the man bleeding and afraid and apologetic locked in his head.

After that, it was time to move on. Sam had to head north. He'd hurt the suited man and killed Jakob within a few minutes' walk of each other. He needed space between himself and the crime scenes. And now, since Violet had been to his alley, the closer Sam was, the easier he'd be to find.

He was careful when he started to travel north. Without his backpack, everything had to be tucked into his pants or jacket pockets, including the guns. If a vigilante or cop looked at him for more than a passing second, they'd see the extra bulkiness weighing him down, and shit would all go downhill. If the cops saw the guns, they'd put him in cuffs and ask him if he was the guy who'd murdered the pawn shop owner, or if he was the one who'd attacked an asshole in an alley. If the vigilantes saw them, they wouldn't ask anything before starting to attack.

The farther away, the less suspicious his overly full pockets would look. Farther away, the only thing they would wonder about him was why he hadn't flocked to the underpass like the rest of the hobos. So he walked. Quietly. Not bringing on attention. Eyes to the ground. Only doing what he needed to.

Halfway through the first day going north, he was able to steal a man's watch. They were walking in the same direction at a crowded intersection and Sam grabbed his wrist like they were holding hands. When the man tried to pull away, Sam flashed the revolver in his belt. The man started shaking and was suddenly fine with the watch sliding off his wrist. Sam walked beside him for another half block, hand ready to draw the gun, until the sidewalk became thick with pedestrians again and he was able to scoot away in the opposite direction and turn a corner before the man started yelling that he'd been robbed.

Sam leaned from side to side between the two cars to stretch his knees. His legs were sore from the full day of walking north. He rose to look at the electronics store again and saw a woman wheeling a cart out of the automatic doors. It was filled with an Xbox and some DVDs or maybe games. Nice big box meant it would be expensive. Maybe he could get some money for it. Sam shrank back between the two cars and watched her through the windows of an SUV.

She pulled a ring of keys from her purse and opened the trunk of a car near the back of the poorly lit parking lot. As she passed him, Sam stood from between the two cars and pulled the revolver on her. She froze, her eyes big like quarters.

Sam motioned to the shopping cart with the pistol and pointed to himself. Every time he waved the gun, she flinched and a look of fear crashed across her face. The woman gave the shopping cart one big shove and sent it Sam's direction. He nodded to her and waved the gun again, watching her shrink with every movement.

These people were all easy. So coddled and safe that at the first sign of danger, they'd give up anything they could to stay safe. This woman, the man with the watch. At least the suited man in the alley pleaded and begged for his life. These people put up no sign of a fight. No sign of bravery. They deserved to have things taken from them. They didn't understand how badly other people needed the money they tossed away.

After leaving the parking lot, Sam threw his jacket over the Xbox and rolled the grocery cart through less travelled streets. Less attention, more safety. Anyone walking past would be able to connect that he hadn't bought the items on his own. Even this far from the crimes down south, a vigilante wouldn't wait to ask questions before attacking him. He needed to turn the grocery cart into cash quickly.

A digital bell rang as he entered his second pawn shop in a week.

The man behind the counter looked up from his phone as Sam rolled the grocery cart to the front of the store. He glanced at the Xbox and DVDs still protected by shrink wrap and grabbed a clipboard off the desk behind him. "Do you here certify that these are your items to sell? Please sign here." Sam scribbled a line and checked a few boxes. The man didn't even check what he'd written before folding the page and sliding it under the cash register. "That's two hundred in store credit, one fifty in cash. What do you want?"

Unlike Violet, Sam took the time to make sure the bullets he was buying actually fit the guns he had. The cashier loosely held a pistol in Sam's direction the entire time, not even bothering to look up from his phone. Smarter than Jakob, even if he didn't have anything to worry about. Sam was only there to do business.

When he left, Sam wrapped the guns, cash, and boxes of bullets in his jacket, tucking the bundle into the corner of the grocery cart closest to him. He stood outside the pawn shop, not sure which way to go. The exhaustion of the day finally setting in. All the miles walking north. The constant avoidance of vigilantes and cops. And now, with his jacket being used to cover his weapons, the cold. He hadn't thought this part out.

He needed to find somewhere to rest. And to hide. To unload all of his new toys so he could relax and stay warm in his jacket without worrying if vigilantes or cops were hiding in dark alleys waiting to attack without question if they saw he was carrying a gun.

Shelters wouldn't let him in. The second he walked in with the weapons and cash, they'd call the cops and he'd get hauled off to jail.

It had to be somewhere he could stay for a long time. Not an alleyway like before. That was only good for a few days at a time. Somewhere like the underpass where he could build a shelter for himself. Where he could keep his things when he was gone during the day trying to get food and money.

On a quiet street corner, he sat down and took his shoes off. His feet throbbed with pain. Raw patches had rubbed into his heels as the day went on. He massaged his toes, popping them and trying to make the swelling go down. It felt like weeks since he started walking through the hard, concrete city. This city with all of its people that threw away their money on useless shit.

They were all the same. Living in these nice buildings with air conditioning and feather mattresses and security systems...

A low hanging fire escape on an apartment building seemed to wave at him as he rubbed his heel. *Security.* Nothing was safer and more secure than having a quick way to get away from people chasing him. How had he missed this at every building he'd passed on his way north? His eyes followed the fire escape's zigzagging path all the way to top of the building. Sam slid his shoes back on and climbed it, step by step, going faster. He emerged at the top and smiled.

This could be the spot. Away from people, away from the vigilantes walking the streets. The gravel on the roof would be a little rough when hot, but the towering buildings around might be able to give some shade.

And those buildings also had a clear view of the roof. If someone saw him there from another building, the landlord could check during the day while Sam was gone, throw away all of his shit, and call the cops on him. Not an option. He took one last look around the roof before crawling back down the metal stairs.

At this point, a door stoop would be fine. Just somewhere for the night where he wouldn't get rained on. All to be kicked off in the morning as usual. Screamed at. Like a rat.

None of this shit would ever change. He'd always be a bum, no matter how many guns or how much money he had in his pockets. He could walk the entire city in circles and never find a place to stay. That's why the underpass existed. Too few places, too many hobos. And he'd been screwed out of that because he'd tried to help them.

No matter what he did, none of it would change. He pulled the revolver out of his waistband and held it down by his side as he took slow steps. He spun the cylinder while he walked, feeling the new bullets in each chamber. Laid it flat in his palms in front of him. It would be such a simple thing. Nothing would change. He already didn't have anywhere to go. This was the way it always should have gone.

A chain link fence rattled as a truck drove by. He looked up from the pistol. Across the street stood a fenced off building, half burnt out, half reconstructed. Sam went to the fence and looked through. A yellow sign was nailed to a post in front of the building with the words "WARNING" and "CONDEMNED" in bold letters. He tossed the bundled jacket with the ammo and money over the fence and climbed.

The double front doors were loosely chained together and he was just able to squeeze through. Sam held the gun out in front of him, pointing around at the dark room. Nothing moved.

He climbed the skeleton of a staircase up to the second floor. The wood beneath his feet screamed. He waited for the sound of footsteps coming to check the noise. Silence.

Nothing was there. No hobos. No construction tools. The place hadn't been worked on in months. There was some trash around the construction site—enough that it looked abandoned, but not lived in. No one would wander through to steal his things. No one would kick him out when construction work started in the morning.

He ignored the weight of his legs and searched each floor, looking for a reason not to stay. At a point, the construction changed into charred remains of the building, wood ending in blackened charcoal tips wherever the fire had eaten through. And still, there was nothing. It was perfect.

He hid three of the guns in different areas, shoving most of the money and bullets behind a stack of old plywood. The revolver and a few twenty-dollar bills stayed tucked into his waistband, just to be safe while he was out. The exhaustion weighed on him, making every step more difficult, but his mind was shaking off the despair from just minutes ago. He had somewhere to live. There was only one more thing he had to do before he rested. The night would be better for this than the day.

It was more difficult to get things done in the middle of the day as a hobo. The city was alive and people were out, walking around. They ignored him until he came too close or showed up somewhere he wasn't supposed to. But the night brought comfort. The night meant darkness and a sense of safety. And he would blend right in with all the others still awake at this hour.

The bright lights of the Walmart hurt his eyes as he walked in.

Pop music playing through the speakers was only interrupted by requests for help at a front register. The other people in the store were all insomniacs and minimum-wage shelf-stockers. No one gave him the usual disgusted looks because of his clothes and dirtiness and his face that he'd been told was so scary. He was there to spend money like anyone else.

He wandered through the rows of shelves, unsure where everything would be. He couldn't remember the last time he'd been in a Walmart. Couldn't remember the last time he'd had money to spend at a store. But he was here now. Sam had things to buy. Water. Food. He wouldn't have to worry about his meal for the night. It would be covered. Paid for and purchased.

Peanut butter, baked beans, cans of soup, a camping cot, and even a bottle of red wine. And he still had almost thirty bucks left over after he checked out with his full cart. When he got home to the construction site, he feasted on peanut butter, gobbling up big finger scoops followed by gulps of wine until his stomach couldn't handle anymore. He went to sleep on the cot he'd set up on one of the unfinished levels, nothing between him and the sky.

He wasn't lying on the ground, hard cement hurting his head, worried someone would pass by and take everything he owned. Wasn't listening for Davey's people or the cops or vigilantes to come looking for him. Cars passed with the occasional honk or screeching brakes. Every once in a while, people shouted at each other. Laughed.

The sky above him was black and empty, full of nothing. The construction site silent. It wasn't an underpass cramped with hobos all crying or talking to themselves as he tried to sleep. Or the doorway to a rich person's house. Or steps to a church that a pastor would kick him off before the next service.

There was no one but him. This was Sam's shelter. Home.

CHAPTER EIGHTEEN

JESSICA

Jessica rearranged her breasts and checked her makeup before knocking on the door. He was a tits man, which was good because she didn't have much of an ass. He opened the door, talking on the Bluetooth attached to his ear, and waved her in. Officer Parker was wearing loose boxers and a wifebeater undershirt a size too small. When he turned to walk into the living room, she saw his back hair flooding out of the shirt's collar, trying to escape. He disgusted her.

Once he got off the phone, he didn't apologize or even say hello. He sat down in his La-Z-Boy and patted his knee. She forced her mouth to smile. He was too comfortable with the setup. She would have to change something soon. Make him work for it. Or at least appreciate that he was even getting to touch a woman in the first place.

She straddled his knee, facing away from him. She laid back on his chest, grabbed his hands, and slid them from her legs to her breasts. He squeezed too hard. She started rolling her hips to distract him. "Hey big daddy. You have a tough day at work?"

He said he did, and then made a bad joke about it not being the only thing that was hard. She wanted to remind him that he didn't do shit while she was working her fourteen-hour days. That it didn't take a lot of effort to sit behind a counter and assign numbers to pieces of evidence. But she kept her mouth shut and focused on her business. Pushed back against him and gasped as if she'd never felt a dick before. His stupidity was a necessary part of the arrangement.

Whenever Jessica ran low on any of her drugs—weed, blow, smack, anything—she gave him a call and, for the fee of one or two fake orgasms, he turned off the lights in the evidence locker for her, blinding the camera inside and wrote up a bullshit reason why his key card registered as entering the room. When new evidence came in, he underwrote the weights on drugs, ensuring she would get a certain amount per bust. Not enough to start dealing in the big leagues, but she was able to supply small dealers and hook up her friends for a fee.

It was an overly cautious routine, his writing up an excuse why he'd gone in the locker so she could fill baggies of drugs while wearing night vision goggles in a pitch-black room, but they'd never been caught. She was making more money than she ever could as a cop, he was getting sex he wouldn't be otherwise, and everyone was happy. She only took the best quality shit to sell, and none of her customers knew where she got it. A small side industry with no investment other than dealing with Parker. She was printing money by fucking a slob.

She supposed there should be some weight on her soul, or guilt on her conscience, but honestly didn't give a shit. Her body wasn't a temple. It was a tool to do whatever needed to be done. If she had to let some fat hairy fuck flop around on her for a few seconds to make thousands of dollars, that was fine. She just had to deal with the rough tit grabbing. He was a stubborn dummy and got upset if she ever asked him to try something different.

As she lowered herself down his body, she noticed that he'd trimmed his pubes. Maybe he was actually starting to care about his hygiene. It would make life less disgusting for her if that was the case.

As Parker leaned back and ran his hands through her hair,

she wondered if Violet was having any luck finding Sam. There weren't many women in Johanson's book of vigilantes. If she turned out to be decent, it could help him with someone subtler for the underpass. Johanson would owe Jessica, and probably wouldn't complain if she upped his price for the nose candy. A price increase, plus convincing him to buy an extra eight-ball a week would add up to a couple hundred bucks a month, and Johanson's habit on its own could pay for the majority of her mortgage. Parker whispered something to her as he led her to bed.

Some of her other users helped cover her car payments and utility bills. Even with the 0% interest she got from the Bank of Under My Mattress, if she kept moving the way she was, slow and steady, she would be able to actually move somewhere outside the city and retire by the time she turned sixty-five.

Parker was lasting longer than usual tonight, so she whooped it up a bit to make him feel like a big stud. The grunts and groans came soon after.

He snorted mucous and rubbed his nose with the back of his hand as he rolled off of her. "You wanna stay the night?"

"Oh, I'm sorry baby, I have an early breakfast meeting and didn't bring a change of clothes. I wish I could," she said. Where the hell was her underwear? More than a few pairs had disappeared in his apartment. The perverted bastard probably hid them in a drawer as soon as they were off her body. She should just stop wearing them when she came here.

"You have more breakfast meetings than anyone I've ever met," he said, watching her quickly pull her clothes back on. She didn't care about pumping her breasts up now that he was finished.

"Have to find time for meetings when you're busy tracking down criminals all day."

"My lady, the super cop."

He called her that sometimes. *My lady*. It made her uncomfortable. Did he think this was anything more than a transaction of ass for access? She never wanted to ask. She wasn't sure what the answer might be.

She let him kiss her goodnight in case he was in his emotional state. Her inventory of pot was low right now and she needed to grab a couple ounces from the closet tomorrow. He had to keep feeling good about the deal. She couldn't afford for him to lose interest.

Jessica had parked her car a few blocks away from his place. There was no such thing as being too paranoid when coming here. She didn't want a superior officer driving by to notice a car that looked even similar to hers outside of Parker's building. Besides, it gave her a reason to spend a few more minutes walking in a part of town she didn't come to often enough.

Parker was somehow able to afford a place in the one nice neighborhood of West Ham where the hills began their rumblings that grew into the mountains a few dozen miles west. Residential buildings were nestled between the slow rolls of hills, like East H had been picked up and dropped in the middle of a skyscraper city.

She never realized how much she liked Parker's neighborhood until she and her husband got the divorce. Her new condo was a roach-infested place, squeezed into a building squeezed into a city block. That fucking cunt, Sam. If he hadn't attacked her. If he hadn't made her lose the baby. If he hadn't destroyed the bottom half of her face in a way that made it difficult for her husband to look at. Her life would be so different. She'd still be sneaking around, stifling her disgust at fucking Parker to get access to drugs and selling them whenever he was on call, but it was never a necessity back then. Just an opportunity for some extra money she could keep for herself. Now she couldn't afford for the drugs to only be a side occupation.

If her husband hadn't been in such a rush to leave her, maybe she could have found a place in this neighborhood. She would have had to sell more drugs to afford it, all while avoiding running into Parker, but it was a good neighborhood, peppered with mom and pop restaurants and local grocery stores. When the weather was nice, people took walks at night on the brightly lit streets and listened to loud pop music on the radio and paid twelve dollars for a cone of gourmet ice cream.

But now she was stuck. Couldn't get out of her lease without paying a fee she couldn't spend the money on, couldn't afford to buy a new place, couldn't do anything but continue on the road that was in front of her. Selling heroin to surgeons and coke to party-goers, as long as the goal was still clearly in focus. Retire at sixty-five. Own a nice house. Read some good books.

Her jeans rubbed uncomfortably on the bare skin below her hip bones that was no longer protected by cotton underwear. She readjusted her pants as she sat in her car. Took a deep breath and reminded herself why she drove half an hour to fuck a disgusting bastard who lived in a better neighborhood than she did, all in order to steal and sell the same drugs she was paid to get off the street. If the shit you deal with is worth what it brings, then your balance is in the positive. If the pain is worth the reward, then it's worth the investment. She wanted those commas in her bank account. Needed them. If she had to put in a little work to increase that balance, so be it. She enjoyed having that balance in the positive.

CHAPTER NINETEEN

VIOLET

Violet groaned as she collapsed on the floor of her tent. She laid there for a moment before wrenching her shoes off and tossing them by the soup can filled with loose change. They usually smelled bad, but now they were rancid. Her feet cracked as she flexed her toes. The hours of walking around the city looking for Sam had added up. Her knees ached and circles of skin on the bottom of her feet had loosened into blisters. Even her body was trying to tell her what her mind already decided. There was no point in continuing the search. Sam was gone.

The past three days were a blur of alleyways, shelters, and abandoned buildings, none of them with any sign of Sam. Violet came home twice for food and extra cash from the soup can, but those were just breaks. She refused to stop. Money signs danced across her eyeballs whenever she thought about Sam's face. She had to be the one to find the bastard. It shouldn't be that difficult to locate one person outside of the tent city.

The first place she checked after accepting Jessica's terms was where she and Sam split the money from the pawn shop. She shook her head at her stupidity as she looked down the long, empty alleyway. Of course it wasn't going to be that easy. The bigger the payday, the harder the job, and two hundred fifty dollars meant she was going to have to put in the work.

She walked through the alley three times, searching for any clue or hint of where Sam had gone. A business card or a book of matches, like in the movies. But it was just another trashway in West Ham, same as all the others. Air thick with the rotting smell of leftover food people didn't want to eat because they were already too full. Dark puddles of God knew what—water, booze, bodily fluid. Graffiti tags covering the walls. Pieces of a broken phone someone had thrown away. Nothing to show that she and Sam had been here dividing up stolen goods after murdering someone.

No. After Sam murdered someone.

She saw Jakob's bloated corpse in her mind. The swollen lips and face and eyeballs, dark red from burst blood vessels. Limbs twitching like a dying insect's. It was still hard to believe he was dead. Not because Jakob had been some saint, but because she had been there and couldn't do anything to stop it.

Jakob always acted like he and Violet were great pals and he was giving her a break with deals on what she dropped off, but that was only in comparison to the other pawn shops around town. Her engagement ring and wedding band were worth a hell of a lot more than the six hundred dollars she was offered. When she saw them in the jewelry display selling for eight grand, Violet had nearly killed the man herself. She'd never do it, but in that moment, months ago, a flash of anger pushed the idea to the front of her mind—fingers tightened around his fleshy throat, ignoring the croaks for help. But none of that had happened because Violet wasn't an animal. She wasn't a killer.

And then there was Sam. Sam had throttled the man to death, completely without needing to. He didn't know Jakob, didn't have a problem with him, only thought it would be easier to live if Jakob was the one to die. It had to happen, he'd said. He was doing it for their safety.

He'd said that right here in this alleyway. Dividing up guns and money with a smile on his face. Happy that they'd done a good job and already forgotten that he'd just killed a man.

What would Sam buy with all that money? Violet had been fighting the itch to get lost in the dim lights and hazy cigarette smoke of a gambling hall, but Sam wasn't interested in cards. Maybe food? West Ham was packed with fast food spots and places to load up on cheap groceries. It would be a waste of time to look everywhere Sam could find something to eat.

Where had he gone? He already had the guns and bullets from the pawn shop and the jacket he'd stolen from the Salvation Army. What else was there for Sam to buy?

Maybe he wasn't buying anything.

Maybe he was using those guns to break into someone's house in a quiet area of town. He needed somewhere to stay. Killing didn't bother him. Nothing was stopping him from doing it again to lock down a place to find shelter. It would be impossible to track him down from a trail of breadcrumbs and clues. So Violet just started walking. Looking.

The other alleys in the area were as empty as the first. She visited shelters. Checked under nearby bridges that weren't as livable as the tent city in her underpass. All came up empty. But she forced herself to stay patient. Check out one area and move on to the next. Eventually she had to find Sam. Find him and turn him in to the police for hundreds of dollars.

Her mouth had dried at the numbers Jessica was throwing around. Two hundred and fifty dollars. Get out of jail free. Money. Things she could get, just for doing the right thing—find Sam and do whatever needed to be done to prevent him from killing again.

Violet winced as she put her boots back on. All those hours of walking and no result. At least Jessica didn't join her on the search. She would have mocked her and asked if she really knew Sam or was just trying to get attention like the other hobos and vigilantes.

She was one of them now. A vigilante. She had accepted terms from the police and was declared one of them. But she had nothing to do. No crime to fight. No people to help. What a waste.

Why did she think she would be successful? The police trained for months to do this kind of job and were paid well for it. Way more than the couple hundred dollars Violet would be getting. Enough money to buy cars and houses and send kids to private schools with crisp uniforms of navy-blue sweaters. And real vigilantes, the ones people knew about and took pictures of in the streets like celebrities, had turned down the same job for much better terms. She should have opened her damn eyes.

She was a homeless woman who had thrown her life away in pursuit of cards on a table. Not a vigilante protecting the city. Not a cop hired to help. They were the people really responsible for keeping the city safe. The bending of the rules that Jessica and Johanson had done, working with the leader of the tent city and coordinating with vigilantes - those things were necessary to keep people safe.

Violet wasn't necessary. She was homeless. A nuisance to the rest of the city. Vigilantes were little more than useful tools. And now she lived in both of those worlds. Violet, the houseless hero. Violet, the homeless vigilante. What a joke. She was just a roadblock to these people.

Forget the casinos. She needed a stronger distraction tonight. She grabbed the wad of cash out of her soup can and left the tent, not even bothering to zip it closed.

The Lamplighter was good about serving the homeless early in the week when it wasn't too crowded, but the same bartender who politely nodded when she walked in tonight would yell at her like a dog any time she stepped through the door between Thursday and Saturday. No bar needed a bunch of bums scaring away the real, money-filled customers.

The lone bartender pulled out a large bottle of whiskey and filled a glass in front of Violet as she sat at the bar. "Strongest, cheapest?" The common call of drunkards. She nodded and took the bills out of her pocket. It was appreciated when tent citizens paid before getting their drinks here. The whiskey burned down her throat, the bitterness of it biting all the way to her belly. The unspoken piece of the strongest, cheapest rule was "tastes like shit," but she wasn't here for the taste. A solid drunk could make anything taste good. And tonight, thanks to Jakob, she had the money.

There were only two other people in the bar. An old boozer and a drunk kid who couldn't have been older than seventeen. Sad country music crooned out of a jukebox in the corner and dim lighting helped hide all but the drunkest of moments. She finished her first drink and put bills down for a second.

Violet saw them there, flattened on the table like they were in the cash register at Jakob's. They were faded. A little torn. These little rectangles were the things Jakob had died for.

She shook her head. No. She had to take responsibility for what happened. She'd been at the pawn shop. Led Sam there. Told him about the cash and the guns. These were the things Jakob had been *killed* for. It was dirty money. Murderer's money. But if she could find Sam on her own and help the city, she'd get cash—good, clean cash that would pay for all that guilt to disappear.

Sam was the murderer. Sam. Not Violet. She could find him, somewhere in the city. She had to. That would take care of her guilt. The money wouldn't hurt either.

The bartender had just slid the second glass of whiskey to Violet when the teenager raised his voice and yelled, "What're you, some kinda queer? Get your hand off me, man." Violet turned in her chair and saw the older man with his hands up like someone pointed a gun at him.

"I'm not touching you, kid." His words came spilling out of him like a waterfall. Without holding on to the bar, he started weaving in his chair. The Lamplighter should have cut him off a long time ago, but it was one of those places that didn't mind letting its customers buy as much as they wanted.

"You just told me you'd suck my dick for another shot of

tequila. The fuck do you think that makes you? Did you hear that, man?" the kid asked Violet. "He said he was gonna try to suck my dick!"

"I guess that makes me... someone who tells bad jokes?" the man chuckled and upended his glass.

The bartender pulled a baseball bat out from some hidden place and laid it flat on the bar. "Settle down or leave," he said. There was more annoyance in his voice than threat. "I don't care what you do in your own private time, but it's not going to happen here." Violet sipped her whiskey. *Drinks and a show tonight.*

The kid flipped off the bartender. "You can go fuck yourself." He was the kind of aggressive sexual drunk that turned up in a lot of Violet's card games. Get them a little liquored up and they start hanging onto people, kissing them on the cheek, and talking about titties. "You know what, fine. I'll leave. But if you want to settle things up, old man, I'll be outside." The man didn't respond, just blinked, droopy with booze.

"Did you hear me? I'll be outside."

The man chuckled again and stood. He let out a small burp, then grabbed onto the bar with one hand, his chair with the other, stumbling toward the teenager, trying not to fall. Then he smiled. And vomited on him.

The kid screamed in disgust, and hit him with an open-handed slap. The man laughed a deep belly laugh, spittle and puke rolling off his stubbled chin. The bartender started yelling for them both to get out. Violet fought the rolling feeling in her stomach.

She'd always been a sympathetic vomiter. If she ever saw or heard someone get sick, she knew that if she didn't get away, she'd puke too.

The man started gagging to vomit again, and Violet felt her lurching stomach signal it was about to blow. Violet pushed the old drunk out of her way as she ran to the door. The man fell to the ground as she escaped the bar. The cold air helped her hold the whiskey down. She put her hands on her knees and breathed slowly. She needed to keep her stomach calm. There was whiskey inside that she'd already paid for and needed to finish. In through the nose, out through the mouth, she breathed, begging her stomach to settle. The kid opened the door, arms held wide, and walked toward Violet.

"Lady. Lady. Dude, thank you. That guy was gonna kill me or something. You saved my life." Violet backed away as the kid tried to hug her, eyeing the moist vomit on his clothes. Her throat started closing and stomach re-clenched.

"It's not a problem. You're fine. Go home," Violet said. The kid nodded, his brow furrowed and eyes cloudy.

"I think I'll do that. Thanks again. For saving my life." He wobbled past Violet down the street. Saved his life? What an idiot.

Inside, the old alcoholic lay sprawled out in a booth, unconscious and snoring, while the bartender cleaned his vomit. Violet sighed. The faster it was clean, the faster she could get back to her drinking. She gagged, put her shirt over her mouth, and helped wipe up. The bartender nodded in appreciation and poured two shots of whiskey on the house when it was all clean. Violet took them and sat at the bar, as far as possible from where the old man had vomited and sipped on her whiskey.

Now this was stuff she could enjoy. No bitterness or stomach pain. Just a nice, smooth burn.

Had she really saved that kid from being killed? Was this her reward? She couldn't remember the last time someone bought a drink for her. And that skinny kid wouldn't have stood a chance in a fistfight.

The drunk had already vomited on the kid. Why was he coming closer to him? To hurt him? He was at least twice the size of him, and Violet knew some tent citizens that could still throw a mean punch when drunk. The teenager was an idiot, but he was right. If Violet hadn't knocked the drunk down, the kid would have been hurt. Probably killed. She polished off a shot of whiskey and nodded to herself.

Yeah. The drunk old man threw up on the kid to get him

off guard, and then was going to beat him to death for insulting him. But Violet saw what was going to happen and knocked him to the ground to protect the kid—a child, really. The innocent child. Violet had just saved his life. She tossed back the last of her whiskey and asked for another. Only three days on the job and she'd saved an innocent child's life.

Maybe the whole vigilante thing wasn't so hard.

PART TWO

THE PERMANENCE OF THINGS EARNED

CHAPTER TWENTY

TAYLOR

SOMETHING WOKE TAYLOR before his alarm sounded. He kept still and listened to the early morning noises as his mind cleared, searching for what had jarred him from his sleep.

No dogs barked. Birds had all flown elsewhere by this time of year. The only intrusion was the occasional rumble of a car driving by or a dumpster being emptied. Everything natural had hibernated. Hamington belonged to the humans now.

He stood and stretched before the cold could convince him to close his eyes and pull the comforter back over his body. He dropped to the floor and panted out short breaths as he counted push-ups. Muscle soreness was constant since the beginning of his new workout regiment, but now his joints only creaked when he first woke. Once he was warm, everything seemed to work better. No aching lower back or wrist soreness from computer work. Just an ease to things. After the pushups, Taylor moved on to other movements. Quick squats, crunches, and yoga-inspired twists to limber up, the fog of sleep dissipating with every rep.

He dried the sweat off his face with a towel when he finished then tossed it on the bed to use again after his second and third workouts of the day. The usual pang of regret hit as he remembered how heavy and tired he used to feel after any kind of physical activity. His heartrate had already returned to a resting pace and his muscles felt refreshed. It had taken a gun in his face to motivate him to become healthier and stronger. He'd wasted too much of his time at restaurants eating foods that acted as teasers for his taste buds instead of fuel for his body. If he'd been stronger, maybe he could have fought off that mugger.

Taylor rubbed his hand against his head in frustration. The short hair still felt unfamiliar under his fingers.

After weeks of salves and medical ointments to speed up his recovery time, the stitches from the attack had dissolved, his wound healed, and the hair over the injury had started growing. He took clippers to his scalp a week ago to even it all out to a short length. He tilted his head, examining himself in the mirror at angles.

It made him look different. In the past, his hair had always been longer. Product was necessary to keep it from exploding in all directions and dropping down over his eyes. Alice had said the semi-slicked back look was professional on camera.

The new cut made his face seem thinner, more utilitarian. Almost military. Taylor didn't mind, but apparently Jake thought the audience would. When Taylor returned for his first broadcast after the injury, Jake pressured him out of the studio and into his office to talk. Taylor tried to wave him away as he reviewed the night's opening lines on the teleprompter.

"No, don't worry about that," Jake said. "Brad can sit in for you again. Let's chat." Brad smiled prettily at Taylor over Jake's shoulder as he settled into the anchor chair. He'd filled in for Taylor while he recovered from the attack and looked too comfortable as he cleared his throat and loudly read the words Taylor had just been practicing.

Taylor followed Jake down the hallway to his office. Stacks of paper settled in disorganized piles on his desk and the floor surrounding it. Trophies and glass awards were lined up two and three deep in a shelf against the wall. Jake collapsed into his chair and reached for a stress ball on his desk. He eyed the side of Taylor's head where the gash could still be seen as a bright pink scar line through the newly trimmed hair.

"I just want to chat for a second, if that's alright," Jake said. "You've been gone a while. How are you feeling? Injury all healed up?" Taylor pressed his lips together to keep silent. Jake knew exactly what the status of the injury was. He'd asked for an update almost every day as he gave Taylor more items and questions to get out of the Hudson interviews.

"I know that's not why you asked me here."

Jake shifted in his seat. "Have you been watching ten o'clock?"

Taylor shrugged. He'd watch the opening segments when the broadcast featured whatever violent crimes and attacks needed to hook viewers in for the rest of the hour, but his attention faded after that. The longer he was out of the anchor chair, the less interested he was in the puff pieces that dominated the nightly news and the more he focused on what was happening in the city. Things that Hudson could have stopped if he were twenty years younger and a few limbs more intact. "Of course I do."

"This kid. The new guy," Jake motioned to the monitor on his desk. The anchors beamed at each other, then at the camera, welcoming the viewer to the broadcast. Jake scratched the patchy beard he was trying to grow. "He's good. Just graduated from college and has some really good instincts. He and Vanessa seem to have great chemistry too."

"Sounds like a great stand-in."

"Yeah, he's been..." Jake sighed and tossed the stress ball on his desk. "Look, are you really going to make me spell this out? Maybe... don't rush the recovery process. Between Alice and now this whole... incident, you've had a really tough past six months. Take your time getting better."

Taylor shook his head. It wasn't his fault he'd been attacked. Wasn't his fault that his life had been threatened and he was rushed to the hospital where they had to shave his head to sew his head back together. "So what, you want me on permanent vacation? Just step away from everything? Are you letting me go?"

Jake's eyes widened. "Oh no no. Keep on with the Hudson interviews. By the time they're done and the piece is edited together, you'll be good as new for broadcast and we'll get you back on the air. Hey, maybe it'll even be your big homecoming piece. How does that sound?"

Taylor hadn't been back to the station since then, but the frequency of Jake's emails and texts never faltered. Ask him about this. See if he'll tell you about that. Jake needed Taylor for access to Hudson, but not on a TV screen scaring his viewers with the constant reminder that they could be attacked any time they left the house.

It took time, but eventually Taylor was able to ignore the frustration of getting kicked out of the anchor role and focus on what was important. Each interview reminded him that Hudson was the key to understanding what happened to Alice. Whether it was the old man reiterating how easy it was for anyone to pick up a weapon and go to war against crime, or that the law system in the city had adapted to unofficially encourage vigilante justice, every aspect of what happened to her seemed to flow back to Hudson as the architect of it all.

The longer they spoke and the more information he could get out of the man, the closer Taylor felt to Alice. It was an odd thing he'd never been able to really comprehend. He wasn't searching for acceptance or a way to forgive the man who had shot her. Those things would never come. Understanding what drove vigilantes was the closest he could get. Forcing himself to look deep into the details of the world Hudson had made, hoping something would click and he could understand why this nightmare of widespread vigilantism had stolen his wife. It was a sweet torture he brought on himself, but he had no other options. He hadn't been there when she died. He didn't have any other sacrifice to give.

Taylor didn't wear a suit to the meetings with Hudson anymore. That was too formal for their relationship now, and the tailored clothes felt smug while he sat next to the old man confined to his wrinkled hospital gowns and loose-fitting sweaters. There were times when Taylor even felt a level of respect between the two of them. Hudson was becoming less of an enemy to interrogate and more of a puzzle to solve.

Taylor grabbed his workout bag and note-taking materials as he left his townhouse. A skullcap kept his buzzed head warm as he padded through the light snow. At each street corner, he glanced toward the entrance to the alley where he'd been mugged, the dark, gaping mouth widening as he came closer. He refused to change because of things he feared. This was the route he always took before the attack, this was the one he would continue to take.

He tried to force himself not to pause as he entered the dim, unlit corridor, but there was always a moment's hesitation. What if he was there again? What if the man decided to actually shoot him this time?

Taylor turned the corner, muscles tensed.

Empty, as usual. No one in sight.

He stepped over spilled trash and standing water as he walked through the alley, stopping himself from staring at the bricks still stained with his blood from the attack. When he emerged to the other side of the alley, he felt lighter. Cleansed. He took a deep breath. Now the day could begin.

When he arrived at the Hudson House, Linda answered the door alone. Hudson always dismissed when this happened, saying he didn't want to go through the process of being carted up and down the hall just to welcome him, but his daughter didn't have interest participating in his secret keeping anymore. "He wasn't able to make it into the wheelchair today," she said.

When they walked into the sunroom, Hudson looked up at him from the hospital bed adjusted to prop him up at an angle, instead of from the table by the window. He motioned to the chair at the bedside and turned down the volume of the police scanner at his bedside table reporting a 10-57 at a convenience store in West Hamington. His voice rattled as he said, "I hope this is alright. I'm just too damn comfortable to get out of bed this morning."

"Hey, your house your rules. Why do you always listen to that stuff?" Taylor asked, pointing to the police scanner.

Hudson tried to look casual as he shrugged. The monitor wires and hospital gown pulled against him. "What if a mob of criminals is heading our way? Or terrorists are attacking city hall? We should be the first to know."

"No super-villains are coming, Hudson. You just like listening to bad news."

"I like to listen to the world. It's not my fault that everything going on out there is bad," he said before erupting into a phlegm-laden coughing spell. He spat a brown glob into a plastic bottle half-filled with mucous then took a deep breath, his lungs briefly at peace from their rattling after ejecting their contents, and swept his eyes around the sunroom.

It seemed brighter today. As the snow fell outside the glass cube, the clean white blanketed everything, blocking the view of West Ham. "It's a beautiful thing," Hudson said. "Like we're in a snow globe, but inside out." He shook his head and refocused on Taylor, pointing at the duffel bag he'd placed by the chair. "Working out after today's session?"

"Krav Maga. Already did a little work this morning, but there're always a few more rounds waiting."

Hudson nodded and looked out the window again. "Good, good."

There was no longer time for the niceties of Hudson gingerly asking if Taylor's nightmares about the mugging had gotten any better or if he was still going down the alleyway. Both of them knew exactly why Taylor had started trying to get in better shape. Sudden noises made him jump, he stayed overly cautious about his head, and it only took a few times for Linda to learn she shouldn't come up from behind him.

With every meeting, it felt like their conversations were becoming more about the techniques and approaches to fighting criminals, abandoning the historical, highly detailed discussions of Hudson's origin. Without the luxury of time, their conversations had become blunt and honest.

A few weeks after the attack, Hudson recommended Taylor try self-defense training. He swore it would be helpful if Taylor ever had to use what he'd learned, and the sense of security that he could defend himself if necessary was worth the time on its own.

After long sessions peppered with Hudson's prodding and asking, Taylor finally signed up for a membership at a new self-defense studio within walking distance from his townhouse that had been littering his mailbox with flyers for free classes. He considered lying to the old man to get him to stop asking, but with his forced sabbatical from the station, it wasn't like he had anything better to do with his time. Hudson nodded his approval when Taylor told him he'd started taking Krav Maga lessons, but didn't seem impressed or surprised. "I started studying Krav after a few months as Hudson when I realized I needed to know how to fight, not just throw my body around and hope for the best. It ended up being the basis for most of my fighting."

The self-defense style specialized in incapacitating attackers with and without weapons. They covered knives and guns and fistfights, but Taylor was most interested in close-quarters gun disarms. He imagined his attacker. The smile. The hot breath. What he could have done if he'd been able to defend himself. How lucky he'd been that something worse hadn't happened that day.

It made him push harder. Concentrate his efforts on improving his skills and fitness. His free time was spent working out and practicing his takedowns. He couldn't remember the last time he'd been out for drinks with friends.

The routine consumed him. Fitness in the morning, sessions with Hudson during the day, defense technical work at night. There was little to worry about beyond that. He cooked for nutrients, not taste. Ran for endurance, not pleasure. He'd reduced his life down to an intense core. Everything beyond the necessary was superfluous. If he couldn't protect himself, what was the point of anything else?

After the day's session he took a cab back into the city, ignoring all the questions that regularly came with being picked up at the Hudson House. He bought the standard coffees at the shop near his townhouse and waited for her to arrive. Sometimes it took her more than an hour to show up, other times, when there was a lot she wanted to cover, she walked in almost on his heels. Today he had enough time to review his note before she came through the door, brushing off snow that had settled on her jacket.

"We really can't meet anywhere closer to a middle point?" Linda asked as she settled in the chair across from him and wrapped her hands around the warm cup of coffee.

"I like this place. And besides, you're the one who wanted to do this and break his rules. I just happen to be working near my house."

Linda pulled out a notebook of her own and flipped to the latest page. Only a few weeks after the Hudson interviews started, Linda had walked Taylor to the door at the end of a session and asked to meet somewhere nearby to talk. "I have no idea what's going on," she said. Her eyes were red and brimmed with tears. "Every single thing he's told you is different than what I've heard before. There's a casualness in his voice when he talks to you. He never talks to people that way. Never. I just couldn't stand sit back and not know what was going on anymore." She'd confronted Hudson about the new stories and the rules. Her hands shook at first when she started telling Taylor what happened, but they steadied quickly.

"He told me he was doing it on purpose. It's not dementia, it's not Alzheimer's. He's telling you these things differently because he thinks you need to hear them that way. He didn't want to tell me, but I wouldn't drop it. I mean... it's not like he can leave the room to avoid the question." She wiped at her eyes with the heels of her palms. "And he looked at me with that... that Hudson face they always put on the magazine covers. That scowl like I was some kind of villain. I just don't understand what's happening. Please... help me understand. I can't let him die and not know."

So they started meeting after the sessions. To compare notes and the day's recordings to determine the truth in the middle of the lies. And to understand why Hudson finally wanted to have his story told, whatever it may be. They said they wouldn't meet more than a few times, just until Linda knew why Hudson was changing his stories, but it had become ritual now. The two of them talking over coffee, trying to make sense of the lies they'd been told.

CHAPTER TWENTY-ONE

SAM

SAM SLURPED DOWN the last drops of soup. His tongue traced the inside of the aluminum can before he tossed it toward the pile of other empties by the grocery cart. It would be worth its weight in gold at the recycling center. His stomach rumbled for more. He dug through the cart, searching under the bags of fabric and bullet boxes and garbage, but didn't hold out hope. It was filled with a lot of things, useful or not, but no food.

There had been good runs lately. He'd stolen a hand powered space heater that saved his life during December nights. A kerosene-fueled stove he needed to find a new tank for every few weeks. Some clothes. A few purses. Nothing that kept his wallet as comfortable as the pawn shop, but he couldn't go any bigger. It had to be enough.

It took a week of living at the construction site for him to decide to stop stealing from stores. Another big robbery would bring too much attention, and unless he left the neighborhood and went a few hours away from his new home, people were more likely to figure out who he was and where he was staying every time he stole. Complaints would be sent to the cops about a thieving hobo that wasn't living in the underpass. It wouldn't take long for them to check the area, raid the construction site, and find his new home.

He'd turned the place into a multi-floor condo. Over the months he'd lived there, he kept bringing back things people had thrown away, making it more and more comfortable. He slept on a mattress someone had tossed because it had a stain on it. A broken cabinet he'd found on the side of the road was now his pantry. On the unfinished floor above him, he set up a bowl to catch and store water when it rained. He could live here forever if he was able to keep finding food. But food was where he was having trouble.

He shook his head whenever he thought about his trip to Walmart in October. It was stupid. Buying all that food and feasting on it. Not saving, not considering it'd have to keep him for months. It took too long to realize he needed to ration. There was no money left from the pawn shop job. No one like Violet who would help him find another opportunity like it. No way to get more food. He'd have to survive on scraps and what food his leftover loose change could get him.

Sam shoved the grocery cart over, dumping out all the trash he'd collected when he thought he'd found something useful and began tossing the empty soup and vegetable cans in. He'd been saving this trip until he didn't have any other options. The more cans he brought at once, the more money he'd get for them. After loading the cart, he checked through his garbage one last time, making sure there hadn't been a full can of tomato soup or green beans hidden inside.

Nothing.

He wrapped himself tight in his jacket, patting the right pocket and waistband of his pants to make sure his guns were there. He always kept at least one on him in case the cops or vigilantes came. The others were hidden around the construction site in hallways and under ledges. He was ready if someone found him.

He rolled the grocery cart out of the construction site, snow settling on the blanket covering his aluminum treasure. The cold bit at every inch of exposed skin. He raised his collar higher, hunched his shoulders, and started walking.

The kid counting Sam's cans at the recycling center was baby-faced and pimply. He was too excited to be working a counter dealing with garbage that homeless people gave him. When all the cans were out of Sam's cart and in a bag behind the counter, the kid popped open the register and said, "Alright, that's twenty-one cans for two dollars and ten cents! You have a blessed day, now."

Sam didn't move. The kid had a mannequin smile slapped on his face as he extended the two wrinkled bills across the counter. "Two ten?" Sam asked. The smile wavered. "Is this a joke? Those cans are worth more than that. What the am I supposed to do with two dollars?"

"I-I'm sorry, sir. That's what the rules say. Ten cents per can."

Sam clenched his jaw. Bullshit. Fucking bullshit. It wouldn't be enough money.

His eyes pulled to the register that was still open as he gripped the gun in his pocket. There were a few bills in there. Definitely more than two dollars.

But the moment he took the gun out, his soup cans wouldn't be worth anything. He'd never be able to trade trash for cash here again. His fingers released the pistol grip and took the money from the kid's hand. He looked relieved and told Sam that God blessed him on the way out of the store.

The cheapest food nearby was at a local gas station. They had enough pre-packaged microwaveable meals to fill his stomach until he figured out the next move. Hot dogs on rollers and plastic-wrapped ham sandwiches on thin layers of bread. After buying a refrigerated burrito, he still had a few coins clinking together in his pocket.

He heated it in the gas station's microwave as the pictures on the instructions said to. He slid into a booth by the window and sank his teeth into the burrito. The first bite was hot, scalding his mouth with the melting cheese. He breathed through the pain, blowing out steam. Like a choo choo train, he thought. The snow kept falling outside.

He took another bite and the cashier yelled across the store at him. "Hey, man. You can't eat in here. Go outside."

"Just give me two minutes. It's snowing outside. I'll leave right when I'm done."

"No, you need to get out now."

A man in another booth met Sam's eyes then quickly looked back at the paper he was reading while working through a morning hot dog. If Sam wore nicer clothes, it wouldn't be an issue. If he had a job and a newspaper and a credit card, he could eat as much as he wanted, wherever he wanted. He finished his burrito on the concrete curb beside the road, hoping the snow would stop. His jacket kept him warm for now, but probably wouldn't much longer. The shoulders were tearing at the seams and holes had shown up from snagging on fences and barbed wire. If he didn't find some tape or string to fix the jacket soon, it wouldn't even be worth giving to another hobo.

The burrito filled his stomach in the hollow way Sam knew wouldn't last long. He licked his fingers. All of this, just to feel full. Just to feel content for one meal. After the pawn shop, he was able to eat like a normal human being. The fear of starvation didn't hide behind his thoughts when his stomach growled. He missed the absence of fear. The absence of worry and concern. It was bad now, but he couldn't go all the way back to how it was before. Hunting for scraps in the trash and begging for leftovers. He'd known what it was like to have food ready and waiting whenever he wanted it.

His hands were turning a pale, patchy pink from the cold. He shoved them into his pockets to get rid of the stiffness in his fingers. The grip of the pistol was warmer than the air outside.

He pressed the trigger of the Glock in his pocket, pushing up against the tension it would take for the gun to go off. Wondering what it would feel like to fire. There hadn't been a reason yet. If he started shooting his gun just to try it out, he'd have to find a new neighborhood. Gunshots in the construction site would attract attention. Stupid. Not worth it.

But maybe staying in one place was a bad idea. It kept him from doing what he needed to survive. If he left the construction site and used the cart to move around, looking for new places to stay every night, he could do whatever he needed for money and food. He might even get a job if he found something good enough while wandering the city. The construction site was neutering him from doing what needed to be done. His stomach kept nagging.

No food. No money.

He gripped the pistol tighter. The decision was already made for him.

He paced outside the gas station, blowing air into his hands to loosen his fingers up while waiting for the store to empty. Through the window, Sam saw the last customer paying for her coffee at the counter. He held the door open for her and walked in. "Back again already?" the cashier from earlier laughed as Sam passed the counter. Another worker mopped the floors by the coffee machines, humming along to whatever song was playing in her headphones. Sam grabbed a stack of sandwiches and burritos and took them back to the counter.

"Oh, man! Are we a little hungry today?"

"Guess so," Sam said.

The cashier rang the food up and asked if he wanted a bag. Sam nodded while he pretended to feel around his pockets for his wallet. The cashier gave him the total and Sam shoved the Glock in his face.

"Money. Bag. Now." The man threw his shaky hands into the air, eyes darting around the store. Surrendering hands couldn't help Sam. He slammed the gun on the cash register and yelled, "Let's go!" In the side of his vision, Sam saw the other employee moving toward the back hallway of the gas station. He reached into his waistband and pulled out the revolver he always kept there, pointing it at her. He shook his head.

The cashier dropped his hands down and punched buttons one at a time to unlock the cash register. Not fast enough. Sam shot the fridge behind him. The kick of the gun was heavy. The glass shattered and cans hissed as beer poured onto the floor. His face felt flushed. "Now!"

The drawer opened with a ding. Sam returned the revolver into his waistband, pushed the cashier back, and grabbed the tray, dumping the money into the plastic bag. He fired the Glock into the ceiling above the cashier. The man dropped below the counter and Sam slammed his shoulder into the door, running out into the parking lot. He stuffed the pistol in his pocket and sprinted away keeping the plastic bag tight in his fist.

Two blocks was all he needed. Two blocks then he'd turn a corner and walk normally and fade into the other pedestrians. He had to get far away, and quickly. Sam held the bag to his chest as he ran. If it ripped, he'd thrown away his home for nothing. The construction site was too close—he couldn't stay there now. He breathed heavily. Feet pounded the sidewalk.

One more block. One more block and he'd be fine. He'd be fine, then he'd get his things from the site and start roaming. Start over from scratch.

He turned the corner after the block and collided into someone solid. He fell and dollar bills tumbled out of the plastic bag. He grabbed as many as possible and started rising to run again when a voice yelled, "Don't move!" Sam froze halfway up from the ground and turned toward the voice.

A sneer crossed his face. He'd hidden from them the entire time he was in the construction site. Months of peace without worry. All to run into one after robbing a fucking gas station.

The nut job was wearing tight, brightly colored spandex all over his body, ignoring the snow. He held a taser in one hand and slowly reached toward the handcuffs on his belt with the other.

"This is a citizen's arrest, declared by The Hamington Hunter. Drop the bag and put your hands in the air."

This guy. This fucking guy whose testicles had probably shrunken into his own body to avoid the cold was trying to put Sam away. He had a toy taser and handcuffs and a fucking costume he'd probably bought at a Party City to play superhero in. This was not the person who would bring him down. This was not the way it would happen.

Sam stood all the way up. "Now drop the bag. And slowly put your hands in the air," the vigilante said in a rehearsed deep voice.

The people on the street stopped to watch. A few pulled out their phones and started recording. This wasn't life or death to them. It was a game. Something to share with their friends. These fucking people. This entire fucking city. They were all trying to take him down.

Sam let go of the bag and his hand was in his pocket before it hit the ground. His finger wrapped around the Glock and electricity tore through him. His body was on fire. A horrible screaming static blared between his ears. He dropped. Muscles tensed and he heard someone groaning. There was nothing but the pain. He forced his eyes open wide enough to see the vigilante still aiming the taser at him, squeezing the trigger. This was it. He was going to prison if he couldn't get past the shock. He had to do something.

The gun was in his hand. All he had to do was aim. Through the pocket. He rolled his body. Through the pain. The vigilante came closer. The screaming pain. Sam fired. Someone yelped. The static in his head stopped. The vigilante stumbled backward and pressed a hand to his leg. It came away bloody. The taser was limp in his other hand. It was all Sam needed. Move through the pain.

He stiffly pulled his arm out of his pocket and fired two rounds in the man's chest. Blood splashed in the air. He fell onto his back, coughing, eyes wide. Red poured onto the snow-covered sidewalk. The people around screamed and ran.

Sam ripped the taser prongs out of his chest and tried to stand, his body still tense from the shock. His leg collapsed under him, his own blood dripping onto the pavement. The first shot must have grazed his leg. He tried standing again, bracing himself for the pain. Needles ran up his leg. He pointed the gun around. No one had stayed. Scattered like pigeons after the final gunshot dropped their Hamington Hunter.

Sam's first step felt weak and sore. How much blood was he losing? He couldn't worry about it now. The vigilante wasn't moving. The blood spitting out of his chest was slowing and his open eyes stared at the sky. Sam grabbed the plastic bag of money, backed around the corner, and ran as fast as his limping would allow.

CHAPTER TWENTY-TWO

JESSICA

A STREAM OF curses rang from Johanson's office across the hall and her name followed. Jessica bolted from her chair, thinking back to the last time she'd sold him coke. Was something wrong with the product? Had she shorted his weights too much?

He was hunched forward, hands planted on his desk, eyes wide as he stared at his computer screen. His scowl deepened when he saw her. She'd never seen him like this before. He shoved himself away from the desk and motioned for her to look at what he was watching. The video replayed.

It was snowing. A vigilante in tights yelled at a man, proclaiming he was under arrest, then tased him. The girl recording the video cheered and yelled at the vigilante to get that asshole. The man waved to the crowd like a politician.

But the video continued. Three shots fired and the vigilante collapsed and the girl started screaming as the perp unsteadily stood up. He panned the gun around and the recording became a mess as she ran away. Johanson scrolled the video back and paused on the man's face. Bile rose in Jessica's throat. The scars on her face itched. It was him.

When the pawn shop owner died in October and Violet mumbled her way through her proposal of terms, claiming she could take Sam down, Jessica wondered how the man that had ruined her life could possibly be around every corner and under every rock. She'd brushed it off as a result of the job. They were opposites. He was a violent human being and she was paid to make sure the violent ones were punished. It was only natural that they would come in contact with each other. But now it was happening again, and this time it felt more like a curse than an expectation.

"That's him, isn't it? The guy who attacked you and killed that pawn shop owner—the one your hobo was supposed to find," Johanson said. There was no need to respond. She couldn't keep the emotions off her face. Johanson snapped a picture of the screen on his phone and started texting someone.

"You said your girl could get this done, Jess," he said as he typed, "and now I've got a video floating around of a vigilante bleeding out in the streets in Midtown after getting capped by an underpass hobo and I'm telling another hobo to come help. What the fuck are we doing here?"

She ignored the question and leaned over him to restart the video again.

After Violet was activated, she managed to stop a few crimes and Johanson put her into the regular vigilante rotation. She was given a burner phone and reported to the station every other week to receive her terms. Violet texted Johanson back immediately. She'd be at the station soon. Jessica's stomach clenched. This was supposed to be over weeks ago.

Johanson always told Jessica how open Violet was about the fact that she'd been unable to find Sam. It didn't make anyone happy, but she was productive enough in other areas to keep her around. She stopped a few bar fights that could have led to something more, grabbed a few purse snatchers, and was now acting as the vigilante contact in the tent city after the last one, Silky O'Sullivan, broke into a civilian's home in search of a man he claimed was assaulting the homeless. With every criminal Violet apprehended, she received a little more leeway. Criminals off the street made Hamington a safer place. But she still hadn't provided the one thing Jessica truly needed: Sam. The pawn shop had been in her precinct and each day he wasn't behind bars was another that he could be doing shit like this.

The video was set on auto-replay. The vigilante was suddenly alive again, waving at the crowd and acknowledging their cheers before getting blown away. In only a few hours, the clip had reached thirty-five hundred views. It wouldn't be long before the local news picked it up and made a ridiculous scare piece to terrify citizens into staying home and watching more of their programming. "Crazed, homicidal hobo murders vigilante in cold blood—are you in danger? Find out at eight." The video played again.

Despite getting shocked by what looked like a military-grade taser, Sam had somehow been able to control his extremities long enough to take an accurate shot, then fire twice more in a small grouping before escaping the scene. He was still psychotic, still lethal, and had now killed another person. Yes, people were absolutely in danger.

Violet arrived a short time later. She looked better than the last time Jessica saw her. Her clothes, while dirty, were newer and less damaged than what Jessica remembered her wearing. She stood taller and the veins and cords of her neck weren't as visible from the lack of food. And most importantly, she didn't stink nearly as much.

Jessica showed her the video. Any confidence gained over the past months withered. She blinked at each of the gunshots. Her body visibly tensed when she paused on the full view of Sam's face.

"When did this happen?" she asked.

"This morning. We didn't know it was Sam until this video came out."

"Where?"

"North of here," Johanson said. "Corner of 16TH and Main. He robbed a gas station and killed this vigilante as he fled the scene.

Guy who called himself The Hunter." He smoothed his eyebrows, probably looking for something to do with his hands to avoid strangling Violet. "He was good. He was a good man."

Violet scratched at her hair. Jessica spotted dandruff falling to the floor and had to look away. "I hadn't made it that far north yet. I've been trying to take the city section by section. You know, going outward from the underpass, but that area wasn't for another few weeks. There was no way I could have found him up there."

Excuses wouldn't be enough. They were paying her. More specifically, they were paying her to find someone she'd claimed she'd be able to find and bring in quickly, without a lot of noise or attention.

This wasn't quick. This wasn't quiet. Jessica thrust a finger in her face.

"This is bullshit, Violet. This should have been handled weeks ago. You should have found him when I first gave you your terms. The longer it takes, the less interested I am in your relationship with him. I can offer the same terms to anyone on the street. Do you understand? You are not special. You haven't been able to find him, even with everything you claim to know about him. Now you and everyone else are on even ground. And trust me, I'm a lot more willing to pay people that have proven they can do their fucking jobs."

Violet whined like a baby. "You can't have expected me to find one person outside the tent city in three months. It'll take time. He could be anywhere. But I'll go north. I'll keep looking. I swear I can do this." Her eyes chased between Jessica and Johanson, looking for forgiveness or sympathy. Jessica let her silence speak for her. Do your damn job, you fucking sewer-rat.

Violet double-checked the location of the gas station and left with the image of Sam frozen on the computer screen, eyes half-lidded and teeth bared in pain. Jessica breathed shakily, hoping her anger at Violet had covered her reaction of seeing Sam's face. How could she respect the scared, clean police officer barking at her for not doing her job while she was the one doing the dirty work?

But fuck that. Jessica's fear wasn't an issue here. She'd lost a child because of Sam. She'd been disfigured because of him. Fear was permitted. What could not be allowed was Violet's bullshit.

She had the balls to talk back to her, in her station when she was the one screwin up. Jessica needed to straighten her up. Remind her who she was speaking to. Johanson spent too much time recruiting and talking the delicate politics of vigilantes and police instead of pulling back on the leash with a choke collar and telling the nut jobs how this whole deal worked. That's not how Jessica operated. There were a million poor, greedy fools in the city that would kill for Violet's opportunity. That was a fact. She saw it every day.

Over lunch, she winked at Parker and brushed her hand through her hair three times. It was the second time this week, already the fifth time this month, that she needed to visit the evidence locker. Her business was growing. Parker was having to underweigh the drugs more aggressively whenever they were entered, which lately hadn't been often enough. There was a limit to how harshly she could cheat the system. If the timing was wrong and an officer checked needed to reference the drug records for a case before she took her share, it wouldn't be difficult to notice a bag of cocaine was recorded as 750 grams when it looked more like a full kilo. And if Parker got caught altering weights, her business would be the least of her problems.

Minutes before three o'clock, she left her office for the evidence locker with her backpack, a place she would never go for her desk job. Parker flipped the closet's light switch and tapped his key card against the pad as she walked up, unlocking the door for six seconds. She thanked him by rubbing her hand on his crotch as she walked past. He quickly closed it behind her and she pulled the night vision goggles out from her bag. Her eyesight filled with a sickly green tint and the goggles re-calibrated to the lack of light.

She'd hit the limit on pills and blow two days earlier. There hadn't been any busts since then, so she couldn't take any of that. She'd have to settle for restocking weed. She checked Parker's recorded weights and put the most recent addition of weed on the scales. Something wasn't right.

The numbers were the same. There wasn't any leeway for taking product with her.

She clenched her teeth. Did Parker screw her? What was she supposed to sell if he turned back on their agreement? Should she punish him? Or remind him that his dick wouldn't fuck itself?

She turned the block of pot over, rotating it around to try to find something that could fix the situation. Anything. She paused and breathed heavily. It was worse than Parker not overweighing the drugs. He'd done his job, just like always.

She'd already been through this block. Through the entire section. She slid the block back on the shelf and grabbed the entry log hanging by the door. No new additions of product for weeks. The city of Hamington was dry. No drug busts meant no new product supply to steal from. How could she have been so stupid to not notice? She picked blocks off the rack, measuring each one. Every damn piece of evidence was tapped out. Matched perfectly with Parker's weights.

Voices outside the closed door carried into the locker as she finished checking the logs. Parker was talking to someone about a football game, making loud tackling sound effects and yelling about a cheap hit. Jessica delicately hung the clipboard on its nail by the door, listening to the conversation. Her heart pounded. If Parker couldn't distract whoever he was talking to and they came in to find her wearing night vision goggles in an area she didn't have access to, she'd be screwed. Her mind raced for excuses to explain what she'd been doing in there.

Eventually the voice went away. She slipped the goggles back into her bag and tapped the inside of the door twice. Parker coughed. They were clear. She came out and he pantomimed wiping sweat off his forehead. He'd managed to convince the detective he was talking to that he needed both his ID and his badge for access to the closet, not just the ID. "And I told him, you know, I don't make the rules. I just have to make sure they're followed. He wasn't real happy about that one."

Jessica's heart slowed to its normal pace. She let out a shaky breath and thanked him for keeping an eye out for her. She started walking away but then turned back and gave him an earnest kiss on the cheek. In that one moment, he'd actually saved her. She'd needed him and he'd done his job well.

Parker only nodded and turned back to his computer screen, not feeling the difference between that kiss and the quick ones she gave him after nights in his apartment.

CHAPTER TWENTY-THREE

VIOLET

VIOLET KEPT SEEING the video play before her eyes. A vigilante, just like her, killed. Sam limping away. The teeth, yellowed and crooked, sharp like a snake's, bared, growling. He had become an animal. Something that had struck out and killed another person because Violet hadn't done her job. Since this vigilante thing started, she'd stopped more fights than she could count, broken up drug deals, caught a few robbers, but none of that mattered because she couldn't do the one thing she needed to balance the scales.

Sam had finally used the bullets she stole from Jakob, and they'd found their first target. Or maybe second or third. There hadn't been any other deaths linked to Sam between Jakob and now, but there was no way of knowing what he'd done.

The subway turnstile sang a polite tone as it read her pass and allowed her access. She didn't feel the sense of joy it usually gave her, signaling she could afford a ticket. Sam had stolen that. The pride that came with money in her pocket was gone. She wanted that feeling back. The only way she could get it was to double down on her efforts and find Sam. Any blood that continued to flow from his hands was Violet's fault.

A group of vigilantes waited outside the yellow-taped gas station while the cops finished inside. Violet stood on her toes and peered over the shoulders of people who had already gathered around the crime scene.

On one side of the caution tape stood black-uniformed men and women, interviewing the employees, taking pictures, and dusting for fingerprints. A team used tools to wrench something out of the metal framework of a beer refrigerator.

On Violet's side, a rainbow of uniforms was worn by people of all shapes. Some she had seen before, but the others were either new or from a more northern section of the city. She recognized Big Bus, a giant of a man who wore a yellow rain jacket and a black bandanna over the lower half of his face, members of the Hero Club—a group of teenagers that volunteered and tried to help the community, but rarely did any fighting—Blazer Man, armored in green chain mail over a bulletproof vest, and Church, a woman wearing a surgical mask and a religious habit rumored to be a Catholic nun before starting to fight crime. There were a dozen others, all talking and comparing costumes and weapons. It was a sight Violet never got used to. Real life wasn't supposed to look like comic books. These people were out of place in the real world.

Instead of looking stoic and fearless in a skyscraper or underground cave, they blew warm air into their hands and bounced on the balls of their feet, waiting for someone to arrive with hot chocolates from the Starbucks down the street. Violet could understand a mask, or body armor like Blazer Man's, but most of the costumes were useless. They offered no protection, no disguise. Just admission to the party. She pulled her hockey goalie mask from her waistband and became the vigilante version of herself.

Big Bus waved a hello to her and she nodded back. "Any idea when they'll be done?"

"Not yet. It shouldn't be much longer though since no one was hurt at this scene," Big Bus said. "Cops've been here for a while, but you never know when these people are going to finish. If the wrong shift comes on, they can take hours just to do a standard crime scene check in order to get their work hours and leave for the night." He spat on the ground and rubbed saliva into a patch of ice with his boot, waiting for her to agree.

"Oh, yeah," she said. She exhaled deeply and shook her head. "The, uh, the people of this city deserve better."

Big Bus nodded his approval. They stood in the cold, talking about crimes, vigilantes in the news, and the new Chipotle around the corner until night came and the police decided they were finished. As they pulled the police tape out of the way Big Bus muttered something about them punching their time sheets at the station. A single officer stayed behind to make sure the employees didn't get harassed by the people dressed in costumes, but he looked bored and disinterested as the vigilantes rushed forward. The cops had finished their job and the gas station was now open for business.

Violet stood back as the vigilantes began examining the building in an attempt to find something the police hadn't. She'd never come into a crime scene like this before. It felt wrong. Inauthentic. Everyone was so desperate to be someone special. To be the person who did what the police couldn't. The excitement of getting their faces on the news for solving a crime was more important than helping the victims of the crime.

In the video Jessica showed her, Sam carried a bag filled with sandwiches and money. Violet walked to the deli cooler and was blocked by vigilantes trying to analyze the fingerprint dust left by the police or figure out which kinds of sandwiches he had taken with him. Maybe he took all the ham sandwiches because he has a big industrial refrigerator. No, no, he took the burritos because he's going to the barrio and wants to have something to bargain with the homies for safe haven.

Violet shook her head. None of them understood the stabbing hunger of being homeless. Sam hadn't carefully selected food by cuisine or calorie count. He'd have grabbed what was the closest within reach and taken as much as he could carry.

She left the deli cooler and stood in line for the counter. No one was paying for food, just waiting for their turn to stand where Sam held up the cashier. A group of them were arguing that Sam had shot a bullet over the man's right shoulder into the beer fridge, which would explain all the tools the police had used in there. They were wrong about this one too. Sam had probably taken the money by force, fired a blind shot over his shoulder, and run out of the store. Across the street, gone west two blocks, then turned north where he ran into the man he'd killed.

The Hunter's murder location was still taped off. Vigilantes wouldn't be able to get there for another few days, well after the trail had gone cold.

"No!" she heard someone whine, "It's my evidence! Let me take it!" A lanky teenager in street clothes and a wolf Halloween mask was arguing with the remaining police officer while his buddies tried to calm him down. He clutched a laptop under his arm. The cop looked tired.

"Son, this is a computer from the back office. I don't care if you think it's evidence or not, it has nothing to do with the crime, and I can't let you steal from a store."

"But I'm not stealing! I'm helping find this murderer!" His voice was muffled by the plastic mask over his face.

Church, the nun-turned-vigilante, slid up to the kid and grabbed his wrist. She tore the laptop out of his hand and tried to give it to the police officer. "I'm sorry about that, sir. I'll take care of this child."

The cop crossed his arms. "Don't give it to me. Make him put it back where he got it, Church, or I'm arresting him for theft."

"But I'm not stealing! I'm helping!"

"Look, I don't care what you think you're doing. You're breaking the law and you're lucky I haven't already cuffed you. Put it back and get the hell out of here."

Church tucked the laptop under her arm and turned the kid around. Vigilantes that had finished their investigations watched the teenager, sipping on convenience-store cappuccinos and laughing.

"Why is this funny?" Violet asked Big Bus.

"These jerks. They'll come into a crime scene, try to steal stuff, and claim it's for 'evidence.' The cops never let it happen, but they try almost every. Damn. Time. You have to love the audacity and stupidity of youth."

Church dragged the teenager to a corner of the store and started scolding him. Finger-pointing and condescending like a true pro trained in the religion of guilt. Violet had to get out of here. Sam hadn't left any sign of where he'd gone and stupid people in stupid situations made her angry. She turned to tell Big Bus she would see him around when she heard a crash.

Church was splayed on the ground, trying to keep hold on the teenager, surgical mask barely hanging on to one ear. "Get off me, bitch!" He swung his arm away from her, skewing his mask upward. He snatched the laptop from the tile floor and sprinted through the entrance. Vigilantes chose to help the groaning Church instead of chasing the kid. The cop yelled at him. He left the store and ran after him. People fussed over Church, making sure she was alright. That she hadn't broken anything in her fall. That she'd done the right thing by trying to stop the kid.

From outside, there was another cry of, "Stop! You're under arrest!"

Two loud pistol shots followed.

The vigilantes in the store froze. Violet felt her skin crawl. She didn't want to leave the store anymore. Didn't want to see what had happened.

Church's face squeezed into a mask of wrinkles and she started crying. Others seemed to shrink. The optimism of solving the whodunnit mystery leaked away. Their dress-up party was over. Blazer Man took slow steps toward the door, ran out, and started screaming.

"Oh... Oh *God*! What did you do? Someone call 911! Are you fucking kidding? You shot an unarmed kid! You piece of shit!

What the fuck did you do? Call 911!" Big Bus darted outside and his large voice echoed Blazer Man's. The Hero Club joined. Others followed. A multi-headed beast screamed at the police officer.

Violet couldn't move. How had this happened so quickly? Everything was fine, and then that kid tried to steal something and now he was... dead? Seconds ago, he'd been alive. A breathing, whining child, too immature to make decisions that would affect the rest of his life. And now... A cold wave covered her. She felt like she would vomit. This was her fault.

One way or another, it was Violet's fault. If she'd found Sam, there wouldn't have been a murdered vigilante earlier today. A child wouldn't have been searching for opportunities to steal. That child wouldn't have been gunned down by a police officer.

She left the gas station numb. Her brain didn't register the mob a block to her right. The screaming sirens and flashing lights didn't bother her. All she could see was Sam's face. Sam's reassurances that everything was going to be alright. That the job was going to go smoothly and quickly and no one would get hurt and that everything would be better afterward.

The walk back to the underpass was dark and cold and miles long, but that was the way she would travel. She didn't deserve the luxury of the subway. The hockey mask weighed heavy in her hand.

CHAPTER TWENTY-FOUR

TAYLOR

Voices from the television greeted Taylor as he walked through the door of his townhome, calling out the names of the local anchors as pre-roll for the nightly news coverage played. He took deep breaths as he peeled off the skull cap he'd donned during his run to stay warm. Taylor engaged the locks behind him and grabbed a towel from the chair by the door, wiping sweat off his face. He alternated between long gulps of water and stretching his legs as he stood in front of the TV. It was hard to disagree with Jake about the new kid in the anchor chair. From the segments Taylor had seen, Brad was good-looking with easy charisma and natural camera ability. He flexed his voice at the right time, flashed his teeth to enjoy light moments, and slightly pursed his lips during stories about the government, signaling his disapproval and earning the trust of his viewers. He was good. There was no legitimate reason to rush Taylor's return to the anchor chair. It was clear his job was in danger.

Maybe it was having competition for the first time or the seclusion he'd forced himself into after Alice died, but the more time he spent with Hudson, the more they talked about it, and the more he realized the old man was the only reason he still had a job at all. Jake cared about little else than the interviews during their calls. Whenever Taylor brought up visiting the station or coming in for a night back in the anchor seat, Jake turned the conversation to keep the focus on Hudson. Taylor found himself tuning in for his old time slot more often, keeping it playing in the background—even through the heart-warmer stories at the tail-end of the segment about community service or opportunities to adopt a pet. Maybe he could learn something from Brad that would help him get better. Or maybe he was just looking for some finite sign that the job would never be his again and he shouldn't worry about it anymore.

As the station trumpeted its dramatic opening theme, the cameras faded in on Brad, his face stern and brow furrowed. "We have breaking news in the vigilante murder that occurred earlier today on the corner of 16TH Avenue and Main Street. A new report states that a second vigilante has been shot, a member of Uptown's Hero Club, as a result of an altercation with the police at the site of the original crime. Of course, this is a continuation of the story that our Action News 3 team exclusively brought you earlier today, in which the vigilante known as The Hamington Hunter was shot and killed during an armed robbery. That suspect has still not been found by police."

Taylor took a gulp of water, keeping his eyes glued to the screen. He hadn't heard about the vigilante from earlier today. It must have happened during his visit with Hudson. Brad cocked his head and allowed his eyebrows to drop, emoting a subtle sadness. It was textbook, but he was doing it well. The kid knew the right buttons to push.

"If you have any information on the murder suspect from today, we encourage you to please call our tip hotline below. We're going to show that bystander video of the incident now to help with identification. Parents, if you have children in the room, please have them leave. The following video is graphic and viewer discretion is advised."

The cup slid through Taylor's fingers. Water splashed onto his legs. There was no forgetting that face. The empty stare of the eyes. The twisted, growling mouth. He watched the man lock up when shocked and then shoot the vigilante three times in the chest. Stumble up. Limp away.

Taylor couldn't move.

Brad warned the audience that the man was armed and extremely dangerous, and no one should attempt to approach him. If they saw the suspect, they should call the police immediately. The camera shifted over to Vanessa who pressed on, talking about the city council's meeting on pollutants in the Baldwin River. Taylor's hands shook.

He could have been the dead man they were reporting on. If the hobo had fired that gun instead of just hitting him with it, the station would have featured a somber memorial for their murdered colleague instead of a quick opener with a tip hotline scrolling across the screen.

Their story wasn't enough. This man was a killer and they'd devoted only a two-minute segment to his crimes. Enough time to lock the viewers into the news cycle, but not enough to make them aware of how dangerous the problem was. No one seemed to take it seriously. It had been months since the mugging and the cops still hadn't put him behind bars, the vigilantes hadn't taken him off the streets, and this was the result. A man, dedicated to helping others, was dead while his murderer stayed free. A kid, somehow wrapped into this whole thing, killed at the scene of the crime.

It was terrifying to think about. The man had been tagged directly in the chest with a taser and was still able to shoot his gun. Taylor's head throbbed. His fingers traced the scarline where he'd been pistol-whipped. There was nothing he could have done that day to escape the mugging. He knew nothing then. But if that bastard tried to attack him now... there would be a different result. He'd only been training for a few months but knew he could defend himself from people like this who felt they didn't have to obey any laws or moral rules.

He imagined the man's hand, gripped tight against his tie.

Swiping it away. Redirecting the gun, breaking the trigger finger, turning the gun on him, cocking it and taking the safety off. If the man took one step toward him, Taylor would have squeezed that trigger and ended his life, no question.

The vision was clear in his mind, like the memory of something that actually happened. He'd thought about it too many times. About what he could have done to make a difference. About the pain. And his weakness. Something about this news story pushed that fake memory away. He remembered the fear. Taylor ran his hands over his buzzed head. On the TV screen, Brad and Vanessa threw back their heads and shared a laugh.

He needed air. His feet pounded the down the stairs and he yanked open the front door. The cold air swept in, covering him like he'd dunked himself in an ice bath.

He paced the sidewalk outside his townhouse, his breath a cloud under the streetlights. Part of him wanted to go to the alley where he'd been attacked and stand there in the darkness, reminding himself he was safe and that no one was there waiting to ambush him. The other part wanted to run as fast as possible in the opposite direction. His mind tumbled over the options—hunt for danger or run from it. Those two were the only choices.

There wasn't an answer. There couldn't be. He ran when Alice was killed. Ran all the way into a quiet secluded shell to try to make himself feel better with knowledge. Comfort himself with the understanding of why people made the choices they did.

Knowledge didn't help him in that alley. But if he went the other way and pursued that danger, he could end up dead like the vigilante from the news. Or worse, like Hudson. Broken and helpless. Dependent on the people around him.

There was nowhere for Taylor to move. No one for him to even talk to. Jake would tell him to stay still, stay quiet, stay home and heal for the next day's interview. Hudson would tell him confronting the fear would be the only way to get past it, even if he got hurt in the process. And Linda would...

What would Linda say? Why did he even consider it?

So many people seemed to disappear after Alice died. Their mutual friends didn't want to see Taylor and be reminded of her. His colleagues quickly adjusted to his focus on pursuing Hudson and left him to his obsession. Of the few who were around now, Linda was the only one he couldn't predict the response of. Taylor found himself scrolling through the recent calls on his phone until he got to her name. His finger hovered over the screen as he paced in front of the townhouse. He pressed down firmly.

The sharp spike of volume when she answered caught Taylor off guard. He pulled his ear from the phone and could only barely hear her yelling "Hello?" over the crowd in the background of the call. "Hello? Taylor?" He stopped from yelling into the phone to help her hear over wherever she was. His street seemed sleepy and quiet by comparison. "Hey, hold on one second," he heard her say. The noise of the group lowered in the background.

"Hey, are you still there?"

"Sorry, is this a bad time?"

"No, I just got roped into a get-together with some old nursing school classmates. What's up? Did you figure out something about Dad?"

"I... that guy. The mugger. He killed someone. They showed a video of it on the news tonight."

"Oh. Wow. Are you okay?" The rest of the crowd noise in the background quickly faded. A door closed on Linda's side of the call. Taylor imagined the quick, choppy strides she took into the coffee shop every day bringing her into a different room from the rest of the party.

"No. Yeah. I don't know. I'm kind of shaken up. They zoomed in on his face and I think I had a mini-panic attack." His teeth felt dirty as he spoke. This wasn't information he needed to share. He barely knew her. This was the kind of thing he would have told Alice.

"But they got him on video and put it on the news, so the vigilantes and cops will be all over him now," she said. "They have a specific person they're looking for instead of the description you gave, so they'll get him faster. You've been doing your self-defense thing Dad recommended, right?"

"I'm still going almost every day, but I don't know if that—"

Taylor heard someone banging on the door and calling Linda's name from the other side of the phone. "Sorry," she said, "we were on our way out the door. If you're okay, can we talk about this tomorrow?"

"Yeah… yeah, no problem. Of course." They said their quick goodbyes and Linda ended the call to go with her people. He put the phone back in his pocket and turned in a circle, looking out at the darkness beyond the streetlight's range.

She was right. The man wasn't a faceless criminal anymore. He'd been seen. Broadcasted to the city. People would know. Someone would find him.

Taylor walked up the steps of his townhouse and looked back out at the quiet street. No one walked the sidewalks. Cars passing on the closest intersection didn't turn down the road. The dark was calm, like it had nothing to hide.

He went back inside, started turning the knob for the deadbolt, and froze. It felt like running. But just because he was going back inside didn't mean he was fleeing the situation. One decision didn't result in the complete elimination of another. There could always be a middle ground.

He turned the deadbolt the other way, leaving it unlocked. Taylor would sleep safely in his home tonight. But if someone wanted to come for him, let them come.

There was a set morning routine for visiting the Hudson House. Taylor fielded similar questions from different awestruck cab drivers, all wanting to know why he was special enough to speak with the great man himself. He showed his ID to the security camera before the gate slid open. As he walked up the drive to the house, he revisited their previous conversations in his mind. On some days, if the timing and light was right, the sun wouldn't reflect off the glass walls of Hudson's hospice sunroom, granting

Taylor a view of the old man fussing with his blankets or the bed-side police scanner. By the time he reached the top of the drive, Linda and Hudson would be there waiting for him with the front door open.

The door was closed today.

He shuffled his feet, reached his hand out to turn the door-knob and drew it back. The door hadn't been closed since the first day he'd visited. Taylor dropped the heavy knocker once and after a few moments heard the locks inside the door sliding.

Linda opened the door, wincing at the light, and waved Taylor in. "He's asleep." She turned and started walking down a hallway he hadn't been down before, leaving the door open for Taylor to close.

If it weren't for the large stainless-steel appliances, the kitchen would have passed as a breakroom in a hospital. Nurse's bags hung on the wall by the oven. Spare sets of scrubs were piled on top of the stove. Instead of a KitchenAid mixer or a coffee machine, monitors flashed different spiking stat lines and numbers. Cabinets had bold labels applied to the doors identifying what medicines were inside and what time of day Hudson was supposed to take them. There was no way of knowing the last time a full meal had been cooked in this room.

Linda grabbed a bottle of Advil off the kitchen island, tapped two pills into her palm, and swallowed them.

"Long night?" Taylor asked.

She kept her eyes on the kitchen table. "Long night. I needed to blow off some steam. Blew off a little too much, it feels like."

Taylor nodded and kept roaming around the room. A baby monitor in the corner broadcasted the wet, half-drowned breaths of Hudson sleeping down the hallway.

"What, you're not going to ask why?" Linda asked.

"You can tell me if you want. I've just never seen you like this before. I don't just mean hungover, but not... you know. Revolving around Hudson."

She leaned her head back and let out one loud laugh. "Now *that* is funny."

"Sorry, I don't meant that—"

"No no," she put her hand out to stop him, "you're correct. Actually, I only went out last night because of him."

Taylor thought back to their call. She'd asked if he'd heard anything about Hudson. If he'd learned anything about him. Like it was one of their coffees after an interview, trying to find out why there were so many versions of Hudson's stories.

"What do you mean?" he asked.

She put her hands on the kitchen island and leaned forward. "You know," she exhaled deeply, "we're a couple of idiots."

Something felt wrong. "What happened, Linda?"

"We keep thinking about why we hear different stories from him. Your version of the fraternity brothers beating up some guy named Dennis, versus my gang members assaulting a beggar. My story about the men in the park compared to yours. It's not a medical problem. No dementia or Alzheimer's or brain tumors affecting the hippocampus. We know he's lying. But why, oh golly gee, why is he lying to us, Taylor?" she started rubbing her temples. "He doesn't care about fame. He never has. Why do you think he doesn't let cameras in? It's because he just cares about who he's talking to. When he's saying these things."

He didn't speak. She looked up and met his eyes. He didn't recognize the expression locked on her face. It was an anger or an exhaustion with the entire situation. Something happened last night that pushed her here.

"Good lord, maybe you're the only real idiot here. I'm talking about *you*, Taylor. Whatever version of the stories the truth is, whoever's version is, he's changing these stories for you. Because you're here now asking all the questions."

The breathing from the monitor was loud in Taylor's ears.

"He had a bad reaction to some of his medicine yesterday," she said. "Not sure if it's too strong for him as he gets weaker or one isn't mixing well with something else, but he said things."

"Like from the stories?"

She shook her head and smiled. The sides of her mouth turned down. Linda went to one of the bags hanging on the wall and pulled out her phone. She rubbed an eye with the heel of her hand.

"I started recording him when I take care of him, like you do, so we could compare our two versions of the stories. Usually it's nothing. Instead, yesterday, this is the lovely gem I got." She slid her finger across the screen to a specific moment in the recording. She'd probably listened to it enough since yesterday to know the timing of every word.

Hudson's phlegm-laden voice spoke from the phone as she laid it on the kitchen island. Taylor took steps toward it. "I always wanted a daughter," the voice said. "Daughters are irreplaceable. But I wanted a son too." He sounded weak, like someone who'd just woken from a long slumber.

"We can talk about this later. You need your rest," Linda's voice replied from the recording.

"I love you very much, and love having a daughter, but you can't replace a daughter. I can't replace you. You're compassionate, like your mother. And I love that. But you could never follow in my footsteps. Maybe someone else can. A son of sorts. Like a moon. A sun of the night."

Linda kept her back to Taylor, but in the reflection of the oven, he could see her pressing her fingers to her eyes either to hold back tears or a migraine. Taylor paused the recording. Linda turned back to him. "Is it clear now?"

This was supposed to have been his way of understanding the purpose behind his fiancée's death. Facing and overcoming what caused it was the only way to move past it. He'd tracked down the source of the vigilante movement that she'd been lost to. Talked to him for months. Felt like he was gaining the understanding he'd been looking for. Making his peace with things. And it was all a farce. This entire time.

It hadn't been from a lucky chance that Hudson wanted to

tell Taylor his life story. It wasn't a fortunate career result of hard work or a turn of events in his pursuit of that understanding. This entire time, it was a sick old man coming up with whatever bullshit he thought would impress the most people through a TV interview to inspire more people to become vigilantes.

Why hadn't he seen it? People always make themselves seem bigger or better when they know others will be watching. Why should he have ever expected the truth from this man? These conversations with Hudson weren't going to help Taylor understand Alice's death. They were just made for more people to do the same thing that led to it.

Taylor turned and left the kitchen, taking long strides to the sunroom. Linda behind him told him to stop and wait as she caught up to him. Hudson's breathing followed them through the house, echoing from the monitors set up to listen for any subtle change in his breathing or extra liquid in his lungs or desperate cries for help if he were in pain.

Taylor shoved through the doors to the sunroom. Hudson's one eye flashed open. Linda asked Taylor to stop one more time as he walked across the room to Hudson's bedside. He didn't have the sleepy look of old sick men stuck in their bed. His eye was bright and alive, aware for any danger.

"I know what you're doing," Taylor said.

Hudson glanced at Linda then turned back to Taylor. "What are you talking about?"

Linda grabbed Taylor's arm and tried to pull him away from her father's bedside. He did not move.

"You've been lying to me." Taylor's teeth bared themselves as he tried to hold his voice down. "You've been lying to us."

"Define a lie for me," Hudson said. Taylor felt Linda go rigid next to him.

"Dad, you have to stop. You can't do this anymore."

"I honestly don't know what you're talking about."

"How many gang members did you fight to help that beggar?" she asked.

"Six," Hudson said automatically.

"You told me it was four of your fraternity brothers," Taylor said.

Hudson's jaw rolled back and forth like had options of what to say. Seeing what tasted right. "Yes, I did."

"So which is it?" Linda asked. There was sharp desperation in her voice.

His jaw started rolling again. It shouldn't have to be a decision-making process.

Taylor almost wanted to tell him to ignore the question. He was an old man who had been asleep. He was confused. Taylor could call a cab and come back tomorrow, ready for another day of history lessons and self-reflection. Pretend like this day hadn't happened and everything could stay the same.

"I guess... the answer is that it doesn't matter."

"What do you mean it doesn't matter? Of *course* it matters. If the world is going to know your story, it has to be true," she said.

Hudson shrugged. "Fuck my story."

Linda shook her head. "Nothing about this makes sense. I'm sorry, but I will never understand you. You're... you're *dying* in a hospital bed because you threw your body in front of every possible threat aimed to hurt someone else. Those are the people you're going to be lying to. That's the world you're going to be lying to. So why, all of a sudden, does it not matter anymore?"

"Your next answer better be a very good one," Taylor said. He could feel heat rising in his cheeks.

"Alright, hold on now," Hudson chuckled. The liquid in his lungs turned it into a cough. "That's not what I meant." Like it was a simple misunderstanding. Easy to clear up.

Hudson breathed deeply, rattling the phlegm in his lungs. "In the Bible there are two versions of how God created humans. The first is that man was created after everything else, the same way the rest of the world was created: with the 'Let Us' or 'Let the' language. Just another thing to add to the planet, but we were the thing made in his own image.

"The second version is that after he finished making everything, he rested and then realized nothing was growing because there was no one to tend the land. So he created Adam to make sure everything would grow, and then he made Eve to be his partner by using Adam's rib."

"I am aware of the story of creation, Hudson," Taylor said. He could feel his pulse pounding through his veins.

"No, now hold on. There are two versions, but people generally combine them. They take the 'made in His own image' part to make themselves feel special, and they take the 'made from dust' part, because it explains that we're physically of the earth, and they take the 'made from Adam's rib' part, because men always like to feel like they've won a race and gotten somewhere first.

"The part of the story where humans exist only as the planet's caretakers, to make sure that plants and things grow well, is very rarely talked about. No one wants to be told there's no point to life but service. Growing vegetables and taking care of animals. And most of the first version is ignored as well, where we were just another thing thrown into the mix. These two versions completely contradict each other: one says we were made before God rested, one says it happened after. One says we were made like everything else, the other that we were specifically made to look after the rest of the world. But it doesn't matter."

Hudson pushed himself up in his bed. His arms shook against the weight of his own body.

"The things that are most true in this world are what you believe. Not what happened, but what you believe happened. If you believe something, then it becomes the truth. It's the same as religion as it is with world history, all the way down to individual human relationships. The past didn't happen moment for moment the way history books say it did. Those records were made by the victors of battles. The losers get no say in their story."

"No. I refuse to accept that," Linda said. "If that's the case, then what people will believe about you, and what they consider to be fact, will all be wrong. Why don't you just tell the truth about what happened?"

"That's what I'm telling you. This is the truth. It's the version of the truth he needs," Hudson said, pointing the stump of his left arm at Taylor. "Which is different than the version of the truth you need. But they're both true, because you both believe them."

"And what about when the rest of the world believes what Taylor tells them? Will your daughter be the one stuck with the wrong stories that came straight from the man who told them?"

He waved the question away. "I already said I don't care about what the world thinks of me. And the damn story won't even air until after I'm dead, if it ever does."

Taylor tried to swallow his anger. Hudson refused to understand the effect he had on people, especially the ones still close to him. "Then why the hell are we doing all of this? I came here so the city could know something real about you for the first time, and now it's all going to be a lie? Because you wanted to tell me some bullshit version of your history?"

"No. You are here because you need to hear your truth. Like I said, the rest of the world doesn't matter. I'm through with it. It's irrelevant. But you are not."

The man was talking in circles. Forget the dimensia test results, something had to be wrong with him. "You're not even saying anything, Hudson. Just repeating the same thing and never saying anything at all."

Hudson inhaled deeply and furrowed his brow like he was going to launch into another one of his lectures or wax poetic, and then his body sank. He took quick shallow breaths and placed his palm to his cheek. "I am too tired to argue. Let me... let me just show you."

He motioned to Linda to help him into the wheelchair. She froze, a flash of a grimace or a sneer crossed her face, then she moved into action without comment. The dutiful nurse. Taylor looked outside the sunroom. Signs of life seemed to have fled as winter approached. Leaves had fallen off the surrounding trees, leaving the branches harsh and bare, cracking against each other in gusts of breeze. The grass had dulled from its lush green into a patchwork of browns.

There was nothing to look at, but Taylor refused to turn back. He'd never been here when Hudson needed help getting his wires and tubes disconnected from the equipment around him. Something about it felt intimate for Linda and her father. His heart pounded and teeth were clenched, but it was still not his place. If he didn't respect the man, he'd be just as bad as him.

Hudson cleared his throat and said, "Let's go for a walk."

They left the sunroom and immediately Hudson signaled Linda to turn him down a hallway away from the sunroom and main entrance hallway. They went in silence, the rhythmic bass of the wheelchair rolling over wooden floorboards the only sound. She seemed uncertain of where they were going, never trying to pre-empt his instructions. "I wanted more time before I showed you this, Taylor," Hudson said.

"Showed me what?"

They arrived at a pair of doors that ran from floor to ceiling, at least fifteen feet tall, carved out of what looked like mahogany.

"The library," Hudson said. He rearranged his full arm to reach into his pocket. It emerged with a keyring holding a single round gray tab. His arthritic hand shook as he reached toward a rectangular panel by the door, muscles in his arm strained. It let out a pleasant tone and the doors shuddered as mechanical deadbolts unlocked themselves. Hudson pulled his arm back and rested it in his lap. "Convincing always takes more time than you expect."

He nodded at Linda and she pushed the doors open. Her jaw dropped as lights flickered on inside the room. Taylor heard her whisper something and only realized what it was after he said it himself.

"Holy shit."

CHAPTER TWENTY-FIVE

TAYLOR

Whenever Taylor walked through the Hudson House, he got the sense that the old man hadn't changed much about the mansion on the hill after he moved in. The layout didn't look newly renovated and aside from the medical equipment in the kitchen and sunroom, the furniture all seemed a few decades old. The only sure signs of Hudson's occupancy were the photographs and news articles that had been hung in the hallway, like a museum exhibit had been slid into someone's home. It was all permanent in a way that made Hudson feel like a temporary passerby. But as the door to the library opened, Taylor realized it was because Hudson had spent all of his free time here instead of the rest of the house.

Outside, the hallways were lined with fine rugs, bright pieces of artwork of ships and landscapes, and antique knick-knacks on side tables, giving the house a political weight about it. Inside, the library was a hidden beast. Fluorescent bulbs shone a harsh light on the sheets of plastic hanging from the ceiling twenty feet overhead, shrouding built-in bookshelves packed with hardbacks that lined the walls. The wooden floors exposed throughout the rest of the house were covered by connecting black rubber pads just past the threshold of the door. What looked like dark soundproof paneling ran from floor to ceiling wherever there would have been an exposed wall or surface. An old wooden ladder stood next to a rack filled to the ceiling with weapons. Taylor could see guns and knives, nightsticks and tasers and numerous other pain dealers he couldn't even guess a name for. Tall cabinets with locked doors stood on either side, probably filled with even more violent tools.

Punching bags, targets, and oversized boxing mannequins were scattered around the room. They looked worn, punished to the point of tearing at the seams from countless practice strikes. In the corner, a twin bed with a down comforter seemed alien. It was the one thing not designed to facilitate violence within this black hole of the Hudson House.

"Welcome to the library," Hudson said.

Taylor couldn't find words. Here, inside this majestic mansion, built in one of the most historic neighborhoods in the city, Hudson had continued teaching himself how to destroy criminals well after he'd revealed his identity as the city's first vigilante. "Well, what do you think?" he asked.

"It's... incredible," Taylor choked out. "And terrifying." He looked over at Linda. Her eyes traveled around the room, continuing to see new details of violence, her face drifting between something that looked like anger and disgust. "I guess this is your first time here too?"

She glanced at him and nodded before pointing at a set of targets at the end of a shooting range. "That wall... what's on the other side of that wall?" She looked down at Hudson in his wheelchair.

"One of those guest bedrooms we don't use very often," he said. His face was brighter than Taylor had seen in weeks.

"I had friends sleep in that room when I was a kid. They used to ask me about banging sounds and I never knew what they were talking about. But it was you shooting at a target. Feet from their beds." Hudson's smile faltered but he quickly pointed out the Kevlar layering the wall behind the targets. Linda nodded again. Taylor noticed her dragging her thumbnail across her palm in long straight lines. When Hudson waved forward, her hands released from each other and settled on the handles of the wheelchair. The three of them went further into the library, Hudson allowing silence.

Taylor's eyes chased around the room, trying to take everything in. Two mannequins stood at the back of the room, one donned in a black sweatshirt Hudson described as wearing during the early, untrained years. The iconic costume was displayed on the other. Jeans, boots, shirt, peacoat, gloves, and baseball hat, all in vague, unidentifiable black. The entire set looked ready for Hudson to leap out of his wheelchair and throw it on to run into the dark.

Tears and stains scarred the coat fabric. The filthy boots were covered in dark blood marks. On a mannequin, they were nothing but dirty clothes that deserved to be incinerated. But in the dark, once violent rumors spread about someone with a low hat and a high jacket collar, it was a sight that would make a criminal look for any escape.

If the front hallway, with its posed pictures and framed news articles, was a museum exhibit, the library was a personal memory box. A straightjacket, one arm ripped off and splashed with blood, hung unevenly from the wall. A bicycle chain, ends taped for use as a garrote, framed and hung. Taylor recognized items from Hudson's stories and others that likely made no sense to anyone but Hudson.

It made Taylor feel uneasy. These things had been described to him. The stories that he'd believed were real until Hudson admitted they weren't seemed pretty damn real everywhere Taylor looked. Hudson's truths were backed up by the evidence right in front of him. This was his entire vigilante life in all of the gory, broken details. The kind of stuff Jake would have bear-hugged him for sending a picture of.

He turned to face Hudson. "What is this? What are we doing here?" Linda glanced over her shoulder at them, then turned her attention back to the hooked rack by the weapons cabinet that was covered in dozens of dark hats for different costumes.

Hudson rubbed his head with the stump of his left arm. "I didn't bring you here for the story, Taylor. This is—this has all been—part of a proposition.

"You've been coming here almost every day for what—four, five months now? It doesn't seem like a long time when I say it. But you've been changing. And learning. I'll be honest, and I hope this doesn't anger you, but I never really cared about the story. I don't care if you plaster my scarred-up face on every five o'clock news segment, magazine cover, and front page in the state. What I care about is what is going to happen to this city after I'm gone.

"The vigilantes these days... I don't know. I listen to the police scanner and I hear them doing these things to try to make a big name for themselves. Or to take advantage of someone else's misfortune. Like that kid yesterday who got himself shot. How does stealing a computer help anyone? That's not the point of being a vigilante. That's not why I started doing what I did. After all I've told you, you have to believe me in that regard."

"Hudson, how can I believe you about anything you say? Nothing you've told me is the same as what you've told Linda."

"The details, no. But the journey and the end-results are the same. Your truths are the same."

"Sure," Taylor said. He turned away from Hudson and tried to take in more of the library. Tried to visualize a younger version of the man in the wheelchair running in here after fighting crime, trying to burn off the adrenaline of the night's illegal activities. Linda had moved from the hats to the weapon rack, arms tightly folded across her chest, her nose inches from the glass separating her from all sorts of weapons.

"You agree," Hudson said. "I know you do. And more importantly, you understand. You get pissed off when people hurt others. When they break the law. When someone gets taken advantage of. I see that in you. It's why you were so bothered by the mugging. It wasn't just the physical assault. It got in your head.

"What were you doing wrong that caused someone to attack you? Nothing. Just walking down the street, trying to catch a cab to interview an old man.

"You're a good person, Taylor. And you understand where I'm coming from. When it comes down to it, those are the core qualities needed to do this thing. A clear, black and white view of right and wrong. The belief that someone needs to be responsible for righting those wrongs and protecting the future of Hamington and its citizens. And everyone these days knows that sure as shit isn't the cops."

The man leaned forward in his wheelchair and a grimace crossed his face as the movement strained his body. Taylor saw Linda took slow steps away from the weapons.

"There's no simple or easy way to ask this. I can only ask and hope you understand and see within yourself what I believe. You are *good*. You are *strong*. You are *precise*. And you believe that if someone has the ability to help the people around them, then they should. The only thing that has to happen for the triumph of evil is for good men to do nothing. You are one of those good men, Taylor. That's what I hoped you would be when I first saw you on the news. That's what I learned you were when you came to my home. I don't care about this story you're writing. I don't need it. That's not why I brought you here.

"I want you to take up the mantle of Hudson."

The statement hung heavy in the air.

Taylor heard Linda's footsteps stop. He felt his anger from the sunroom coming back.

He shook his head slowly from side to side. Could feel his chest getting hot. His vision blurred with tears. This was supposed to be his way of coping with Alice's death. His way of grieving and understanding and letting himself get back into his career. And the entire time, he'd been getting played by an old man with other intentions. He choked out, "What?"

Hudson repeated himself.

"I heard what you said, I just don't know how to..."

Linda joined Taylor. Her arms were crossed, shoulders tucked high as if bracing for an impact, her lips squeezed together so tightly all the color had left them.

"Well, I would prefer an answer in the affirmative," Hudson said.

"I don't even understand. *Why*? I... I read the news for a living."

Hudson sighed and he motioned to the room with his arthritic hand. "After everything I've told you about all of this, do you think what I did before really mattered? I was a college kid. Criminals were hurting innocent people and no one else was there to do anything, so I stepped in. I still would if I could get out of this damn chair.

"All of this started because I wanted to help people. It came naturally. Of good, pure intention. Not like these new kids who just want to get on the news to be famous."

"What makes you think I'd be any different than them? I make a living off being seen. Being on television and reading about the actions of other people."

"That's fair. And someone else might have looked at you and assumed you would embrace the more hollow and self-serving intentions of the job these new vigilantes focus on. But the difference is in the way you do that 'reading' about other people. You speak with a tone of disgust when someone was harmed. Or what seems like awe when someone goes beyond what was required of them.

"I didn't make the final decision until you came here. You asked the right questions about whether civilians had been injured or criminals caught and put away. Reacted to your own mugging with an equal measure of fear and anger, qualities that are necessary to stay alive and fierce in battle.

"The point of this job is to help the city and the people who live in it. Instill fear in the hearts of evil men. Because those currently claiming to be vigilant don't care about those traits. They made a mockery of a noble thing, putting on flamboyant outfits and talking to the press to make a brand of themselves instead of being invisible and tackling evil from within. That... self-centered focus has allowed criminals to re-emerge in this city."

Taylor glanced at Linda and could see her eyes narrowing as Hudson went on with his monologue. She couldn't trust him anymore. And none of Hudson's long-winded answers gave Taylor what he was looking for. Maybe it was the wrong question.

He'd gotten used to looking at Hudson's decimated body and no longer noticed when he quickly winced in pain or motioned with the curled up arthritic hand, but now Taylor tried to really take it in. The amputation. The long scar that had stolen his eye. He made no effort to hide his gaze and realized Hudson had quieted.

"And what makes you think I would say yes?" Taylor asked.

"You... you're the last chance I have at helping this city. And the only choice that makes any sense. You stayed here after your fiancée died. The city came around you, helped you. You could have left here, but you stayed. And you've proven to be a better fit than I could have ever imagined.

"When Alice died, you threw yourself into wanting to learn about the vigilantes that took her from you. When you were mugged, you started learning how to protect yourself and committed to that, almost obsessively. You don't put yourself into things halfway. That's why I had the Krav Maga studio set up near your home. To let you dive all the way in, but surrounded by the idea that normal people can affect their—"

"You did *what*?" Linda's interruption was almost a shout. Taylor saw her fingernails digging small divots into her arms. He felt his brow furrow. Heat rose in his face.

The manipulation. Hudson dropping hints about where Taylor should train so he could control him a little more. Leveraging the death of Alice. The man had never brought her up directly before. It wasn't his place to. That was a wound too sensitive to examine. A bruise deep and tender, but still, Hudson had been using it to his advantage.

"Dad, not only is this... insane, but it's completely irresponsible. You set up an entire business to try to convince Taylor to follow in your footsteps? You know what happens after that? He ends up in the same position you're in. No one is built for that. Not even you."

Static was building in Taylor's ears. His breath became shallower. He tried to keep his voice steady. "You do not use Alice as some pawn in your need for a legacy. That is not right. It's not fair."

"And what *is* fair? That doesn't matter here. There's more at stake here than your feelings, Taylor. The life and safety of this entire city is at risk. Is it fair that a gang member kills a little girl during a drive by? That women can't feel safe in the dark because of things that have happened to people close to them? Or that a man suspected of robbery shoots an innocent woman on a walk while he's fighting with a vigilante? None of it is fair. It is up to others to balance those scales and make it that way."

Talking about Alice again. He shouldn't do that. Shouldn't even be saying her name. "Vigilantes aren't invincible to that lack of fairness, Hudson. Is it fair when a vigilante is murdered in the street? That mugger was on the news last night. Because he killed a vigilante. Shot him three times, right here in the chest. The same guy who attacked me could have killed me."

"And if you had been more than just a victim, if you had been a vigilante of the city, you could have stopped that from happening. He might have been in jail for months now, if you'd been able to put him away when he attacked you.

"I won't try to deny it, there is risk involved with this life," Hudson said, motioning to himself. "Horrible, terrible risk. And you're the only one who can decide those risks outweigh the gains. If your personal injuries and trials will be harder to deal with than the fact that you know you could have stopped that mugger. Or a murderer. A rapist, a child molester, any of those monsters. If you devote yourself, there is no limit to what you can do to help this world."

"Don't talk to me about what I can do to help other people. I couldn't even help my fiancée."

Hudson's lips pressed together as if they were the only things stopping him from saying something. He opened his mouth, closed it again, then took a deep breath. "I want you to listen to me very carefully," he said. "I don't want to insult you or anger you when I say this. But Alice is *gone*. I'm sorry, but you can't hide behind her corpse and use her as an excuse to avoid helping this city. She wouldn't want you to do that. You aren't protecting her by not helping the city. You are no one's husband anymore."

A wave of cold came over Taylor. Hudson would not talk about her that way. Like she was one of the hundreds or thousands that had been hurt by criminals and vigilantes in this city. Like he could speak for her about what she would or wouldn't want him to do. Taylor inhaled deeply and let out a shaky breath.

"Now I want *you* to listen to me when I say this. *Fuck you*, Hudson. All we've done this entire time is talk about your life. All about your life, because you're the famous vigilante everyone's trying to copy. You're the one with the house on the hill and the framed newspaper articles and comic book series devoted to him. Under your definition of the truth, I know you now. I know your life. You don't know anything about me.

"Screw you. Have Linda do it if you need someone to take your place. She'll end up crippled like you, and then later she'll be in a grave right next to yours, because that's what happens. The only reason you haven't asked her is because you don't see her as expendable, like me."

Hudson's eyes went to Linda as if he'd forgotten she was still there, arms crossed and silent. Refusing to help the old man while she watched it all building. It was his fight to handle.

"And at the end of the day, you're kidding yourself. One person can't make a difference here. You spent your life fighting crime, and what's to show of it? Like you said, Hamington is still full of criminals. Still packed to the gills and choking with people you tried to get rid of one by one. Nothing changed. You're just an old man, a *fool*, famous because of your... your *insanity*, and you didn't achieve anything you claimed to strive for."

Taylor gave Hudson half a moment to respond, then walked toward the library door. "You're wrong," Hudson called from behind him. "You told me on our first day together: one person can singlehandedly change the city."

Taylor didn't falter in his steps. The rubber matting beneath him silenced his footfalls, but he made sure Hudson could hear the library door slam as he left.

CHAPTER TWENTY-SIX

"P-please. Just a quarter. Anything helps."

The fire in his leg throbbed in a slow rhythm. Moving made the flesh feel like it would pull off his body. Staying still made the heat build and push drops of sweat through his skin. The shivering never stopped.

"Water? Food? Just a little bit of food?"

The few days since the gas station had gotten to him. It was fine at first. Once he'd put space between him and the dead vigilante, he limped into in an alley and hid. Waited to make sure no one caught up with him. It got dark and cold and every time he heard someone come his way, he was able to duck his head down and shifted to cover his face. He'd shot that vigilante more than ten blocks away—far enough that they wouldn't be looking for him in this neighborhood. But now they had his face. Now all the cops and vigilantes were a threat.

The pawn shop had been much better. Simple security, easy to fix, no chance of getting caught. That made his stupidity at the gas station even worse. He should have waited. Planned it out. The place was packed with more tech than the pawn shop owner could have dreamed of. Alarms, motion detectors, cameras, all probably recording to a computer locked up in the back.

And then there were the people on the street, recording and yelling and watching him fight for his life like he was some kind of zoo animal.

In the big picture, the robbery wasn't the issue. He hadn't hurt anyone in the gas station and it wasn't that much money. It was that vigilante. That fucking vigilante who had tried to stop him. Sam had to kill him in front of an entire crowd to defend himself.

Everyone knew you could kill someone in self-defense to protect yourself. That's exactly what Sam had done. A judge or jury or lawyer couldn't argue that. The guy shot him with a taser and was going to handcuff him and take him somewhere. But of course the cops wouldn't see it that way. Wearing spandex meant you got to beat anyone you wanted into a coma. It was bullshit.

The pawn shop owner's death had been all on Sam and Violet. He knew that. It was a risk they had to take. They robbed the place, got him out of the secure office, and Sam did what he needed to do so they wouldn't get caught. But he was so much more likely to get screwed here.

In the alley, long hours passed. He kept waiting for his energy to come back so he could move to a new place, but all he felt was the leg stiffening up. It must have been the cold. The snow kept falling as he waited for his body to tell him he could leave the alley.

Sam peeled his pants down to look at the leg. The bullet had torn a divot in his thigh that ran halfway to the knee. Blood creeped down, but not enough to worry about bleeding out and the muscle would heal in a while. It could have been worse. He tucked his knees close to his chest and leaned his head against the brick wall of the building behind him. The throbbing in his leg kept him awake longer than he expected.

When he woke, he stretched and rubbed the leg feeling for the gunshot. A bolt of pain ran from the gash to the top of his head and he had to fight back vomit. The immediate burning from the gunshot was gone, but a low heat had moved in. He felt weak. Tired. He unbuttoned his pants and checked the leg again. It had kept flowing overnight, caking the inside of his pants with black dried blood all the way down to his shoe. He scraped some of it away from the wound and a sharp pain responded. The skin beneath was an angry red, shiny and swollen. Something white was mixed in with the newly flowing blood. His fingers came away sticky after he touched it.

Sam sucked air between his teeth as he pulled his pants back up. A soreness spread across his chest and he felt the holes where the taser's barbs pierced him. He remembered ripping the needles out as he limped to the alley, leaving small bleeding holes. They were sensitive, but nothing compared to the gunshot.

This was too much to deal with all at once. He'd seen guys recover from gunshots without a problem, but all the small injuries added up. It wouldn't let his body fix itself. He had to do something. If he could get some bandages, find somewhere to clean all the cuts and injuries, they would get better.

Sam used the wall behind him to steady himself as he stood on his good leg. He slowly put pressure on his right, testing it out. The knee buckled and he almost fell. He couldn't stay here and wait for it to get worse. He had to get moving.

He kept his hand on the wall to stay steady and took a hobbled step forward. Felt cold sweat blossom on his face. Pain turned his stomach. But there wasn't another choice. Another hobbled step. He felt dizzy.

Sam put his hand on his injured leg. He could feel the puffiness of the swelling through the fabric of his pants. He had to move. *Move.* Bile rose in his throat with the next step. He ignored it. Took another. There wasn't another choice. He kept his hand on the wall, holding his weight.

Each step was a battle. One sent sharp pain up his right side. Another sent his head into the clouds, forcing him to hold onto the wall. Eventually, the breeze at the mouth of the alley cooled his skin. Sam let out a rough breath. The sun was high. He'd missed rush hour. He could do this without being recognized. He could do it.

Being in the open made him push faster. The limp. The blood on his clothes. His face that Violet always said people couldn't forget. It wouldn't take much to be recognized. And it would take next to nothing for another vigilante to decide he was an easy target.

He took a break after a couple of blocks. Collapsed on a corner, hiding his face, holding his hands out like he was asking for change. The tent citizens would be out right now. People passing by might ignore him like he was just another one of them, wandering far out beyond the limits of the underpass. The sweat from his forehead formed a small puddle on the sidewalk. His mouth was dry. Faster. He needed to move faster.

It took a few more blocks to make it into a drug store. He grabbed a cart, leaned on it to take some weight off the leg, and limped down the first aisle in front of him. He grabbed a bag of chips off a shelf. A bottle of water. Wrenched it open and drank half of it in long gulps. Turned into another aisle and grabbed thick sweatpants, a hat, and a long-sleeve shirt with the Hamington skyline across the chest. Bandages on another aisle. Something in a tube that looked like it would help the gash.

He took slow steps to the front of the store and slapped down a few bills from the gas station as the cashier stared at the blood splashed on his pants. Sam looked down and saw it looked damp, like the cut had opened again. He needed to move faster.

He walked the cart out of the store and the cashier stayed silent, watching him through the window as he left. Sam slid the hat onto his head, low over his eyes. Tore off the price tag. In the next lonely alley, he squatted behind a dumpster and peeled the pants down. He could barely look at his leg. The dried blood around the gunshot was flaking away, leaving a clear view of the puckered skin beneath it. The gash had mostly clotted, but with each movement of the leg, cracks broke through the large scab, releasing new blood. He rubbed some of the cream from the store onto it and it burned. Had to be a good sign. Taped a bandage over the leg. Tucked the bloody pants deep in the dumpster.

Changed into the new shirt put the hat back on low over his eyes and drank the rest of the water.

What now?

He couldn't go back to the construction site. Not even to get his things. It was too close to the gas station. Everything there was lost. The rags, old cans, zip ties and even the other two guns. Stupid. He should have been patient and stashed the pistols somewhere first. But even losing the guns didn't hurt as bad as losing the construction site.

The place looked dangerous, all fenced up and protected by barbwire. No one else ever came there. The quiet had been good for him. He was able to sleep and eat without another hobo staring at his food like a buzzard. He'd even read a picture book a kid forgot at a bus stop. He'd never been much for reading, but it was nice to be able to sit and look at the colorful pictures. He went through it a few times before using it to start a fire. And then he'd finished that last can of soup.

He didn't want to shoot the vigilante. But he had to. It was either that or never see the outside of a prison again.

Keep moving. He had to keep moving. He'd found a place before, it could happen again.

Sam breathed deeply and stood. He hissed as his leg gave out, the grocery cart the only thing stopping him collapsing. The steps were slow, but the cart would help.

The cream would work. It was something medical, so it had to work. A doctor wasn't an option. They'd connect the gunshot and the vigilante and he'd be handcuffed to the hospital bed before they even got his name. No doctors. No hospitals.

He always liked being alone. Friends and family used to always get in the way of what he needed to do. He grew up on his own and was able to keep that up on the street.

But what if there was no way to fix this on his own? Who would help him?

Davey would watch him bleed out with a smile. Maybe Violet? Sam had gotten her all that money and offered her the guns.

Helping him make sure there was nothing really wrong with his leg was the least she could do to repay Sam for the extra gambling money. And she had fucked up on the bullets. Sam had to buy the right ones with his own cut of the pawn shop. Violet still had a debt to pay.

But that look. That look she gave him as she refused to touch the guns after the robbery. Disgust and weakness and fear. What if she'd gone to the cops and ratted him out? Or worse, to Davey? It wouldn't be surprising. She was a big enough pussy to run and tattle. Think she was doing something good.

Sam looked down at his leg as he crossed an intersection. The new pants were already dotted with red, the bandages soaked through with blood. His muscles loosened when he saw it. Almost lost his balance. There was no decision to make. Pray the money had cleared Violet's conscience or bleed out or die of infection.

Sam liked to take time with his decisions. Think about the choices. Other options.

There wasn't time or options here. One stupid mistake left him limping down the street without a home. Again. Just like when he'd attacked that cop in the underpass.

He'd give anything to slow things down. Let him think about the decisions he needed to make. But there was no time.

He held tightly onto the cart, pushing it against a street sign at an intersection. He let his head fall back and looked up at it. Blocks and blocks and blocks away from the underpass. At this speed it would cost him a full day. Hopefully not so long that his leg stopped working. It'd be easier to go through the subway using the gas station money, but they were always packed with cops standing guard. No cab driver would pick him up. A grocery cart-peddling hobo limping his way through the snow above ground would look more normal the closer he got to the underpass.

The fastest way there was through one of the main shopping streets. Always a pain in the ass, especially this time of year. Families came out of one store and right into the one next to it, their arms full of bags and presents and receipts from Christmas, Hanukkah, Kwanzaa, and whatever new holiday people celebrated now. Everyone stumbling around in the cold, looking to exchange the three hundred dollar tech gift because it didn't have all the features or the five hundred dollar coat because it didn't fit just right. Not caring that three hundred dollars could feed Sam for months or that a jacket didn't have to be exactly perfect to keep your body warm.

They made sure plastic covered their bags, keeping the snow from making them wet. Covered their hair, so the perfect curls Mommy had spent so much time on with Little Lucy wouldn't deflate before the end of the shopping trip. Stepped around puddles to make sure their shoes, the things that were made to give their feet protection, didn't get wet. Dozens, hundreds of these families roamed the streets, vulturing and looking for the best replacement for the shit they didn't need.

Sam stood at the crosswalk with his grocery cart, holding a bag of chips for when his stomach settled, waiting for the signal to cross. He pulled the hat lower. Didn't want to see the people not seeing him. Not even realizing they didn't see him as their eyes scanned past without pause, just washing around him, like a stream around a rock. Invisible. Worthless.

The walking light changed and the crowd moved forward on to 9TH Street, passing him with enough space to make sure his smell didn't rub off. A Salvation Army Santa Claus rang her bell on the corner. Another rock the stream moved around. Even the people who dropped their pennies into her bucket didn't look at her. Didn't nod when she thanked them or wished them happy holidays. Just winced if her bell rang too close to their heads.

The woman in the Santa suit looked old and tired. She was probably even colder than Sam was, standing there in the wind, guarding the pennies of rich people. She saw Sam and nodded.

But she was better than him. She was able to stand firmly in the stream, collecting whatever the water brought her. He was barely able to keep floating with the current.

Sam brought a handful of chips to his mouth and crunched down, hoping they would help him get to a woman named after a color who lived in a pit of waste under a bridge.

CHAPTER TWENTY-SEVEN

JESSICA

JESSICA CONDUCTED HER business differently than most dealers. Their normal night meant being posted up in trap houses with no less than other four people—one to guard the door, two for protection inside, one to do the business—and waiting for the money to come to them. Customers always knew when and where to find their dealers, what to expect from their product, and how to avoid police and vigilantes on the walk home. It was an easy, efficient, and consistent way to do business. And it was stupid.

The moment those dealers made themselves stationary targets, the heat began to grow. It only took one cracked out junkie stumbling out of a dilapidated building, or a night of too much foot traffic, to tip off vigilantes. New traps were taken down every other week, the dumbasses inside either beaten to shit by the costumed crazies or arrested and losing their entire stash in the process. Whenever those arrests were in Jessica's precinct, the drugs were taken to her station, Parker underwrote the weights, and she rebalanced the scales before scheduling drop-offs in public places to her clients. Easy, efficient, consistent.

Except when it wasn't.

Nothing had arrived in almost a month. Every drug weight

matched the log. She'd heard a rumor of a drug bust on the out-skirts of town earlier in the week, but Parker lazily denied it, say-ing she could check the entry log for herself if she didn't believe him. She spent half an hour—longer than she'd ever risked before—checking the packages and weights and entries in the evi-dence closet. Hamington was in a drought.

Until there was a bust, she would have to shoulder her utilities and meals and car payments all on her paltry government salary. No money could be added to the safe at the back of her closet. Nothing could be added to her tropical island retirement fund.

She sat cross-legged on the floor in front of the safe, eyes locked on the loading icon on her phone screen, waiting for her account balance to show. The mortgage payment was next week and the gas tank was close to empty. When the number popped up on her phone, she stared at it, imagining it had only halfway loaded. Maybe it was only counting one portion of her checking account and then the other would show. She closed her eyes. Put her phone on the ground and rubbed her face. Didn't really have another choice. She dialed the combination into the safe and pulled open the heavy door.

Stacks of money and files lined the shelves. In the back was the safety stash she'd tucked away in case she couldn't get to the evi-dence closet for product. Or a time like this.

Jessica took inventory of the product she had. There wasn't much. Maybe one night's worth of selling. But Hamington had an economics problem she could take advantage of. Nothing was on the street and she could rocket the hell out of prices for the night. Simple economics, supply and demand. She grabbed the burner cell off the shelf at eye-level and turned it on for the first time in weeks.

It took longer than usual to crank up. The phone vibrated as dozens of texts and voicemails loaded. She read through a few then deleted them all. It wasn't worth tracking down the people who'd tried to contact her earlier. If they didn't get in touch while the phone was on, they were shit out of luck. This stuff would go fast tonight. She typed in the numbers of her most consistent customers and shot off a text. "The store is open." It took all of forty-five seconds for the phone to start buzzing.

Even without the ease or consistency of trap houses, her clients always came back. Her quality and price beat everyone else's. She was discrete, didn't act scared or suspicious of mall rent-a-cops or passersby, so no one stopped her as she gave hollowed-out books stuffed with drugs to her customers and they slid a few bills into her hands, one after another.

She kept her clients higher end. Less drama and concern for violence. Some weed for a college student or a little bit of coke for a party-going surgeon, everything in between. She only added new customers on referrals and only started selling to them after she used the police network to dig into their backgrounds. Worst case scenario, if one of them did screw her, she had enough information to give it right back.

Her schedule was fixed less than half an hour after she sent the first text. On busy nights like these, she had to meet her clients closer together than she preferred, but it was the only way she'd get to everyone in one night.

It all had to be planned carefully, timed down to the minute. If a customer didn't show, that was too bad for him. The drought would do the work for her tonight. Wouldn't matter if she blew a buyer off or felt like the deal site was compromised and she denied the action. She was the prettiest girl at school that all the boys wanted to get with. Picking and choosing who got to was completely up to her.

On the way to her first buyer, she got another text asking for a hook up. When she got back to her car after selling to the first guy, she had three more, all of them she had to turn down. People were desperate for that wintertime high.

It was easy to get tempted into using this time of year. Everyone had their happy families and celebrated the holidays by laughing so toothily she wanted to scream. She'd been close to that once. Close to that big happy family holiday with a husband

and child and grandparents, but now her biggest holiday concern was that her biggest buyer was calling after the cocaine was already scheduled to run out.

"Jackie. Been a long time. I need some winter wonderland. What's available in the store for me?" She dealt under the name Jackie Brown. Another paranoid security measure, but if someone caught wind that she was a cop, her customers leaving would be the least of her concerns.

"I'm all out tonight. Should've called me earlier."

"Damn, man. You know you're my main connect for that shit. The fuck am I supposed to do now?"

"Figure it out yourself."

Dammit. Usually she'd be able to re-up the next day, filling her coffers with whatever was in demand to get the business back. That was not an option now. She could dip below Parker's recorded weights if she had to, but that was a risky short-term option. She'd just have to be patient. Tighten up the belt and budget for a while.

Jessica met most of her customers in different places so no two could run into each other. Those kinds of people, the lawyers and doctors and businessmen, usually fell into the same circles. Keeping them separate was just another level of paranoia that had its place in her business.

The rest of them, the smaller buyers, weren't worth traveling to individually. She wasn't going to waste her time driving around the city for people asking for a few pills or a nug of weed. Instead, she scheduled tonight's meetings in one of the main crowded shopping areas, timing them down to the second. 8:48 in front of Best Buy, thirty seconds for the deal, ninety seconds to get in front of Anthropologie, thirty seconds for the deal plus thirty seconds to remind Reggie that they were making a business transaction and if he kept staring at her tits while buying, she'd break his arm and delete him from the customer list.

She hated that 9TH Street ended up being the best place to do business. Families and loved ones walking arm in arm, bundled from the cold, streets and sidewalks packed tight all the way across. But there the crowds were heavy enough that two people standing and talking wouldn't call for interest. All she had to do was hand a hollowed-out book or a small shopping bag to her customers when they gave her the money and she was golden.

Todd was scheduled to be the first buyer in this area. She leaned against one of the stores when she got to the meeting spot and watched everyone throwing their inheritance at retailers. She felt him slide up next to her and heard him whisper in an Elvis voice, "Hey, pretty mama." She let herself smile.

"Hi, Todd. Just an eighth, right?"

"That's correctamundo." He stared at a couple dragging two screaming children down the street. "Why the hell did you want to meet here, of all places?"

"It's busy. Officers on duty in this area are told to watch for shoplifters in high-end boutiques, not deals in front of cheap outlet stores. We'll be fine here."

"You sure it's not so you'd have an excuse not to break out your scales? I think you were a little light last time."

"I've told you a million times. I have no reason to be light. My connect is solid and ruining my relationships isn't worth the extra ten or twenty bucks I'd get from skimming off the top. If you have a problem with how much I put in your Christmas stocking, you can change religions." She grabbed the copy of *Harry Potter and the Sorcerer's Stone* from her bag and thrust it into his hands. "Ho ho ho."

He peeked inside. There wouldn't be any complaining coming from him. It was some of the best looking OG Kush that had come through the station in months. She'd saved it for a big sale or a thank you to a big buyer, but the drought had limited her options for what to do with what she had. She didn't let him know it would be her last sell for the foreseeable future. He slapped her five and slid a fifty into her palm.

"Excuse me." They both looked in the direction of the voice.

Shit. Rent-a-cop. Now. Of all the times. During the first drop on this street.

These security guards were the kind of guys who failed to pass the police exam but still felt like they needed to be a goddamn superhero, yelling at everyone that wasn't walking the straightest, tightest line. "Ma'am, may I see your ID?"

"I'm sorry, is something wrong?"

He stared at her and adjusted the weight in his body, resting his hand on his hip holster. Textbook technique. A technically non-aggressive movement since the officer was just resting his hand, that also had clear intentions. It was an easy to way to remind people who was in charge of the situation. "Ma'am, just your ID please. Don't make me ask again."

"As far as I know, it's not illegal to wait for your cousin to go shopping, is it?" It was the best she could come up with.

The security guard's hand went from resting on his pistol to wrapped around the grip. Todd took a step back. "Ma'am. You were loitering here, and now I've found your behavior with this man to be suspicious. This is the last time I'm going to ask politely. Your ID."

Jessica glanced at Todd. Don't run. Don't you fucking run. If he ran, they were fucked.

She pulled out her wallet. There weren't any other options. This rent-a-cop motherfucker. So much for Todd buying from her. Hasta la vista, baby.

When her wallet flipped open, the star and police ID were clear in the fluorescent streetlights. The color drained from Todd's face.

"Are you happy now?" she asked. The security guard looked at the star and his shoulders dropped.

"I'm uh, I'm really sorry about that ma'am. The clients just told us to be really careful around here tonight."

She waved him off. "It's fine. Thanks for protecting all of us helpless shoppers." She wrapped her arm through Todd's and pulled him away. He felt tense. Resisting being this close to a cop after she'd just given him drugs. If he could just shut up until they got further away, they would be fine. They walked in silence for a block, passing a few happy families, a hobo, and some tourists. Jessica checked her makeup in a compact and used it to look over her shoulder. The security guard hadn't followed them.

Todd opened his mouth, his eyes watering. Before he said anything and started weeping, attracting attention, she interrupted him. "It's fake. See? I know a guy who does good fake IDs, and the star I got from a costume store. I didn't even know police actually had stars in real life. Lucky I was right, right?"

Todd looked like he was about to vomit. "I don't give a shit if you say it's fake. That was too easy for you. Too close. I'm gone." He turned and walked away from her—faster than a stroll, but not quite a run. She gritted her teeth as he disappeared in the crowed. He'd been one of her most consistent clients, buying at least twice a week.

It was too bad. But he'd made her late. The night's business had to continue.

CHAPTER TWENTY-EIGHT

VIOLET

THE ALLEY WAS dark with sharp shadows. Empty, with a natural echo that let Violet hear things on the street clearer. It was a common spot for pickpockets and thieves to pass when leaving the crowded shopping area on 9TH. She would wait there, listen, then attack. It was a pattern she'd used a dozen times to stop criminals. Like a cop on patrol.

Quick footsteps came closer to where she crouched just behind the opening of the alley. These were different than the light, rhythmic padding of someone running for exercise. They sounded choppy. Hard and flat on the pavement. She heard short panicked breaths of someone sprinting. Violet reached to the small of her back and grabbed the hockey mask tucked into her waistband. Someone shouted as the runner knocked past them. All doubt left her mind. Her muscles tensed as she prepared to leap into the open.

The runner let out a shocked cry and his step faltered as Violet knocked her shoulder into the man's chest and wrapped her arms around him. They staggered another few steps together before falling, Violet refusing to let him shove past. The stolen bags hit the ground as the man started throwing punches. Most hit Violet on the back, weak and without threat. She kept her head tucked down and moved up the runner's body, never fully letting go. The man swung awkwardly and landed a solid right hook to Violet's jaw. Her hands automatically released their grip and she rolled off the thief.

She wasn't great at fighting. It was her biggest concern when she agreed to become a vigilante. She'd stayed out of trouble in the underpass because she knew she'd never win a confrontation. There was always someone else who had fought more and knew how to punch harder. Unlike most of the other people living down there, Violet's childhood didn't involve defending herself against thugs on the street. Usually, a life like that was a blessing, but after things went downhill, it meant she didn't even know how to defend herself once she started living in the underpass.

After the night in the bar, knocking the drunk out of the way of the teenager, Violet thought she could handle herself in a fight. Every one she got in for the next month proved that wrong. Her eye swelled up, and she was out of it for a week because she couldn't see. She healed and things went well, stopping a few muggings and assaults, then her collarbone had been hurt. She didn't have a doctor to visit and it started feeling better after a few weeks, so the only thing to do about that was rest while looking for Sam. She was getting the hang of it now. Like learning when to fold and when to push the bet as hard as possible.

Violet caught the man's legs as he tried to get up and run away. Pulled him back down. Her body naturally responded to the next punch, leaning away from it, allowing less force to strike her. Her own fist came back, cracking down on the man's chin. She blocked a strike that came in with the right. Her punches poured down on the man, slowly wearing him down. She swung an elbow to his temple, and he went limp, thudding into a bleeding pile on the concrete. Steaming breath poured out of the hockey mask. Her head rang like bells. But she had done well. She dragged the man to his hiding spot and put the stolen bags next to him. She texted the only number on her phone, telling Johanson the perp's crime and where to pick him up. She sat with the unconscious man in case he woke, prepared to hit him again if she had to.

As she fit the man into the back of the squad car, Johanson let a fifty dollar bill float from his hand to the ground. He glanced at the money, at Violet, then back to the bill on the ground. He winked as he drove off.

Violet stared at it, watching it quiver in the cold breeze. It slid an inch. Her hand darted down to snag it. The softness felt good between her fingers. She uncrumpled the bill and nearly stumbled backward as she made eye contact with the white man on the paper.

Fifty bucks. Her biggest terms she'd been paid out so far. Usually there was a ten to be collected somewhere on the ground after Johanson picked someone up, or a twenty if the criminal was a serious dirtbag, but never a fifty. She was moving up in the world. She'd add the fifty dollars to what she already had in his tent. Almost a hundred to her name now.

It had been so long since she'd had that much money. She didn't even know what to do with it. More clothes, for sure. A better work jacket for the winter, so she could move easily and stay warm. Maybe a new tent?

She shook her head at the last thought as she took off the mask and started walking home. With a hundred already saved up, it was only a matter of time until she could afford a real apartment off the money she made from vigilantism. They'd never been specific about terms for stopping general crimes, but it seemed like the more people she caught and gave to the police, the higher the terms got. Soon she could rely on it like a steady paycheck. The one thing holding her back from getting into the big bucks was Sam.

Her mouth curled. Sam.

They had expected Violet to bring him in. Or at the very least, supply information that helped another vigilante finish the job. But no one had found him, no one had seen him. Not even a whisper of a rumor. And someone else was dead. A poor kid, stupid and greedy, shot in the back because Violet hadn't found Sam quick enough. That was on her. She was getting better at her job, but still wasn't there, wasn't good enough. If she was, that kid would be alive today.

The warmth from the underpass grew as she descended the steep decline border. Tent citizens gathered around barrels hot with flames, rubbing their hands together, warming pre-packaged meats, and laughing in the comfortable heat. They did the same thing every winter with their little bonfires. There were always dangers and small incidents, drunks knocking over a barrel or someone getting burnt, but nothing serious enough to change their minds.

The circles around them stayed too tight for many people to stay warm. People got forced out, then had to work around the group to try to find a way to get closer, which forced someone else out and so on. They looked like snakes, wrestling in the mud of the underpass, all trying to get to a rat that had fallen in.

She stopped short of his tent, the underpass's warmth helping her toes finally regain feeling. Her stomach dropped. She felt lightheaded. Something was wrong with her home.

Davey made it clear that stealing in the underpass would be punished, but the more money Violet had in her tent, the less she trusted the other tent citizens. She began adding security measures to make sure no one had come in while she was away.

She always zipped the tent, tied the strings at the bottom in a specific way, and covered them with a welcome mat she'd found in a trash pile. It wasn't like the alarm or the front door she used to forget to lock before she was homeless. That was an automatic habit that became difficult to remember as part of a daily routine. Violet forced herself to be conscious about her tent's safety every time she left. The zipper handle at the bottom turned at a ninety-degree angle to the ground. The laces, double knotted then looped inside of each other. The top of the W in the "Welcome to Our Home!" mat lined up perfectly with the bottom of the tent.

It was all wrong now. The zipper was down, but not all the way, the handle dangling freely. The laces were covered by the mat, but sloppily peeked out from underneath it. Someone had tried to make it look like they hadn't been inside. She thought a shadow moved inside the tent.

She glanced over her shoulder and put the mask on again. No one here knew she was a vigilante, and she wanted to keep it that way. People would mock her or ask her to help with their problems. Either way, more attention was never a good thing.

She quietly slid the welcome mat away from the tent. The laces weren't tied. She took a breath. Threw the zipper up and leapt in, her arms reaching for a throat. She found one and a laugh followed.

"Where the fuck'd you come from," Sam asked, his voice froggish through Violet's grasp, "little league practice?" Violet's hands loosened for a moment and Sam pushed her off. He was here. On the floor of her home. Her heartbeat picked up speed. Skin tingled with adrenaline. She wasn't sure if she felt lucky or terrified.

Her mind returned to Jessica's office, months ago. The argument finally settled by Johanson, deciding on terms of $250 and two nights out of jail if she caught Sam. All those months of work, walking and searching and fighting, and he had just shown up in her tent. Just walked in and sat there on the ground. He couldn't have known she was searching for him. He wouldn't have made it that easy. There had to be something else he was here for. She could use that. Just needed to wait for the right moment.

Sam was coiled up in an easily defensible position, crouched with his back against the tent. Violet couldn't leap forward to attack. Nothing within reach could be used as a weapon. She had to be patient. "Oh, this is just something I found around Halloween," she said, tossing the hockey mask onto her cot, "I've been using it to scare people walking on 9th." Sam laughed and his shoulders seemed to drop with relaxation. It was something she would never do, but probably exactly what Sam would if he'd found a mask.

"Ah, that's funny as shit. Always with the jokes, Violet."

"I'm never about the jokes, Sam. What are you doing here?"

Sam rubbed his leg. "I need your advice. And then I'll be out of here, I promise." He gingerly slid his pants down. Starting high on his right thigh, some kind of wound ran almost to his knee. It looked irritated and red. As it went lower, the gash became angrier, reaching veiny fingers outward, covering more skin.

"Jesus. That's... that's pretty nasty," Violet said. It looked almost like two separate injuries, starting as a burn and then turned into something more devastating. She started feeling bad for him, then remembered the video of Sam firing a pistol through his pants pocket, the gun probably flush against his leg, burning the skin. She heard the shots in her mind, tinny from the phone recording. Pop. Pop. Pop. "What happened?"

Sam's response was delayed. "It doesn't matter. Do you think it looks infected?"

Violet took a step forward and leaned closer, closing the attacking distance. Sam didn't react, just continued grimacing and staring at the gash. "I'm not sure about the area higher on up, but closer to your knee, here... that's pretty textbook for infected cuts. What happened?" she asked again.

Do it. Force him to do something. Eliminate any regret.

"There was this damn barbed wire fence that I tried to climb over. Bad idea."

Lie.

"Where were you trying to break into?"

"This construction site I've been living in close to the river."

Lie.

"Gotcha," Violet said. She sat next to the bag of cans in the corner of his tent, trying to look relaxed. "How are you on food these days?" Another delay in Sam's answer. There was a reason he never played cards. His tell had the subtlety of a kick to the groin.

"Pretty good. I sold those guns we got. So that, and with the money from the pawn shop, I've lasted pretty well. I still have another month or so where I can live off cold Spaghetti-O's."

That was the last lie Violet would let herself listen to. He hadn't sold the guns. He hadn't been living in peace. He was a murderer.

Violet nodded to Sam and started rustling through her junk pile in the corner of the tent while Sam continued. "Yeah, it's no underpass, but this construction site is pretty good. I think it's abandoned. No one ever comes around to bother me, no other homeless people have checked it out yet, it's pretty nice. But that's why I wanted to check with you about what you thought with this scrape. I know you've been buddies with a couple of guys that bit it after they got shit infected, so I'd rather be—"

Violet turned and swung the bag of cans. Sam blocked it out of instinct, but didn't expect the bottom of her boot that caught him in the nose. There was a satisfying crack, and she swung the bag again. He caught it this time, and raised his arms, expecting another kick to the head, but she knocked him in the ribs. Sam stumbled against the side of the tent, tipping it on its side.

He thrust his hand into his jacket pocket and it came out with a gun. Violet grabbed the arm with both hands. Pulled the upper arm toward her and the forearm back. Sam leaned forward with the torque of the arm. She kneed him in the face, then pulled the lower arm back further. It resisted against the joint and her weight. She pushed hard. Sam groaned, his face crunched in pain, swinging wild blind punches wherever they could land. There was a loud pop as the arm went limp. Sam tried to tackle Violet with the arm that worked. She shrugged it off, pushing him to the other side of the tent.

If this had happened a year ago, Sam would have ripped her head off. Now, she fought on the street against people who knew if they didn't win the fight they'd go to jail or worse. Fear made a person more desperate. Desperation made them punch harder. Sam didn't have that right now. He was injured. Surprised. He came in lower, trying to tackle her, and his face was met by a rising knee again. Violet laced her fingers together and raised her hands high. They came down on the top of Sam's back twice. The second one knocked his breath out. He rolled onto his chest.

Violet stomped on the injured shoulder and stomped again after Sam screamed. She would never be involved in another murder because of him. She swung her foot into Sam's infected leg. He howled like an animal.

She dropped a knee on Sam's back, pinning him to the ground. The fist of Sam's good arm swung wildly behind him, weak with pain, barely making any impact. Violet grabbed it and pinned it under her knee, tying up Sam's legs with his own. She started raining down punches on the back of his head, with each one, a satisfying pain searing through her knuckles. Sam's face slapped the tent floor with every strike.

"Violet, stop!" Sam cried out in pain. It was not an option. He was a murderer to be punished. Money to be taken. And he deserved to be torn apart. Blood puddled under his face, bubbling from his mouth. Sam yelled at her to wait, stop, please.

Violet didn't wait. She had to get her terms.

CHAPTER TWENTY-NINE

TAYLOR

By the time the taxi pulled up to his townhouse, Taylor was shaking. He'd alternated between clenching his fists and stretching his fingers the entire drive, trying to steady himself and bring his anger down.

That bastard. Using Alice against him. Playing him for months, talking about his past, his legacy, all to try to manipulate him into following the insane path into vigilantism. The very thing that had gotten Alice killed. It was demented. Cruel.

His hand automatically pulled some bills from his wallet and handed them to the driver as he closed the cab's door. Inside, he dropped his things on the floor and collapsed on the couch. Stared at the ceiling.

The insanity of it all almost made his mouth curl into a smile. What else was there do than laugh at the situation? A crippled superhero asks Taylor to take on his breed of crimefighting so his legacy won't die, insulting the memory of his fiancée in the process, causing Taylor to lash out and explode. Like a child with a temper or some sort of melodramatic comic book crescendo.

He groaned and leaned forward. What was he going to tell Jake? He couldn't go back to the Hudson House now. Not after calling his interview subject a fool and slamming the door on the way out. Taylor was supposed to be a professional and Hudson was an old man, probably delusional from his medicine and cabin fever, living in a fantasy world. There would be no reason for Jake to keep Taylor anymore. Not after tonight, and especially not with Brad waiting in the wings. He had Taylor's job in all but title at this point, and it couldn't be much clearer that Taylor was only still on the payroll for the sole purpose of this interview.

No job at the station, no Alice, no parents, no one who wanted to be around him since he was just the sad widower that reminded them of a tragic, violent death. Nothing anchored him to the city of Hamington. Maybe he could start at a new station in town. He could remind them of how the city responded to his loss, boosting his ratings to a new level, and...

Waves of nausea crashed inside of him. What was he doing? Thinking about using Alice's death as a way into a new job? A sour taste filled his mouth. Once he told Jake that the interviews were done and he'd failed at getting Hudson's full story, there would be no excuse or reason to stay in Hamington. None.

He grabbed his phone off the floor to call Linda. She'd already texted him, telling him to meet her at the coffee shop later that day. He tossed his phone onto the coffee table and rubbed his eyes. Turned on the TV and let the sounds and shapes try to drown out the memories from bubbling up again.

The call from the police. A body on a sheet. Her friend covered in a thin blanket, eyes glazed over, looking at an invisible something on the ground, as she sat on the curb twenty feet away from where Alice had been shot in the head. And when she looked up at him, the questions on her face. Where was he? Why did this happen? Why did he let this happen to her?

Identifying Alice at the morgue. Her face swollen from quickly stitching up the entry point of the bullet. Her quiet, pale face.

Taylor turned the volume on the television up until it hurt his ears. Dug his palms into his eyes until Alice's face was blurred out by stars and colors in a deep black.

Linda was already seated at a side table, hands wrapped around a paper cup, when he walked into the coffee shop. They didn't have long before the place closed. The employees were tired, wiping down tables, and having their own cups of coffee to wake up. It had turned dark outside and the streets were busy. He went straight to her and joined without ordering.

She glanced up, then back into the black of her coffee. "What a day, huh?"

"Sure," he said.

They settled into silence. He got up and ordered a cup of coffee. Came back.

Silence. Two of the employees laughed about something.

"You wanted to meet me here," he said.

She nodded, took a sip of coffee. No steam drifted off its surface.

"When I was little, I loved that Dad was a superhero," she said. "It was a secret I couldn't tell other kids. They would all argue whose dad was stronger or could beat up someone else's dad, but I just had to sit back. They didn't know they were all arguing about who would come in second place in a fight with my dad. I didn't hate what he did until he started making mistakes."

"Like what?"

"Like..." she took a deep breath. "Like when he lost his arm. My mom told me. She woke me up, said we had to go to the hospital because he'd been hurt. Her eyes were all puffed up from crying.

"And then a few years later there was the leg. Same situation, but you kind of come to expect something else bad to happen at that point. By the time he lost his eye, Mom was gone. She couldn't take it anymore. And after all that, it never really made a difference. There were always more people to fight. Criminals to take down or mobster organizations to topple.

"I didn't want a normal childhood then. I was proud of my dad and what he did. But now, looking back, I just wish we'd had a backyard to play in together. A swingset he could have pushed me on instead of a training room I wasn't allowed in. Gets a little less romantic when people you care about start paying the price."

Taylor nodded. "I used to be able to imagine life being like that. Swingset, playgrounds, all that stuff. Alice and I would have a kid. I'd brew the coffee while she made breakfast and the kid watched cartoons. Chaperoning a first date. Playing baseball in the backyard. I mean, I don't even like baseball, but those are just the images you get. You know? When Alice died, all those things died with her. I've been trying to figure it out since then."

Linda thumbed at the coffee sleeve around her cup. "Why did you want to talk to him so badly if you feel like your wife died because of vigilantes?"

His voice stabbed out of his throat. "She did die because of them. If that crap hadn't spilled over into East H from the west side of the river..." He shook his head. Took a deep breath. Saw the red stain blooming on the sheet over her face. Why get angry about it again? "I thought if I was able to talk to him and understand why he started everything I could logically think through how the city benefits from vigilantes and that Alice was... an unfortunate accident in the grand scheme of something that has done other people good. Separate my personal story from the facts of how vigilantes help the city overall. It was a dumb idea. That was never going to be possible."

"You can't find logic or morality in something that's driven by people without it. I mean, come on. Even now, do you think what my dad did was logical? Take a step back and look at all of this. He's on a hospital bed, in all likelihood his death bed, in a mansion and he's asked you to become the next Hudson and join him in a hospital bed right next to him, because he wants to be remembered.

"*Remembered*. The guy who has an entire comic book series based on his adventures feels like he doesn't have a way for people to remember his legacy," she laughed. "But that's what we come back to though. The insanity of this whole thing."

Linda ran her hands through her hair. "The truth is, I'm not enough for him. Call him overprotective or misogynistic, but I think he wanted a son to follow in his footsteps. You heard that recording. After all I've done for him, it's not enough because in his eyes I can't be the next Hudson. That's why he brought you in. Which means..." she inhaled deeply. "I have to ask a terrible favor of you."

Taylor's brow furrowed. Linda kept her gaze on her coffee, refusing to look up at him.

"My father is dying. He hasn't been a great one, but he's still my dad and there's no replacing that. I don't know how long he has. Could be weeks, could be months. But he is going to die. I want to make that time as comfortable as possible for him." Linda drank the rest of her coffee. Put her cup down on the table and continued staring at it.

"What is it? What are you asking me?"

She met his eyes. "I want you to agree to become Hudson."

"What?" he shouted. The few people left in the coffee shop turned and looked at them. Taylor raised his hand in apology and faced back to Linda.

"Hear me out. Not to actually become Hudson," she said, "just... tell him you will. Keep coming back for interviews. We both know he doesn't have long."

"Why the hell would I do that? He-he just mocked me and my dead fiancée, has been lying to both you and me for months, and now I probably won't have a job because of him."

"That's why I described this as 'terrible.' There's nothing making you agree to it. It is a favor I ask for my dying father. No matter what he did in the past, if his last interaction with people is him failing to convince you to become Hudson, he'll die thinking his entire life is a failure. I don't want that to happen."

Silence lingered between them. A barista came by, pardoned his interruption, and told them the shop would close in five minutes. Linda nodded politely. Taylor didn't move. More silence.

"Do you honestly think he ever wants to see me again after today?" he asked quietly.

"If you say you want to become Hudson, I don't think he would hold anything you've ever done against you."

They got up from the table and threw their cups away. The employees locked the door behind them as they went outside.

"I'm sorry to ask. But just think about it," Linda said. She squeezed his upper arm and walked away. He turned to walk back to his townhome.

It wasn't just a favor. It was a lie to comfort an old man who had insulted Alice's death. He'd been the one to start vigilantism in this city. He was more than partially responsible for her.

Maybe tangentially. He hadn't been the one to pull the trigger. He'd been retired. And if the cops had done their jobs and put the thief in jail, a vigilante wouldn't have been in East H in the first place. Maybe they'd done good in the past and stopped more criminals from coming across the river. Or maybe they encouraged violent people and made things worse. The only thing he knew was that Alice was dead.

The two of them would never have the life together that they'd talked about. A peaceful life with a nine o'clock bedtime. A house in East Hamington close enough to the river to be convenient, but far enough away that the lights of the city wouldn't keep their children awake. Soccer games, boy scouts, Easter egg hunts. Those fantasies were gone. Slain.

Hudson had been right. There was no idyllic life once he clocked out of work. No peaceful, strong relationship to go home to. Everything had been about her before and even after she'd died, that hadn't changed. It was about trying to understand why it happened. Dedicated to it. But there was no way he would ever come to understand it. She was gone, he was alive, and that's all there was now. No more hiding behind Alice.

She was gone. He was alone in this city.

And Hudson was right.

The world spun around him. He wanted to punch something. Scream.

A body under a white sheet.

He ran. Sprinted. His shoes beating the sidewalk, jacket pulled tight across his back. He lost track of the streets he passed, weaving between cars, barely hearing their horns and screeching tires. They didn't matter. A red flower blossoming under a white sheet. Things like that no longer mattered. A pale, swollen face.

Alice was gone.

His lungs burned, muscles tightened, and he pushed forward. Between buildings and people and cars, street over street, he ended up at the river.

Couples sat, scattered over the riverbank. Watching the moon. Or the stars. Or whatever else was out there. He doubled over. Put his hands on his knees. Coughed out hot breath that rose like smoke. Sweat clung to his skin and clothes. He stood tall, arms on his head, trying to catch his breath. The darkness of East Hamington looked back at him. The light from behind him reflected off the Baldwin River.

The people east of the river had all tucked in their children and gotten into bed, reading the day's paper before going to sleep. In West Ham, time didn't dictate when people rose and slept. Taylor never tired this early. Maybe he was never built for living in East Hamington.

A woman's giggles carried across the water. Her lover tickled and kissed her. Taylor couldn't be here with these people. He inhaled through his nose. Exhaled shakily. Felt his heartrate slow. He turned to walk through the lights of the city, painfully bright in the nighttime. His chest burned and he didn't have the energy to run.

CHAPTER THIRTY

SAM

HOLY FUCKING SHIT. She was selling him. Fucking selling him. Like a slave.

As Sam was loaded into the car, the cop gave Violet a smile, a pat on the back, and a roll of Benjamins bigger than his fucking cock. After everything Sam had done for her—the money and the guns and all that other shit—Violet had tossed him away. Like a sandwich wrapper. Torn up and useless after getting to the meat inside.

She tried to explain while they waited for the cops to show up, Sam's arms, legs, and mouth bound with duct tape, shoulder screaming, while she sat cross-legged in the corner of her tent. "The cops," she said, "they're paying me to bring you in. I've been hired as a vigilante." With that stupid, *stupid* fucking look on her face, like she actually knew what she was talking about.

Hired as a vigilante. Bullshit. She was like a bounty hunter on TV. They were going to pay her for their dirty work, then throw her out.

A whore, selling herself to pigs.

While the cops stood with Violet beside the squad car and talked, Sam had to lean forward in the backseat to avoid putting pressure on the arm she had twisted into that angle. It felt broken.

And she didn't have to do it. She could have stopped when Sam told her to, but instead, she pulled harder and now the arm hung limply in the handcuffs while Violet stood as the center of attention in the middle of a bunch of cops. Glowing like some award winner.

She had no idea. No idea that they were laughing about how stupid she was. About how easy it was to convince a dumb hobo to do exactly what they wanted. Sam met her eyes through the glass. She came over to the cruiser, placed her hand on the window, and told Sam she was sorry, but this was the right thing to do.

Sam peeled back his lips. "I'm going to eat your heart."

These fucking vigilantes. They were ruining him. If he didn't have to shoot the one from the gas station, if he didn't have to go to Violet for help, he'd still be sitting in his construction site, warm and safe and not bothering anybody. This wasn't his fault. He only did what he had to when these vigilantes got in his way.

He leaned his head on the fence between the back seat and the driver and started banging it. Anything to stop him from thinking about the friend that had just sold him or his infected leg or his broken arm or how long he was going to be stuck in a small concrete box. A cop outside slapped the window and told him to shut up and sit back. "Fuck you," Sam yelled. He would get in trouble for that later. Probably beaten. But he didn't care. His life was done. They were going to toast him for the vigilante murder. Probably the shop owner too.

No, not that one. They wouldn't have paid Violet if they'd known she was the one who planned the robbery. He could use that. Just needed to be smart. Test the waters and find out what they knew. He tried to ignore the static and robotic voices coming from the cop's radio.

It always surprised Sam when he met people who didn't know that jail and prison weren't the same thing. Prison was the concrete block in the sky with barbed wire fences and M16-armed guards and lifers. The place where criminals were cooped up for decades but were still expected to easily re-adjust to the real world once released and a random judge decided they had "paid their debt to society" by using all of society's tax money.

Jail was the lockup. The drunk tank. The place people are stored to be close to the police station and the courthouse if they aren't rich enough to post bail. Security didn't come in low or maximum levels, it just was what it was. Sam had been there a few times on small shit that never panned out to prison time. Inmates were less aggressive because they actually still had something to live for and a chance to get through their trials without being shipped away.

Sam was brought into the jail through the back door and dropped down on a bench. A chain snaked through his cuffs and connected him to the two men next to him. Each time they yanked the chain to add a new prisoner or unlock one, his shoulder burned with pain and he had to fight a wave of nausea.

It was like every other jail he'd been to. Phones ringing, new arrests pulling and spitting at cops, rich brats accused of drunk driving looking like their world was ending. Everyone fighting back from being dragged down the hall by a cop or refusing to answer questions. All trying to make a point. Their emotions made them stupid. He would be better. Violet had surprised him in the tent. Sam let his guard down and paid for it. That was not a mistake he would make again.

A fat cop shoved her hands in his pockets, looking for a gun or knives or mace or a bomb or even a dangerously sharp toothpick. The gun he'd taken from the construction site was still in Violet's tent and he didn't have anything on him but his coat. She took off his shoes and belt started asking him questions. "Are you sick or ill? Have you ever tried to commit suicide? Ever thinking about killing yourself? Do you feel that way now? Have you recently lost a loved one? Do you know why you're in custody?" At first he thought about each question and answered, then he just set his answer to "no" and ignored everything that followed. They weren't interested in keeping him safe or healthy. She didn't care what his answers were. They just wanted to follow the rules shoved down their throats to avoid a lawsuit.

The cop walked him past the rubber-walled room used for the suicidal and into a standard holding cell. When they uncuffed him, he didn't rub his wrists like every other whiny bitch who ended up in jail, he just let them throb and swell. He wouldn't give them the satisfaction of seeing him in pain. When he said his shoulder felt broken and leg infected, the cop told him he'd have to deal with it for the night because the doctor was gone for the day.

He waited.

There were no clocks on the wall. No way to tell time except the buzzing of alarms telling inmates to line up for count and get in their cells and go to sleep. It felt like days, but probably only a few hours passed when he was taken out of the holding cell. Waves of pain washed over him every time he limped down hallways to have his mugshots and fingerprints taken, then back to the cell. He asked about getting his phone call and no one responded. He didn't know anyone with a phone, but everybody on TV got a phone call.

He waited.

Someone else dragged him from the cell and brought him to what he thought looked like a standard interview room. There was a one-sided window, metal table, three metal chairs, and a camera wired in the corner. He laughed and shook his head. He wasn't getting arrested for murdering someone, he was in a rerun of *NYPD Blue*. He could feel the heat coming off his leg without touching it.

More waiting. Trying to scare him. Loosen up his tongue for questioning.

Two officers came in, like a standard good cop bad cop pair. They weren't even trying to get creative with him. They thought he was a poor hobo who'd never seen this on TV before.

One cop was the guy who picked him up. The one who patted Violet on the back for being a good girl and chuckled as he gave her the reward money. The other, a woman with a nightmare web of scars flowing across her chin and mouth like a river. He couldn't take his eyes off it. He motioned his chin toward hers and asked, "The fuck happened to you?" It took effort. Sweat was building on his forehead.

Her mouth twisted into a very small, close-mouthed smile. The man put his hand on her arm. He said, "My name is Officer Johanson. This is Officer Sanders. I have no reason to look out for you here, but I would highly recommend you don't ask that question again."

Sam scoffed. Someone was sensitive about her ugliness. Sanders sat at the table and her eyes fell over him. He refused to look away. The bitch was going to be bad cop. He had nothing to fear from her. She leaned forward. Spoke slowly. "My name is Jessica Sanders. Do you recognize that name from anywhere?"

It hit on something from the past he couldn't fully remember. Fog sat heavy in his skull. He didn't respond. She leaned back and shrugged. "That's fine. You may not remember me, but I know you, Sam DeWitt."

His stomach dropped. What the fuck was this? No one knew his last name. He hadn't given it at booking. He only used his first name on the streets. Nothing else. What the hell was going on here? Johanson stood a distance behind her. He wouldn't be jumping in. He was there to stop her if she went off the rails. Good cop.

"Look," Sanders said, "we have a lot to charge you on, so let's go over it. Most recently, we have armed robbery and second-degree murder. People like their costumed nutjobs in this city. That certainly won't sit well with the jury, especially since you were caught on camera doing it. A bit further back, we have a robbery and a first-degree murder. Not as emotional for a jury as the vigilante, but the DA should be able to tie the trend together pretty well there. That premeditated murder charge alone will put you in the pen for twenty-five years.

"Next, we have assault on a police officer, which juries *also* don't take lightly." She tapped the scar on her chin. Sam's brow furrowed. Then he saw the night again in his mind.

Climbing the fence. Leaping off of it, attacking her. Slamming her face into the wooden planks. Thinking the tent city would rally with him and throw her out. Running out of the underpass into the night. *Shit.*

"And last but not least, we have yet another charge of first-degree murder. This one against your drug dealer, two years ago, as well as constructive possession of drugs with intent to distribute. Your friend Violet tipped us on to that one as well. It's so sweet that you confided in her when you were both living under that bridge together."

His dealer. He'd almost forgotten the feeling of the cracking spine vibrating up the baseball bat. The blood splashing on his face.

"So in all, that is a lovely total of *seven* charges for you, Mr. Sam DeWitt. Only a couple have to stick for you to live in prison for the rest of your life. So it's really up to you which one you'd like to discuss first." The scar on her face screwed up into a Halloween mask as she smiled.

He slumped. The vigilante, he could have said was self-defense. The shop owner, he could have blamed on Violet. He had to take the gas station robbery because he was on tape, but no one died there and he could have gotten off on good behavior. But the dealer. It was so long ago he'd almost forgotten about it.

He'd come home from being out getting food and saw the cop cars lining the block of his apartment block, lights flashing, engines running. They'd tracked him to his apartment and raided it when they thought they'd caught him. The baseball bat was still there, the drugs were still there. It was the reason he'd gotten on the street in the first place. And now it was a pretty package, all wrapped up to send him to fucking prison.

"Lawyer," he said.

"Not a problem," Johanson said from the back of the room.

"Do you have one we can contact for you or do you need a public defendant?"

"What the fuck do you think?" Sam asked.

The bitch smiled like a predator. Using a public defendant on this many charges would be as good as trying to do it on his own. The lawyer would make a deal with the cops to trade information for time out of prison, but Sam didn't have any information to give. The best he'd be able to do was one life sentence instead of multiple.

The arraignment was the next day. Sam didn't even know what that word meant. He sat in a courtroom, his leg on fire with pain, as people talked about him like he wasn't there. Half of what they said didn't even sound like English. His lawyer, a washed-up idiot who had been tossed out of his old firm for a terrible trial record, sat him down in a private room in the courthouse afterward.

"I'd ask you if you want the good or bad news first, but there's really only bad news. They haven't offered you bail and the court is going forward with all charges."

"I don't have anyone to pay bail for me anyway," Sam said.

The lawyer clicked his tongue in an annoying fucking way and scribbled something on a notepad. "Got it. So now I have to tell you. Things look very bad for you, Sam. One option is that we can change your plea to guilty and potentially negotiate a shorter sentence in exchange for any information you have on criminal enterprises."

"What does that mean?"

"I believe you would call it 'ratting out.'"

"I don't have anyone to rat out. I'm on my own."

The man cleared his throat. "Alright then. In that case, let's operate under the assumption we'll keep that not guilty plea and work from there. Start from the beginning, please. Tell me every-thing."

Sam lied to him at first. Said he wasn't at the drug dealer's home with a baseball bat, slamming it into his skull, that he wasn't the one who bashed Sanders' face into the ground, that he only shot the vigilante because he thought he was about to die.

The lawyer took off his glasses and rubbed his eyes dramatically. "Look," he said, "if I'm going to help you at all—either by pleading these charges or by getting you through a trial—you need to tell me everything. None of your stories make sense. The facts don't fit. And if I have to do this with one hand tied behind my back, I can tell you, without a doubt, you will be in prison for the rest of your life. I need you to tell me everything."

Sam wasn't used to this. This telling the truth and relying on others. He didn't like it. But there was nothing else he could do. He cleared his throat told his story to the lawyer. Everything. Probably too much.

He told him about his mother giving birth to him on the dirty floor of their apartment. Getting picked on by kids that could actually read. Clawing out a bully's eyes. Joining a gang to make sure his mom had food, and getting thrown out because he was too violent. Mugging people to pay for his family's meals. Getting hooked on crack and then heroin. Killing his dealer for overcharging him. Escaping to the underpass and then running after he hurt Sanders. Killing the shop owner for guns and money. The construction site. The gas station. The vigilante. Violet. The money.

When the story was coming to an end, the lawyer looked tired and bored. This was the guy who was supposed to keep him out of prison? But when he got to the part about the cop paying Violet, his eyes opened wide. He scratched notes on his pad and asked more questions. How much money? Bills or checks? Did they look familiar with each other? Comfortable? And this was the woman who planned the pawn shop robbery?

When the lawyer left, Sam asked the police if the doctor was available to look at his injuries yet. His leg was oozing now. They told him the doctor was already gone for the day. He'd be back tomorrow. But fuck them. Every day without treatment, his lawyer said, could be used as ammunition against the cops. Against Sanders.

Despite his nice bed and heated cell and building to sleep in, her smile kept him awake some nights. She would be coming for him. But he'd survived that bitch once. Now he just had to do it again.

He waited.

CHAPTER THIRTY-ONE

TAYLOR

TAYLOR LET THE knocker of the Hudson House drop heavily. He released a shaky breath and wiped his palms on the side of his pants. There was no way to guess how Hudson would react to him here. He could invite him in and the day could go as usual or he could tell him the interviews were over and he never wanted to see him now that he'd rejected his proposal.

Linda opened the door without Hudson beside her and let Taylor in without a word. She motioned toward the sunroom and didn't follow as he began walking down the long hallway.

Hudson was still asleep. Or at least, the semi-deep rest that was his version of sleep, easily interrupted by noise or movement. Taylor approached the bed quietly, but it was no use. Hudson's eyelids slid open. His remaining eye stared at Taylor and the wet empty eye socket shined in the light of the room.

The look on his face. Was it shock? Anger? After their last conversation, he probably hadn't expected Taylor to return. "I... I'm sorry about last night, Hudson," he said. The man blinked. Stayed silent. "I know that it wasn't an easy decision, offering me... your name. The mantle of Hudson. It's just a lot to try to take in. I wasn't expecting it and after everything that happened with Alice... yesterday wasn't a great day for me."

The old man cleared his throat and pulled at his clothes, readjusting himself. "You don't have anything to apologize for. Most heroes don't immediately embrace the opportunity to do what they can. You're not unlike the majority of people who joined in vigilantism after me."

Taylor nodded, hoping Hudson would keep talking or Linda would come in to distract the situation. He still hadn't decided what to do about Linda's request and didn't know what to say next. It would be an insult to the memory of Alice if he tried to make this man feel better about his legacy. Turning away and letting go of the idea that he was involved in her death would go against why he'd been looking for him in the first place.

Finding Hudson to understand what happened to Alice had been everything to him. But now that Taylor knew Hudson would never say what he needed to hear to get to the core of what drove a vigilante, he felt different. A sense of lightness. Fuzzy around the edges now that the goal he had was gone, along with all its strings and anchors dragging him to come to peace with what happened. Now he was just drifting.

"You were right," Taylor heard himself say. "I've been trapped under this memory of Alice. Hamington tried to help me after she died. Tried to pull me out of it, but I refused. And when you made me realize that, I turned around and I took it out on you. And I'm sorry."

Hudson nodded and rubbed a crust of sleep off a corner of his eye. "So you're not here to talk about my offer."

Taylor pressed his tongue against the back of his teeth. Words caught in his throat. A terrible favor. Lying to a dying old man to make him feel better. Taking both of them further from the truth that Taylor came here for in the beginning. There had to be somewhere in the middle. Keeping the truth while helping this man feel accomplished at his end.

"Honestly, I don't know what I'm here to talk about."

Hudson grimaced as he pressed a button and the bed adjusted to a more upright position. His eye was clear now, the sleepiness absent from it. "If you're not here for what we spoke about the last time, then unfortunately you and I no longer have business together." He reached his curled arthritic hand forward as far as his arm would allow.

A handshake to say goodbye. That was all it would take and then this would be over. No more internal struggles about Alice and trying to come to peace about how she died. No reason to worry about a man's contentment with his life's work. He could start over and find something new for himself. By himself. Away and apart from the rest of the world. A slate so clean there would be nothing and no one to make him feel guilty about it.

No one. A vacuum of a life surrounded by a city he wasn't prepared to leave. Forced to find a new job, a new career. Something that would help people even less than being a news broadcaster. Nothing that made a difference in the city like Hudson had.

He shook his head. These thoughts. The longer he stayed in them, the more they'd keep spiraling into dangerous places. "I have to do something to avoid losing my mind. Something... positive to take out of this. I can't just let her go. I have to have a reason for it."

The words tasted bitter in his mouth. When had her death changed from something that happened to her, to something only about him? He'd become so self-centered. Focused only on making himself feel better.

What Hudson did wasn't for personal gain. Unlike today's vigilantes, he hadn't pursued the publicity or sponsorships when he was crawling in the dark looking for bad people. Those opportunities had all come searching for him after he was done. It wasn't egotistical or flashy. It had been a need to protect his city and he did so the only way he knew how. Who relied on Taylor now?

In a few weeks, with the new kid Brad already getting settled in front of the camera, no one would remember Taylor. They'd talk to themselves about the former news anchor whose fiancée died and the city tried to support before he turned away from them. Then it'd turn into a memory of something tragic happening to someone who used to work for the news. And then it would be nothing.

Hudson and Linda were the only people he really had a connection with now. Maybe that's why he'd been coming here to the Hudson House so often. Following the old man's recommendations so closely. He was someone to talk to about this. To listen to as he told his stories and anecdotes about his world. The only thing stopping him from continuing as a vigilante was his body. It was failing him, and his daughter, and Taylor all the same. They wanted more time with him. More than he was physically able to give. But they would be able to continue on without him. They didn't rely on Hudson.

And that was exactly what had given him permission to do the impossible. The Without people relying on him, he had had the freedom to do what sane people should not.

"Nothing is positive or negative, Taylor. You just have to make a choice as to what is right and wrong." Hudson's arm started to drop as his muscles tired.

Maybe it wasn't a bad thing, a negative thing, to plan on moving on. Or to do what was right... to act without personal gain. Saying goodbye to the memory of Alice to help an old man, instead of honoring someone who was already gone. If he did that, Hudson would never leave him. The act of telling Hudson he would carry on his legacy would never go away. Taylor placed his hand on top of Hudson's and moved it back to rest on the hospital bed. The skin on his hand felt soft and fragile.

What did he have without the people in this house? What options were there for moving forward? He let out a shaky breath.

"Our... our business isn't finished."

Hudson's lips tightened. They seemed to shake as his remaining eye watered.

Taylor clenched his teeth. He felt like he was on the precipice of a long fall.

"Say it. There is nothing heavier and more costly than a name. I need you to say it."

Whether it was a lie or a truth, the man needed his peace at the end. He had prepared himself for this life. A life of violence and death and pain, if for nothing else, because there were no other options to move forward.

"Yes," Taylor said. "I will become Hudson."

CHAPTER THIRTY-TWO

VIOLET

THE PHONE HADN'T made any noise since she'd turned in Sam two weeks ago. She used to get texts telling her a crime had been committed near the underpass, or to go patrol a certain area lacking police numbers, or to report in to the station to talk. Now there was nothing. She still charged it in fast food restaurants and soup kitchens to make sure Johanson could get in touch with her, but it stayed silent. It gave her too much time to think.

Her mind kept going back to the fight with Sam in the tent. He had come to her, trusting her to help him, and she'd taken advantage of that. Beaten an injured, desperate person. A friend? No. Maybe in the past, but not anymore. He'd gone too far too many times. But what options did he have? After the mistake of attacking the cop in the underpass, he had just been doing what he had to do to survive. Of course he was desperate. That didn't change what he did, but it also didn't make him evil at his core.

Terrifying? Yes. Dangerous? Absolutely. He needed to be removed from the streets before he hurt anyone else. But the way he'd begged her to stop and she'd kept punching him. The back of his head a clear target for every shot she wanted to take. She could have stopped earlier and held him until the cops came. Why did she keep going? To try to prove something to him? Or to herself?

A red fog had come over her and she pounded him until he lost consciousness. Who was the dangerous one then?

It was exactly what Johanson and Sanders wanted. It took longer than expected, but still, the job was finished and she should have been given something else to do. So why the silence? Without messages from that phone, there was no support. No payment, no way to buy food.

When Johanson gave her the phone, he made it clear Violet was not to contact him unless she had a perp. They would get in touch with her when they needed something. Violet expected them to call right after Sam got to jail, but after two days of checking for missed calls and getting no action on the phone, she thought about breaking the rule and calling. Johanson had threatened to stop offering terms, but if there weren't any to lose, what was the point of just sitting there?

She forced herself to wait. Be patient. It had only been a few days. She just needed to wait or find a criminal to bring Johanson to her.

After the post-Christmas rush, the city was quiet. It seemed tired from the holidays and even criminals were hiding from the cold. Violet walked her usual areas, hockey mask tucked in the waistband under her shirt, waiting for something to happen. Wishing a criminal to show up and let her force the conversation with Johanson. Still, nothing.

The phone finally buzzed almost three weeks after she'd given Sam to them. The text didn't list any crimes or terms, just told her to come to an intersection a block away from the underpass later that night. It was strange, but she sent an immediate OK back. Her money can had gotten dangerously light over the past few weeks. She couldn't afford to second guess anything from the police. A cruiser was parked at the corner when she arrived.

Her muscles tensed. Cops never came to the underpass unless they were looking for a perp hiding in the tent city. She walked up to the car slowly, ready to fight if someone tried to surprise her. The street was poorly lit and at an angle out of sight from the tent city. She flinched when the car door open and Johanson stepped out. He waved Violet over with a smile. This didn't feel right. Didn't feel safe.

"Hey, Violet. How you doing?"

"I'm... fine." Police did not come here. Police did not contact her just to talk. Violet turned her head to glance behind her, looking for another cop around the corner waiting to grab her. Take her out of the situation now that she'd done her job. "What is this?"

"What's what?" Johanson asked. He came around the car and walked toward her. Violet took a small step backward.

"This. What are you doing here?"

"Jesus, right to business these days I guess," Johanson said. "Look, I've been moving some money budgets around and I wanted to come here in person to ask you something. I want you to be the official vigilante for the underpass and the surrounding areas. You'd be responsible for making sure the people that live here stay safe and criminals aren't hiding within your territory. We'd pay you a bi-weekly stipend as long as crime stats consistently decrease and ask you report in once a week. Other than that, nothing changes. We'd still offer you terms for specific people we want you to bring us, just want to give you an incentive to keep doing what you're doing. This could be a huge help for getting you off the streets eventually. What do you think?"

Her heart was pounding. She glanced over her shoulder again for someone hiding. It was too good of an offer. A salary. A job. And she didn't even have to leave her home or change what she was already doing.

"You serious?"

Johanson shrugged. "Of course. Why would I joke about something like that?"

Violet forced her shoulders to relax. This was what all the hard work was for. This was the payoff for all the miles she'd wandered the streets, fighting criminals, bringing Sam in. She shouldn't reject it. There was nothing to think about. Nothing to consider. It was a royal flush.

"I'm all in. One hundred percent."

Johanson smiled and came toward Violet with his hand out. She automatically took a step back. Johanson stopped and pursed his lips. Put his arm back by its side. "Well that's all good, then. That's fantastic. That'll help us avoid going in and creating negative relationships with the homeless, and you can help lead and manage the activities going on down there."

"Lead? What about Davey?"

Johanson rubbed the stubble on his cheek. "Davey's doing a fine job. We don't want you to replace him. Just... help him along. And whether you want to tell him about our deal or not, that's up to you. We tried to have Silky O'Sullivan operate down there without notifying Davey and look how well that turned out. For all of our concern that Davey would feel pressured by a police contact challenging his authority, it was still Silky we ended up having a problem with after he attacked that guy he thought was kidnapping homeless people."

"Davey's a good person," Violet said. "I'll let him know. Besides, if even Sam knows I was paid to get him arrested, Davey should know I'm doing something similar for the underpass."

Johanson's face froze. He didn't respond. Just stood there. Like some kind of statue.

"What do you mean 'Sam knows'?" The words rolled out of Johanson's mouth slowly. There had been a shift. This was not the vigilante coordinator. This was not someone proud of her for a job well done. This was a police officer talking to a dirty hobo. Violet glanced around. She was very much alone.

"Well, you know. I told him I was a vigilante and was being paid to bring him in."

"You told him what?"

The air was static. The oxygen was being sucked out of her lungs. What had she done wrong? This was a job with the police department—what was the problem with that? What was there to hide from?

"Did I do something wrong? You gave me that money right in front of him. If it was a secret why would you have given it to me then?"

"Jesus Christ, I don't know, Violet. I owed it to you from a thing we did one time. I felt bad that you live under a bridge. It was a loan. He was hallucinating from the beating you gave him. That's one tiny thing and there are a million goddamn reasons to explain why I would have given you money. But you flat out told him that we hired you as a vigilante and were paying you?"

Was that not open knowledge? Since he first met with Johanson and Jessica, all the talk had been about terms and criminals and vigilante justice. There wasn't any secrecy or hushed voices. She and Jessica drove around the city talking to vigilantes. She didn't know how the small details worked with their relationship. All she'd done in the past was stop guys from committing crimes and keep them in place until the police arrived. Once they did, Violet got money, a pat on the back, and that was it.

"How was I supposed to know this was a secret? You never tell me anything!"

"Because... you're... an *idiot*! And usually, when it comes to idiots, the less they know, the less they could fuck me. But apparently that's not the case in this scenario."

A tent citizen caught Violet's eye as he passed the police cruiser on his way to the underpass. He looked worried. It was never good when someone from the tent city was yelled at by police, especially right next to the bridge. This was the closest most cops would come after Sam's incident with Jessica. Violet wished he would stay close. Being alone felt dangerous here.

Johanson sighed and rubbed his face. "Who else knows?"

"What do you mean? I told Sam and now I told you that I told Sam. I don't go around yelling that I'm a vigilante, living alone and unprotected in an underpass tent. You may think I'm stupid, but I'm not that stupid."

"So no one else knows that you told Sam... what you told him."

"No one."

"You didn't tell any other cops. You haven't told Jessica."

"You're the only one I talk to. How would I have told anyone?"

"Got it. Got it," Johanson said. His eyes searched for something in the dark sky above. "Look, let me tell Jessica... what you've done. What you told Sam. And don't bring it up to her unless she says anything to you directly. She gets even angrier about this stuff than I do. And if it gets back to me that you've been running your damn mouth, don't think I won't have a problem bringing you in. You may think you're hot shit, picking up a couple of small drug dealers and stopping muggers, but you're nothing. I could find a million Violets in this city. And you're lucky I still need you in this area."

He slammed his car door as he started driving away. The siren sounded twice to get a group of homeless people out of the way as he turned the corner. It was a bunch of crap. How was she supposed to know paid vigilantism was a secret? No one had told her that before.

Maybe she just wasn't as good at evaluating situations as she thought. Johanson hadn't told her getting paid was a secret, but she should have been able to figure it out for herself. She wasn't a cop, and was being paid by cops to do a cop's job. Looking at it straight forward, something was out of place. But there was nothing she could do to change that now. Just keep her mouth shut in the future and work to keep getting terms.

Davey's shack trembled when Violet knocked. It was better than a tent, but she was amazed the place could stand against even a light breeze. Davey came out, brushing his teeth. Violet couldn't remember the last time she'd seen him without a toothbrush in his hand or tucked into his shirt pocket. He was obsessive about his teeth, constantly telling tent citizens that the best way to a good first impression was a healthy smile.

"Wasn't sure if you heard, but Sam's been arrested. It happened a few weeks ago. He's not going to be a problem anymore."

Davey spat the toothpaste out in a thick white glob. His eyes went wide like a cartoon's and he held his arms out. "That's great news! How'd they find him?"

"Well, that's actually the main reason I came by. I was the one who stopped him. I've, uh, been working as a vigilante. Stopping bad guys—well, criminals—getting them to the cops." *Getting paid to do it.* She stopped herself before the words tumbled out. Stupid. "I should have told you what I was doing. I'm sorry for not being honest. But I think there's an opportunity for us here."

Davey didn't interrupt. The only sound coming from him was the brushing of teeth. Violet asked, "What if I became sort of a... resident vigilante for the tent city? I could work in the underpass and the areas around it. If people start fighting or getting worried about something, I could calm things down. I don't want to take over your position, I'd just be more feet on the ground. Eyes up close and personal with the problems. You'd still have your contact with Jessica, and I'd call a different cop if the police ever needed to be involved."

Davey kept brushing, the foam in the corner of his mouth growing. Violet hated talking this much, and now the silence answered her. "So basically what Silky did before he went crazy, right?" Davey spat out another glob, this one mostly just saliva. "We don't really like the police coming down here. Especially after what Sam did. If there were any disputes, I'd prefer they were settled internally. Within the community—tent citizens all fending for themselves and representing themselves. But this is a good middle ground. That's important here, that compromise. It'll be good to have a little weight to swing to settle things down, but if someone doesn't care about the community they're a part of, they can be shipped on to the police for them to deal with."

The brush entered his mouth again, dry aside from spit. "I think it's a good idea."

There it was.

A salary offer. Approval from the underpass. Guaranteed food, guaranteed water. And eventually, when it wasn't worth throwing herself into danger anymore and she'd saved enough money, she'd get out of the underpass and into an apartment. Into a home.

They should have given this to her earlier. The police didn't have any idea how to handle the homeless and their lack of knowledge made them overly cautious about making decisions.

But Violet was agile. A single person. She could show up to a tent if there was an argument, get it settled, and send it up to the police if she had to. She could make sure people living around the underpass didn't harass them. No one could use it as a police-free hiding place after committing a crime. No one could say it was a lawless group of hobos leeching off Hamington. Violet was there to make sure of that. She was an official extension. A weapon for the police.

Instead of reading books that night, zipped up in her tent and closed off from the rest of the city, she sat on the doormat outside, hockey mask tucked at her back, listening for disputes. Listening for violence. Listening for any way she could be of some assistance.

CHAPTER THIRTY-THREE

JESSICA

SHE THOUGHT SHE would have gotten accustomed to it by now. Johanson was sick of hearing about it. Hell, she was even tired of talking about it. But the smell of homeless people made her gag. The thought of them sleeping in garbage, surrounded by soiled diapers and half-eaten hamburgers squirming with maggots triggered a gut reaction.

She knew it was unfair. They couldn't do anything about it and some of them even made attempts to wash themselves. But even when she spoke to the cleaner ones like Davey, she tasted acid on the base of her tongue thinking about how long it had been since they'd even seen a bar of soap. Roaches probably crawled over that toothbrush he was always using. A half-assed attempt at hygiene.

Germs and disease and sickness ran rampant down there. It was like the homeless method of depopulating the tent city. Weaker, older bums got sick and never recovered, leaving space for the healthier ones. Six months later, some of those healthy hobos would be the sick ones making room for new hobos, and so on. It was a cycle that somehow never seemed to clear them all out.

The image of those dying hobos flashed through her mind as she walked by the underpass. She breathed through her mouth and refused to imagine what organisms or bacteria were landing on her tongue. Tried not to let her face bend into a disgusted frown. She took small steps down the decline into the mud of the tent city.

The corner where Sam had attacked her was still there. The wall. The platform of pallets puzzled together like some kind of stage. She turned from it quickly and walked deeper into the tent city before her memories took over. She asked a group of hobos warming their hands by a burning barrel if they knew where Violet was. One pointed toward a tent and started whispering to his friend when Jessica left, probably asking why the police were coming into the underpass to talk to her.

None of the officers came down here. Not after what Sam had done to her. There was an understanding that once you walked down that decline, your badge didn't mean shit anymore. No respect would be given, no authority would be allowed. The tent city was an illegal squatter community that couldn't be officially acknowledged by the government. If the police couldn't even admit it existed without risking being sent to the hospital, how were they supposed to have any kind of control over it?

She tapped one of the tent's support poles with the toe of her boot. "You in there?" A rustling sound came from inside as Violet swam through garbage. Her head popped out of the front flap and she flinched when she saw Jessica. They hadn't spoken since Sam had killed the Hamington Hunter. Jessica nodded toward the border of the underpass. Violet zipped her tent and tucked things under a welcome mat before leaving. They didn't say a word until they'd come up the incline and were far enough from the tent city for prying ears.

"Look... I want to thank you for bringing Sam in. I'm not sure if you know, but he's the reason my face looks the way it does."

Violet nodded without a word, her eyes never meeting Jessica's. They were too busy watching people pass by. Across the street, down the block, in the shadows. She was the same as other vigilantes Jessica had met. Paranoid. It was disconcerting that the people fighting crime had the same visual cues as criminals checking for cops or opportunities to score. Always aware, always watching.

"How's everything going with his case?" Violet asked.

"His court date's coming up soon. He's using some piece of shit public defender that doesn't know the difference between his armpit and his asshole. Sam won't be a problem for you or me anymore. Won't be a problem for anyone. Someone's going to make him a wife in prison and then his multiple life sentences will get a hell of a lot shorter." She couldn't wait to see the look on Sam's face as he realized he had no power in the courtroom. No control. But for now, she'd settle for him knowing what was slowly coming his way. That there was no way he could stop it.

After what happened in the underpass, her therapist said her anxiety attacks and nightmares and sense of guilt came from a case of PTSD. Feelings that she shouldn't have been in the underpass that day doing her job. A survivor's guilt that it was her fault she'd been attacked, not Sam's. She'd surprised herself with how little she'd reacted to seeing him during processing at the jail. Cuffed and injured, he had no command of the situation. She was the one in control.

It was cathartic, laying all of his crimes out in front of him. Seeing the look of fear when he realized he'd attacked the wrong cop. When he realized she hadn't rolled over and crawled into a hole, hideous and injured because of what he'd done. After the interrogation, she left work early and let herself cry before pouring herself a drink. She was alive. She was healthy. And she was a professional that was going to move past a workplace injury and do her fucking job.

"I understand you have bad blood with him," Violet said. "I get that. He's done terrible things. But more than that, honestly, I think he's just really desperate. He got into drugs at a young age and didn't have a lot of options. He strikes out at people when he feels like he's being backed into a corner, and he's terrifying. But at his core, I really don't think he's a bad guy. He's desperate and that's what makes him so... dangerous. You don't have to hate him for what he's done."

Jessica felt like the air had been sucked out of her lungs. Heat rose in her face. Her hands curled into fists, the nails digging into her palms while Violet kept talking.

Words kept flowing from Violet's fat mouth as her eyes kept dancing around, her head on a pivot looking for criminals. "There's a difference between the people that kill or rob because they have to and those that do it because they don't know any better. That wasn't Sam. He didn't have any alternatives, so he did what he could. It was still against the law, and it doesn't justify the horrible things he's done, but don't hate him for the fact that he was homeless and starving without options."

Jessica felt ready to explode. "*What*? Just desperate? Let me tell you something. I questioned him when he first came in. He had no memory of who I was, or what he did to me. I have to deal with this *fucking* face every day because he didn't like that a cop was doing her job. Usually, horribly scarring another person for life is a thing people remember. He's being charged with assault of an officer, drug possession, two counts of robbery, and three murders. *Three*! Don't give me some bullshit about striking out when backed in a corner. He's an evil human being that deserves to be torn apart by other evil people in prison.

"In fact," she said, heat still rising up her face, "once the trial's all done and the media isn't focused on the case anymore, I plan on forcing myself onto his visitation list, just so I can watch him wither away into a shell of himself for someone to break apart and get to the inside. He deserves every bit of what's coming to him, so don't you try to tell me I should feel any sympathy for him."

The nerve of this bitch. Johanson needed to lock her down and tell her what the fuck was up. They couldn't afford another underpass vigilante go off the deep end. It didn't take much to hop across those lines from vigilante to ill-advised criminal.

"I came down here to thank you for helping me get justice on an evil person, not hear that I've done something wrong by doing the right thing."

A pair of hobos walking to the underpass diverted their eyes from her as they passed, craning their necks to pretend like they hadn't been watching. Violet noticed it too. She watched them as they walked down the decline into the underpass. A cop yelling at a hobo outside the underpass wasn't anything new, but immediately pulling your eyes away from a cop in an attempt to seem casual was the most obvious criminal tell in the book. A bad poker face, Violet had called it before. She reached behind her back for something. "Are we done here?" she asked. Her eyes were still aimed toward where the two had entered the underpass.

"Yes. We're finished." Jessica watched her descend back into the tent city, limping, probably from a recent fight. She pulled a hockey mask over her face as she walked down the decline. She'd become fully indoctrinated in the insanity. Probably wouldn't live more than another year. She'd gain confidence too quickly, think she was invincible, and end up getting shot in the back in a careless moment. It happened more often than Johanson liked to admit.

Another hobo passed as Jessica was about to turn the ignition of her cruiser. They were like rats. Cockroaches. All running back into the dark of the tent city when the daylight bled out. One almost jogged toward the underpass as he passed her car, scratching at his neck and pulling at his shirt collar. It was a sight Jessica knew well. Anyone who'd ever been around a crackhead for five minutes knew those habits.

She moved her car around a corner, grabbed a jacket, and found a view to see who was returning to the tent city. Over the next ten minutes, more and more of them filtered back into their dirty home. Almost all of them showing signs of addiction. The sweating, the paleness, the scratching. These were people looking for their fix.

Was someone down there selling? Or was every pathetic sack of shit in the underpass an addicted, addled mess?

She zipped her jacket all the way up to cover her uniform. The cop shirt and badge wouldn't let her see anything. Nothing alerted a group of criminals to stop what they were doing like seeing a uniformed police officer watching them. She stood at the lip of the underpass. Nothing seemed out of place. There were the tents, the fire barrels, the people wrapped up in blankets sleeping or talking or eating. No one going around selling drugs or booze. They just kept filing in.

Another ten minutes passed. Twenty.

The temperature was dropping. She shivered and realized her fingers were losing feeling. What the hell was she doing, standing in the cold and watching these people? There was nothing to be gained from seeing addicts huddle around a fire before slinking into their tents to sweat through their withdrawals.

A final few hobos descended into the tent city, the steady flow trickling down now that the day was over. Most went straight to their tents to pass out and start the process all over again. Some walked toward the fire barrels to warm up.

A group standing by a barrel welcomed one hobo more excitedly than any of the previous ones, patting him on the back and smiling and laughing. They stayed around the barrel for another few minutes as the new guy walked around the fire and talked to each of them. Shook their hands. And then, as if on a schedule they split ways to their tents. Shakily. Scratchily. All of them around that barrel.

Holy shit. This place. It was a fucking gold mine. There were all sorts of life's rejects here. People with job problems. Gambling debts. Alcoholism. Mental illness. And then there was the good one, the most important one—addiction.

These people weren't like the ones she sold to now. If her customers didn't get their weekly 8 ball or supply of Adderal, their partying wouldn't be as much fun, but they could survive without it. These people could die if they didn't get their fix. Shit and shake themselves into oblivion. There was a reliability to that kind of business. A factor of necessity and recurrence.

It'd take effort. Some adjusting of how she got product—more crack and crystal, less weed and cocaine—some flexibility with their lack of money and ability to pay quickly. A little tolerance for dealing with the disgusting rejects of the city. But she could make a killing.

Cops hadn't come down here frequently since she'd been attacked. The only vigilante that gave a shit about the place was Violet and Jessica owned her. There was no reason not to attack it. Take it for her own. She could choke out the current dealer by selling under his purchase cost. Develop a payment and delivery system that would allow her to never step foot in the cesspool. If someone was going to get rich off this scum, it ought to be her since she was the one who'd been left for dead there. Repayment for everything she'd gone through thanks to this place. And at the end of it all, they'd still be passed out in the mud, high on product like they were now, but she'd be living on an island, sipping a pineapple drink with an umbrella and an extra shot of rum.

CHAPTER THIRTY-FOUR

TAYLOR

Taylor groaned as he sat up. Everything hurt. Everything always hurt now. He thought he would adjust to the soreness, or it wouldn't come as often, but the harder he pushed himself and the harder he trained, the more familiar the aching in his muscles and joints became.

The visits to Hudson had changed. Instead of telling his stories and knowledge like a professor, the man insisted on hearing about what Taylor was doing, how he was training, what he was eating to improve his body. The first time Taylor lied and told him he'd been following his instructions Hudson saw through it yelled at him like he was a child. "Do you think I'm trying to get you killed? That's exactly what's going to happen if you go out there without proper training."

There wasn't a way around it. Somehow Hudson could tell if he was skipping the gym or not sleeping enough to let his body heal. Taylor either had to follow through on the training or not visit Hudson at all.

At first, he told himself that that he'd made a promise to Linda and he was going to see it through, even if that meant spending all of his time training under the critical eye of Hudson. Then it became habit. He enjoyed pushing himself. Enjoyed feeling better somewhere underneath the soreness, knowing he could defend himself while walking down the street if someone attacked him. Then it became the clearest way to separate himself from the past. He wasn't sitting at a desk reporting the news. He wasn't researching how to grieve for a loved one. He was improving himself.

When he was still regularly getting in front of the camera as a news anchor, he would eat a light breakfast after he woke, visit the gym for sit-ups and bicep curls while watching the morning news segments, shower, then get to the station to work on whatever story he would be reporting later that night. It was easy and comfortable.

Now he was up hours before the sun. He ran through dozens of bodyweight movements to help the lactic acid filter out of his muscles while drinking a quart of water and preparing for the five-mile run that completed his morning ritual. After the run came half an hour of yoga to improve ligament flexibility and a large breakfast balancing proteins, fats, and carbohydrate macronutrients. Depending on the day of the week, he would either pack his bag for Krav Maga classes then catch a cab across the river or go straight to train in the library while Hudson supervised from his wheelchair in the corner of the room. The old man could still yell that Taylor had screwed something up when he wasn't drowning in his lungs.

Somewhere along the way, he stopped calling Jake to send the progress reports on the interviews and switched to emails. Then those got shorter with each day until it didn't make sense to waste time trying to come up with something to talk about. The only indication he still had a job was the direct deposits that landed in his account twice a month. It wouldn't surprise him if those stopped without warning.

At this point, what did it matter? Hudson was right. Alice was a shadow over everything, including his job. If he woke up to find out that Brad had been permanently given the anchor's seat, maybe it would be a good thing. Force him to get outside of the shadow that hung over his time there.

Linda still met him at the door of the Hudson House when he arrived, but that was where most of their interactions ended. Since the training had picked up, she'd stopped asking him to meet for coffee. Maybe she was angry at him. He'd followed through on the lie more enthusiastically than they'd discussed. But this was her fault for suggesting it in the first place.

Of the weapons in the library, Hudson had used only a handful during his career. The rest had been post-retirement gifts from self-defense companies or shipments from sponsors who had begged him to license their products. The variety was good for Taylor. It helped him research what felt natural. What he would feel confident using if he were on the street and someone tried to attack him again. Taylor imagined his attacker's face, teeth bared, pulling back to slam the metal of the gun into the side of his head, only for Taylor pull out a weapon of his own.

For the non-lethal approach, there were sap gloves, filled with eight ounces of steel shot that allowed him to punch through concrete blocks without added force on his bone structure. Stun gauntlets that would shock an assailant on impact. Spring batons, tear gas grenades, more and more. On the other side of the room, the lethal weapons hung on racks. Pistols, shotguns, assault rifles, and SMGs all in a row. Knives ranged between finger-length switchblades to machetes that could be used as small swords. Taylor trained with them all. He pummeled and diced mannequins in the library. Shot hundreds of targets to shreds against the wall Linda had pointed out the first time they visited the library.

The hand-to-hand weapons came naturally to him after his Krav Maga training. The sap gloves were heavier, stronger versions of the UFC gloves he normally used. The baton was easy to hide and acted as an extension of his arm. Concealability was a key factor to everything. Every time he shot targets on the firing range, Hudson ended the session telling him if he dressed in the standard Hudson uniform of dark jeans and a black peacoat, he couldn't have any weapons attracting attention. A man with two guns strapped to his back when wearing a skin-tight spandex outfit was a hero. If that same man with assault rifles wore the street clothes of Hudson, he would be considered a terrorist.

It was easy to slip into the lie. After his shoulder started to get sore from target practice, he'd rerack the weapons on the wall and remind himself he wasn't going to be patrolling the streets with guns or knives or any other weapons. Now that he was familiar with them, maybe he'd have the self-defense gear on hand for walking around the city, but this was mostly just for Hudson. Just for show.

After a few weeks, Hudson missed the first training session in the library. And then a few days later, he missed another. Linda brushed off Taylor's questions about what was happening and just said, "Don't be stupid. You know he's sick. You don't have to keep doing this."

He pushed to continue on without him. He'd made a promise to Linda to help her father find peace before he died. Taylor wasn't going to let her down now that Hudson was getting worse. These were the important days of the lie. Making sure Hudson felt like he had an impact at the end of each day, in case something terrible happened to him in the night.

There was a struggle to the days without Hudson. Taylor wanted to get better now that he was getting stronger and more adept with the weapons, but without the presence of the wheelchair-bound totem telling him how to progress, or how to improve his fighting technique, the only practice he could use was repetition. Breaking down an attacker's pistol was easy when that attacker was a mannequin frozen in place. An actual assailant wouldn't be that kind. He thought about the alley. The man who attacked him, slamming the gun against his head. Taylor had to push harder.

When Hudson wasn't there, Taylor had to resort to researching tactics online. He watched police training videos of how to take down aggressors, read articles on pressure points that would incapacitate a criminal, studied how to talk his way out of an arrest. He built up a library of techniques and methods in his mind, but he knew if someone attacked him again, he'd have a hard time remembering those strategies through the fog of adrenaline. The human touch in his training was being lost.

For all the resources and weapons on hand, he was nothing more than the other vigilantes on the street. Lonely men and women who thought they could change the world.

The library felt emptier without Hudson. At first, it was odd to even be in the house without the man at his side. Taylor adjusted to it, but he missed talking to him. If there was anyone who could push him through what he was doing, it was Hudson. Every time he stayed in the sunroom instead of coming to the library, Taylor tried to visit him, but Linda appeared out of a hidden corner or seemingly empty hallway and stopped him just short of the doors.

"You don't understand. I need to see him. I feel... lost."

"Taylor, he's not your coach," she said. "It was your decision to follow through this much. If you can't do it without some sort of guidance, maybe you shouldn't do it at all. He can't see you train now. You don't have to keep going."

It pushed him even harder. He lived and breathed for the idea of the combat. If he wasn't going to get advice from Hudson, he had to do it on his own. Had to live in it. Bathe in the training and violence like warm sunlight. Imagine what he'd have been able to do if he was there when Alice was killed.

After his Krav Maga sessions, he stopped at the grocery store to buy lunch before returning to Hudson's. The salad bar was his first stop, putting down a base layer of lettuce and grabbing spoonful after spoonful of cubed meats and nuts and hardboiled eggs. One day he saw his co-anchor and said hello to her. She stuck her hand out for him to shake and said, "It's always nice to meet a fan."

He looked down at her outstretched hand. "Vanessa. It's me. Taylor Gardner."

Her eyes searched his for a moment, then she breathed out, "Oh my God, I'm so sorry! I barely recognized you, you look great! How have you been? A little time off looks like it's been good to you!" She remembered the name of the co-worker who had sat next to her for two years, but not the face. It was her job to act respectful and composed when reading even the worst news. Lying about how good it was to see someone wasn't too far of a stretch.

Taylor didn't worry about his appearance anymore. He kept his hair buzzed short. Whenever it started getting long, he imagined the hobo grabbing it and shoving him against the dumpster in the alley. He used to have a desk jockey's pudginess that viewer testing said was relatable, now he was lean and prepared for battle. The lack of rest darkened his eyes and paled his skin.

He was no longer thick, soft Taylor Gardner. That man wouldn't have been able to stand in the cold all night on look out, prepared for whatever may come. He wouldn't have had the mental or physical stamina to train for hours on end or be comfortable with the idea of harming someone if he had to.

That version of Taylor wasn't him anymore. He wouldn't call out to old friends in the grocery store, couldn't worry about his fiancée and the life they had lost. That was in the past and he had to move forward. They were distractions. They had no purpose in the world of Hudson. And that's where he lived now.

With no one else around him, nothing holding him back, holding him accountable for dressing up in a coat and tie and combing his hair, Hudson was the only purpose. The only goal.

In the library, deep within the house east of the river, he clenched his fists and struck a wooden fighting mannequin. Again. And again.

Taylor would have winced from the impact. Hudson did not.

CHAPTER THIRTY-FIVE

"Okay, let's review this again." It felt like the hundredth time Sam and Frye had gone over it all. It had to be more for the lawyer's sake than Sam's at this point. Even though he dressed nice like the lawyers on TV, giving him information was like pouring water into a cracked cup. Everything slowly dripped out, eventually getting bone dry and having to be refilled with the exact same shit. "First, the drug bust: you were…"

Sam stared at him. The mole on Frye's face, the way his mouth got wet in the corners, the thick glasses. Even looking at him pissed Sam off. That cop really had done the job right, sticking him with this guy. No judge would be able to get past the throat clearing and the nose rubbing and foot fidgeting. He was fucked.

"Sam. Samuel. It's very important we review this. We can't have you misspeaking when you're on the stand. Everything has to line up."

He wanted to slam the man's face against the desk. Sam pushed his jaw forward. Felt his neck strain. "Don't worry about me. I've got it all down. During the bust those years back, I wasn't the dealer. I moved out of the apartment months ago, but the landlord didn't file the paperwork. The stuff in the apartment wasn't mine since I was already living on the street and wasn't trying to take it."

"And the drug test..."

"Yeah, and the test I took when I got arrested shows I don't have anything in my system. I don't do anything with drugs."

"Good. That cuts your link to the murder. Next, the assault on—"

"Do you really think just telling these people I didn't live there anymore will make them think it wasn't my apartment?"

Frye smoothed his tie. "Well you said you didn't have many personal items there, right? At least things someone would be upset about leaving behind? Fingerprints say you were there, plus drugs at levels that indicate intent to distribute, but there's nothing to prove your ownership. I can try to say it's circumstantial, but you don't have an alibi. No records of living on the street. It's the best I can do. Now, please. The assault on Officer Sanders."

Best he could fucking do. Story of Sam's life at this point. Put it on the damn gravestone when all of this was over. He had to be better than this guy if he was going to survive here. "After recently relo... re-locationing—"

"Relocating."

Sam forced the words out as his hands gripped together under the table. Fancy law degree thought he had to step in whenever Sam couldn't remember a word. "After relocating to the streets, I experienced a brief mental breakdown and attacked Officer Sanders. Now that I have recovered my state of mind, I am terribly sorry that I did such a thing. But due to the... the..."

"Superficial."

"Superficial damage to her face, she's been chasing me down to get revenge for what I did during my impaired mental state."

"Beautiful," Frye said. "Remember to really play that up. Not guilty by reason of insanity won't play without that being spelled out well. Juries have been relatively lenient on defendants with mental issues recently, so this is really the lynchpin of our entire argument."

Sam didn't know shit about this stuff. He'd always been able to defend himself with his fists. But now he was forced to talk out the issues people had with him. His attacker would be wearing a suit fifteen feet away with cops all around. How was he supposed to fight against that? And Frye was supposed to be the one protecting him?

It would be almost impossible to get out of all of this clean. If it wasn't Violet, it would be the cop. If it wasn't the cop, it would be the ghost of drug dealers past from years ago. Something was around every corner and the only one who could help was Frye. The twitching idiot Sam would have to find a way to pay if he did somehow stay out of jail.

The lawyer had thrown around the idea of pleading the case out, which would probably wind Sam up with only one life sentence that could be shortened to thirty or forty years with good behavior and volunteer work and meetings with psychiatrists. He had listed the options to Sam in a bored voice, like trying to decide what candy bar to eat during his lunch break—nothing seeming very appealing, but it was nice to have choices. At the end of their conversations, Frye always put his jacket back on, shook Sam's hand, and walked into the open sunlight. Sam was re-chained and escorted back to his cell.

Jail wasn't as bad as he'd expected. He had no control over when he did anything or the people he was around or the random bunk searches or the bars on the doors or the lack of time outside. But he had a bed to sleep on, a roof over his head, and three meals a day. If they pled the case, he would have a lifetime of this. Guaranteed shelter and food, traded off for not making decisions for himself. Or he and Frye could fight the case and pray for a good jury that would say he was innocent of all crimes.

A crazy longshot. But it would mean no more cops chasing him. A clean beginning. A longshot, but possible. He would only have the clothes on his back, but he'd still have a jacket to keep him warm. And he'd never have to step into one of these concrete boxes again.

Frye's voice, nasally and clogged, brought him back. "Next, there's the pawn shop. For that, we're going to say..."

"I committed the robbery under pressure from Violet. She was the one who killed the owner because he'd screwed her on deals in the past. It started with Violet and the owner playing some arcade game and then she threw him on the ground, choking him while telling me to rob the place or I'd be next."

"And you conclude with?"

"Find Violet and get her fingerprints. They'll match the prints from the arcade game, if the cops did their jobs."

"And finally, the vigilante."

"I did rob the gas station. That was out of desperation. The vigilante was searching specifically for me after Officer Sanders ordered him to."

"Ordered? What do you mean 'ordered?'" Frye asked, practicing his own lines.

"When Violet handed me over to the police, she was given a wad—sorry, a large sum—of money. She told me that she and other vigilantes were hired by the police to work outside the law. Specifically by an Officer Johanson and Officer Sanders. They illegally took me into custody."

"At which point, the prosecution goes on the defense, not knowing we would take this route ahead at all, and we reach for a mistrial. Very nicely done, Sam."

It was nicely done. He didn't need Frye to tell him that. While practicing for the stand, Sam remembered he was good at memorizing shit. He should have been an actor or something. Make millions of dollars by reading words. It felt too easy, like a few days of practicing responses to questions would be enough to keep him out of prison. But Frye was the only lawyer he had and if that's what he said he had to do, that's what he would do. Anything Sam could do to help the weak-looking man defend him. Maybe it would be different if he had money to pay a real defense lawyer out of an office in East H with an intern to cart around his paperwork. But those weren't the cards he'd been dealt.

Dealt cards. He felt a smile crawl across his face. It was the stupid kind of thing Violet would say.

Sam had gotten over his anger at her while in jail. Turn in your friend to make easy money and not worry about getting chased by the cops? No question. Sam probably would have done the same thing if their positions were switched. But that didn't change the fact that Sam was on the short end of Violet's plans, even after the years they'd been through together on the streets.

Maybe there was no love in Violet's heart for Sam. Maybe the friendship Sam stole and killed for didn't exist. If they went to court, he'd throw her connection with the police back at her, in front of the judge and jury and everyone else in the courtroom. That was the best way to do it. Sanders, Johanson, Violet, they'd all go down. If he pleaded out for a few comfortable decades in prison, nothing would happen to any of them. Was it worth putting himself in a box to make sure the others got sent to theirs too?

"Have you thought any more about if we should make a deal or not?" Sam asked Frye.

"The public defendant in me says we should," Frye said. He laced his fingers and perched them on his tub of a stomach. "It'll be easy and you stand much better chances of eventually getting out of prison. With a trial, the entire process will take a long time. In full transparency, I won't get paid any more. And there is a very large chance you'll be in prison the rest of your life.

"But the big-time defense lawyer in me says there's a chance we win and you don't go to prison at all. Then you'll get a fat settlement for pain and suffering and I come back to the real world of law. At the end it's entirely up to you. I'm comfortable with either way forward." He pushed his glasses farther up the bridge of his nose and pinched his nostrils. A deep sucking sound came from his sinuses.

Sanders was right. Sam didn't stand a chance with this guy. No spine. No chance of getting out of this situation, even if he pleaded the case. There wasn't a question here. He'd been on the run his entire life. He ran from home as a kid. Ran from his old gang. Ran from cops and murders and drug deals and robberies. All of it had dropped him here. Running had never worked before. Why would it now?

No, he had to take them on. Headfirst. Go down in a nasty ball of flames, scorching and burning as many people as possible. They would all burn, with him standing in the center. There was no other option. They had to burn.

CHAPTER THIRTY-SIX

VIOLET

NO MATTER HOW she tried to distract herself, Jessica's words continued to ring in her skull. *I want to watch someone break him apart and get to the meat inside.* She'd said it with such anger. Such disdain. She wasn't happy with the idea of Sam just getting put away, no matter how long he would be in jail. She wanted him to get assaulted and killed in prison. Reveled and delighted in the idea. But she didn't know Sam the way Violet did. He'd never allow someone the upper hand on him.

He was a terror. Always working, always moving. It's what he'd been trying to do with the pawnshop robbery. It was a move made through lack of options, and it went further than Violet was comfortable, but she knew Sam felt it was the only way for the two of them to survive in the underpass. That same desperation drove him to murder.

There were nights when Violet couldn't get the images out of her head. Jakob's legs flailing as Sam strangled him to death. Slamming against the floor. Scratching and pressing Sam's face away. It was an evil thing that Sam had done. But if someone took a chance on him and worked to help him get out of his cycle of violence and anger, he might be able to climb away from the path he was on. It wasn't his fault he'd been the child of a meth addict in a bad neighborhood, or that the only childhood role models he had were the gang members that lived in his apartment block. Maybe if he had two married parents with a golden retriever and a private school education he wouldn't be as violent or quick to anger. Definitely not as desperate.

But rehabilitation and second chances weren't what the police were there for. They wanted someone dangerous off the street and didn't care if a shitty lot in life explained what Sam did. So Violet did the job they asked her. Turned in a criminal and the soup can of cash got heavier. Sam trusted her on the pawn shop job and in return she took him to the cops. He kept saying he was trying to help her, but as soon as he put his hands around Jakob's throat, everything turned upside down and they weren't on the same side anymore. There was no forgiving Sam for dragging her into that pawn shop, but after everything they'd gone through, handing Sam over to the police still hurt.

Violet didn't know the backgrounds or life stories of the other criminals she turned in to the police. She didn't want to know. It was a job and it got her money. That's all that mattered. Not whether or not Sam was right that she was just a bounty hunter. Or if Violet was to blame for the pawn shop and everything that followed because she gave Sam the information he asked for. She helped get criminals to the cops and got paid for it. Eventually, she'd get off the street because of it. None of the rest mattered.

Being checked on by Johanson and Jessica didn't help her get any work done. If she had to make herself available every time they dropped by, it defeated the purpose of being a vigilante in the underpass. The more tent citizens saw her talking to cops beside their cruisers outside the underpass, the less comfortable they would be around her. It was becoming harder to find out the things happening in the underpass that residents didn't want the police to know about.

So when her phone buzzed and signaled a text from Jessica, she almost threw the damn thing out of the tent to die in the snow. But she didn't have an option. Jessica and Johanson were necessary evils. The only way for her to get the money she needed to escape the underpass. "Meet me at 0230 two blocks from regular spot. Won't be in a police vehicle," it read.

Jessica had only come by a few times since she'd told Violet how excited she was about Sam's future in jail, but it had never been in the middle of the night like this. She always came in a cop car and official uniform during the bright of day. Why now? Did Johanson tell her she'd told Sam about getting paid? She started pulling on her boots and stretched her joints out. Patrolling the area would keep her mind awake. Ready for whatever was coming to her.

Outside of the underpass, snow came down sideways, blown in hard lines that pummeled anyone stupid enough to venture out into it. Violet kept her jacket buttoned tight and squinted in the wind. Her eyes watered and lips cracked. Bad weather that kept people inside usually gave criminals free rein to rob and deal with fewer witnesses, but this was too rough for even them. There were no disturbances in the neighborhood surrounding the underpass or active underground casinos to stake out and survey. She was almost disappointed. Something about attacking criminals made her feel like she was making the underpass and the rest of the city better. Without criminals to stop, she was just like everyone else.

It was a familiar feeling. The pressure to never stop moving forward or else she'd fall behind. It was the same one she had every time she joined a card game to try to drag herself out of the money hole she'd dug.

A car behind her tapped its horn. She turned and the SUV flashed its lights. She hadn't noticed it before. When she came closer, the passenger door opened. She got in rubbing her hands together, hoping the feeling would come back to them soon. The dashboard lights turned Jessica's face a bright red Violet couldn't see from outside the car. The color changed the scar on the bottom half of her face into a Halloween mask, alternating between deep valleys and unnaturally smooth plains. Someone on the radio spoke in low volume. Violet nodded to her and blew into her hands. Jessica stayed silent. Cocked her head to the side while continuing to look out the windshield at the swirling snow outside.

"Can I trust you?" she asked.

"I... feel like I've earned that. After Sam and everyone else I've brought in."

Violet felt her muscles tense. She'd learned when situations were close to turning bad and something smelled wrong about this.

"I don't feel like I can." Jessica turned to her, half her face illuminated in the bright red of the dashboard, the other hidden in darkness. "Violet, I like you. That's no bullshit. You and I won't ever be friends or get together outside of work, but you do your job well and I respect that. So I wanted to give you a heads up. There have been talks. Whispers and rumors really, that there's a drug dealer staying in your tent city, even though you've been working there as a resident vigilante for almost a month. That makes Johanson... uneasy."

Violet scanned through the roster of tent citizens in her mind. Did more live there that she was unaware of? Davey didn't allow the obvious addicts into the city. He said they brought violence and attention which were best avoided whenever possible. The only drug users allowed were the ones going through planned detox, forced to get clean because they couldn't afford their poisons.

She shook her head. "No way. I spend too much time down there—hell, I live down there—looking for things going down to miss someone dealing. The only trouble I've seen lately has been people getting too drunk or shoplifting or getting in fights. Nothing like a drug ring."

"Are you saying you're not good at your job?"

She sucked her lips back behind her teeth. No one could do the job she was doing. Balancing the connection between the tent city and the police while still acting like a normal tent citizen during the daytime. It was important no one down there knew what she was doing, or else they'd clam up so much that she'd quickly become worthless. Jessica and Johanson weren't making that easy.

"No. I'm saying it doesn't exist."

"My source says it does. So now there's a conflict. Between the two of you, who am I more likely to believe is wrong? Or worse, you do know of a drug ring down there and you've just decided not to get rid of it. Enjoying the profits a little too much?"

Jessica punched the lights on in the car. Violet winced in the bright white light.

"What are you—"

"Show me your arms." Jessica shoved the sleeves of her jacket up and inspected the soft skin on the inside of her elbow for track marks. Violet yanked away from her hold.

"I don't mess with any of that stuff," she said, rolling the sleeves back down.

Jessica brushed hair from off her face. The full light of the car exposed dark circles under her eyes. "Okay, okay. There's only one step from here. You have to find whoever is selling drugs in the underpass and bring them to us. Because right now Johanson isn't listening to me. He thinks you're involved. I've tried to tell him you aren't and you're doing a good job, but you need to help me convince him. So you need to find the dealer or Johanson is going to cut you loose." Violet saw herself fighting criminals, bringing them to the front steps of the police station, only to be met by Johanson with his arms crossed, shaking his head. No money for the help she gave. No money for the food she needed.

Was Johanson setting her up? Making her pay for what she slipped to Sam?

"Terms? I haven't been getting many from Johanson lately."

"You don't understand. I'm helping you out here. Going behind my own colleague's back. If he knew I was talking to you about this, he'd rip me a new one. You cannot discuss this with him at all, or you and I won't be able to have these conversations anymore.

"I think you're telling the truth and you really don't know

what's happening in your backyard. Do this and prove to me that you're not protecting the primary dealer of the area that's been assigned to you, then you'll earn back Johanson's trust and solidify mine even more."

None of this made sense. Neither of them came into the underpass. At most, they parked outside and asked her questions. Violet was always on the lookout for crimes going on down there. There was no way Jessica was right. Either Johanson was trying to cut her off or someone was selling them lies to get her in trouble.

It had to be Davey. It was the easiest answer. Maybe he felt like Violet was taking too much authority. She thought the two of them had been working well together, avoiding stepping on each other's toes, but what if that was an act? No, that couldn't be it. Davey didn't know about the vigilante connection with the cops and he didn't have anything to gain from telling them there was a dealer in the underpass.

"Where are you getting this info?" she asked. "This can't poss—"

Jessica put her hand up and shook her head. "I've said too much. I can't tell you anymore. Do your job. Take out the dealer. Or this relationship is over."

She wanted to punch something. Jessica had her by the throat. If she kept pressing, she'd lose her terms. If she lost her terms, she lost her right to the title of vigilante and the only thing that made her any different than everyone else living in the underpass. If she wasn't a vigilante, what was she? Just a hobo who got in fights?

There was no way to argue. If there was a drug dealer in the underpass managing to hide from Violet, she'd find him. If there wasn't, she'd have to get creative. Find a dealer from West Ham. Restrain him. Maybe beat him to the point he couldn't speak. Break his jaw or cut his tongue out. Beat him until he couldn't deny he'd never been anywhere near the underpass.

"Fine," Violet said. "I'll find him."

CHAPTER THIRTY-SEVEN

JESSICA TURNED THE car on to signal for Violet to leave, but more importantly, to start filtering out the sickly sweet smell of her sweat and dirt. Violet didn't seem to notice the air fresheners she'd hung in front of all the vents in the car or the plastic wrap she put over the seat to stop her stench from sinking into her car like it had in the office. She refused to let Violet's odor chase her around the city.

She looked scared when they started talking. Too nervous about the situation to do anything other than keep her eyes on Jessica's face as she spoke. Waiting for Jessica to bark at her like every other cop she'd dealt with while living in the underpass. As she shut the door and walked back toward the underpass in the snow, her head down like a whipped dog, Jessica knew she had her.

She'd done a good job getting Sam arrested—probably the first thing she'd done right in years. It was something she should've felt proud about and showed that she was actually worth the air she breathed. The cops hadn't been able to find Sam after any of his crimes. And then along came this little hobo who managed to get him back to the underpass and attack him when he least suspected.

Of course, she couldn't tell Violet any of that. The moment she complimented her, Jessica would lose power. Instead, she insinuated Violet wasn't good at her job, that her performance at the responsibilities she'd earned was subpar, and Violet wanted to prove her wrong. It was easy. Malleable clockwork like a starving child doing anything it could to get a piece of candy.

It was a beautiful plan. By getting Violet to take out the current dealer, Jessica would have no competition, a hungry customer base, and a perfectly scheduled notification once the territory was available for takeover. As long as she didn't disobey her orders and speak to Johanson, she'd be fine. Johanson knew she got blow for him and a few other friends but wasn't aware of how big of a player she'd been before the drought hit.

Thanks to Violet and this new plan, she'd be able to recover from the drought almost completely. And more. This new business would let her get into the dirtier drugs most of her customers avoided while the supply on luxuries was still down. The narcotics division of the force hadn't seized any of her usual products in the past six weeks, but crystal, crack, all of that backwoods and inner-city shit was still arriving into the evidence closet like clockwork. The drought just forced her to adapt earlier than she wanted. Jessica always knew she'd only be able to skim off the top of the same drugs for so long before someone noticed the weight discrepancies.

She drove along the river, stopping sometimes to look across at East H. What was there to do until Violet found the dealer? She was so used to constantly working. Either at the station or selling late at night. Whatever she had to do to keep Sam's face out of her mind.

She'd kept it together when she saw him at the station, but afterward she went back home, locked the door, poured a drink, and ran her fingers along the scars until they turned numb. Tried to put down enough whiskey to kill the brain cells holding on to the memory of what happened.

Forget the drink now, she just needed a good lay. Someone

to really bang her brains out, leaving them splattered against the headboard. Make her forget about the evidence closet's limits and the operation she asked Violet to take on and Sam DeWitt's sharp, sneering face. She scrolled through her phone at a red light, looking for someone who could give her what she needed.

The light changed from red to green twice before a car behind her honked. She drove around the corner and pulled over, hitting the emergency light out of habit. Swiping up on the names in her phone faster and faster. No one from the contact list jumped out at her. The only person she knew could do the job was Parker, but that wasn't even close to the definition of a good time. She wasn't sure that the flopping he did even met the definition of sex in general. But there was no one else.

He was groggy when he answered, confused about why she would call him this late.

She dropped her voice into a low moan. "I need it. I need you, baby. So badly." Whatever desperation she felt like he needed to hear.

She heard Parker move the phone and fumble it from one hand to another. "I already have someone over here," he said. His voice came through muffled, like he had his lips pressed against the phone and was whispering. "Maybe... maybe we can do something next week."

The call ended. The headlights flashed along to the polite emergency rhythm in the car. Dark to light. Tick tick tick.

Fat, flopping Parker turned her down. Her very last resort and he had completely shut her down. And there was someone with him.

She almost checked her phone to make sure she'd called the right person. He turned her down? *Parker?* The man with the sweaty upper lip? The man tiger-striped with stretch marks? Who the fuck did he think he was? And what kind of disgusting slut had he convinced to share his bed?

Jessica punched the emergency light button and the ticking sound shut up. She couldn't let her thoughts get ahead of her.

He'd only said someone was there. Not that it was a woman or someone in his bed. Maybe it was a family member in town. Or a friend. Or something.

No.

It was a woman. Another woman. And she had given Parker what Jessica thought no one else would.

What if he wasn't going to need her at all anymore? What could she do or give him in exchange for the drugs if not her sex? She had all these plans. The house on the river she'd already drawn blueprints for in her mind. There was the boat, a small catamaran that would be docked on the water, waiting for her to sail on the breeze while she drank her morning coffee. That life suddenly didn't seem so clear. The image blurred.

There was no other way to get the drugs without Parker. Those plans revolved around whoever this woman was and whether Parker felt obliged to return Jessica's call. The life she'd planned and wanted after she quit the force all depended on if Parker remembered how good of a job she'd done in the past. If not, none of it would matter to him anymore. Her source would be gone. She'd be back to where she was before all of this started.

Everything she'd been working toward and planning all hung by a thread. One sweaty, fat thread.

CHAPTER THIRTY-EIGHT

HUDSON

THE NIGHT USED to be his time. Darkness would wrap around him like a blanket and change him into something more than human. A legend. A protector. Now, its silence was a reminder of how little he could offer the world.

During the day, there at least was activity. Medicine to take or conversations to have or any number of smaller matters to tend to before he died. And on top of all that, there was Taylor's training.

The young man had committed to the process entirely. Some nights he'd fall asleep on the library's corner cot after hours of weightlifting and technique training and cardio and boxing, but there was only so much Hudson could do besides voice his approval or correct a misstep. He was locked into his damned wheelchair, unable to walk Taylor through the techniques and methods that used to come so naturally.

Linda tried to get him to rest as often as possible, but he could never tolerate more than a quick recharge. Some days she wouldn't even let him leave the sunroom, even though he wasn't sleeping. He tried to listen for when Taylor came and left, seeing if he could tell how hard he worked from how tired his footsteps sounded. He stayed awake for those moments. Any excuse to avoid sleeping. He hated losing too much time to sleep. Hated the feeling of waking and knowing that five or six more hours had drifted out of his grasp while he'd been unconscious.

Nothing was worse than the long, lonely sleep that came with the night. Linda didn't come by the sunroom to give him medicine. There were no sounds of Taylor training in the library. The low, static voices of the police scanner were all he heard and the only company he kept were his ghosts.

After Taylor accepted the mantle, Hudson considered recanting the offer. He stayed awake for three nights and remembered every fight. Revisited every injury, from ankle sprains to his dismemberment. It took him over a week to recover from the lack of sleep, and he was still unsure if it was the right decision. Linda had made a good point. Now that he'd convinced Taylor, was this really the life he wanted to bestow on another person?

He saw stories of other vigilantes in the news, but they were misrepresentations. Never telling the truth about the dirty, violent things that happen in the dark. They likely didn't know. The news only focused on the charismatic men and women who thrived under media coverage, and of course, only on their victories. There would be no reports of a vigilante, dressed in all black, finally crawling away from a captor that tortured him for weeks, defiling him, beating him, amputating his leg, only escaping by clenching his teeth down on what his kidnapper was trying to force in his mouth. There would be no stories of police officers begging vigilantes for help, too afraid or annoyed to risk their own lives for the city because they weren't paid enough. No reports of vigilantes breaking into a house, killing its residents in an attempt to clean up the city, only to realize they'd murdered the wrong people.

The world didn't understand them. Didn't understand the reasons they existed. And how could they? Most of the vigilantes didn't understand it themselves.

When he started, it was a question of morality. Other people ignored what was needed of them, endangering others and not living up to the expectations asked of them. It was his responsibility to pick up the slack. Each man has a duty to safekeep his neighbor. Hudson had just taken his a little further.

He readjusted in the bed. A new dull pain had settled deep inside his lower back over the past few days that he could never settle into. His mind turned over as he tried to distract himself to help fall asleep. What motivated Taylor to change his mind and accept the mantle?

Hudson knew he would never find out. That was something private to keep hidden deep inside like a motor, continuing to pound along when everything fought against him. But he thought it was a matter of love. Or rather a lack of it.

Taylor seemed to always be in pursuit of someone to love him. To need and respect him. When he lost Alice, his search began again. Now that he'd accepted she was gone and it wasn't his fault, he was looking to get that love from the city. What other options did he have? Hamington was the only thing Taylor had any semblance of a connection to.

He was proud of the kid. Taylor's motives were purer than his were in the beginning. Protect the thing that gives you what you need, protect the things you love. Hudson's first steps as a vigilante were reactions to anger. Punish people who break the law. Make them realize they all lived on an even playing field. Everyone had to follow the same rules as the man next to him. And when reprimanding the law breakers wasn't enough, his vigilantism evolved to trying to bring them justice on his own. Balance broken laws with broken bones.

It had taken years for that mentality to graduate from punishing individual people to the larger, city-wide protection Taylor was already approaching the world with. It was those kinds of things that washed away all of his uncertainties about Taylor following in his footsteps.

Taylor aspired to make the city he loved better, but he still feared for his life in a way that would make him move faster, think smarter. No one held him back. No Alice. No family. No job.

Those bastards at the news station began severing their connection with him they day they told him to take time recovering from the mugging. Asked him to only report if there was news on the Hudson interviews. What a crock of shit. They were preparing to toss him to the wind as soon as he delivered the recordings and write-ups of their conversations. Hudson stepped in where they had failed. Gave him a purpose.

Hudson readjusted in bed again. The lower back pain wasn't bothering him—he'd had enough pain in his life that he could handle a low throbbing ache—but it was present enough to not allow him to fall asleep. All this money in this big house and he still couldn't buy enough meds to push it away.

He had too much in the bank. Linda already told him she wouldn't accept money from the actions she felt had killed him. The endorsements and salaries and payments from the police. She hated all of it.

Back before he was bedridden and Taylor was still writing letters about interview opportunities, Hudson dug up information about the police terms system. The strange thing that lived somewhere along the line of bail bondsmen who turned into bounty hunters who turned into vigilantes. Back when Hudson was around, police officers had quietly pooled together money as a thank you for doing their job faster, despite not being completely within the law. Now it was some sort of instituted system, official in all but the loudest, top-heavy conversations of government.

He'd avoided telling that to Taylor. He didn't need to get distracted by the money flowing to these people. All he needed to know was that Hudson had gained a reputation from criminals and a respect toward the peacoat and ball cap from the police. Rumors spread about a man in all black hunting down criminals. Breaking down doors without notice, beating men into submission, doing all the things police couldn't, despite having all the evidence that said they should. The fear of being found by the Man in the Black scared some out of committing more crimes and others into making stupid mistakes, simplifying the cops' search for them.

Hudson chuckled to himself as he stared at the ceiling. A sharp pain went through his side. He grimaced, held his palm to it, and breathed out slowly. Tried not to focus on it. Directed his mind somewhere else.

Taylor. The most recent in a long line of reporters that had tried to dig into his story. As Hudson had started doing more good, and rumors began circulating of his actions, a special report came out in the newspaper questioning the Hamington Police, asking if they were using the vigilante known as Hudson as a tool and ally. If they were purposefully allowing him to continue operating without any kind of punishment. The Chief of Police publicly denied any connection, which did nothing to his relationship with Hudson except force their meetings and conversations to be more discreet as criminals kept winding up on the doorsteps of police stations, bound, injured, and unconscious.

Other vigilantes began appearing. Some deliberate rip-offs of Hudson wearing all black, some deciding to do things their own way. Halloween costumes were sold year-round to people who felt they needed a superhero outfit to make a difference. Organized vigilante groups took down local gangs. Individuals stopped worrying about being mocked for their costumes and intentions and threw themselves into the city's crime headfirst. It was the Wild West of Hamington.

There was a man who called himself Washington One who worked exclusively on financial crimes. Another, Peacock, cracked down on prostitution before he was killed by a pimp. All of the people dressing strangely and creeping in the night had an effect. The number of crimes decreased. The cops received fewer distress calls as criminals were dealt with on the streets. The police force was reduced to its lowest number in decades, all while the high brass continued to deny any knowledge of vigilantes in the city.

Even now, all these years later, in this uncomfortable

deathbed, he was proud of it. Like a mother of spiders as her brood left its nest and went out into the world. He created this insanity, and all he personally had to show for it was a house on a hill. But it helped the city.

There were always exceptions. People went too far. Those who tried to use the leniency around vigilantes as an excuse to get revenge or commit their own crimes. More than a few disgruntled ex-employees assaulted and delivered their former bosses to the police station, claiming that the company had been stealing or money laundering or simply overpaying their corporate executives. It became more common to settle disagreements with fists than words.

He'd moved the city along in its evolution. It was always a violent place, but that violence was hidden. Shoved down deep into the shadows of parks in the early hours of the morning, or in the underpass, or the rough intersections of difficult neighborhoods. All Hudson did was drag it out into the daylight, bleeding and screaming where vigilantes could do something about it.

At least, the good ones could do something about it. He didn't agree with the way most of them operated now, with a fist in one hand, a cell phone in the other calling the media so they could get on the news. That wasn't the point. That wasn't what it was all about.

Now he could make sure Hudson returned. To bring the focus back to the criminals. Protect the innocent. Revolutionize how this city approached crime. Again. He didn't care about the name or the legacy or any of that shit, but the title of Hudson brought weight to it. The legacy of Hudson as a vigilante was important, not Timothy Hudson the person. People would listen to what Taylor did. What he told them. And if he could convince the public, and the other vigilantes, and remind them that fighting crime was more about the city—more about the victim—than the perpetrator or the hero... then that was a legacy worth leaving.

A familiar popping sound came from his hip as he readjusted, his fake hip moving in a way the rest of his pelvis didn't agree with. It was usually quickly followed by Hudson sucking down air through his fake teeth into his liquid-filled lungs, trying to gasp in enough breath to ignore a large dull pain. That's all his life was now. Dull pain.

A weight pushed against his lungs and he tried to breathe slowly against it. Another new pain. But it would pass soon.

Days when he wished he would die in order to escape it were more frequent than the days he wanted to live a little longer. But now things were different. The years of waiting around the house for a reason to continue had passed. There was a legacy now. At a minimum, there was potential for one. He wanted to watch Taylor grow into his shoes. Make an impact on the city. Become bigger than he ever could by staring into a teleprompter. Taylor was ready for it. Hudson was returning.

CHAPTER THIRTY-NINE

TAYLOR

As he watched the phone vibrate, Taylor tried to come up with another reason why someone would be calling him from the Hudson House at four in the morning. It would be Linda. For this, it had to be Linda.

Maybe she was worried about someone lurking outside the gates. Or she couldn't sleep and wanted to talk to someone. Or even rolled over in bed and accidentally called him. But he knew why the phone was ringing. He let it go through to voicemail in a last effort to delay the urgency.

It rang again. He placed his hand on the phone, wondering what her voice would like. Choked up? Drunk?

He answered the call and waited for her to speak. He listened to her breathing on the other end of the line, heavy and steady and calm. "It happened," she said. A rock sat in his stomach. His mouth twisted into a knot.

It wasn't unexpected. The opposite of that, really. Over the past weeks, it had become a waiting game to see just how long Hudson's body and lungs could hold out. Taylor stopped sleeping on the cot in the library after Linda asked him to give their family a little privacy at the end. It was coming. He knew it, she knew it, they all did. But that didn't help with the pain.

Taylor had been given the chance to learn from a legend, squeezing every last drop of knowledge out of him before he passed. When he received that email from Linda so long ago, he'd been hoping for the opportunity to break him down and show the world that he wasn't the man from the stories of determination overcoming despair and evil. People loved a hero being brought down to their level. Larger-than-life characteristics like those from Hudson's stories rarely survived the interviews that thrived on magnifying flaws. But within the shell of the legend Taylor blamed for Alice's death, there was a human being. Someone he could relate to. A friend to talk to and rely on.

As a child, Taylor only knew him through the comic books and lunch boxes and Saturday morning cartoons. Now, he saw the real effect of Hudson's life—all of the vigilantes who protected and served where the police continued to fail. And then he eventually saw him as the mentor he became. From a behemoth to an old man in a wheelchair. Interview subject to a lecturer in a hospital bed. And now he was nothing. Dirt. Fertilizer.

He thanked Linda for calling and apologized. He was about to hang up when she said his name. Her voice was distant, like it belonged to a sleepwalker. "He left something for you. A letter in a sealed envelope. He managed to write some for a few people and stuffed them under the mattress. No one found them until... well, until they came to get his body. I'd like to get this done with quickly, if that's okay. It'll be a busy few days coming up. I'll see you in a few hours."

The call ended. He smiled at the idea of Hudson scribbling away at night while listening to the police scanner. Always about the dramatics, the old man. That had been apparent even from the start. He would take long pauses, more to pull Taylor into the stories than to catch his breath, weave in and out of his personal narrative like a professional storyteller. His timing was excellent, making jokes at the right moment or reenacting fights with gestures and punches in the air. And now he had put a bunch of letters in sealed envelopes under a mattress. The man thought he belonged in a Faulkner novel or something.

Used to think.

Taylor had trouble focusing on his morning workout routine. He paced the pushups too quickly and it was hard to gather strength for pull-ups. His run slowed after he winded himself. He tried interval sprints. Air squats. Handstand holds. Anything to keep his mind on breathing and working and pumping his legs to outrun the image of Hudson dead in his bed, lying on top of a stack of letters. He quickly threw on clothes after showering and slid a baseball hat on his head.

What was in the envelope?

The cab driver scoffed when Taylor asked him to drive to the Hudson House. "You and the rest of em," he said. "I been driving you vigilante fanboys out to East H all damn day. No one's getting return fares, so I'm wasting my time driving back and forth across the river. Absolutely ridiculous."

"What are you talking about?"

The driver glanced in his rearview mirror. "That's why you're going right? Because Hudson died yesterday?"

Taylor froze. "How did you know that?"

"You serious? It's all over the news. Another celebrity death, another news cycle. I don't even get it. What is it about this guy that's got all of you so fired up?"

"I'm not... I'm not a fanboy," Taylor said. It felt wrong talking to a stranger about Hudson's death. How did the news get out so quickly? How did anyone find out? "He was a friend of mine. I've been working with him for a few months."

"Yeah, sure. Just make sure that if you get included in the will, you remember who drove you today."

Traffic was backed up across the bridge. The suburban roads were clogged with cars parked blocks and streets and miles away. Everyone coming to the Hudson House to give their condolences. The cabbie let Taylor out half a mile from the house while his car idled and the line of impatient visitors behind him grew.

Horns honked and people yelled and no one could move an inch. It was like West Ham had flowed across the river into pristine, quiet East H.

He heard the crowd before he saw it. Vigilantes in costumes and fans with signs and children on parents' shoulders all mixed in together. A crowd where there had always been silence. He gritted his teeth. This wasn't a concert. A man had died. A man that had done a lot of good for these people. And now they were just hoping to catch a last glimpse of the famous guy in the big mansion as he got wheeled out under a sheet.

Police cruisers and news vans were parked all over the lawn outside the gate of the house, churning grass into mud. Barriers were set up to cordon off the visitors, keeping them yards away from the fence. One section of the metal barricade had flowers and candles and pictures and news clippings and dozens of black baseball hats piled up in front of it. A child took his off, put it on the ground with the others, and held his fists to his eyes as he started crying.

All of them were there. The local stations 2, 7, 13, and 68, reporters from neighboring states, even a few national channels. Broadcasters stood with the house behind them, trying to frame the perfect shot, almost yelling into their microphones to be heard over the crowd, more concerned about their meticulously phrased news segment that would be replayed over three time slots than they were about Hudson's death itself. Vultures trying to feed off the carcass of a hero. He heard the fact sheets being read as he walked by. "Timothy Hudson, better known as the former vigilante 'Hudson' passed away early this Tuesday morning. Sources have not yet disclosed the cause of death, or..." None of them noticed him listening in as he walked past.

A hand on his shoulder.

He turned, clasped the wrist. Twisted downward. The attacker gasped in pain. "What the shit, Taylor?" The man winced as he pulled against his grip. He had a familiar face and besides resisting the arm hold, wasn't fighting back. Taylor let him go, trying to remember the man's name.

He took a step back and said, "Jesus, man. You pull that karate shit on everyone you see or just your old co-workers?" It clicked. Bill. The cameraman who had been such a jackass on the first day of the Hudson interviews when he found out there wasn't going to be any visual to the story. He'd finally gotten his excuse to film about Hudson.

"Sorry about that. I, uh, you just shocked me a little bit."

"No problem, man," Bill said, rubbing his wrist. "How've you been? You look good. New haircut. I like it. You at a different station now?"

"No. Well, I'm fine. Just wasn't expecting to deal with all of this. I'm still with Action 2, I'd just been mostly working on the Hudson story before he died, so I wanted to pay my respects."

"Got it, got it. It's kind of crazy, all this, right? I mean, you start interviewin' him only a few months ago, and now he kicks the bucket? Timing's just a bitch."

Taylor nodded. What was he supposed to say to that? That he, and everyone else close to him, knew this had been coming for a long time? That Bill should speak with more respect? There was nothing to say. No conversation would explain why he and the rest of these people were here when Bill was just trying to get the station's big clip of the week.

"Hey uh... you know, he was the one that didn't want us filming, right? You were still working on the story—maybe they'd let us in now? Get some exclusive footage to show over the interview audio you have?"

The roar of the people outside the gate churned in his ears. Taylor turned and walked away before he lost control and punched Bill in the jaw. His voice followed him as he walked away, still talking, asking where he was going, if he'd said something wrong, and at the end of it suggesting Taylor crawl back into the hole he'd disappeared into for the past six months.

He shoved his way through the crowd to get to the front barrier where policemen lined up, arms crossed and ready to defend themselves if the barricades flooded over. Badges and blue shirts were the only things allowed past the metal barricades. The vigilantes who had crossed over the river to East H to pay tribute were told to stay in the crowd. Maybe it was because of the cameras. Maybe the police didn't want all of the vigilantes to get out of control.

None of the cops listened to Taylor as he tried to get their attention. He waved and shouted as they strolled in front of the barricade until eventually he decided to just climb over the metal railing. One of his legs had crossed over when two cops grabbed his arms and began shoving him back into the crowd. "Hey, hey, stop! I'm supposed to be here!" he tried to explain.

"Oh, yeah. You and every other asshole this side of the Baldwin," one cop said.

Taylor held on tight to the barricade to stop from being pushed back into the crowd long enough to say, "Call up to the house. Tell Linda that Taylor Gardner is here. I'm a family friend." The shoving stopped. The other cop leaned in closer.

"What'd you say your name was?"

"Taylor. Taylor Gardner."

The cop nodded, saying his name was on an expected visitor list, and helped him over the barricade without apologizing for almost shoving him into the mud moments earlier. A flood of people behind him started trying to crawl over as well, yelling that they needed to be let in too. Cameras flashed and voices grew louder as Taylor approached the security box.

When the gate opened, he heard a reporter yelling over the noise. "We are now seeing a man walk through the gates, into the Hudson compound. We are unsure of who this man is, but you can trust that CityView News 68 will bring you the exclusive."

The walk up the drive had become familiar over the past months, but the crowd beyond the gate transformed it. It was alien now. No longer a silent, steady walk up a hill, bordered on both sides by cherry blossom trees, but a dark tunnel, hidden from the light of day with jackals howling at the bottom. He made the mistake of looking back only once. The roaring grew, the cameras flashed, and the sea of people swelled. He went around to the back door of the house that led into the kitchen. There was no point in giving the newscasters more visuals to gossip about.

The front door he usually went to was a solid slab of majestic oak wood with a brass knocker crafted into the face of a lion. The back door was some sort of plastic wooden mix, tucked into an alcove used mostly for making deliveries and care workers sneaking cigarette breaks. Taylor knocked on the back door's window, a thin plastic sound resonating from under his knuckles.

Linda looked worse than she sounded on the phone. Her eyes were bloodshot and swollen, her hand clutched an over-used tissue. "Back door, huh? That's a first." Her voice had the thick fuzzy sound that came with crying too much.

"It's a nightmare out there. I've never seen anything like it," he said. She nodded in acknowledgement and locked the door behind him as he walked in.

"Do you want anything? Coffee? Tea? Water?" A desperate look was painted across her face. Now that Hudson was gone, she didn't have anything to do. No one to care for or worry about. He told her a water would be fine and she jetted to the sink to pour a glass.

The monitors that used to show a symphony of information with beeps and flashing lights were all quiet and dark. Linda had pulled out some of the boxes to pack the equipment but only looked to have started on a few pieces.

The house felt different without him.

Emptier.

It was unsettling.

They went to a window by the front door and peeked through the closed blinds. "I don't know who called these people," Linda said. "Someone got in touch with the press this morning and told him he'd... died. I want the hospice agency to fire everyone who worked on the last shift. It's bullshit." He took a sip from the glass and she asked if he wanted anything else.

"Look, Linda… I'm really sorry. I know it wasn't unexpected, and it's been a long time coming, but that doesn't make it any easier, and I'm just… I'm really sorry about your dad." Her eyes narrowed as she nodded again, trying to keep her eyes from over-flowing. She'd been nodding at everything he said since walking in the door, her head bouncing back and forth like it was attached to a spring.

"I appreciate that. You know…" she sniffed and rubbed her nose with the tissue, "at least this means you don't have to keep up that stupid lie anymore. We did what we needed to do. I think he felt good at the end. That he thought you were going to step in for him. I know it wasn't easy, but you'll never know how much it means to me that he finally had some peace when he went."

It was Taylor's turn to nod silently. The lie. The invitation that he could just turn it off now that Hudson was gone. "Can I um," Taylor cleared his throat and blinked his eyes clear. "Can I see the letter? I want to read it."

Linda motioned toward the doors of the sunroom. Closed. Stopping the light from flowing into the rest of the house's main hallway. He couldn't see the framed pictures or articles on the wall anymore. The walk up the hill was no longer peaceful. Doors Hudson liked open were shut and dark. A million little things were already different. Linda refused to cross the threshold of the sunroom and pointed at the seat Taylor usually took during his talks with Hudson.

The bed was no longer in the middle of the room but pushed against the back wall's outer doors with the rest of the medical equipment, waiting to be picked up by a rental company. Despite the windows letting him see out on the property and across the river to West Ham, the sunroom felt smaller without its living centerpiece. Death hung in the air. A sweet smell not completely unlike fungus and shit, as if the body started decomposing the moment his heart stopped beating. Taylor wasn't afraid of it. But he wasn't comfortable in it either.

The envelope lay on the side table, the handwriting of his name on the outside sloppy, like something a child would scribble by holding pen to paper in a clenched fist. He realized he'd never seen Hudson's handwriting until now, but the weak, curved letters didn't surprise him. The lack of mobility left in his hand coupled with arthritis in the joints probably made it painful to write.

The letter was short. Three thick black lines of ink covering the center of the page. Jagged and difficult to read, some words gave Taylor trouble. But he refused to let himself get frustrated. This was his last interaction he'd ever have with the man. He tore open the envelope and read.

TAYLOR,

SORRY I COULDN'T SEE YOU BECOME HUDSON. YOUR TRAINING IS GOOD TO WATCH. GETTING STRONGER. PROUD. YOU ARE READY. LIBRARY IS YOURS. GO TO WORK. BUT NEVER FORGET PROV 4:27. DO NOT BECOME ME. DON'T LET IT CONSUME YOU. SEE YOU ON THE OTHER SIDE.

THE FIRST HUDSON

He'd memorized the chapter Hudson told him about. The one his father read him when he was young and started down this path. Its twenty-seventh verse read, "Do not swerve to the right or to the left; turn your foot away from evil." He re-checked the letter to make sure he was reading it correctly then used his phone to make sure he wasn't mistaken.

The last communication Hudson had for him was to not be evil? No words to encourage him helping people in Hamington. No affirmation that he'd made the right choice. Had Hudson seen something in him that he thought would spoil and rot? Had Taylor done something to disappoint him? The questions were all open-ended now.

He reread the letter twice more. Maybe Linda was right and now he could leave all of this behind. Turn the interview audio into a powerful memorial piece. Get his life back. He slid the letter into his jacket and closed the doors of the sunroom behind him as he left, not wanting the death smell to follow him into the rest of the house. Linda waited beyond the threshold with her arms crossed. Her cheeks shone red and swollen. "Well?"

What was there to tell her? He wasn't sure what the letter meant. It was obviously written in his last few days of near-death delirium. A warning of avoiding evil and the plea not to become too much like him, plus the gift of the library. Taylor reached for the only thing that would satisfy her. "It... it was nothing really. He basically just said that I could keep the stuff in the library. Kind of disappointing to be honest. Anti-climactic, I guess."

Linda nodded, her eyes not coming up from the ground. Her shoulders dropped, like some tension had been released. "I'm fine with that. What was I supposed do with all of that stuff anyway?" she laughed.

They stood, no words passing between them. All the time they'd spent together was because of her father and now there was nothing new to share.

What was a world without Hudson? The city knew him as the hero who sacrificed his own life and well-being to give them a safer place to live. Taylor knew him as the damaged man that came after all that. Despite the fact that he'd been holed up in his high castle on the hill, nursing his declining health for years, he'd been a symbol of something uncompromisingly pure and good.

That was just a lie the city convinced itself of. Taylor knew the truth. He'd heard the stories of the violence and pain and all the unglamorous details of life that came with tracking down criminals and living only to harm other human beings.

But he was the creator of what had improved the lives of many.

The effect he had on Hamington was real and permanent. Even if the old man thought the new vigilantes were too focused on themselves, they were still strangers willing to be injured or killed for other strangers. Citizens dedicating themselves and their livelihoods to creating a better home for their neighbors.

Would that change now that Hudson was gone? Now that the news channels would broadcast that the invincible man—the ideal of vigilantism—had died because of his work? Taylor didn't want to know. Even with the vigilantes Hudson had inspired, the city needed all the help it could get. Whether that meant he would get back in front of the news camera to keep the public informed of what was happening in their city, or stepping into the vacuum and taking up the mantle of Hudson to inspire and serve and protect.

Taylor broke the silence in the house first, turning to walk into the library. The massive doors swung open. He watched the lights blink on to reveal the tools of violence. He grabbed an equipment bag and started loading up, the words of the letter moving through his mind. There were parts of the bible verse he'd have to file away for later. Save for when he could understand what Hudson had meant. But within the confusion, it was clear the old man was right about at least one thing.

Training had to be over now. It was time to get to work.

ACKNOWLEDGEMENTS

When I started writing this story, I had no idea what I was getting myself into. Maybe it'd be an entertaining side project in my free time. Something to do so I could say there was a direct product from my undergrad degree in Creative Writing. Now, more than half a decade later, I'm finally starting to realize how crazy I was to start this "little side project in my spare time," and how many people had a hand in it becoming what it is today. There are so many to thank from this entire process, in no particular order, that I don't really know where to start.

Mark Behr – thank you for your scholarship and foundation building. I know you told me to start with a short story because a full novel would be too overwhelming. Oops. I'm sorry it took too long to be completed for you to get the chance to read.

Dominic Wakeford—thank you for your patient editing and fielding of questions from a first-time novelist. Your words and feedback provided a level of confidence that helped see this story to the finish line.

Natasha MacKenzie—thank you for the incredible cover design work. A book is always judged by its cover, and you did an incredible job interpreting this sprawling story into one image.

Phillip Gessert—thank you for the formatting and typefacing work necessary to make this story legible in all of its various configurations.

Robin Treto—thank you for your patience while I bored you with how eight hours of writing went every day in our Atlanta apartment. Your early legal advice was core to the realism of the story.

Lillian Askins Lalo—thank you for explaining the completely unknown world of television journalism to me. Your helped create the foundation on which these characters stand.

Crimson Fist—thank you for walking me through what drives you to be a real-world superhero. Your insight was fundamental to the early development of characters in this story.

John Reimers—thank you for teaching and dealing with all of my ups and downs through my most formative years. I hope this gets added to your list of books you recommend to your students.

Jane Barrilleaux, Oliver Haynes, Norman Jetmundsen, David Kristoph, Will Russell—thank you for your early feedback when this story wasn't anywhere near finished. The thoughts you gave were formative to the book you're holding today.

Mom and Dad—thank you for your constant encouragement and understanding when I refused to let you read anything until the final ink had dried. More importantly, thank you for not laughing and canceling the checks when I told you I was going to get a degree in Creative Writing.

Caitlin—thank you for everything. You've dealt with me talking about the people in these pages for longer than we've been married. Your opinions and guidance during this process have kept me sane and helped drive this story to what it truly was intended to be. Thank you for understanding when I go through my periods of not wanting to do anything but work. You're an amazing partner and parent and I never could have done this without your support.

I'm sure I've left out people who have had a positive impact on this project, and for that I apologize. I hope you'll still be willing to field my incessant questions for the next go around.

Hudson will be back. Stay vigilant.

Will Bowron
August 2014—December 2021

WILL BOWRON lives in Birmingham, Alabama, with his wife Caitlin, daughter, cat, and dog. He received his BA in Creative Writing from Rhodes College and MBA from Emory University. When not reading, writing, or watching soccer, he works for his family's coffee and tea company. *Vigilant* is his first novel.

9 789898 548230